"What's wrong
around the fire

She sat up and drew her knees up under her cloak. "Nothing. I'm fine."

"You use that word far too often. How can you be fine?"

"You have a point. I would love a cup of hot tea and a cracker. Any chance that Dale left some in his toolbox?"

"I'll check. Chamomile or Earl Grey?"

Her eyes widened with surprise. "Jesse Crump has a sense of humor."

"Don't look so amazed." He stoked the fire.

"I noticed it was snowing again while I was on the porch. Heavily. No one will be able to follow our tracks, will they?"

"Nope." At least she understood why help wouldn't be coming.

"So, what do we do?"

"The hardest thing of all in a survival situation. Stay put."

Her eyes grew wide. "When you say survival situation, are you telling me that we are in serious trouble?"

There was a long silence. "*Ja*. We are."

After thirty-five years as a nurse, **Patricia Davids** hung up her stethoscope to become a full-time writer. She enjoys spending her free time visiting her grandchildren, doing some long-overdue yard work and traveling to research her story locations. She resides in Wichita, Kansas. Pat always enjoys hearing from her readers. You can visit her online at patriciadavids.com.

Living on a remote self-sufficient homestead in North Idaho, **Patrice Lewis** is a Christian wife, mother, author, blogger, columnist and speaker. She has practiced and written about rural subjects for almost thirty years. When she isn't writing, Patrice enjoys self-sufficiency projects, such as animal husbandry, small-scale dairy production, gardening, food preservation and canning, and homeschooling. She and her husband have been married since 1990 and have two daughters.

USA TODAY Bestselling Author

PATRICIA DAVIDS

&

PATRICE LEWIS

Their Amish Agreement

Previously published as *Shelter from the Storm*
and *Amish Baby Lessons*

LOVE INSPIRED
INSPIRATIONAL ROMANCE

LOVE INSPIRED®
INSPIRATIONAL ROMANCE

Recycling programs for this product may not exist in your area.

ISBN-13: 978-1-335-42695-6

Their Amish Agreement

Copyright © 2022 by Harlequin Enterprises ULC

Shelter from the Storm
First published in 2019. This edition published in 2022.
Copyright © 2019 by Patricia MacDonald

Amish Baby Lessons
First published in 2021. This edition published in 2022.
Copyright © 2021 by Patrice Lewis

For questions and comments about the quality of this book, please contact us at CustomerService@Harlequin.com.

Harlequin Enterprises ULC
22 Adelaide St. West, 41st Floor
Toronto, Ontario M5H 4E3, Canada
www.LoveInspired.com

Printed in U.S.A.

CONTENTS

SHELTER FROM THE STORM   7
Patricia Davids

AMISH BABY LESSONS   225
Patrice Lewis

SHELTER FROM THE STORM

Patricia Davids

This book is dedicated to all the men and women who work in neonatal intensive care units across the country. You care for the least of God's children. May you know abundant peace and joy in your work.

For thou hast been a strength to the poor, a strength to the needy in his distress, a refuge from the storm, a shadow from the heat, when the blast of the terrible ones is as a storm against the wall.
—*Isaiah* 25:4

Chapter One

That couldn't be Gemma Lapp.

Jesse Crump turned in his seat to get a better look at the Amish woman on the sidewalk waiting to cross the street. She was wearing a black Amish traveling bonnet and a long dark gray cloak. She was pulling a black wheeled suitcase behind her. He couldn't get a good look at her face. His driver and coworker, Dale Kaufman, pulled ahead when the light changed, and Jesse lost sight of her. There was nothing outward to suggest it was Gemma other than the Amish clothing but something about her, perhaps her small stature, reminded him strongly of the woman he wished he could forget.

"What's the matter?" Dale asked, noticing Jesse staring behind them. "Is something wrong with the load?" He slowed the pickup and trailer carrying two large garden sheds.

Jesse turned around to stare straight ahead. "I thought I saw someone I knew."

"That Amish woman waiting to cross the street?"

Dale knew Gemma. Jesse hoped he had gotten a better look. "*Ja*, did you see who it was?"

"I saw she was Amish by her clothing, but I couldn't see her face because of that big black bonnet. Who did you think it was?"

"Gemma Lapp." He had been thinking about her lately. She was on his mind far too often. Perhaps that was why he imagined he saw her.

Dale glanced his way. "You mean Leroy Lapp's daughter? I thought she was in Florida. Boy, that would be a great place to live during the winter, wouldn't it? Have you ever been there?"

"*Nee.*" Jesse was sorry he'd said anything. Most of the three-hour drive had been made in silence, the way Jesse liked it, but only after Dale tired of Jesse's one-word answers to his almost endless chatter.

Dale accelerated. The ancient truck's gears grated when he shifted. "It could be that she's on her way home for a visit. The bus station in Cleary is just down the block from that corner."

"Maybe."

Dale shook his head. "Nah. Leroy would've mentioned something if she was coming home. That girl is the apple of his eye. She was always easy on the eyes if you ask me. Too bad she got baptized before I had the chance to ask her out."

Jesse scowled at Dale. The man wasn't Amish, but he worked for an Amish bishop. "If you want to keep delivering sheds and supplies for Bishop Schultz, you'd better not let him hear such talk." It was the longest comment Jesse had ever made to the man.

Dale's stunned expression proved he got the point.

"I meant no disrespect, Jesse. I like Gemma. You know how Leroy is always rattling on about her."

Jesse leaned his head back and stared out the window at the homes and small businesses of Cleary, Maine, flashing past. He had eavesdropped on Leroy's conversations about Gemma a few times. He knew about her job in Pinecrest at a pie shop, about the large number of friends she was making among the *Englisch* and Amish folks, and how much she loved the ocean, but he had never asked about her himself.

Bishop Elmer Schultz—like most of the men in their community, including Jesse—had a second occupation, in addition to being a potato farmer. The bishop owned a small business that made storage sheds in various sizes. Jesse had worked for him since coming to Maine three years ago when the community of New Covenant was first founded.

Starting a new Amish colony anywhere was filled with challenges, but the rugged country of northern Maine had its own unique trials. Here, more than anywhere, a man had to depend on the people around him in times of trouble. There was no certainty that the community founded by Elijah Troyer could survive. Elijah had passed away two years ago. Nine of the original ten families remained and more had come the past summer.

The move to New Covenant, Maine, may have been a difficult choice for some of the families in the community, but not for Jesse. He had jumped at the chance. In Maine he didn't have to hang his head because he wasn't as smart as some or because he was bigger than everyone else. In Ohio he'd been known as Jesse the Ox since his school days.

The child of a single mother, he'd been orphaned at

thirteen. He quit school and became a hired man with no hope of owning his own land until he answered an ad in the Amish newspaper seeking hardy souls willing to settle in northern Maine and offering a small parcel of land as an incentive. The beautiful scenery of Maine and plenty of hard work soon overshadowed Jesse's memories of his unhappy early years. Until Gemma Lapp managed to reopen those old wounds with her sharp tongue.

He could still see her standing with her arms crossed and her face flaming red as she sputtered, "Jesse Crump, you're as big as an ox and dumber than a post."

All because he had rebuffed her offer of marriage.

She had barely been twenty-one at the time, not old enough to know what love was, but she'd taken the notion that she was in love with him. He'd suffered through weeks of her attempts to gain his affection. She tried everything from fresh-baked pies delivered to him at work, letters full of her newfound love, even getting her father to hire him to do handiwork on their farm, where she was always close by, chatting about how wonderful it would be to marry and have children.

He was almost eight years her senior and not interested in settling down until he had enough land to support a family. Her proposal wouldn't have been so bad if they had been alone, but they hadn't been. A half dozen people overheard her offer, his pointed rejection and her scathing words in reply.

The snickers, taunts and jeers that had made his school years and young-adult life miserable were only in his head but in that moment, Gemma had unlocked feelings of inferiority he had lived with for years and worked hard to overcome. If she saw him that way, surely others did too.

He kept to himself after that day, hoping her remarks would be forgotten, but they stayed stuck in his head, even though no one else echoed them. He strove to avoid being anywhere near Gemma for the next six months. *Big as an ox and dumber than a post.* It wasn't until she left New Covenant that he stopped hearing her words. In spite of her comment, he hadn't disliked Gemma. She was loyal to her friends. She was a hard worker. She had a good sense of humor, but she was also headstrong and willful.

It had been nearly a year and a half since the embarrassing incident. He thought he'd put it out of his mind, but it seemed he hadn't.

Gemma's father, Leroy Lapp, worked with Jesse at the bishop's business. Leroy had recently been chosen to become the community's second minister. The influx of six new families in the spring had swelled the congregation, making it more than Bishop Schultz and his first minister, Samuel Yoder, could manage. Especially now that plans were underway to start their own Amish school.

"Maybe she's making a surprise visit," Dale said when the silence stretched too long to suit him.

"Maybe you could drive faster. It's almost noon."

"What's your hurry? We've got all day."

"I've got to get back before the bank closes. I need to get a cashier's check for the earnest money the auction company requires I put up before I can bid on the property I've got my eye on. They want ten thousand dollars to prove I can afford the land."

"Oh, right. The land auction. I almost forgot about

that." Dale shot Jesse a sheepish glance and focused his attention on the road.

The farm Jesse owned was small, but he had plans to expand. The money he'd made building sheds over the last few years would help pay for more land. He had his eye on eighty acres that bordered his property to the west. It was fertile land ready for planting in the spring. He couldn't ask for a better piece of property. It was going up for auction the day after tomorrow. The auction company required earnest money in the form of a cashier's check or cash before anyone was allowed to bid and Jesse wasn't about to miss out on the opportunity of a lifetime.

He gazed out the passenger's-side window at the farms that lined the highway, interspersed with heavy forests already covered with the first snow of winter. His thoughts drifted from the land he intended to purchase back to Gemma. If Gemma did come to visit her family in northern Maine, it wouldn't be in the middle of November. Gemma didn't like the snow. To hear her tell it, she didn't like much of anything about Maine.

He was sure his name topped the list of things she disliked most about the North Country.

"There won't be another bus going that way until the day after tomorrow."

"Are you sure?" Gemma stared at the agent behind the counter in stunned disbelief.

The tall thin man with thick glasses stopped writing in a logbook of some sort and peered at her over the top of his glasses. "Of course I'm sure. I work for the bus company."

She held up the flyer she had picked up in Boston.

"The schedule said there is a bus going to Caribou every day."

"Look at the small print. There is, until the fifteenth of November. After that, bus service drops to every other day until the fifteenth of April. Today's bus left two hours ago. Won't be another one until the day after tomorrow. Next," he called out, leaning to look around her.

Only one elderly man stood behind her. He held out a piece of white pipe. "Do you have a J-trap that will fit this size and PVC glue?"

"I sure do, but you'll need cleaner, as well." The agent came out from behind the counter and led the man to the plumbing section of the hardware store that doubled as a bus station in Cleary.

Gemma waited impatiently for him to come back. When he did, she clasped her hands together tightly, praying the tears that pricked the back of her eyes wouldn't start flowing. She couldn't afford a motel room for two nights. "I don't have much money with me. Are there any Amish families in this area?"

The man behind the counter rubbed his chin. "Let me think."

The Amish opened their homes to other members of their faith even if they had never met. She would be welcomed, fed and made to feel like one of the family. The command to care for one another was more than a saying. It was a personal commitment taken seriously by every Amish family, no matter how poor or how well-to-do they were. Many times, she had seen her mother stretch a meal for three into a meal for twice that many when Amish travelers appeared unexpectedly at their door. She waited hopefully for the clerk's answer.

He shook his head. "Nope. Not that I'm aware of anyway."

She sniffed as her vision blurred. "Thank—thank you." She started to turn away, humiliated by her runaway emotions. They were one more unhappy part of her horrible situation.

"You might check with the sheriff," the agent offered with a hint of sympathy in his tone. "He may know of some."

She managed a half smile for him. "Where do I find the sheriff?"

"I'll call him for you. He's usually home for lunch at this time of day. You are welcome to wait here." He gestured to a wooden bench sitting in front of a large plate-glass window.

She nodded, unable to speak for the lump in her throat, and wheeled her suitcase over to the bench. Sitting down with a sigh, she moved her suitcase in front of her, so she could prop up her swollen feet. She leaned her head back against the glass and closed her eyes. After two solid days on a bus, she was ready to lie down. Anywhere.

"Miss? Excuse me, miss."

Gemma opened her eyes sometime later to see the agent standing in front of her. She blinked away the fog in her brain. "I'm sorry. I must have fallen asleep."

"You've been snoozing for a couple of hours. The sheriff just got back to me. He's been working an accident out on Wyman Road. He doesn't know of any Amish in these parts. You've been here for quite a while. I thought you might like something to eat. You mentioned you were short on funds, so I brought you a burger from the café down the street." He held out a white paper bag.

"*Danki.* Thank you. That's very kind." She sat up surprised by the unexpected gift. What did he hope to gain by it? She rubbed her stiff neck and waited to hear the catch. "It smells *wunderbar.*" She slowly took the bag from him.

"You're welcome to use our phone to call someone. The store will be closing in an hour, but the diner down the street stays open all night." He sent her an apologetic glance and walked away.

She bit her lower lip to stop it from quivering. She could place a call to the phone shanty her parents shared with their Amish neighbors to let them know she was returning and ask her father to send a car for her, but she would have to leave a message. It was unlikely that anyone would check the machine this late in the day.

Besides, any message she left would be overheard. She knew two women who checked the machine each morning for the sole purpose of keeping up with the local gossip. Unless she gave a reason for her abrupt return, speculation would spread quickly. If she gave the real reason, even Jesse Crump would know before she reached home. She couldn't bear that, although she didn't understand why his opinion mattered so much. His stoic face wouldn't reveal his thoughts, but he was sure to gloat when he learned he'd been right about her. He had called her a spoiled baby looking for trouble and said that she would find it sooner or later. Well, she had found it all right. A thousand miles away from him in Florida.

No, she wouldn't call. She didn't want to make her parents the center of conjecture about her return or have them bear the expense of hiring a car to fetch her. What she had to say was better said face-to-face.

She was cowardly enough to delay as long as possible. Her appetite gone, she put the burger bag on the bench beside her.

She didn't know how she was going to find the courage to tell her mother and father that she was six months pregnant and Robert Fisher, the man who'd promised to marry her, was long gone.

Jesse and Dale delivered both sheds as promised, but the second customer wasn't ready for them, despite having chosen the date and time for them to arrive. The two men spent an extra three hours helping the owner clear the area where he wanted it. They even leveled out a gravel pad for him before setting the building in place.

Jesse joined Dale in the cab of his ancient but prized pickup when they were done. Dale's expression showed his annoyance. "I can't believe we did all that work for him and then he claimed it was included in the price of the shed instead of paying us. What a rip-off. There are always a few dishonest folks who think they can stick it to the Amish and get away with it, because the Amish won't come after them for the money."

Jesse understood Dale's frustration, but his faith required him to forgive those who would do him ill. "Give thanks that you are not like him. It is better to be a poor man than a dishonest one."

"It's a good thing I'm not Amish. I'm gonna get my money and I'll get yours too. I have a brother-in-law who works for an attorney. I'm not afraid to go after someone who cheats me." Dale turned the truck key but nothing happened. He tried again with the same result. He glanced sheepishly at Jesse. "Don't worry, I've got this."

He hopped out of the cab and reached behind his seat to pull out a large toolbox. "This old heap has taught me to never go anywhere without my tools."

He raised the hood and propped it open, disappearing from Jesse's view. A few seconds later, he looked around at Jesse. "Loose battery cable. Try it now."

Jesse scooted across the bench seat until he was behind the wheel. He turned the key and the truck roared to life. Dale dropped the hood, pushed his toolbox behind the seat again and got in as Jesse moved back to his side of the seat. "Are we heading back, or do you want to get a motel room tonight and start fresh in the morning?"

A glance at Dale's face told Jesse his coworker was worn-out. "We'll get a room."

As eager as Jesse was to get back, making the long drive this late wasn't practical. Tomorrow afternoon would be soon enough to have the bank issue him a cashier's check as earnest money for the auction the following day. He needed the land to expand his farm. It could be years before another piece of farm ground so close to his own came up for sale.

Dale grinned. "Good. Let's get something to eat too."

"Sure." Jesse was getting hungry. The sandwich he'd packed for his lunch was long gone.

"I know this great little burger place just off the highway downtown. Our crew used to eat there every chance we got."

"Crew?" As soon as he asked the question, Jesse knew it was a mistake.

"I worked two summers for a logging company up the way. Didn't I ever tell you that? The pay was good, but the hours were long and the work was dangerous.

The first week I was on the job, a tree fell within inches of my head. Inches. That was just the start of it."

Jesse was sure he was about to hear everything that had happened to Dale during those two years. He settled himself in resignation. Hopefully dinner would put a halt to Dale's storytelling.

As they drove back into town, Jesse searched for the Amish woman, hoping to see her face and prove it wasn't Gemma. The streets and sidewalks were almost empty. He didn't spy anyone in Amish clothing. Dale pulled the pickup and empty trailer into a parking lot off the main street. When he opened the door, Jesse got a whiff of mouthwatering fried onions and burgers. If the fare was anything like the aroma, they were in for some good food. His stomach growled in anticipation.

He followed Dale inside the small diner, ducking slightly to keep from knocking his black hat off against the doorjamb. Several people were seated at tables and at a counter. They all turned to look. He should have been used to the stares, but he never got over the feeling that he was an oddity. An Amish giant. At six foot four, he towered over Dale, who was five foot eight at the most. Jesse's hat added another two inches to his height, and his bulky black coat made him look even bigger.

He happily took a seat in a booth where his size was less noticeable. His friend Michael Shetler once told him he needed to hang out with bigger friends. Good advice, but the problem was there wasn't anyone his size in their Amish community.

A waitress came over and pulled a pencil from her dark curly hair. "What can I get you?"

"Two of your lumberjack burgers, two orders of fries and I'll have a soda. What do you want to drink, Jesse?"

"Water."

Dale winked at the waitress and grinned. "The Amish like to keep things simple."

She ignored Dale and focused on Jesse. "Are you with the Amish lady waiting at the bus station? Oscar, the bus station attendant came over a little while ago and bought a burger for her. He said she had missed her bus and didn't have enough money for a motel. She was hoping to find another Amish family in the area. He asked me if I knew any and I don't."

"We aren't from around here," Dale said.

Jesse hesitated a few seconds, then stood up. "Which way is the bus depot?"

She pointed her pencil up the street. "It's not really a depot. The bus line just has a desk in the hardware store."

He touched his hat. "Thank you. Go ahead and eat, Dale." He couldn't leave without offering aid to another member of his faith. He would pay for her motel room and make sure she had money to use for food if she needed help.

He walked out the door and up the sidewalk to the hardware store. A bell tingled as he walked in. A quick glance around showed him a woman in Amish clothing sitting on a bench near the other end of the store. She sat huddled in her seat with her head down and her hands gripping her handbag as if someone might tear it from her grasp.

He stopped a few feet away, searching for something to say, to ask if she was okay, if he could help and he finally settled for a simple "good evening" in the native language of the Amish, Pennsylvania *Deitsh*. *"Guder nacht, frau."*

The woman looked up. He stared at her familiar face in astonishment. "Gemma?"

Her eyes widened. "Jesse?"

The color left her cheeks. She pressed a hand to her lips and burst into tears, leaving him with no idea what to do.

Chapter Two

What was Jesse doing here?

Gemma struggled to control her sobs. He couldn't have looked more stunned if he tried. His expression would have been comical if she could have found anything funny in her humiliating situation. How much worse could this day get?

The bus agent hurried over. He knelt beside her and offered her a box of tissues while glaring at Jesse. "What did you say to her?"

Jesse's face became expressionless. "I said goodevening."

The agent's scowl deepened. "That's not enough to make a woman cry."

"I reckon it is when I say it."

"It's—it's okay," Gemma managed to reassure the helpful man between hiccuping sobs.

She reined in her distress and raised her chin to meet Jesse's gaze. The surprise of seeing him had caught her off guard. His size, as he towered over her, made her feel small and insignificant. Like always. "Hello, Jesse. What—what are you doing here?"

"Delivering sheds. And you?"

She looked away. "Going home. I missed my bus."

He shoved his hands into the pockets of his coat. "Dale Kaufman and I are returning to New Covenant in the morning. You are welcome to ride along with us. I'll get you a room for tonight. Dale's truck is down in front of the café. If you would rather not ride with…us, I'll pay for your room as long as you need one."

He turned and left the building without waiting for her answer. She drew a deep breath and blew it out in a huff. She wanted to get home, but she didn't want to spend hours sitting next to Jesse. Nor did she want to be beholden to him. He had only offered to pay for her room because they were both Amish. He hadn't done it because he cared about her.

Once she had imagined herself in love with Jesse. Was it only a year ago? It seemed like a lifetime had passed. She'd done everything within her power to make him notice her. What he had seen was a pesky child not a woman. Her declaration of love and marriage proposal didn't win her the kiss she'd been hoping for. Jesse had laughed at her and called her a spoiled baby. She'd been humiliated, brokenhearted and furious. She had said some cruel things she didn't mean. As it turned out he'd been right.

She picked up her sandwich bag and lifted the handle of her suitcase. She tried to hand the box of tissues back to the agent.

Her kind protector shook his head. "Keep it. You might need it. You don't have to go with that fellow if you're afraid of him."

That made her smile. "Jesse Crumb might break a foolish young girl's heart, but he wouldn't hurt a fly."

Pulling her suitcase behind her, she left the building and walked toward the café. The autumn wind was cold where it struck her face. It carried the promise of snow. Why people had chosen to settle this land was beyond her. The Florida coast was so much nicer.

Dale Kaufman came out of the building as she approached the vehicle. Jesse was nowhere in sight. Dale grinned. "I sure am surprised to see you, Miss Lapp, and in Cleary of all places. How did you end up here?"

"Cleary is the northern end of the major bus line. I was supposed to take a local bus up to Caribou, but they only run every other day in the winter. One more thing about this state that makes life difficult." She pulled her cloak tightly around her shoulders, making sure to keep the material gathered loosely in front so her pregnancy didn't show.

"So why come back?" Jesse asked as he walked up behind her.

"That's none of your business." She made her tone as sharp as possible. The last thing she wanted him to think was that she still had a crush on him. She'd gotten over him a long time ago. Well before she met her baby's father, she had realized her infatuation with Jesse had been more about being the last single woman in her group of friends than finding her soul mate. There had been only two single Amish fellows in their community back then. In her opinion, Jesse had been the better choice.

He arched one eyebrow but didn't say anything. That was Jesse's biggest problem. He never had much to say. Especially to her. How could she ever have considered him attractive? Sure, he was tall with broad shoulders, curly black hair and the most beautiful sky blue eyes fringed with thick dark lashes, but looks weren't everything. An attractive man needed an attractive personality. Jesse had the personality of a fence post.

No, she was being childish again. Just because he hadn't been blinded by her charms last year was no reason for unkind thoughts about him. Jesse was a quiet man and there wasn't anything wrong with that. He was about the only man she knew who didn't have a hidden motive.

Robert Fisher, her former boyfriend had been a handsome smooth-talking flirt. She had been a naive, easy target for him. His attentions soothed her wounded pride and made her feel beautiful and loved. Except it was all a lie. He seduced her and left town the day after she told him she was pregnant. Like a fool, she had waited for him to return. It took months for her to accept that he wasn't coming back. It was a lesson she took to heart. He was the last man she would trust unconditionally.

Returning home was hard. She had already been baptized into the Amish faith. She would be shunned when the bishop learned of her condition, but that wasn't as frightening as having a baby alone. She wouldn't be able to eat at the same table as her parents and they wouldn't be able to accept anything from her hand. She wouldn't be included in church activities for as long as her shunning went on. She was prepared for that. She fully intended to confess and ask forgiveness and pray the bishop chose a short period of shunning for her to endure.

Jesse held out a motel key. "I got you a room. Number eight. I'll take your suitcase." One arched eyebrow dared her to reject his offer.

"Danki," she murmured.

Dale glanced between the two of them. "Have you eaten, miss?"

She raised the white paper bag. "I have my supper."

"Goot." Jesse walked toward the motel, carrying her suitcase as easily as if it were empty instead of packed full of all she owned.

She nodded to Dale. "I'm grateful for the lift home."

"My pleasure. It's a long trip, and I sure will enjoy having someone to talk to for a change. Jesse don't say much."

"I know." She followed Jesse to the room at the very end of a motel that had seen better days. The Gray Goose Inn's paint was peeling in multiple spots and the windows were dingy. The sidewalk along the front was cracked and lifted while the neon light on the sign out front flickered dimly.

He held open the door and set her suitcase inside. "We'll leave at six."

"I'll be ready." She swallowed her false pride and stared at her fingers clenched around her purse handle. *"Danki,* Jesse. This is generous of you. I will repay you, I promise."

"It's nothing. Why come back? Your *daed* says you like it in Florida."

Had Jesse asked about her? She found that hard to believe. "I do, but I got homesick."

As soon as she said the words, she realized they were true. She missed her parents and her friends, even if they didn't miss her.

Bethany, Gemma's closest friend, had married last winter and all she talked about was how happy she and Michael were and how blessed she was to have found the man God had intended to be her husband. Gemma's first cousin Anna Miller was the same way. She and her new husband, Tobias, had arrived in New Covenant a few weeks after Bethany's wedding. The two women had nothing on their minds except setting up house and starting a family. Two more young married couples moved to New Covenant at the same time. The women all enjoyed one another's company and often visited between houses. Gemma was the only single woman among them.

Gemma had been happy for her friends, but it hadn't taken long to realize she'd become a third wheel. The sad odd person out with no one of her own. Without the prospect of marriage and the memory of making a fool of herself over Jesse popping up each time she saw him, Gemma decided to escape to the Amish settlement in sunny Pinecrest, Florida, to find her own soul mate. What a mistake that had turned out to be. A shudder coursed through her at the memory of her betrayal by the man she had met down there who claimed to love her.

"Are you back for good?" Jesse asked. Was there a hopeful note in his voice? She glanced at his face. His grim expression said she must have been mistaken.

She looked down and shrugged. "I haven't decided."

Her lower lip quivered. The council of her mother was what she wanted and needed, even as she dreaded revealing her condition. She had no idea what she was going to do about the baby.

Jesse stood as if waiting for something else. She glanced at his face again and caught a look of tenderness before it disappeared. His usual blank expression took its place. Underneath his brawny build and his reclusive nature, Jesse had a soft heart. While he avoided the company of most people, he was known for taking in wounded creatures and strays. Was that how he saw her now? If so, he was more astute than she gave him credit for. She glanced down to make sure her full cloak hid her figure. "Thank you again for your kindness."

"The bishop would expect it of me. Gemma, is something wrong?"

She couldn't look at him. "I'm tired, that's all."

"Then I'll say good-night."

Unable to reply, she went inside, dropped her cold supper in the trash and closed the door, shutting out his overwhelming presence and her irrational desire to bury her face against his chest and give in to her tears.

It was still dark when Gemma left the motel room a few minutes before six o'clock the next morning, pulling her suitcase behind her. She could see her breath in the chilly air. Snowflakes drifted gently down from the overcast sky. Winter was tightening its grip on the countryside. The contrast between the sandy beach and ocean waves where she had been three days ago caused her to shiver. Had she been foolish to come back? Maybe.

She had her emotions well under control for the moment. A good night's sleep had erased the ravages of the tears she'd cried into her pillow after Jesse left her. Washing her face with cold water had removed the last bit of puffiness from around her eyes. She was ready to face a few hours in Jesse's company.

He was standing beside Dale's battered yellow pickup waiting for her. Without a word, he took her bag and stowed it in the bed of the truck and held the door open for her. She got in. He climbed in after her, taking up more than his share of the bench seat. She scooted farther away.

Dale got in and handed her two white paper bags identical to the one the bus agent had given her. "I got some breakfast burritos for us to eat on the road." The aroma of toasted tortillas, sausage, grilled peppers and onions filled the air in the small cab, making her stomach rumble ominously. Her morning sickness was more like any-time-of-the-day sickness. It struck without warning. She handed one of the bags to Jesse and swallowed hard, hoping she wouldn't get sick.

Dale kept up a steady line of chatter as he drove northward on the highway. Jesse ate his meal in silence. He took a swig from a bottle of water, recapped it and put it back in the bag. "Aren't you going to eat yours?" Jesse nodded toward the paper sack on her lap.

"I'm not hungry. You are welcome to it."

"Danki." He took the offered bag and finished off her burrito.

Dale chuckled. "He's a big man with a big appetite. It must cost a fortune to keep him fed. No wonder he hasn't found a wife. The poor woman would never get out of the kitchen."

The heat of a blush rose up her neck and across her cheeks. She cast a covert glance at Jesse. He was staring straight ahead. A muscle twitched in his clenched jaw. He hadn't forgotten their last conversation.

After weeks of dropping hints about her feelings for Jesse and her desire to get married, she had finally confronted him point-blank and proposed marriage with disastrous consequences. He'd laughed at her and told her to go home. She had countered by confessing her love and throwing herself into his arms. He'd abruptly

put her aside. The scowl on his face and his words still
echoed in her mind.

*You're not in love with me. You're a foolish, spoiled
baby looking for trouble. One day you will find it unless you learn humility.*

She wasn't proud of her reaction. She said things she
hadn't meant, but she was sure Jesse had meant what he
said. He'd walked away, shaking his head, leaving her
crushed and fuming. Her humiliation had been complete when she learned some of her friends had overheard their conversation. Her parents had been appalled
as the gossip quickly spread. Rather than face it down,
after a few months she had packed up and moved to
Florida to start a new life.

The sad part was that she really had liked Jesse. It
was knowing that he had been disgusted by her behavior that hurt the most.

She dared a glance at him, but his attention was focused out the passenger's side window. She clutched the
front of her cloak and sat quietly beside him as Dale
chatted away about his ex-wife and her poor cooking.

About thirty minutes into their trip, it began snowing heavily. Fat flakes smashed themselves against the
windshield and were swept away by the wipers. As the
snow became thicker, Dale grew quieter and concentrated on his driving.

Ahead of them were several semi–tractor trailers.
Dale hung back to keep out of their spray. Suddenly the
last truck in line went into a skid on the bridge ahead.
The rig jackknifed and clipped the rear end of the truck
in front of it as it tipped over. The sound of screech-
ing metal reached her as both trucks hit the sides of
the bridge. Dale maneuvered his pickup off to the side

of the road. Both men got out. Gemma saw the flickering of flames through the windshield that was being quickly covered with snow.

Jesse paused to look at her. "Stay put." He slammed the door shut and jogged away with Dale into the snow.

Gemma had no idea how long she sat in the truck. She prayed silently for all the people involved. The sirens of rescue vehicles announced their arrival before they pulled up alongside her. With police and firefighters on the scene, Dale and Jesse finally returned to the vehicle.

"Is everyone all right?" she asked Jesse as he opened his door.

"Both drivers survived."

Dale knocked the snow off his boots before climbing in behind the wheel. "That is a mess. The bridge will be closed for hours yet. You should've seen Jesse pull the door open on that tipped-over cab and lift that fellow out. If it weren't for him, that guy would be toast."

Jesse stared straight at her. "Sometimes it pays to be as big as an ox."

She didn't know how to reply. He continued to stare at her for a few more seconds, then he looked away. She was left with the feeling that her long-ago comment had hurt his feelings. Had it? She'd only been concerned about her own humiliation at the time.

Not that it mattered. Once news of her condition got out, he would be eternally grateful he had avoided her bumbling advances.

Jesse stared straight ahead. He had given Gemma the opportunity to apologize for her painful comments about him. Either she still believed he was big and dumb or she didn't care about his feelings. She once claimed to love him. If she still harbored tender feelings for him, she was hiding it well. His Amish faith demanded that he forgive anyone who had wounded him. He thought he had done so, but having her so close beside him proved some of his resentment remained.

He had been taunted and ridiculed about his size since his school days. He wasn't the smartest kid in the class, and he knew it. That only made him try harder. He endured the teasing until one day in the fourth grade he hit his antagonist in the face. Wayne Beachy had ended up with a broken jaw. Filled with remorse, Jesse never allowed his temper to take control again. Enduring teasing was far less traumatic than seeing the results of what his fists could do.

That was why his continued resentment of Gemma Lapp troubled him and why she was never far from his thoughts. He didn't understand his reaction. He only knew she made him uncomfortably aware of his size and his lack of intelligence. Gemma was tiny compared to him. Her sharp wit had made her a favorite among the young people in New Covenant. It was only after her best friend, Bethany, married Michael Shetler that her wit took on a cutting edge.

He should've been glad when she decided to move to Florida, but he hadn't been. For some unknown reason, he had missed her.

She looked at Dale. "What now? Do we wait here, or do we go back to Cleary?"

"I might have a third option."

"What?" Jesse asked. He had to get to his bank before the close of business today.

Dale half turned in his seat to face them. "You remember that I told you I used to work for a logging company in this area?"

Jesse nodded. "I remember."

"About two miles back, there is a logging road that cuts off this highway and goes about twenty miles back into the hills. It comes out on this same highway about twenty-five miles up ahead. I figure it'll be rough in places, but we'll lose less than two hours of time, which will be better than sitting here waiting for the bridge to be cleared. What do you think?"

"What about the weather?" Jesse asked.

"The snow is letting up. We'll stay ahead of it."

"I say go for it," Gemma said. Clearly the last thing she wanted to do was spend more time than necessary with him.

"What do you say, Jesse?" Dale asked.

"I've got to get home by this afternoon."

Dale grinned and turned the pickup around. "All right, folks. We are about to see some fabulous Maine backcountry wilderness."

Dale had been right. Not about the weather, the snow continued, but about the beautiful scenery and the road being rough. It was more of a trail than an actual road. As they bounced along the narrow track through towering pine trees, Jesse and Gemma were constantly tossed against each other. He had been in many uncomfortable situations in his life but none as uncomfortable as trying to remain indifferent to the little woman continually apologizing for jamming her elbow or her shoulder into his side.

She wasn't doing it on purpose, but that didn't make it any more comfortable. He was tempted to slip his arm around her and pull her tight against him, but he didn't. She might think he was trying to take advantage of the situation.

They reached a more open area, and Dale picked up speed. Suddenly, a bull moose galloped out into the road directly in front of them. Dale swerved. Jesse threw his arm across Gemma as he braced for the impact. The moose sprang forward at the last second. Dale missed him but lost control of the pickup and careened into the trees. The front wheels hit a large fallen log and stopped abruptly, throwing them all forward. Gemma slipped from under Jesse's arm and cried out as she hit the floorboard.

After a few seconds of stunned silence, Jesse pushed himself away from the dash and back onto the seat. "Gemma, are you hurt?"

She had ended up in a crumpled heap on the floor. Dale was slumped behind the steering wheel.

Gemma looked up at Jesse with pain-filled eyes. "Something's wrong with my ankle. I think it may be broken." She tried to lever herself up. He stopped her with a hand to her shoulder.

"Are you hurt anywhere else?"

"Give me a minute." She flexed her neck, shrugged her shoulders, then opened and closed her hands. She shut her eyes and pressed a hand to her midsection.

"What is it?" he asked, concerned by her stillness.

Sighing, she held out a hand. "It's just my left foot. Help me up."

"How bad is it?" He lifted her gently to the seat. The movement caused her to grit her teeth as a deep frown creased her brow.

"Bad enough, but I think I'll live. Are you okay?"

"A few bumps and bruises." His right arm hurt where he had braced it against the dashboard, but it was likely a strain and nothing more. He was a little surprised she had asked.

Turning to the driver, Gemma touched his shoulder. "Dale? Dale, are you okay?"

He moaned and sat back, raising a shaky hand to his head. "I'll get back to you on that. What happened?"

Jesse rubbed his shoulder. "The good news is you missed the moose. The bad news is that you struck something else." The front end of the truck was tilted up at a fifteen-degree angle.

"Anybody hurt?" Dale blinked rapidly as he tried to focus.

"Gemma thinks her foot is broken. I'm fine. How about you?"

"Other than an aching noggin, I think I'm okay." He pushed open his door and looked down. "Wow. This is not good."

Chapter Three

Dale turned off the vehicle, got out and squatted to look under it. His expression told Jesse he wasn't happy with what he saw. Jesse had to force open his door to get out by hitting it with his aching shoulder several times. Gemma stayed put. Her foot had twisted under her awkwardly when she was thrown to the floor. Jesse's arm had kept her face from smashing into the dashboard.

Jesse and Dale conferred outside. Dale took out his cell phone and held it up, turning from side to side. He slipped it back into his pocket and came to the open driver's-side door. "Do you think you can walk, Gemma?"

She shook her head, turned sideways and lifted her legs onto the seat. Her right ankle was twice as big as her left one. She peeled down her stocking and hissed at the pain. Her ankle was already turning black-and-blue. "I doubt I can stand on it, let alone walk."

Dale scooped up a handful of snow and held it against the bump on his head. "This truck isn't going anywhere. The front tire has busted loose, and the body is high centered on a boulder. It's going to take a tow truck to lift it off. The problem is, I don't have phone service in this spot."

"What are we going to do?" Gemma looked around them at the thick forest.

"We're gonna have to hoof it to where I can get cell service and call for a tow truck. Maybe we can fix a crutch for you."

She shook her head. "I'll wait here. Even hobbling, I'd only slow you down."

Jesse glanced from Dale to Gemma and back to Dale. "I don't think we should leave her by herself. I could go, and you could stay here."

Her eyes widened, and she gave a tiny shake of her head. "I'll be fine alone for a few hours." Her smile was half-hearted at best.

He pulled a large blue handkerchief from his pocket, packed it full of snow and handed it to her. "Put this on your ankle. It will help the pain and swelling."

"Danki." She took the compress from him and placed it around her lower leg.

Jesse turned to Dale. "I'll stay with her. Are you sure you are up to the hike?"

Dale managed a lopsided grin. "Fortunately, I have a hard head and my legs are fine." He blinked hard as he stared at his watch. "It's only a little after nine. I don't think we drove much more than ten miles, do you?"

"If that far."

"Even if I have to walk all the way to the highway to get service, which I know I won't have to do, I should still get back with some help before two o'clock."

"We'll be fine." Jesse tried to decide which would be more uncomfortable, waiting in the cold for Dale's return or sitting beside Gemma in the truck for an unknown number of hours.

Dale reached under the seat and pulled out a moth-eaten green army surplus blanket. "This should help keep you a little warmer." He shook it out and handed it to Gemma. She spread it over her legs. Her thin socks and low-cut walking shoes were suited for winter in Florida, not for winter in Maine.

Jesse looked up at the sky. "At least the snow has stopped."

"For now," Dale said. The men exchanged worried glances. They had watched the local forecast on the TV before leaving the motel. They were calling for more snow and the possibility of a blizzard in the coming days.

"Is it safe for you to walk? What if you get lost?" Gemma asked and nibbled at the corner of her lip.

Dale winked. "I'll be fine. All I have to do is follow the tire tracks back the way we came."

Dale sent a speaking glance to Jesse and jerked his head toward the rear of the vehicle. The men walked to the back of the truck to converse out of earshot. Dale pulled his gloves from his pocket and put them on. "It's going to get real cold for her just sitting. Use the heater for fifteen or twenty minutes at a time. The truck has enough gas to run all day if you don't waste it."

"Right. I'll take care of her."

Dale patted Jesse on the shoulder. "I know you will. What I'm saying is, get her talking. That way she'll have less time to worry about her situation. Women need more reassurance when things go wrong."

That hadn't been Jesse's experience. The women he

knew handled the unexpected as well if not better than most men. "I'll do my best."

"Make sure to keep the muffler clear of snow when you run the truck. I don't want to come back and find you passed out from carbon monoxide poisoning or, worse yet, dead."

"I know what to do."

"Okay, see you soon." Dale staggered a few steps before Jesse caught up and steadied him.

"Maybe I should be the one to go."

"I'm fine. You know as well as I do that the bishop and her father would much rather a fine, upstanding Amish fellow stayed with her instead of a not-so-up-standing non-Amish guy like me."

He was right, but Jesse hated to admit it. "Okay, go."

Jesse watched Dale as he walked off until he was out of sight, then he returned to the pickup, praying Dale could make good time in getting them help.

Gemma pulled her cloak tightly around her shoulders. It was growing colder. She studied Jesse's face as he got in the truck beside her. "You look concerned. Are you worried about Dale?"

"I'm sure he will be fine. *Gott* is watching over him." He tried to make his words sound encouraging, but he missed the mark.

It was clear he was concerned for his friend. She could only offer him small comfort. "You're right. I can pray for him, even if I can't do much else."

Jesse nodded to her foot. "How is the ankle?"

"It hurts, but I will be fine here. If you hurry, you can catch up with Dale. I know you'd rather go with him."

"Can you turn on the heater?"

She lifted her chin. "Of course I can."

"Do it."

She stared at the unfamiliar array of gages and knobs until she found the word *heat*. She pushed the slide over, but nothing happened. She glanced at him sheepishly. "Okay, how does it work?"

"The truck has to be running."

"That means turn the key, right?"

He nodded. She grimaced as she scooted behind the wheel and turned the key. Nothing happened. "What am I doing wrong?"

"Probably a loose battery wire." Getting out, he moved to the front of the vehicle and lifted the hood.

"I'd like to know how he expected me to figure that out," she muttered. How often did battery cables come loose?

After a few minutes, he stepped to the side. "Try it now," he called out.

She did, and the engine roared to life, startling her. She pushed the slide over to High. The air came blasting out of the vents. Jesse walked up to the open passenger's-side door. She turned the knob the other way and the flow of air died down. She looked at him, knowing he was testing her, and she was failing miserably. "It's just blowing cold air."

"The engine has to warm up."

Annoyed that she was looking foolish at every turn, she glared at him. "You could've told me that."

"You could have admitted that you don't know anything about running a truck. Did you realize that you have to keep the exhaust pipe free of snow or you will die of carbon monoxide poisoning inside the cab?"

"I didn't. You just love rubbing my face in my ignorance, don't you?"

"That's not true. Can you say the same?" He slammed the door shut and walked to the rear of the vehicle.

Gemma's irritation quickly gave way to guilt. She was in the wrong. She would have to apologize. She shouldn't have snapped at him. Nothing was simple anymore. Every step she took pushed him away, when that wasn't what she wanted. She moved until she was sitting with her back against the driver's-side door and stretched her legs across the seat. In the side mirror, she saw Jesse kick a clump of snow away from the rear tire. He was angry with her.

Why was it that they couldn't have a civil conversation? They were going to be alone together for hours. She watched him pace across the trail behind them with his arms crossed over his chest. She could see his breath rising in white puffs. The snow had started falling again. She couldn't expect him to stay out in the cold while she enjoyed the warmth of the truck. It was clear she was going to have to make the first move. She folded her hands across her abdomen.

She had abysmal judgment where men were concerned. Robert was a prime example. He'd spoken about love and marriage, but he'd used her and cast her aside as soon as she gave in. She betrayed the vows she had made at her baptism and lost her self-respect for nothing.

Love and marriage were out of the picture now. She was about to become an unwed mother. Someone to be pitied. To be talked about in hushed tones, pointed out as an example of what could happen to girls should they stray. She wanted to bury her face in her hands and cry.

Tears slipped down her cheeks, but she scrubbed them away. They solved nothing, but she couldn't stem the rising tide of her remorse.

When Jesse had his anger under control, he glanced at the truck. Gemma's head was bowed and her shoulders were shaking. Was she laughing at him? He'd been the brunt of her teasing before. He'd give a lot to know what she found funny in their current situation. As he walked past the truck bed, he caught the smell of gasoline. Leaning down, he checked under the truck but couldn't see anything wrong. The undercarriage was resting on a snowdrift but the smell of gas was stronger. He wished he knew more about trucks, but he knew enough to be sure it was dangerous to run the vehicle if the gas tank was leaking.

He pulled open the cab door. Gemma wasn't laughing. She was weeping. His anger evaporated. "I'm sorry, Gemma. Don't cry."

"I can—can cry if I—I want to." She wouldn't look at him as she sniffed and wiped her nose with a tissue from the box on the dash.

"We need to turn the truck off. It's leaking gas."

Her eyes widened. She quickly turned the key and the engine died. "Is it dangerous?"

"Not unless something sparks. We'll have to get by without the heater. I'm sorry I hurt your feelings. Please forgive me."

"I'm crying because my ankle hurts."

He sighed heavily. "Then I'm sorry I made your ankle hurt worse."

"Go away," she snapped and sniffed again. He took a step back. She looked up and held out her hand. "I didn't mean that, Jesse. Don't go. Get in here where it's warm. You'll catch your death out there."

"I'm pretty tough. A day in the cold is nothing new for me."

"Please?"

He got in the truck, gently lifted her injured leg and placed her foot on his thigh. "You should keep it elevated. Is the snow pack helping? Am I forgiven?"

She bent her other knee and scooted forward an inch to make her position more comfortable. "It's hard to be upset with someone who is being kind." She rubbed both eyes with her hands.

"I will make it a point to be kind more often. I think we should get your shoe off, but that is up to you."

She bit her bottom lip and nodded. "I'm already crying. I guess now is as good a time as any."

She braced herself, but he was incredibly gentle as he pulled her shoe off her swollen foot. It immediately relieved some of her pain. He placed her shoe and sock on the dash and settled her foot on his leg again. "It needs to be taped up."

"With what?"

He opened the glove compartment and pulled out a roll of duct tape he had noticed yesterday. "This might work. I'll need to put your sock back on. I don't want to plaster this to your skin."

After a few minutes, he had fashioned a crude brace for her foot. "How is that?"

"Okay. Better I think."

"Warm enough?"

"The blanket helps."

"I don't know how. It has more holes in it than a

cheese grater." He reached over, tucked it tightly around her shoulders.

"How long do you think it will take Dale to get help?"

"It's hard to say. Four hours, maybe less."

She leaned her head back against the glass and untied the ribbons of her bonnet. "Then we won't be rescued anytime soon."

"You might as well try to get some rest."

Far from sleepy, Gemma closed her eyes anyway, but she could feel his gaze on her face. She endured it as long as she could. She opened one eye. "What are you staring at?"

"I was trying to figure out what is different about you."

"I've got a suntan. The sun actually shines during the winter in Florida, unlike this place, which is dreary from late September until May."

"You think these beautiful snow-covered pines are dreary?"

"I do."

She could see he was disappointed with her answer. If he thought the snow-covered woods and gray skies were beautiful, then he was odder than she had imagined. She waited for his next comment. She had never had this much of a conversation with him before. When he didn't say anything else, she closed her eyes but her throbbing foot allowed her to sleep only fitfully. Sometime later, the cold roused her. She raised her head and found Jesse rubbing the frost off a spot to see out.

"Are they here?" she asked hopefully.

"Not yet."

"Oh." She leaned back and pulled the blanket up

around her shoulders. "Can we have the heat on for a while?"

"I don't think we should risk it."

"Not even for ten minutes?"

He shook his head. "I checked the gas gauge a half hour ago and the tank is almost empty. I know Dale filled up this morning before we left the motel. If the gasoline has pooled under the truck, we could start a fire. Or worse."

"Worse?"

"An explosion."

That would be worse, she conceded silently. He knew more about vehicles that she did. She was cold, but she trusted his judgment and didn't push the issue. "It's snowing again."

It wasn't a question. The windshield was covered. He moved her foot off his lap and opened his door. "I'm going to check the trail for any sign of them."

"That seems silly. You can't see much outside and you'll only get colder."

"Moving around will help me warm up."

"Oh, okay. That makes sense. I wish I could join you."

A gust of wind blew in the snow as he got out. It settled on her blanket and sparkled in the dome light. He closed the door and she shivered. She might not be able to walk but she could still move. She spent the next few minutes swinging her arms as she bent and straightened her good leg. It helped a little.

Relief surged through her when Jesse opened the door again. She hadn't realized how safe his presence made her feel. "Anything?"

"Nothing."

"They should be here soon, shouldn't they?" She waited for his reassurance.

"The snow will slow them down. The wind is picking up out there too. Parts of the road could be drifted over by now."

A chill slid over her skin that had nothing to do with the temperature. "They will still be able to reach us, right?"

Chapter Four

Dale should've been back by now. Something must have gone wrong.

Jesse didn't say that to Gemma. He had scanned the trail behind them for any sign of movement or the sound of another vehicle approaching. There was nothing but the wind in the trees and the snow flurries that continued to worsen.

It was past two o'clock and the temperature was dropping. He had to make a decision and soon. The first rule when stranded in the wilderness was to stay put, but he had to get back to New Covenant tonight or lose his chance to purchase the land he wanted. The bank would open at eight in the morning. The auction was set to begin at nine o'clock. He could still turn over the earnest money before the bidding started as long as he made it home tonight and got to the bank as soon as it opened.

"Any number of things could have slowed Dale down. We might have to head back soon," he said.

Without gas, he couldn't run the truck's heater. While the cab gave them protection from the wind and snow, without heat, it would be like staying inside a cold tin can. The forecast that morning had called for temperatures to drop to near ten degrees. It was going to get very cold tonight.

"What do you mean by heading back?"

"What I said. Don't worry about it."

"You need to work on your communication skills." She scowled at him but fell silent, and he was grateful. He got out before she could grill him.

Another ten minutes passed. The visibility dropped to fifty yards as the snow moved in. He would have to go now while he still had a trail to follow. If Dale had reached help and someone was coming, they would meet each other on the road. If for some reason he hadn't made it, Jesse could still get Gemma back to civilization before dark and get to New Covenant before morning.

She was a small woman, but he doubted he could carry her all the way to the highway. He needed a sled and he saw only one option. Dale wasn't going to like it.

Jesse walked to the truck and opened the driver's side door. Even huddled in the blanket, he saw Gemma shiver. She looked at him hopefully. "Is Dale back?"

"Nee."

"What are you doing?"

"Taking us out of here." He closed the door.

He was amazed at the number of tools Dale had crammed into his battered metal toolbox. There was even a short-handled ax, which had dozens of uses in the wilderness. He quickly removed the bolts that secured the hood to the vehicle. With it free, he tipped the curved hood onto the snow and pushed it back and forth. The rounded edges at the front made it a perfect sled. He fashioned a harness from the tie-down straps to go over each shoulder.

Gemma had rolled down the window and was watching him. She wore a wary expression. "Let me rephrase my question. What are you making?"

"A sled."

"For me to ride on?"

"That's right."

"Will you fetch my suitcase for me?"

He shook his head. They were running out of time. "I'd rather we left it here. That way I don't have to pull unneeded weight."

"I understand, but there are some things I need from it before we go."

He shrugged and grabbed it out of the back. She opened the door and took it from him. *"Danki."*

He stood for a few minutes trying to decide the best way to cushion Gemma's ride. Sitting directly on the cold metal would quickly make her uncomfortable. What he needed was a couple of quilts. Lacking those, he decided a cushion of pine boughs might do the trick. Taking Dale's ax, he walked into the woods looking for a young white pine. Their needles were soft and flexible. He found what he was looking for and brought back an armload. He dumped it onto the overturned truck hood. It was about the best he could do for her.

He stepped up to the truck door. "We should get going. I want to reach the highway before dark."

"I'm almost ready."

She had her back to him. She had taken off her cloak and put on two more dresses over the one she wore. She looked as plump as the bishop's wife. She put a second *kapp* over the one she was wearing and then tied her traveling bonnet over both. "Without warmer clothes, layering is the next best thing. I'm afraid I'm wearing most of the extra weight you were concerned about pulling."

"Don't worry about that. It's a *goot* idea." He was surprised she'd thought of it. "Do you have any gloves or mittens?"

She lifted a pair of socks from the seat beside her. "These will work as mittens."

"Okay. Are you ready?"

She nodded. "As soon as I put on my cloak. We should take the water bottles with us." She grabbed the plastic containers from the dash. One bottle was half-empty. The other one was full. She scooted across the seat toward him and gathered the wadded blanket to her chest.

He rubbed his gloved hands on his trouser legs. He was going to have to pick her up and carry her due to her injured ankle. He knew she understood that without him saying anything because her cheeks were already bright red. He could tell his face was a similar color. He had never held a woman in his arms. That Gemma was the first one made him doubly uncomfortable.

He slipped an arm under her knees and around her back. She curved one arm around his neck as she held the water bottles and blanket with her other hand. He lifted her out of the truck and held her against his chest. She barely weighed anything. He never imagined holding her would feel so amazing, so comfortable.

Speechless, he stood gazing at her face framed by her dark bonnet. Freckles he had never noticed before dotted her nose and cheeks. Had the Florida sunshine made them more noticeable? Her eyes remained downcast. She smelled fresh, like sun-dried linen and faintly of flowers and coconut. It had to be the shampoo she used because Amish women did not wear perfume of any kind. He wanted her to look at him. To know what she was thinking. His feet refused to move.

A gust of wind made her turn her face into his shoulder to avoid the driving snow. The desire to hold her closer and protect her from anything that threatened her surprised him.

"Are you sure this is a *goot* idea?" she asked.

"Maybe, maybe not."

He quickly realized holding her in his arms for any reason wasn't a good one for him. Emotions he'd worked hard to keep hidden were stirring just below the surface. Gemma was not the sort of woman he could care for seriously. She was flighty, and she rattled his thinking.

The wind dropped away. She raised her face to gaze at him. Her luminous green eyes, fringed with thick dark lashes, were as trusting as a child's. "I will try not to be a burden to you."

"You weigh about as much as a bird. You are not a burden."

"I meant I won't be whiny and childish."

"You are hurt, and this isn't going to be a fun-filled sleigh ride, *shpatchen*." The name fitted her. It meant "little sparrow." A tiny creature bold enough to attack a cat that came too close to the nest.

Her lips curved in a soft half smile. "My grandmother used to call me that when I was a child."

It warmed his heart to see her smiling. "Don't worry, Gemma. Everything will be fine."

Despite her throbbing ankle and the biting cold, Gemma relaxed in Jesse's arms. He must not think too badly of her if he could call her by a childish nickname.

She didn't remember the last time she'd felt so safe. Especially around a man.

Until this minute, she had believed any chance of friendship between them had been ruined by her impulsive actions last year. Nothing she could say would undo his opinion except to behave in a manner he expected of a humble Amish maiden. Though he didn't care much for her, she had no doubt he would do his best to protect her and make the journey back to the highway as quickly and safely as possible.

He settled her on his pile of pine branches on the overturned hood. She scooted around until nothing was poking her unbearably and nodded. He took the blanket from her and draped it around her shoulders, pulling it tight beneath her chin. "Ready?"

"I'm ready. Should we leave a note telling Dale where we have gone in case we miss each other?"

"The road is narrow. I don't see how we could miss each other." He walked to the front and slipped his arms through the loops he had made from the tie-downs. He started forward and Gemma grimaced with pain at the jolt. She grabbed at the branches under her with both hands. He looked back.

"I'm fine. I'm fine," she said quickly.

"You don't look fine. What will make it less painful for you? I don't know how long this walk will take, so think about that before you say *fine* again."

He was right. There was no need to suffer more than she had to simply to impress him. "Maybe if I had something higher to sit on and a way to keep my foot propped up a little."

"Will the toolbox be high enough to sit on?"

It was about a foot tall and just as wide. "I think so."

She scooted to one side. He placed the toolbox toward the back of the hood and rearranged the pine insulation on it. Taking the ax, he cut another armful of branches and arranged them as a padded rest for her injured leg. He helped her settle onto them. "How is that?"

"Better. Now all I need is something to hang on to if the terrain gets rougher."

"It will get rougher." He cut another piece of webbing, fashioned it into a big loop and attached it to the front of the hood. He gave her the webbing to hang on to the way she would hold the reins of a horse.

He slipped into his harness and started walking. The seat and padding for her foot made it better but it was a far cry from comfortable. Knowing there was nothing she could do to help Jesse, Gemma gritted her teeth and held on, determined not to complain.

The snow flurries grew heavier. A layer of white soon covered her blanket and the pine needles around her. The wind sent the fresh snow snaking across the trail where breaks in the trees offered access. Jesse's makeshift sled moved easily over the snow, but he couldn't avoid the dips and hollows that jolted her.

They'd gone several miles before her fingers grew numb despite the socks she was using as mittens. She tucked one hand inside her cloak until her fingers stopped stinging, then switched hands to warm the other one. While it helped some, she was soon switching them every few minutes. She tried warming them both at the same time, but the sled hit a drift and she toppled over backward. Jesse was beside her before she managed to right herself.

"Are you okay?"

She sat up and repositioned her aching ankle. "I'm fine."

"What happened?"

"I wasn't hanging on because I was trying to warm my hands inside my cape. I'm sorry."

"Sorry for what? Giving me a break? It's not such a bad idea." He looked around and spotted a place where he could sit on a toppled tree. A group of thick cedars behind it provided a windbreak. He maneuvered the sled up beside them. He knelt at Gemma's side and pulled off his gloves. "Give me your hands."

He peeled off the socks she was using and sandwiched her icy fingers between his warm palms.

Her hands disappeared between his large ones as he gently rubbed the circulation back into them.

Gemma's hands were small and amazingly delicate. They were also ice-cold. His determination to keep her safe grew tenfold. "It shouldn't be much longer. I think we've come at least eight miles. I can't believe we have more than two or three miles left to go."

"I don't see how you can follow the truck's tracks in this snow."

The tire tracks had been obliterated by the blowing snow miles back. "I can't, but I'm sticking to the road." The wider opening between the trees had been his only guide for the past hour.

He realized the socks Gemma had been using for mittens were wet. Putting them back on wouldn't do her any good. He needed a way to keep her upright without having her hang on to anything.

He cut free the webbing she had been holding on to. "What are you doing?" she asked.

"You'll need to keep your hands inside your cloak."

"If your intent is to dump me out in the snow, just say so."

"That's a ridiculous thing to say." He set about making a smaller loop on one end.

"And removing my only way of hanging on isn't silly?"

"You can't put the wet socks back on."

"They will work for a couple more miles," she insisted.

"Nope."

"Fine. Leave me here and go get help."

"Don't be absurd. I'm not leaving you. Raise your arms."

"Why."

"Because I asked you to."

She folded her arms across her chest. "Not until you explain to me what you're doing."

Even cold and miserable, she could be obstinate. He sighed heavily. "I'm making a smaller loop to go around your body. I'm going to fasten the other end of the strap to the front of the hood and pull it tight. That will keep you from falling over backward in the rough places."

"That's all you had to say." She held out her hand. He gave the loop to her. She slipped it over her head and settled it under her arms.

"How is that?" he asked.

She pulled her hands inside her cloak and leaned back several times to test the strength and tension. "It's fine."

"Fine enough to last a few more hours?"

"It's getting dark already."

He held his arms wide. "Want to spend the night here?"

"Of course not. Are you worried that we haven't met up with Dale yet?" Giving voice to her concern made the situation seem even more dire.

"I have enough to worry about getting you to safety." He pulled on his gloves, slipped into his harness and started trudging forward again.

Although Gemma had always been impressed and intimidated by Jesse's size, she had never considered how strong he actually was. Walking through the knee-deep snow and pulling the sled had to be exhausting and yet the only break he had taken was to ensure her comfort. His determination was amazing as he struggled through deeper and deeper snowdrifts. He fell to his knees once but got up and kept going. As darkness fell, Gemma shivered in the increasing cold. The snow finally let up. The clouds overhead thinned out and the thin sickle of the moon cast the landscape in harsh shadows of black on white. She huddled over as low as she could get but the wind still found her and sucked away any warmth from beneath her blanket. When she had reached the end of her endurance, she heard Jesse as he muttered something that sounded like "Finally."

She raised her face to see a break in the trees ahead. She was ready to cheer if her teeth would stop chattering long enough. Her elation died a quick death as Jesse pulled her sled into the open. There wasn't a highway in front of them. Only the remains of some kind of building in a small clearing. A cabin maybe. A chimney jutted above part of the roof that hadn't fallen in. She didn't remember seeing a place like this on their way this morning. Could they have passed by and she just hadn't noticed the building? She listened but didn't hear the sounds of traffic. Nor did she see any lights.

Jesse dropped to his knees and bowed his head. Fear sent a surge of adrenaline through her aching body. "Jesse, are you okay? Where are we?"

He looked back at her, but his face was in the shadows and she couldn't read his expression. "We're lost."

Chapter Five

Jesse couldn't believe what lay in front of him. Not safety but desolation. The ruins of a second building were nothing more than odd blackened timbers sticking upright through the snow. A pond sat frozen and silent at the bottom of the clearing. A dead cedar tree stood between the house and the pond. There were no signs of life anywhere. He didn't bother calling out.

Somehow, he had made a horrible mistake. He had no idea where he had taken a wrong turn. It was his fault and his alone. He'd been in such a hurry to get back to New Covenant that he'd left his good sense behind. They should have stayed with the truck. They might have been rescued by now.

He wouldn't be at the auction in the morning. The land he'd hoped to buy would go to someone else. Now he was lost in the wilderness and, worst of all, he'd brought Gemma with him into this dangerous situation. He sank to his heels as the magnitude of what he had done overwhelmed him and bowed his head.

Please, Lord, give me the strength to overcome this disaster. Help me keep Gemma safe.

He repeated the phrase over and over in his mind, searching for the solace he needed. "Jesse, you have to get up."

It wasn't the voice of his heavenly Father, but rather the voice of the little sparrow on the sled. If she had once thought him as dense as a post, he had certainly proved her right. His bold assertion that he could get them back to the highway was nothing but an empty promise.

He looked at her over his shoulder. Would she forgive him for putting her life in danger? "I'm sorry, Gemma. I don't know where I went wrong."

"That doesn't matter, Jesse. We need shelter. We need a fire." She could barely talk because her teeth were chattering so badly.

She was right. Now wasn't the time for remorse and self-pity. He struggled to his feet and pulled the sled toward the cabin. The snow had drifted as high as the front porch. The structure blocked the wind from the north. He stepped onto the floorboards carefully. They seemed solid enough. He slipped out of his harness and pulled open the front door. It scraped along the floor but opened wide enough for him to get inside.

It was too dark to see much. The smell of charred wood filled his nostrils, but the ceiling seemed intact and the interior was free of snow. As his eyes adjusted to the gloom, he saw a stone fireplace dominated the center of the space. It was a double-sided type open to two separate rooms. The cabin would provide the shelter they needed if he could get a fire going.

He went back outside and lifted Gemma from her sled. She was shivering violently. He carried her inside and lowered her to the floor. "I'll get a fire started."

"You have m-matches?" she managed to ask through chattering teeth.

"*Nee*, but there is a small propane torch with a lighter in Dale's toolbox. I'm right glad we brought it along."

"Me—me too."

He carried in the tool chest and found the propane canister. "Please don't let it be empty," he muttered. He turned the valve on and clicked it once. The bright orange-and-blue flame pushed back the shadows. The room was empty except for some tattered lace curtains on the windows and a small stack of logs beside the fireplace. Using the torch and one of the curtains as tinder, he quickly got a fire going. The flicker of the orange flames catching hold was the most beautiful thing he had seen in his life.

"Thank You, Lord." Gemma pulled herself closer to the blaze. She was still shivering. Jesse helped her sit up and positioned himself next to her. He took off her wet bonnet. The blanket was too damp to be useful, but thankfully, her cloak was dry.

He unbuttoned his coat. "Lean against me."

She was too weak or too cold to object. "You should take off your cloak."

"I'd rather keep it on."

"Okay." The warmth of his body kept the cold of the room away from her. He rubbed his hands up and down her arms to get the blood flowing.

"*Danki,*" she muttered.

He didn't know how long they sat together, letting the warmth of the fire drive the chill away. Eventually her shivering stopped. Her head dropped back against his chest. From her even breathing, he knew she had fallen asleep. He needed to get more wood. He should also take stock of the rest of the house, but for some reason he was reluctant to move. It was more than the simple fact that he didn't want to wake her. It just felt right to have his arms around her. To have her head resting against him with such trust. It was a foolish thought. He already knew what she thought of him. *Big as an ox and dumb as a post.*

He didn't want to wake her. When she recouped her energy, she would realize the full extent of his blunder. He'd taken them out of the frying pan and into the fire, only it was more like out of the refrigerator and into the freezer. He shifted his position slightly on the wood floor. Her breathing changed. He stiffened. Was she awake? He couldn't see her face.

It took Gemma a few seconds to realize where she was. A warm fire crackled in front of her in an unfamiliar fireplace made of rough rocks. She knew Jesse sat beside her with a hand on her shoulder. Her head rested against his chest. The soles of her feet were too warm, so she pulled them to the side. He stopped breathing when she drew up her feet. She remained still, hoping he would, as well. If he knew she was awake, he would move away in a heartbeat. Just for a little while, she wanted to give thanks that they were both alive and pretend he was holding her because he wanted to and not because he was trying to keep her warm.

His breathing resumed. She smiled to herself and closed her eyes. It seemed she was to be granted a few more minutes to enjoy the comfort and security of his embrace. A moment later, a tiny flutter in her abdomen reminded her why she was in this situation at all.

The baby was kicking, proving he or she was okay

despite the difficult ride and grueling temperature Gemma had endured. She hadn't been able to think of her mistake as her baby until recently. It was something she hadn't allowed herself to dwell on before now. The flutter came again. She didn't want to think about the baby or the baby's father. She sat bolt upright. Jesse withdrew his arm as she knew he would.

There wasn't any comfort meant for her. There were only problems to be solved.

"I'm warm enough now," she said. "Do you know where we are?"

He scooted away and stood up. "As I said before, we're lost."

He tossed a log on the fire and lit Dale's propane torch. "I want to check out the rest of the cabin to see if there is anything we can use."

She looked around at the bare floor and walls and tried for a touch of humor. "A cedar chest full of quilts would be nice. However, from the condition of this room, I would say I'm being overly optimistic."

"Ja."

His dry comeback proved her attempt at being funny had missed the mark. Without Jesse next to her, a cold draft began seeping through her clothing. Jesse stared at her for a moment, then went outside. He reappeared a few minutes later, pulling the truck hood sideways through the door and carrying the toolbox.

It was on the tip of her tongue to ask what he was doing, but she decided this time she would just wait and see.

He propped the makeshift sled up against the wall. He went out and returned this time with all the pine branches that had served as a cushion for her. He still didn't offer an explanation, although he did glance at her. She smiled brightly, knowing her cheerfulness and lack of questions would surprise him. He thought of her as a nuisance. If he had it in mind that she was going to be difficult, she would show him she had matured in her time away. His brows drew together as he studied her face. It was the expression she was used to seeing whenever she was in his company.

Still, without comment, he pushed open the door that led to another part of the cabin. From the light he carried, she could see him shove aside a layer of snow. He disappeared into the room. She waited for him to report back. Exhaustion pulled at her eyelids and she closed them. She opened them quickly when she started to tip over. "I am so tired I can fall asleep sitting up," she muttered.

Why was she still sitting up? She wadded her bonnet into a pathetic pillow and lay down on her side close to the fire. Something hard poked her. She withdrew the forgotten water bottles from the pocket of her cloak, sat up and drank one. She set the other bottle where Jesse could see it and lay down again.

Sometime later, Jesse woke her by shaking her shoulder. "Gemma, the floor is too cold for you to sleep on."

She lifted her head. "Don't tell me you found a bed."

"*Nee*, but I have made one."

There was an inviting pile of fragrant, soft pine boughs covered with the blanket made up beside her. "How nice. You are a rather handy man, Jesse Crump."

"I try."

He helped her stand. She sucked in a quick breath at the pain in her ankle. "Sorry," he said.

"It's going to hurt no matter what I do."

"Would you like me to make another cold pack for it?"

She repressed a shiver. *"Nee."*

She hobbled to the bed, lay down and wriggled into a slightly more comfortable position so that she could see him. "Where are you going to sleep?"

He pointed at the fireplace. "In the room on the other side. I can see you and hear you if you need anything."

Sometime while she slept, he had made a brace to hold the truck hood on its side a foot or so past the head of her bedding. It reflected the heat from the fire back toward her and cut the uncomfortable draft she had noticed before. "Did you find anything useful in the other rooms?"

"I found a cast-iron skillet with a broken handle in what was left of the kitchen."

"Did you find some eggs and bacon to go with it?"

He scowled at her. "What do you think?"

"I'm trying to make light of the situation, Jesse. Never mind. Anything else?"

"Nothing useful. I'll take a closer look in the daylight. It appears a fire destroyed the back half of the building. Only these two rooms are intact."

"For which I give grateful thanks to the Lord. What time is it?"

"Around ten o'clock."

"What do you think happened to Dale?"

"I wish I knew. Do you need anything before I go?"

She shook her head and immediately prayed for Dale's safety, upset that she'd barely given him a thought throughout the afternoon and evening.

Jesse crossed through the archway to the other side

of the fireplace. She waited until he had settled himself on his bedding. The outline of his body shimmered in the flames. "Is it possible no one is looking for us?"

"It's possible if something happened to Dale and he didn't reach the highway." Jesse turned onto his side, facing away from her.

The moment the idea occurred to her, it wouldn't go away. What if Dale was lost himself? Or worse. She and Jesse could be stranded for only God knew how long. Was it still snowing? "Will they be able to follow our tracks to this place if someone is looking for us?"

"I don't know that either."

"What do you know?" she snapped.

"I know I'm dead tired and I don't want to answer any more questions about things beyond my control. Go to sleep, Gemma."

"That's easy for you to say," she muttered.

She sat up and wrapped her arms tightly across her chest. They were stranded in some out-of-the-way place and it was possible no one knew they were lost. She touched her head to make sure her prayer *kapp* was still on.

Please, Lord, help us. I know I haven't spoken to You much lately. I've been too ashamed. I'm trusting in Your mercy now for Jesse and Dale. And for my baby's sake, for this child, who is the most innocent among us.

Her panic subsided. She was in His hands. He would care for Jesse and her and the child she carried. She had to believe God would see them through this.

She glanced around the room. Sometime while she slept, Jesse had replenished the wood beside the fire. The bright color on the inside proved the logs were newly split. He hadn't found a cut pile ready to use. He had split it with a small hatchet out in the bitter cold. He had expended a lot of energy to make sure they could stay warm.

"Jesse," she said softly.

"What?" Exasperation filled that one word to the limit.

He almost convinced her to remain silent but she couldn't. "I think you saved my life today. I appreciate all you have done for me. *Danki.*"

He gave a deep sigh. "You're welcome. Do me one favor in return?"

"Stop talking?"

"Ja."

This time his succinct answer didn't annoy her. It was just Jesse's way. She lay down and closed her eyes. The morning would bring light to see by. They would retrace their steps and find the logging road. After that, they would reach safety in a few hours. She would be back in New Covenant by nightfall.

Where her real troubles would make today seem like nothing more than a winter outing.

Jesse woke to a cold draft blowing over him and the sound of Gemma being sick. He rolled off his bedding and got to his feet. Every muscle in his body ached in protest but that didn't matter. Something was wrong with Gemma.

He came around the fireplace. She had somehow made it out the front door and was leaning over the porch railing. He stood two feet away, unsure of what to do. "What's wrong, Gemma?"

She straightened up. Her face was pale. She managed a slight smile as she dabbed at the corner of her mouth with one of her handkerchiefs. "We can rule out that it was something I ate."

How could she be making a joke at a time like this? "Are you okay?"

"As okay as I can be in the situation. Can you help me back inside?" She held out one hand.

"Of course." He swept her up into his arms.

She squeaked in protest but then she laid her head against his shoulder when he ignored her. "I meant for you to hold my arm while I hobble back inside."

"This is quicker." He kicked the door all the way open and carried her to her bedding. After laying her down, he went back to close the door. He returned to her side and thrust his hands into his coat pockets. "What do you need?"

She sat up and drew her knees up under her cloak. "Nothing. I'm fine."

"You use that word far too often. How can you be fine if you just threw up?"

"You have a point. I would love a cup of hot tea and a cracker. Any chance that Dale left some in his toolbox?"

"I'll check. Chamomile or Earl Grey?"

Her eyes widened with surprise. "Jesse Crumb made a joke. He has a sense of humor."

"Don't look so amazed." He stoked the fire, added another log and sat cross-legged on the floor. The auction would be taking place soon. He wondered who would get the land he'd had his heart set on.

"I noticed it was snowing again while I was on the porch. Heavily. No one will be able to follow our tracks, will they…?" Her voice trailed away.

"Nope." At least she understood why help wouldn't be coming.

"So, what do we do?"

"The hardest thing of all in a survival situation. Stay put."

Her eyes grew wide. "When you say survival situation, are you telling me that we are in serious trouble?"

There was a long silence. "*Ja.* We are."

She pressed a hand to her forehead. "I know conversation is hard for you, Jesse, but please spell it out for me and don't sugarcoat it. How much trouble are we in?"

"On the downside, we are lost and away from our vehicle, where they will be looking for us as soon as the weather clears. That is, if Dale made it out. If he didn't, then no one will be looking for us until we don't return to New Covenant. The bishop won't expect us to travel in bad weather. He may assume we have hunkered down to wait it out. In that case, it may be a week or more before someone starts searching. Are they likely to be looking along a remote logging road? I doubt it, unless someone noticed us turning onto it when we left the highway."

"You could've left a little sugar on it. That was the downside. Now, what is the upside?"

"We have a roof over our heads and a way to stay warm."

"That's it?"

"Pretty much."

She clasped her fingers together. "I see."

She wasn't hysterical or crying. Jesse gave thanks for that. She sat quietly, staring into the fire for a few minutes. When she finally looked at him, her eyes were filled with determination.

"I'm going to need a crutch, so I can move around and you don't have to carry me everywhere."

It was a reasonable request. "I can do that."

"Water is important. I drank the last of mine. Did you find yours?"

He nodded once. "I did. I drank it last night too. There's plenty of snow to melt so we won't go thirsty."

"I also noticed some rose bushes growing beside the house while I was outside. If you can gather some rose hips for me, I'll make some tea. Where is the skillet you found?"

"Still in the kitchen. I'll fetch it after I make you a crutch. How is the ankle?"

"Black-and-blue from what I can see of it around the edge of the tape. I didn't take your handiwork off. It hurts when I move, but it will be fine as long as I'm careful."

"How is your stomach?"

She blushed, although he wasn't sure why. "It will be fine." She paused and looked at him. "I mean, it is *goot* now."

He tried to reassure her. "Hope for the best and prepare for the worst. I will take care of you, Gemma."

"I know that. See if you can find anything usable in the other part of the house and bring me that pan packed with snow. I'll need hot water if I'm going to make tea."

Her attitude amazed him. Perhaps he had underestimated her in the past. Or perhaps the worst was yet to come. He was never quite certain where Gemma was concerned.

Chapter Six

Gemma discovered the skillet was a small shallow one, only six inches across, but usable after Jesse chopped a hole through the ice on the pond and scrubbed it clean. He brought in a large handful of rose hips for her on his way back. She removed the seeds and placed the pulp in the skillet filled with melting snow to simmer. Soon the delightful aroma made her stomach rumble. Jesse disappeared outside again.

It was still snowing heavily. She could hear the sound of the wind increasing. It would soon turn into a full-blown blizzard if the storm kept building. The creaking of the old cabin worried her as much as the weather. Was it strong enough to support the snow that was falling? Would it collapse and bury them alive? It had clearly survived a few winters. But would it last through one more? Where would they find shelter if it came down?

To Gemma's delight, Jesse returned a short time later with a long thick branch he had whittled into a crutch. She happily tried it out. It was good to be upright without hopping on one foot, but the crutch was too tall. "Can you shorten it?"

"How much shorter does it need to be?"

"Take off an inch. That should be enough."

He started to whittle at the end. "If I cut off any more I will have to give it to a crippled mouse to use."

"Are you making fun of my size?" She held up one hand. "Wait. Don't answer that. First, I have to apologize for comments I made to you in the past. If I hurt your feelings, I'm truly sorry, Jesse. I wasn't always kind."

"Like when you said I was as big as an ox and dumb as a post? You weren't far wrong, but I forgive you."

"*Danki.* That means a lot. And I was wrong. You may be a big man, but you aren't dumb and it was cruel of me to say that. Now, what were you saying about mice?"

"Nothing." He handed back the shortened crutch. "See if this works better."

She took it and made a trip across the room and back. "This is *goot.*" She wished there was some way to pad the part under her arm. She was still wearing three layers of clothing and her cloak. She didn't want to sacrifice warmth for a little comfort nor did she want Jesse to give her the shirt off his back, which she knew he was more than capable of doing. "Did you happen to find anything we could use as cups?"

He shook his head. "All I found was a broken pint jar. The edge is too jagged to drink out of, but we can melt snow in it. I found a few broken plates, nothing else we can use."

"If you can cut the necks off our water bottles we can use those as glasses."

"That is easy enough."

She lowered herself to the floor in front of the fire. After Jesse was finished with the water bottles, he sat beside her. Gemma folded her apron to use as a hot pad. She moved the skillet away from the fire and after letting it cool a bit she poured the rose hip tea into the plastic bottles and handed one to Jesse. He took a sip and wrinkled his nose.

She smothered a smile. "Did you know rose hips have more vitamin C than oranges? Do you like it?"

"I've had worse. It's not coffee, but it's warm."

Gemma took a sip of hers. "It's better with honey, but it is hot and that makes it taste *wunderbar* to me."

"I'm not surprised. You haven't had anything to eat since supper the night before last."

She grimaced. "I couldn't eat that greasy hamburger. I threw it out."

"When was the last time you ate? Tell me the truth."

"The morning before I arrived in Cleary I had a good breakfast."

"And you let me eat your burrito yesterday morning? What were you thinking?"

"That I didn't want to eat a spicy breakfast and bump about in Dale's truck for hours afterward. My stomach doesn't travel well. I get carsick."

"You weren't in a car this morning."

She didn't want to tell him she had morning sickness, so she skirted around the issue. "Perhaps not, but I was exhausted after a terrible day and uncomfortable night. I'm fine now. I'm even hungry. I could eat a moose if you want to go out and wrestle one to the ground."

He stared at her for several long seconds. "I'm sorry I got us lost."

"It was a mistake anyone could have made. You might remember I was with you. The conditions were horrible. I'm amazed you had the strength to get us this far."

"I thought you would be angry."

"I'm too tired to pitch a fit. Tomorrow I'll harp at you." She took another sip of tea. He made her uncomfortable with his intense scrutiny. A few months ago, she might have been upset with him over getting them lost and taken her frustration out on him. Everything changed the day she found out that the baby's father had left town without a word. She'd had to grow up in a hurry.

What would Jesse think of her when he found out? New Covenant was a tiny settlement. Everyone would know within a matter of days, unless her parents agreed to keep her secret. She couldn't hide it for long unless she left the community. She was already six months along. Perhaps her parents would allow her to stay with her aunt or one of her cousins in rural Pennsylvania. She could have the baby and give it up for adoption. After that, she could return to New Covenant with no one the wiser, except a few close family members. Only, would she be able to give up her baby?

It was the first time she realized that she actually thought of the child as *her baby*. She pressed a hand to her heart.

"What are you thinking?" he asked.

Startled by his question, she shook her head. "Nothing. Why?"

"You looked sad. Are you worried about being stuck here?"

She splayed her fingers over her abdomen under her cloak. There was more than her own life at stake if rescue didn't come soon. "Shouldn't I be worried? You're the one who took the sugar off my expectations when you laid out our situation."

"Maybe I made it sound too bleak."

"*Nee*, I would rather know the truth."

"Food will be our most pressing need soon, although we can survive without it for several weeks."

"What is your plan?"

He cocked his head to the side. "What makes you think I have a plan?"

"Well, you aren't screaming hysterically and running in circles shouting, 'We're going to die!' You managed impressively by improvising a sled to move me, collected firewood and even figured out how to use the truck hood as a draft blocker. One might think you do this kind of thing every winter."

"I get in a lot of hunting by myself, and survival skills are important."

Most of the Amish men she knew hunted for food. A deer or moose was a welcome addition to a family's freezer. "Did Dale leave a rifle in his toolbox?" she asked hopefully.

Jesse actually smiled. He had a sweet smile and a dimple in his left cheek she had never noticed before. "I wish he had."

"What kind of hunting can you do with a wrench set and a screwdriver?"

"Not much, but I can fashion small game snares from my bootlaces. There is always the pond at the bottom of the clearing. It might be possible to catch fish through the ice. It isn't thick enough yet to walk on it. There are cattails I can harvest. The inner bark of the white pine tree is edible, and we have plenty of those around us.

You can also make tea from the pine needles. They're high in vitamin C too. We won't starve if I can help it."

Jesse became more animated as he talked about how to harvest the edible parts of trees, something Gemma never thought she would consider as a part of her diet. She would have to eat something for the sake of the babe. She asked a few more questions to keep him talking. She'd never seen him like this. Where had this Jesse been hiding? Maybe he had just been waiting for someone to listen.

She'd first found him attractive because he was a strong, work-driven man. And to be honest, he'd been one of only two single Amish fellows in the area. Now that she had a glimpse of the man underneath the brawn, she liked him even more.

"How did you learn all of this stuff?"

He suddenly seemed to realize he had been talking too much. "Here and there."

"Come on. Where?"

He looked away and tossed a twig into the fire. "When I first came to Maine, I took some survival training courses the local game warden taught."

"When I first came to Maine I invested in a very heavy coat, fur-lined boots and a lot of books to read. Why are you embarrassed to say you took classes?"

"Because most people don't think a big man like me is very bright."

Shame brought a lump to her throat. He said most people, but he was actually saying Gemma Lapp. "You really like it here, don't you?"

"I love owning my own farm. It's small, but it's mine. I had plans to expand, but that has gone by the wayside."

"Why?"

"Some land next to mine unexpectedly came up for auction. I was determined to purchase it but missed my chance."

"Because someone outbid you?"

"*Nee*, the auction took place this morning."

"If you hadn't stayed with me at the truck, you could have made it back to the highway and gotten home in time."

He shrugged. "There's no way to know that for sure. Why do you hate this country so much?"

She moved a little farther from the fire and stretched out her feet, wincing as she moved her bad ankle. "*Hate* is a strong word. I wasn't prepared for how lonely it could be. I was used to lots of friends and cousins visiting back and forth in our community in Pennsylvania. In New Covenant, I had only two friends. My cousin Anna and Bethany Martin. They both married last year, and they naturally had less time for a single friend."

"And you thought marriage would be the answer for you too?"

Jesse watched as Gemma's cheeks flushed a deep pink. She folded her hands together and stared at them. "I wondered when that would come up."

"It was a joke to you, wasn't it?" He braced himself to hear her answer. "Little woman tames the big ox and breaks him to harness."

Her gaze flew to his face. "*Nee*, it was never a joke."

"Wasn't it?"

"I can see why you thought so. I acted foolishly, but I did like you, Jesse. I do like you. I'm sorry if you thought I was trying to make fun of you or to hurt you. That wasn't my reason."

"So what prompted your pursuit of me?"

"I guess I wanted what my friends had found. They were both so content. You were the best choice out of the single men in New Covenant at the time."

He snorted, unwilling to accept her explanation. "You expect me to believe you chose me over handsome, well-to-do Jedidiah Zook? I'm not stupid."

"I never thought you were, but you can be very stubborn. I reckon I saw it as a challenge. Besides, Jedidiah Zook is no prize. He thinks more of himself than any woman he knows."

Was she telling the truth? Jesse tried to recall the things she had said and done before her stunning proposal of marriage. She'd never shown an interest in Jedidiah that he could recall. Had he misjudged her and her motives all this time? He could believe that she saw winning him as a challenge. That made sense. It was more believable than thinking she had suddenly fallen in love with him. Her confession that she liked him soothed some of his past hurts. He liked her too but couldn't bring himself to say so.

He leaned back on his elbows. "It's all in the past and best forgotten." It was a relief to be able to say the words and mean it.

"Agreed. I was a foolish girl used to getting my own way."

"So what changed you?"

She stared at her hands again. He noticed her fingers were clenched tightly together as her expression grew sad. "We all get wiser as we get older."

There was more to that story, but he didn't want to press her. Something had to have happened in Florida that had changed the brash girl he knew into the somber woman sitting with him now. Maybe one day she would feel comfortable enough to share that sorrow with him.

And why was he thinking about continuing to see Gemma?

When they got out of this mess, he was certain she wouldn't want to spend another hour in his company. "Why don't you take a nap if you're tired? We don't have anything else to do."

"That's a fine idea." She sighed heavily and lay down, turning on her side with her back to him. Her tea sat unfinished on the floor beside her. Was she sicker than she was letting on? There was nothing he could do for her if that were the case. He wasn't used to the feeling of total helplessness.

Jesse was able to venture outside when the wind died down in the early afternoon. He took the opportunity to strip two of the closest pine trees of their bark as high as he could reach. He regretted that his actions would ultimately kill the trees, so he limited his harvest to what they could use in the next day or two. At the pond, he found cattails growing in the shallow end. Pulling up the roots and washing them was an ice-cold messy business. By the time he got back to the cabin, both of his wet hands were numb.

Gemma immediately noticed he didn't have his gloves on. She knocked the cattail rhizomes to the floor and began to dry his hands with her apron. "Are you trying to get frostbite?"

"I was trying to get our supper."

"I would go hungry another night rather than see you wet up to your elbows in this frigid temperature. Do you have any feeling in them?"

"Not at the moment. I'll be okay."

"Come over to the window." She pulled him to the grimy glass where the light was better. She turned his hands over and inspected them carefully.

"Satisfied?" he asked, pleased that she was making a fuss over him.

"You have some blanched skin and some small blisters. I've seen worse frostbite. Go warm them by the fire, but be careful until all the feeling comes back. I don't want you going out any more today. You're trying to do too much. I could go to bed happy if all I had to eat was a few more stewed rose hips."

"Speak for yourself. I like meat and potatoes for my supper."

Her scowl disappeared, and she started laughing. He cocked his head slightly. "What's so funny?"

"You like meat and potatoes but you bring home tree bark and roots. I hope you know how to cook this stuff because I certainly don't. Go warm up. What am I supposed to do with these dirty things?" She stared at the stringy rhizomes on the floor.

"Peel them like a potato. You can use my knife."

Jesse sat cross-legged by the fire with his hands, palms up, on his knees. The dull numb sensation was giving way to painful pins and needles. He took his mind off the discomfort by watching Gemma deal with their unusual food. With instructions from him, she prepared their evening meal. Small strips of the pine bark were roasted on a flat stone in front of the fire along with the cattail roots. She served up the fare on two of the broken plates he had found. She sat down on her bedding with a sigh.

"How is your ankle?"

She held her foot out and wiggled her toes. "The

swelling has gone down some. I should be able to get my shoe back on."

"Stay off of it for a while yet and use the crutch."

She munched a piece of roasted pine bark. "This stuff isn't bad. Kind of sweet and crunchy. It doesn't taste like wood, really. Still, I don't think it will ever make the menu at a fast-food restaurant."

"It's okay for now, but I'll try for some meat tomorrow if the weather is clear. I've seen plenty of rabbit tracks in the snow. I'll set out some snares tomorrow morning and check them tomorrow evening."

"If the weather is clear, don't you think we should try to get back to the highway or the truck?"

"I'm tempted to say yes, but the truth is I have no idea which way to go. I thought I was following the road we came in on, but I could have taken a wrong turn one mile after we left the truck or five miles after we left it. *Gott* was *goot* in leading us to this shelter. We are safest staying put. I will make a distress sign in the clearing that can be seen from the air in case someone is looking for us. The problem is, every time it snows, it will be covered up."

"The next time we end up in a situation like this, I'm going to ask for the sugarcoated version." She pushed her food away.

"Let us pray there won't ever be a next time."

"Amen," she said emphatically.

The next morning, Jesse woke to the sound of Gemma's crutch tapping the floor as she hurried across the room and out the door. A few seconds later, he heard her retching. She was sick again. Concern pushed away his reluctance to confront her about it. He waited until she came through the door and returned to her bedding.

"It's not car sickness. What's wrong with you? And don't tell me you are fine."

"It's not something for you to worry about, Jesse."

Too late. He was already worried. "But you're not going to tell me what's wrong."

"I'm going to be blunt. It's none of your business."

"As long as we are stranded together, I think it is."

Sighing heavily, she lay down and turned away from him. "I'm going back to sleep now."

She had barely eaten anything last night. How sick was she? Maybe what she needed was real food, a hearty broth or rabbit stew. She couldn't stand to lose much weight. She was tiny enough as it was. He took his responsibility to care for her seriously.

He sat up and began to pull the laces out of his work boots. The sooner he got snares set, the sooner he could bring back fresh meat for her. When he had what he needed, he cut one lace in half, using it to secure his boots while he used the rest to fashion another snare.

He quietly left the cabin. Outside, he found it had stopped snowing during the night. He took his hatchet and cut several armloads of pine branches. He arranged them into a large X about ten feet long in the center of the clearing. Satisfied with the result, he took his snares and walked into the woods.

The sound of an airplane in the distance sent him racing back into the open. Were they searching for Gemma and him? He looked up but couldn't see it.

Gemma came out onto the porch. "Do I hear a plane?"

"*Ja*, but where is it?" The sound told him it was

moving closer but the tall trees around them blocked his view.

"I can't see it."

They kept looking but Jesse realized the sound was now moving away from them.

"Where are they going?" He heard the panic in her voice.

"They may be flying a search pattern. If they are, they will come back. We have to pray they fly over our clearing and see the distress sign."

"If we make a signal fire, the smoke will rise above the trees. Shall I add more wood to the fire inside?"

"We need something quicker and bigger." How much time did they have? He could still hear the drone of the engine.

"Jesse, what about that dead cedar?"

He looked around and his gaze fell on the brown cedar tree between the cabin and the pond. It was only about eight feet tall, but it would go up in flames easily and produce more smoke faster than building up the fire inside. "Get me the propane torch."

He raced to the porch. Gemma came out and tossed the canister to him. He rushed to the cedar, turned on the torch and clicked the striker. It caught immediately. He shook the snow from the tree and held the torch to it. The tinder-dry branches caught fire and smoke billowed into the air. He stepped back. The flames quickly engulfed the tree, sending orange flames leaping high in the air.

Gemma hobbled toward him through the knee-deep snow. She stumbled, and he caught her before she fell. She clung to his arm as she searched the sky. "Do you think they saw it?"

Chapter Seven

Gemma clutched Jesse's arm as she strained to hear the plane returning. She prayed fervently for their rescue. "Surely they must see the smoke."

He covered Gemma's hands with his own. "Wait, I think I hear it again."

She caught the sound then too. "Please, dear Lord, let them see us."

Suddenly a small aircraft burst into view, barely skimming the tops of the trees. Gemma and Jesse began to shout and wave their arms. The plane circled back once, and it dipped its wing to acknowledge them.

"They saw us!" Gemma threw her arms around Jesse's neck. His bear hug lifted her feet off the ground. She captured his face between her hands. "We're going to be rescued."

As she stared into his eyes, something changed. His pupils darkened as he gazed at her.

"I'm almost sorry we can't stay a little longer," he said softly.

"Why?" The word sounded breathless as it dissipated in the cold air.

"Because I was just beginning to get to know you."

His revelation gave way to a warm comforting sensation followed by sharp loss. She was in his arms. Exactly where she had wanted to be so long ago, and he was still completely out of her reach. Now more than ever. She didn't deserve this man's affection.

Tears pricked the back of her eyes. She moved her hands to his shoulders and he slowly lowered her to the ground. He didn't release her. She couldn't look into his eyes. "And I have learned a lot about you. You enjoy eating bark. Who would've guessed that?"

"And you like to keep secrets," he said, tipping his head to see her face better.

"At least we don't have to do a lot of packing," she said, trying to change the subject.

He seemed to take the hint. "It may be a while before they can get snowmobiles to us. I should get you back inside."

She looked around for her crutch, but he simply swept her up in his arms and walked slowly toward the cabin. She relaxed in his arms. It would be the last time he held her. She wanted the moment to last forever. He stopped at the porch steps. "We've had quite an adventure, haven't we?"

"We did. I imagine you'll be glad to be rid of me." She bit the corner of her lip as she waited for his answer.

"I think I'm going to miss your scolding but not your rose hip tea."

"I wasn't that hard to get along with, was I?"

"Not at all. Well, not most of the time." He smiled slightly. She caught sight of his dimple again. Perhaps she would see it more often now that they had gotten to know each other better.

"At least we won't have to eat bark for supper again tonight."

He chuckled as he gazed into her eyes. "I can always bring some to your house. You should try it fried in a little oil. It's a lot better that way. I think your *daed* might like it."

She looked down. If only she could enjoy his company at home with her parents. She wasn't sure how they would react to her news. She could be shunned. Until she figured out what she was going to do, she couldn't make any plans. "I'm getting cold. You had better take me inside."

"Oh, sure. The last thing you need is frostbitten toes on top of your other problem."

Her gaze snapped to his. Had he put two and two together and come up with her pregnancy as the cause of her illness each morning. "What do you mean?"

"Your sprained ankle. What did you think I meant?" He walked up the steps and carried her through the door, and then he placed her gently on her bedding in front of the fire.

"It doesn't matter. Can you help me get my shoe on?"

"Sure." He knelt and tenderly slipped her walking shoe over her foot. He pulled the laces snug and tied a neat bow. "How does that feel?"

"Good enough to get home. I'm anxious to know what happened to Dale."

He straightened, took a step back and thrust his hands in the pockets of his coat. "Me too. I sure hope he's okay."

"He must be, or they wouldn't have known to look for us." She glanced at their collection of broken pottery, plastic bottles and the sad skillet missing its handle. "I think I'm going to miss this place."

"I'm ready for my own mattress and quilts."

She smothered a smile. "I'm ready for my mother's home cooking."

It was several hours before their rescuers arrived. Two men on snowmobiles as Jesse had predicted. One snowmobile pulled a sled behind it. Jesse went out to speak with the men. After a few minutes, he brought them in to meet her. "These fellows are members of the Wilderness Search and Rescue Team. Bradley is a paramedic. He needs to check us out before they can transport us."

Jesse and the other rescuer stepped back outside to wait. From Bradley's pointed questions, Gemma knew Jesse had told him about her brief bouts of sickness. Satisfied with her blood pressure and pulse, he examined her foot. "Someone did a nice job of stabilizing it with duct tape."

"Jesse thought of it."

The paramedic cut off her stocking and the gray tape. After gentle probing, he looked her straight in the eye. "This will need an X-ray. You may have a broken bone."

"I'll see a doctor when I get home."

"We will take you straight to the hospital from here. Did Jesse have any injuries that you know of?"

"You should check his hands. They were red with white patches of frostbite yesterday."

The paramedic put his equipment away. "I will have the sled ready in a few minutes. We'll have you both checked out at the hospital. It's protocol."

Jesse came in a few minutes later with a large orange blanket. "This should keep you warm on the ride." He draped it around her and scooped her up again. He carried her out to the snowmobile. She was going to miss this easy familiarity. She knew he would behave very differently once they were back in New Covenant. "Did you ask about Dale?"

"I did. He hit his head much harder than we thought. He made it down to the highway, but he passed out at the side of the road. Someone found him and got him to the hospital. He didn't wake up until the next day. The weather was too bad to look for us then."

Their second rescuer was a teenage boy. "Mr. Kaufman gave us directions to his truck. When we discovered it was empty, we started an air and ground search for the two of you."

"We are certainly grateful for your help," Jesse said as he settled her onto the sled and tucked the blanket around her.

Gemma bit her lip. Had he noticed her rounded tummy? If he had, his expression hadn't changed. The men then covered her with another blanket and strapped her in. It was an odd sensation to be lying flat while the men prepared to get underway. It was even more so once they were moving.

Her view consisted of the blue sky overhead and the tops of the tall pines that bordered the trail. It wasn't long before the speed of the trees zipping past made her queasy. She closed her eyes for the remainder of the trip. When they finally stopped, she opened them to see more men in uniforms waiting for them beside an ambulance.

She was transferred from the sled to a gurney in the ambulance. Jesse was allowed to ride beside her. She was grateful for his solid, calm presence.

Once they reached the hospital, they were taken to separate rooms in the emergency department. The nurse who took her vital signs and asked all manner of questions was extremely kind and curious about her adventure. She gave Gemma a gown to change into and stepped out of the room. Gemma was waiting to be seen by a doctor when Jesse spoke on the other side of the curtain. "May I come in?"

Although the hospital gown she wore was perfectly modest, she drew the sheet up to her chin and turned on her side to hide her growing waistline. "Come in, Jesse."

The concern in his eyes warmed her heart. "How are you? And don't say fine."

"I am wonderfully warm, but this bed isn't the most comfortable. How are you?"

He held out his left hand. He had a bandage wrapped around it. "They say I am in perfect health, except for some small patches of skin on my hand that may slough off. They gave me some cream to use."

"I'm sorry to hear that. The cattail roots were not worth it."

He grinned. "I thought they were pretty good. You just weren't hungry enough to appreciate them. Maybe a little bird like you could live on rose hips, but a man my size needed something more substantial. As soon as they let us out of here, we are going to get some burgers and fries."

"That sounds *wunderbar*."

A young man wearing a white coat with a stethoscope around his neck stepped into the room. He held a clipboard in his hand. The nurse who had questioned Gemma earlier came in and stood behind him. He read silently for a minute or two and then looked up with a smile. "Miss Lapp? I'm Dr. Johnson. It sounds like you have had a tough time of it lately."

Jesse tipped his head toward the door. "I'll be out in

the waiting room. I want to call the bishop and explain what happened to us. I'm sure he is concerned."

The nurse nodded. "I'll come get you when we're finished. You might want to go by the registration desk. They have questions about insurance."

Jesse stopped at the doorway. "We Amish don't carry insurance. Our church will cover what is owed if it is more than we can pay. I'll take care of your bill, Gemma."

"*Danki*, Jesse. My father will repay you."

"I know. I'm not worried about that."

Once Jesse was out of the room, Gemma took a deep breath. "There is something you should know doctor. I'm pregnant."

"Congratulations. We'll make sure to shield your baby while we x-ray your foot."

She managed to thank him. He had no way of knowing this wasn't a happy event for her, and she didn't share that part of her history. He gave her a thorough examination. His friendly smile changed to a look of concern as he listened for the baby's heartbeat.

Gemma started to worry. "Is everything okay?"

"Your little one seems to be hiding from me. Have you noticed any changes? Has there been a decrease in movement?"

"*Nee.*" Her hands clenched the sheet tightly.

"Let's make sure everything is all right with the baby. We'll do a sonogram while we have you down in X-ray."

Jesse placed a call to the community phone booth, expecting to leave a message for the bishop and Gemma's family. On the second ring, someone answered. "Elmer Schultz speaking."

"Bishop Schultz, this is Jesse Crump."

"Jesse, we have been wondering what happened to you. Dale left a message saying you and Gemma Lapp were lost in the wilderness."

Jesse went on to explain the detour, the accident and admitted he was responsible for getting them lost in the woods. He assured the bishop that their injuries were only minor ones.

"I praise *Gott* it was not worse. What can I do to aid you?" the bishop asked.

"If you could arrange for our transportation home that would be great. And let Gemma's family know she is okay."

"I will as soon as I finish speaking with you."

Jesse hung up the phone. He eyed the vending machine in the corner. He strolled to it and noticed a package of beef jerky among the candy bars. He inserted the correct amount of change and enjoyed the snack even while he felt guilty that Gemma hadn't had anything to eat yet. For all his praise of pine bark, it hadn't satisfied his appetite.

He saw the nurse who had been with Gemma motion to him and he hurried to her side. "How is she?"

"I haven't heard a report on her X-ray yet. She's on her way back. You can wait in her room if you'd like."

"*Danki*, thank you," he said, forgetting for a moment that she wouldn't understand his Pennsylvania *Deitsh* language. The room was still empty when he stepped inside. He took a seat in one of the chairs pushed back against the wall.

The doctor came in and held open the door for the people moving Gemma. The doctor caught sight of him. "Mr. Lapp, you will be happy to know that your wife and baby are both doing fine. Her ankle is sprained but there are no broken bones."

"Bobbli?" Stunned, Jesse looked from the doctor to Gemma for an explanation. He spoke to her in Pennsylvania *Deitsh*, so the man wouldn't understand what they were saying. "Gemma, what is he talking about?"

She covered her face with her hands. "I'm sorry. I couldn't tell you. I am so ashamed," she replied in the same language.

"Then this is true. You're with child? You were baptized. You made a vow before the church and before God."

The doctor looked puzzled and concerned. "I don't understand what you are saying. The baby is fine now. As I told your wife, the condition she has will require a cesarean section, but with good prenatal care, both she and the child should come through with flying colors." He laid a hand on Gemma's shoulder. "Don't cry. You are worrying your husband."

Gemma turned her face to the wall.

Jesse found his voice. "I'm not her husband." He got up and walked out of the room.

In the hall, he stopped as a nurse pushed an elderly woman past him in a wheelchair. He raked a hand through his hair.

Gemma was pregnant. Who was the father?

Had she gotten married in Florida and left her husband? Or had she broken her vows to the church? Sadly, the latter was the most likely explanation. She wouldn't have needed to keep it a secret otherwise.

A cold sensation settled in the pit of his stomach. If that were the case, he knew exactly what lay in store for her and her baby. He was the child of an unwed mother.

* * *

Gemma kept her face averted through the first hour of the ride home. Jesse sat silently beside her. Dale had been released too. He sat up front with the driver, a woman the bishop had sent to pick them up. They would be home in another few hours.

"What are your plans?" Jesse asked quietly in *Deitsh* in case they should be overheard.

She glanced at him, but he was still staring out the window at the snow-covered landscape. At least he was speaking to her. Shame almost kept her silent, but she clutched at the olive branch he offered.

"I don't know," she replied quietly in their Amish language.

He turned to stare at her. "You must have some idea."

She kept her voice low, although she didn't think Dale or the driver understood what was being said. "Before the accident, I thought I could put the baby up for adoption. I have family in Pennsylvania that I could stay with. I'm sure there must be an Amish couple who would love to adopt a child in the area."

"And after the accident?"

She gripped her fingers tightly together. "I was worried that something might happen to him or her. For the first time, I started thinking that my mistake was actually my baby."

"The child is not to blame."

She cupped her hands over her abdomen. "I know that."

"Have you told the father?"

"I did."

"Did he offer to marry you?"

"*Nee.* His name was Robert Fisher. He left town

the next day without telling me where he was going. I waited months for him to return. He never did. I have no idea how to contact him. I finally decided to come home."

"I would judge him to be a coward, but it is wrong to judge any man. Only God can know what is in the heart of the person."

There was nothing she could say about Robert that wouldn't make her sound bitter. Jesse looked out the window again. "Do you love him?"

She swallowed hard. "I thought so. He said he loved me. I believed him. I was very naive."

"Life gives the test first and then the lesson is learned."

She had failed the test miserably and couldn't offer anything in her own defense. She had wanted to be loved, but she had been tricked into believing Robert's love was real.

"When this becomes known in the community, you will be shunned unless you make a public confession to the church."

"I know." She dreaded telling her parents more than she dreaded telling everyone else.

"What did the doctor mean when he said you had a complication that would require a cesarean section?"

"He called it a placenta previa. It means the blood supply for the baby will tear open when labor starts." *Please, Lord, protect this child. I didn't want to be pregnant, but I would never wish harm to befall a baby. My baby. Have mercy, I beg You.*

"That is dangerous for the child and for you?"

She found it hard to speak past the lump in her throat.

"He said it was. The nurse gave me a pamphlet to read about it."

"May I see it?"

Gemma frowned. Why would he want to read such a thing? She withdrew it from her pocket and laid it on the seat between them rather than handing it to him. A baptized member of the faith was forbidden to accept anything from the hand of a shunned person, to eat at the same table or to do business with them. Jesse knew that.

He picked it up. "You aren't shunned yet, Gemma Lapp. That is for the church to decide."

He remained quiet for the next few minutes and then handed it back to her. "*Danki.* Will you be able to face the entire congregation and admit your mistakes?"

"I will have to, won't I? If I wish to remain in New Covenant as a member of the Amish faith."

"You could accept the shunning and live apart from the community or become English."

Gemma was surprised by his comment. "To face the shame I have brought to my family won't be easy for me or for them. I won't give up my faith, but it might be better if I moved away."

"You should consider what is best for the child, not only for you and your family."

"I don't know what's best, but I think I want to keep my baby, even if I have to raise him or her by myself. I hope my parents will understand and allow us to stay with them."

He nodded, but his eyes held a faraway look. "A fatherless child faces many hardships, as does a mother without a husband."

There was something in his voice that made her look at him closely. It wasn't a random comment, she was sure of it. "It sounds like you know someone in that position."

He fixed his gaze on her. "I do. My mother was never married."

Chapter Eight

Jesse watched Gemma's eyes widen with disbelief. "Your mother wasn't married?"

"I never knew my father. Not even his name. She never spoke of him."

"How awful. Why? I mean…if you don't mind telling me about it."

He hadn't told a single soul his story since coming to New Covenant, but he heard only sympathy in her voice. "I don't usually talk about it."

A wry smile tugged at the corner of her lips. "I used to think you didn't talk about much of anything. I was happy to discover I was wrong. If you don't feel like sharing, that is okay with me. I won't mention what you have told me to anyone. We are friends now and I value your friendship."

Gemma and her child were facing the same situation his mother had endured. He plucked at the dressing on his right hand, remembering some of the painful parts of his childhood. "My mother worked as a maid for an *Englisch* woman who lived near my grandfather's farm. My grandfather died shortly after I was born. We had no other family. My mother made a public confession and was forgiven. She attended church services, but we never stayed to eat or visit with other members. She avoided people and made sure I did too."

He fell silent as he recalled the day he had asked her why he didn't have a father like the other children. Her answer had frightened him.

She grabbed him by the shoulders, shook him and told him never to ask about his father again. He never had.

Gemma laid her hand on his arm. "That sounds like a lonely existence."

"It was."

"How sad for her and for you."

"It wasn't much better when I started school. I was shy. I didn't know how to act around others. I had trouble learning to read. I was bigger than the other *kinder* my age but not as smart. I tried to keep to myself, but I was teased a lot. They called me Jesse the Ox. The name stuck with me until I moved here."

"Children don't realize how much words can hurt." She looked down at her clasped hands. "I am guilty of using hurtful words."

"Something tells me you have seen the error of your ways," he said softly.

"I hope I have. I'm ashamed of the way I behaved toward you last year."

He shrugged. "I wasn't always kind to you either."

"Thank you for confiding in me, Jesse."

"Your decision will have a long-lasting impact on your child. Make it carefully." Because a child growing up without his or her father's name could feel like an outcast even if he or she wasn't.

"How am I to know what's best for this baby?"

"I reckon you pray on it."

She turned to stare out the window, and they made the rest of the journey in silence.

It was almost dark by the time they arrived at the bishop's business. Jesse was surprised to see the large number of horses and buggies filling the parking lot.

Dale turned around. "It looks like we have a welcoming committee. I guess everyone has heard about our adventure by now."

Their driver pulled the vehicle to a stop in the driveway. The bishop opened the front door, letting the cold evening air pour in. "Welcome back, Dale Kaufman. I'm right glad to have my best hauler returned. You'll have your job waiting for you when you are able to start driving again."

While the bishop spoke with Dale, the door beside Jesse opened and his friend Michael Shetler reached in and grabbed Jesse's uninjured hand. "It's good to see you in one piece. You were found before we even knew you were lost, my friend. God moves in mysterious ways for sure. He spared us a lot of grief and worry."

Michael's dog, Sadie, pressed in to nuzzle Jesse's hand. A yellow Lab mix, she was Michael's constant companion and helped to warn him of the PTSD flashbacks he sometimes had. Jesse patted her head. She was pushed aside by Jesse's dog, Roscoe, a shaggy black-and-white mutt who had shown up at his door last spring. Jesse smiled as he took the dog's head between his hands. "Hello, big fella. I missed you too. Who has been feeding you?"

Michael grinned. "I have. He showed up looking

hungry the first night you were gone. I took care of your stock too."

Michael leaned lower to look inside the car. "I'm mighty glad to see you too, Gemma. Bethany wanted to come but I told her she should wait in a warm house and hear all about it from you tomorrow."

"*Danki*, Michael. Tell her I will come by first thing tomorrow morning."

The door beside her opened. Her father stood waiting for her to get out with a big grin on his face. "*Gott* is good to me. He has brought my daughter home."

Gemma immediately burst into tears. She scrambled out of the car and into her father's embrace. He patted her back awkwardly. "There, there. You are safe now. It's all over. Come, I will get you home to your mother and the two of you can have a good cry together. She sent along your winter coat so you wouldn't catch a chill." He held it out to her.

Gemma took it but kept it bundled in front of her rather than putting it on.

Jesse got out and was soon surrounded by the men of the community, who plied him with questions about the ordeal. He answered them as best he could while he made his way toward the Lapps' buggy. He wanted to speak to Gemma before she left. She was already seated inside when he reached it. She managed to quell her sniffles long enough to extend her hand to him. "Thank you for everything."

He squeezed her hand in reply. "All I did was get us lost. If I can do anything for you, just ask."

She pulled her hand free and looked away. "That means a lot to me, Jesse, *danki.*"

He shrugged. "You were a *goot* companion, except when you were scolding me."

"I should promise never to scold you again, but I fear I wouldn't be able to keep it. Stay safe."

He gazed into her eyes, wishing they wouldn't drift apart but he knew they would. She had her friends and her family. They would take care of her. His job was done.

Gemma's father wiped his eyes with the back of his hand. "You have my gratitude and that of her mother for taking care of our Gemma. She was blessed to have you looking after her." He shook Jesse's hand, climbed into the buggy and drove away.

Jesse watched it disappear down the road. He was going to miss Gemma. That they might never be alone again, might never enjoy the comfort of each other's company again hit him hard. She had a rough journey ahead of her. He wouldn't be able to protect her and her baby.

Michael slapped Jesse on the shoulder. "The bishop has invited us inside for coffee. Come on. We all have questions for you."

Jesse followed Michael inside the front office of the business. Both dogs tried to follow them, but Jesse told Roscoe to stay and Michael said the same to Sadie. It was warmer inside the building. Men began removing their coats. A few chairs lined the plain gray walls. One had been saved for him. Samples of shed materials took up shelf space on one wall. The place smelled of sawdust and paint.

"Why didn't you stay in the truck? That's what I would've done." Ivan, Michael's teenage brother-in-law, offered his opinion.

"That was supposed to be the plan," Dale said. "So why didn't you stay there?"

"The gas tank had a leak. We couldn't run the heater for fear of starting a fire." He explained the rest of their adventure, including his mistake of losing the trail.

Michael punched Jesse's shoulder. "It couldn't have been easy being snowed in with Gemma Lapp." Everyone but Jesse laughed.

The bishop handed Jesse a cup of coffee. He wrapped his fingers around the warm thick white mug. "She was no trouble."

"You're just being kind," Michael said. "I know how much of a pest she was in the past."

Jesse stared at the dark coffee in his cup and thought about Gemma's rose hip tea. He might even miss that. "She has changed."

There were more questions and suggestions for surviving a blizzard from some of the older men. Ivan asked Jesse to teach him how to make rabbit snares. Jesse looked around and realized how thankful he was to be surrounded by friends who appreciated him for his skills and didn't poke fun at him because of his size, except in a friendly way.

"Who bought that eighty acres at auction?" he asked when he had a chance.

"Leroy Lapp did," Michael said. "He got it for a steal."

Jesse managed a wry smile. "Because I wasn't there to bid against him." Gemma's father was a good farmer. He would make the most of the property.

Jesse's plans to expand his farm would have to wait. It was a bitter disappointment, but he accepted it as God's will. One by one, the crowd of men headed for home until only Jesse and the bishop were left in the small office. The bishop took Jesse's empty mug from his hand. "You must be tired. Let me take you home."

Jesse shook his head. "It's not far. I feel the need to walk."

The bishop was a keen man, sensitive to the needs of others. "Is there something on your mind? Is something troubling you?"

Jesse shook his head. He would respect Gemma's privacy and allow her to decide if and when she should confide in the bishop. "*Nee*, good night, Bishop Schultz. I will be in to work tomorrow morning."

"*Goot.* We have many orders to fill."

Jesse walked out of the building. Roscoe was waiting outside the door. He trotted ahead a short distance but came back and barked once. Jesse paused to pet him. Happy with the attention, Roscoe fell into step beside Jesse as they followed a gravel road leading south.

The night was clear, and the stars were beginning to come out. New Covenant had received six inches of new snow, but they had been spared the brunt of the blizzard. The snow and gravel crunched beneath his boots as he walked along with his head down and his hands in his coat pockets. The doctor had warned him that his hand would ache as it was healing, and he was right. But it wasn't his discomfort that occupied his mind.

Gemma was in trouble. "It has nothing to do with me. I kept her safe when she needed me and now she is with her family." Roscoe perked up his ears.

Jesse glanced at his dog. "My responsibility has ended, right?"

He wanted to believe it was true, but he couldn't shake the feeling that she still needed him. They had become close during their time together. He had seen a side of her he hadn't known existed. She had endurance, a sense of humor, a level head. She was a quick thinker. If she hadn't remembered the dead cedar tree, the search plane might've been too far away to see the signal fire by the time he thought of it. She had promised that she wouldn't whine, and she hadn't. She had endured pain and bone-chilling cold without a whimper.

He stopped in the middle of the road. "Why am I listing her good qualities to myself?"

Roscoe sat with his tail wagging slowly and his gaze pinned to Jesse's face. Jesse sighed. "I'll tell you why. Because those are the qualities I hope to find in a wife someday. And that is a ridiculous thought. As odd as it sounds, Gemma and I have become friends."

Still, the nagging feeling that she needed him wouldn't go away. He stared off into the distance until Roscoe whined again. Jesse patted him and resumed walking. There was nothing he could do for Gemma and her baby. He had to accept that.

Chapter Nine

Gemma sat silently beside her father in their buggy as he drove home. The moment she dreaded was fast approaching and she wasn't sure she could go through with it.

"Are you all right, daughter?"

She started to say she was fine but remembered how much Jesse disliked her use of the word instead of an honest reply. "I'm tired, and my foot aches."

"We will be home soon. Tonight, you can rest easy in your own bed."

"That sounds *wunderbar*." If only she could put off telling her parents about her condition until another time. But doing so would only make it harder.

Gemma stared out the window and saw they were approaching Bethany and Michael's house. Bethany stood at the front door. She waved when the buggy drew close enough. Gemma waved back. There was so much she needed to tell her friend. She needed Bethany's advice and her support. Hopefully she would remain a friend after she learned of Gemma's transgression.

The buggy rolled on and Gemma's home came into

view. The tall two-story house, painted white with black shutters, looked inviting with lamplight shining from the windows. Her mother's beautiful flower garden was covered with snow, but she had colorful bird feeders arranged where she could view them from her kitchen window. The big red barn with white trim looked immaculate against the snowy backdrop.

"It's good to be home," she said quietly and realized it was true. She had never appreciated the love and care her parents lavished on their property. The work of tending the flowers, caring for the animals, even painting the barn had seemed like tedious chores. Now she hoped she could do those things again, only this time it would be with a glad heart if her parents allowed her to stay.

Her mother came rushing out of the house when her father stopped the buggy by the front gate. Gemma got down and was immediately embraced by her mother. Gemma kept the coat between them, not wanting her mother to notice her condition. Tears stung Gemma's eyes, but she refused to let them fall. There would be time for tears later.

"It's so *goot* to have you home at last. Come in out of the cold," her mother said as she slipped her arm around Gemma's shoulders and began shepherding her to the front door. Inside the warm house, the familiar smells of home bombarded Gemma. Her mother had been baking. The smell of bread, fresh from the oven, dominated the air but under that, she could smell the scent of cooking chicken, her mother's pine cleaner and the lemon polish she used on the furniture.

"Let me take your cloak."

Gemma handed it over, feeling self-conscious about her growing figure. Her mother didn't seem to notice the change beneath her loose dress. They went into the kitchen, where her mother began fixing a cup of tea for each of them. She had chicken noodle soup cooking on the stove. "Supper is almost ready."

"I've missed your cooking." Gemma took a seat at the table and listened to her mother's happy chatter. Before long, she was up to speed on the inhabitants of New Covenant. Her mother was one who enjoyed gossip and was happy to share what she knew.

Gemma's father came in, stomping the snow from his boots on the porch before stepping inside. He unbuckled his overshoes and pulled them off. He set them on a large tray meant to catch the melting snow beside the door. "It's going to get cold again. My arthritis tells me we're in for a long winter."

"You should have chopped more wood before now," her mother said. "We will run low by next month."

Her father shrugged. "I will have Jesse help me cut and haul some in. He's always glad to lend a helping hand."

Gemma took a sip of tea from the cup her mother handed her. She set it down carefully and waited until her mother served up bowls of hearty soup loaded with vegetables, tender chicken and her homemade egg noodles. A plate held warm mini loaves of bread and a crock of fresh butter. It was the best meal Gemma had eaten in her life despite her nervousness.

When the supper dishes were cleared and her father had refilled his coffee cup, she said, "Please sit down, *Mamm*. I have something to tell you both."

"What is this news?" her mother asked over her shoulder as she rinsed the last plate.

"Come sit down, *Mamm*."

"I can listen standing up."

Gemma bowed her head. "I'm so sorry about this. I didn't know what else to do, so I came home." She looked up to see her mother's puzzled expression slowly change to disbelief. She stopped drying her hands at the sink.

She met Gemma's gazed for a long moment, then tears filled her eyes. "Oh, *nee.*"

Her father stared between the two of them with an expression of confusion. "Oh, what? Why are you crying, *Mudder*?"

"Because I'm going to have a baby." Gemma covered her face with her hands as tears slipped down her cheeks.

"I don't believe it," he declared. "My daughter would not behave in such a wanton fashion."

"I'm sorry, *Daed.* It's true. I thought he loved me and that we would marry, but he left and never came back."

"Who is he? I'll speak to his father and see that he makes this right."

"I don't know who his father is. He told me his family was from Ohio and that's all he told me. I have no idea how to find him."

Her father's face grew red. "Gemma, how could you disregard the teaching of the church? I don't know what to say. How can I hold my head up among the congregation? I am a minister now. I oversee the flock along with the bishop. I will become a laughingstock, a preacher who couldn't raise his own daughter to be chaste."

She shrank from his words. It was what she had expected, what she deserved, but it was still painful.

"Hush, husband. This isn't about you," *Mamm* said quietly when she had composed herself. "This is our child, and she is in trouble."

Gemma wanted to throw herself into her mother's comforting arms.

He rounded on his wife. "Are you not ashamed of her? How will you hold your head up in church when this becomes known?"

"Church is not a place to hold up your head. It is a place to bow low before God."

Some of the bluster left her father's face. Gemma was grateful for her mother's intervention. "I know I have shamed you. I am truly sorry."

Her mother folded her hands together on the table. "Is this the same young man you were seeing in Florida?"

Gemma nodded.

"I thought he was an Amish boy." Her father's frown was back.

"He is Amish, but he had not been baptized."

Daed shook a finger at Gemma. "You have been. You should have known better. And don't tell me I'm wrong, wife."

"You are not wrong, but spilled milk can't be put back in the glass. Many a young woman has lost her common sense in the heat of the moment. It isn't an excuse, but it happens. We must decide what to do now."

"We won't have any success getting someone from here to marry her when word gets out. I'll have my brother in Lancaster find a fellow. There must be some man who will marry her once he learns he will inherit this farm one day."

Gemma stared at her clasped hands. "I don't need a husband."

"What do you want to do, Gemma?" *Mamm* asked gently.

"At first, I thought I could go and stay with Cousin

Shelia or Cousin Donna May and give the child up for adoption when the time came."

"*Ja*, that is a *goot* plan," *Daed* said. "That way, no one has to know about this."

Mamm scowled at him. "You would give away your grandson or granddaughter before you have even looked upon the child's face? Have I married such a heartless man?"

"I don't want to give up my baby anymore. I want to raise my child myself." Gemma glanced between her parents, hoping they would understand.

Her father shook his head. "We have given you everything you ever wanted, Gemma, and this is how you repay us—by bringing shame on our heads. *Nee*. You will not live in my home as an unwed mother. You will marry. I will arrange something as quickly as possible."

"*Nee, Daed*, please. I don't wish to marry." The thought of it made her sick.

He silenced her with a stern look. "There will still be talk when the child arrives early, but having a husband will provide some protection for you and the child from gossip. You will make a private confession to the bishop as soon as possible. I'm finished talking." He rose to his feet and left the room.

Gemma turned to her mother. "He can't make me marry someone I don't know."

"This seems harsh, but I have to agree with him. With a husband, you and your babe will have security. Affection can grow between two people who respect each other and work together for the good of the family."

"I'm not looking for love. It may exist for others but not for me. Not anymore."

"It may feel like that now, but time has a way of healing our hurts."

"There is something else you need to know. The doctor said I will need a hospital delivery. I have something called placenta previa."

Her mother's eyes widened. "I know of this condition. We should ask the midwife in to see you soon. She will know how best to care for you."

Mamm leaned back in her chair. "Finish your tea, Gemma. We will talk more about this in the morning."

Gemma nodded but knew this had only been the first hurdle on her journey. Which way the road led from here was known only to God.

After praying for guidance, something she had rarely done since leaving home, Gemma crawled beneath the heavy quilts she and her mother had made together. Her eyes burned from weeping, and her heart ached worse than her ankle. Snug and warm in a soft bed for the first time in days, she lay curled on her side in a state of half waking. Uncertainty kept her awake. Was she being selfish, wanting to keep her child? Wouldn't it be better to give her babe a mother and a father? Could she marry a man she didn't know? What if they didn't get along? She shivered at the thought. Finally she fell asleep without reaching any decisions.

She rose early the next morning and went downstairs. She found her parents both at the kitchen table. They appeared tired and worn. She wasn't the only one wrestling with the future.

Daed wouldn't meet her eyes and Gemma's heart sank at his cold expression. He rose and walked to the kitchen window. "Someone just drove in."

"Who is it?" *Mamm* got up to put a kettle of water back on to heat.

"I think it's Jesse."

"What is he doing here?" *Mamm* looked at Gemma.

"I have no idea," Gemma said, wondering the same thing.

Jesse entered the house and saw Gemma's father scowling at him. "This isn't a good time to visit, Jesse. Can it not wait until tomorrow?"

"Maybe it could, but I would rather do it now. I have some business I'd like to discuss." He'd spent a restless night worrying about Gemma and her family's reaction. He needed to see how she was getting along.

Gemma's father gestured toward the living room. "Come in and have a seat. Would you like some coffee?"

Jesse shook his head. "I'd like to speak to Gemma for a minute, if you don't mind."

Her parents looked puzzled but got up and left the room.

Gemma leaned toward him. "What are you doing here?" she asked in a small whisper. She looked pale, tired and on the verge of tears.

"I wanted to see how you are feeling. Have you told them?"

"I did." She kept her face down. He wished she would look at him. He wanted to see her eyes.

"And?"

"*Daed* was upset. *Mamm* was sad and disappointed, but she didn't judge me harshly."

"The hard part is over, then. Have you decided what you are going to do?"

"Father wants to arrange a marriage for me to help

quiet the scandal. He's going to have his brother in Lancaster find someone willing to wed me. He is offering to let some fine fellow inherit this farm if he agrees. Apparently gaining good farmland can offset having a sullied wife."

That Leroy was willing to go to such lengths surprised him. "I see. Do you wish to marry?"

"*Nee*. I don't want to spend my life with some stranger. I want to keep my baby, but *Daed* says I can't live in his house as an unwed mother. I've been thinking I might go to live with one of my cousins until the baby is born. Then I will try to resume my life somewhere."

"Somewhere but not here?"

She shook her head still without looking at him. "I don't think I can stay here. My folks will always know what I've done."

"You made a mistake, Gemma. You have to forgive yourself too."

"Perhaps in time." Finally she looked up at him. "Only…"

"Only what?"

A tear slipped down her cheek. "Only I don't want to move away from my family and my friends, and I don't want to marry someone who only wants my father's land. What shall I do?"

He wanted to draw her into his arms and comfort her, but he knew such action wasn't proper. "I don't know the answer. I wish I did."

She wiped her cheek and drew a deep breath. "It isn't fair of me to ask you. This is my problem. I'll solve it. What business do you have with my father?"

"He bought the land I wanted at the auction I missed.

I came to see if he'd be willing to sell it to me for a small profit."

"I hope he will. You missed your chance to buy it because you stayed with me."

"*Gott* allowed it. He must have something else in mind for me."

She laid a hand on her abdomen. "I wish I knew what he had in mind for us."

He gestured toward her foot. "You should go put your foot up so the swelling doesn't come back."

She sent him a tiny smile. "Is that your way of getting rid of me?"

"I thought it was kinder than saying you look worn-out. If we were back in the cabin, I'd tell you to go lie down."

She rose to her feet. "If we were back in the cabin, I'd tell you to go eat bark."

He grinned. "I can bring some over for you later."

Waving her hand, she declined. "I think not. A nap sounds much more appetizing. Thanks for coming to check on me."

"Isn't that what friends do?"

She smiled and nodded. He watched her leave, limping slightly, and then went in to speak with her father.

Leroy was seated in his blue overstuffed chair with his feet on a matching ottoman. Gemma's mother was on the sofa. She rose and left the room without speaking.

Jesse took a seat in a straight-backed chair close to Leroy. "I heard you bought the land that borders mine."

"You heard right. It's a fine piece of ground."

"I thought so too. I had hoped to get in my bid but that didn't happen. Would you be interested in selling it to me? I'm willing to see you make a profit on it."

Leroy ran a hand down his beard. "I can see why you'd want it. Let me think it over."

"Fair enough. That's all I can ask." Jesse rose to his feet to leave.

"Before you go, let me ask you something."

"Sure."

It took Leroy a moment to phrase his question. "A year and a half ago Gemma embarrassed you with unwanted attention. She embarrassed us, as well. Be honest with me. Did she continue that when you were together?"

Jesse shook his head. "She didn't. She was considerate, uncomplaining and worked hard to make the best of a bad situation. No one could fault her behavior. In fact, I came to admire her spirit."

"I'm glad to hear you aren't disgusted with her anymore."

"She has changed a great deal."

Leroy frowned. "More than you know."

Jesse hesitated. He didn't think Gemma had told her parents he knew her secret, but he thought Leroy deserved to know. "I'm aware of Gemma's condition."

"You are?" Leroy seemed to sink into his chair. "How many other people know?"

"Only me. I won't say anything."

Sighing heavily, Leroy glanced at the door his wife had gone through. "It will come out sooner or later. As you might imagine, my wife is heartbroken. We are struggling to know what to do and praying *Gott* shows us the best way to help our daughter. I will speak with the bishop today."

"He is a *goot* man. He will give you sound advice. I should get going. I told him I'd be in to work today."

"Let him know I'll be in later."

Jesse nodded, put on his hat and left. Outside, he opened the door of his buggy and looked over his shoulder at the house. He saw Gemma standing at a window upstairs. He raised his hand in a brief wave. She opened the window and leaned out. "Did he sell it to you?"

"He's thinking about it."

"At least he didn't say no." She closed the window and waved, but she looked sad and lonely. She turned away and once again he was left with the feeling that he should do something to help her.

Her parents were out when Gemma came downstairs. She pulled on her old coat and boots and headed toward Bethany's house, using a stout stick to help her walk. She prayed her friend would be home and the children would be already gone.

Ivan and Jenny were Bethany's younger brother and sister. The responsibility for raising them had fallen to her after the deaths of their mother and later their grandfather. It was Bethany's grandfather who had founded the community of New Covenant. Bethany had been determined to raise the children on her own and continue his dream of a new Amish settlement far from the tourists in Pennsylvania. Then Michael Shetler arrived to take over her grandfather's business. It wasn't long before Bethany and Michael fell in love and were married. Now they were expecting their first child. Bethany was Gemma's dearest friend. She knew she would find comfort and compassion there.

Gemma knocked on her door a short time later. Bethany opened the door wide, grinning from ear to ear. "I was hoping you would come early. Michael left a few minutes ago to see about fixing a clock at someone's home." Bethany grabbed Gemma and gave her a hug. "Promise me you are back for good. I've missed you so much. Tell me everything you have been doing."

"I will tell you everything, but it is not what you expect. Do you have some coffee made? This is going to take a while."

"I have coffee and rolls waiting for you inside. We are holding Sunday services here for the first time. I hope you can give me a hand getting ready. There is so much to do."

It was wonderful to feel welcomed and needed. "Of course I will."

Coffee cups in hand, the two women sat at the table in Bethany's homey kitchen and Gemma laid out the whole sad story of her time in Florida and the trip home. She told her friend everything, including her father's plan to find her a husband.

"My life keeps getting more complicated, Bethany. What should I do?" She waited for Bethany's advice.

Bethany slowly shook her head as she stirred a spoon of sugar into her coffee and started pulling apart a cinnamon bread stick. "Gemma, I can't tell you what to do. I wish I could."

"What good is a friend who won't advise me?" Gemma sipped a cup of strong coffee and prayed it would stay down.

"A real friend helps you see your choices. They don't make those choices for you."

"You sound like Jesse." She took a bite of a saltine cracker.

"My heart bleeds for the position you are in. You know that, don't you? I love the child I carry more each day. I look forward to the birth of my baby as a wondrous event. That you are unable to share the same joy I feel breaks my heart. A baby is a great gift from God."

Gemma reached across the table to lay a hand on Bethany's arm. "I'm happy for you. Please believe that. You deserve the joy a baby will bring you and Michael."

"You deserve that joy too."

"I'm afraid I may find sorrow instead of happiness."

"Why?"

"I didn't want this child in the beginning. I didn't want to be pregnant. But I want it now. I do. I want to hold and love my baby, but I'm afraid. What if *Gott* takes my babe back to heaven?"

Bethany leaned across the table and took Gemma's hands in hers. "Every mother has that fear, but to worry is to doubt *Gott*'s mercy. He will help you bear whatever comes into your life if you open your heart to His love."

Gemma squeezed Bethany's hands. "I know. I'm trying to have faith."

"Have you spoken to the bishop?"

"Not yet."

Bethany smiled gently. "You will be forgiven. You know that, don't you?"

"People forgive, but they don't forget." Gemma shivered inwardly.

"They will in time."

"I have shamed my parents. I can never forget that. I know my father won't. He can barely stand to look at me. I believe it may be best for me to go away."

"A new baby can warm the coldest heart. You'll see."

"Oh, Bethany, I pray you are right."

Chapter Ten

There were two buggies parked in front of the house when Gemma returned home. She recognized both. One belonged to the bishop. The other one was her father's. He was home from work early.

Her parents weren't wasting any time. She drew a deep breath and went in to face them.

They were all seated in the living room. There was a platter of cookies on the end table. They all had cups of coffee in their hands. The bishop wore a stern expression she had never seen before. His wife, Myra, sat beside him with a kindly smile for Gemma. Her parents sat with bowed heads.

She lowered her eyes. "Good morning, Bishop. I trust you are well?"

"I'm in good health, but I am greatly distressed over the reason for my visit today."

"I'm very sorry for the pain I've caused my family and you."

"I believe you, child. Come in and sit down."

Gemma took the only seat left to her, the one directly

facing the bishop. "Would you care for some coffee?" her mother asked.

Gemma shook her head. "I had coffee with Bethany this morning."

"I'm glad you have a friend you can confide in," the bishop said. Gemma wondered how he knew she had told Bethany about her pregnancy.

Her father cleared his throat. "I asked the bishop to hear your confession."

This wasn't what she had been expecting. "I thought only minor offenses were handled in private confessions. I assumed I would have to make a public confession in front of all our baptized members at a *sitz gma*." The *sitting church* was a special meeting held after the Sunday worship was over where only baptized members of the congregation participated. A punishment was chosen if all members agreed. Gemma was prepared to be shunned for a month or more before being accepted back into the church.

Bishop Shultz nodded once. "That is normally the case. While you have committed a grave offense, it is not a matter that has drawn the attention of the whole congregation, and therefore I don't feel it needs to be resolved publicly at a member's meeting. It is your father's understanding that you have repented and wish to once again join our fellowship."

"That is true. I do repent."

"Then begin."

She clasped her hands together and lowered her gaze. She had learned the words of confession in her baptismal classes several years ago but never thought back then that she would have to actually utter the words. "I confess that I failed to uphold my vow. I want to make peace with God and the church, and I promise to do better in the future."

"Come forward and accept the kiss of peace." His wife came to stand beside him as he beckoned to Gemma.

She stood and walked forward. Myra laid her hands on Gemma's shoulders and kissed her on each cheek. "Welcome once again into the house of the faithful."

A second later, she was embraced by her mother. Her father walked away without a word.

Gemma couldn't believe it was over so quickly.

The bishop glanced from her father's retreating figure to Gemma. "Remember that we are only human and none of us are without blemish. Your father wishes for you to take a husband. I agree it is best for a child to have both a mother and a father to nurture and guide him or her."

She thought of Jesse and his story about his unhappy childhood. Would she subject her child to the same unhappiness by staying single? What was the right thing to do? She sighed. "What man wants to marry a wife who doesn't love him? How can that be a loving home?"

The bishop smiled gently. "My grandmother had an illegitimate child and married my grandfather a year later. She told me she barely knew him before their wedding day, but she had faith in her father's choice and faith in *Gott*. I remember them as a happy couple who loved all eight of their children and all twenty-five of their grandchildren. Sometimes we must take things on faith."

Gemma's mother remained with her as her father returned to walk the bishop and his wife out.

"Do you feel better?" her mother asked as she took a seat in the chair.

All was forgiven. It was something Gemma had heard her entire life, but it was the first time she had experienced it. Her spirits rose. "I do feel better, but I wish *Daed* could forgive me."

"He has."

"I'm not so sure. He's barely spoken to me."

"He loves you, but he is struggling to see the path *Gott* wants him to take. Give him some time. Michael and Bethany are hosting the Sunday service. I'm sure Bethany could use an extra hand getting things ready."

"I have already told her that I'll help," Gemma answered softly.

"We'll go over together first thing tomorrow." Her mother looked as if she wanted to say more but left the room with only a backward glance.

Gemma sank onto the sofa. The two things she had been dreading the most had come and gone. All the energy she had spent worrying about telling her parents and telling the bishop left her feeling limp. She was forgiven. She would try hard to become a demure and humble person worthy of the forgiveness that had been shown her.

Getting ready to host church services meant deep cleaning for the home owner inside and out. No room or nook was spared. Because of the large amount of work involved, each family was expected to host the bimonthly meeting only once a year if the congregation was large enough.

Gemma and her mother were getting out of their buggy at Bethany's just as Gemma's cousin Anna Miller arrived in a pony cart. Gemma and Anna had been friends from the cradle and quickly greeted each other with a hug. "Say you are home for good, cousin. It wasn't as much fun without you."

Gemma drew back, suddenly worried how Anna would receive her news. "I have something I must tell you."

Anna squeezed Gemma's hand. "I already know. Bethany told me. I hope you don't mind. I knew something was troubling her and I pressured her until she confided in me. A sin that is forgiven should not be mentioned again and we will not." She laid a hand on Gemma's stomach. "Another baby is coming into the world, and that is a reason for joy."

"*Danki*. I never expected people to be so accepting. I'm humbled by it."

"Not everyone will be. There are some people who will condemn privately before they forgive publicly. Just remember, you have family and friends to support you."

"Friends, but not all of my family. My father isn't speaking to me. He wants me to marry. He's willing to offer his farm as an incentive if it will bring someone willing to wed me."

"His farm? He can't be serious?" Anna looked outraged.

"He won't give it up while he's alive, but he'll leave it to my husband in his will."

"Your father will come around. There is much work to do. Let's get started."

Inside the house, the women gathered around the kitchen table, each one setting her basket on it. Gemma opened the lid of the one she carried and began to pull out its contents. "I brought a few things." She produced cleaning supplies, plastic pails, pine cleaner, rags, sponges and brushes.

"Where shall we start?" Anna asked.

Her mother picked up the pail and carried it to the sink. "I will finish these windows. Where is Jenny?"

"In school," Bethany said. "She'll be home about four." Bethany's sister was ten years old and always a willing helper.

"I'll get this food put away." Anna opened her basket and brought out two loaves of bread and a cherry pie with a gorgeous golden lattice crust. Gemma felt her stomach rumble. Her morning sickness had subsided and her appetite seemed to be making up for lost time.

Next, Anna began unpacking china and flatware that would be needed to feed all fifty church members, along with four coffee cakes. "One for later when we need an energy boost and three for the church meal so you don't have to bake tonight."

Bethany was clearly overwhelmed by her kindness. "*Danki*. This is far too much."

"No thanks are needed. You will do the same when it is my turn to host the service," Anna assured her.

"I will," Bethany agreed.

"What do you need me to do?" Gemma asked, looking over the kitchen.

Bethany took a second to gather her thoughts. "Anna, if you want to start in the living room that would be great. Gemma, perhaps you could help me drag the mattresses outside so I can beat the dust out of them."

Gemma's mother shook her head. "None of you pregnant girls are going to be struggling with heavy mattresses. Leroy and Jesse will be here after work. They will do the heavy lifting."

Gemma couldn't help the little jolt of happiness that shot through her when she realized she was going to see Jesse again today. She thought she would have to wait until Sunday.

The house quickly became a beehive of activity. Walls, floors and appliances were scrubbed until they shone. Windows sparkled and window curtains were washed. Everywhere inside the house, the sharp scent of pine cleaner filled the air.

Bethany stopped beside Gemma, who was polishing the hall table. "Can you believe it? In one morning, these women managed to do more inside the house than I could have accomplished in four days on my own."

"Many hands make light work." A sharp pain in her abdomen made Gemma grimace and bend over. She waited for it to come again, but it didn't. It was a reminder that her pregnancy wasn't going to be a normal one. "Be good, little one. Don't scare me like that."

"Are you okay?" Bethany asked.

Gemma managed a little smile. "I'm fine."

Bethany pointed to the couch. "Sit and take it easy."

"Only if you do."

Bethany plopped down and patted the cushion. "This is me resting. Now, you."

Gemma joined her for ten minutes and then both of them got back to work.

One of Michael's heirloom clocks on the mantel was striking four o'clock when all the women gathered in the kitchen once more. Bethany wiped her forehead with the back of her sleeve. "I don't know about you, but I've worked up an appetite. I believe I will sample the cherry pie. Would anyone else care for a piece?" The coffee cake had vanished before noon.

Mamm smiled brightly. "I thought you'd never ask."

"I'll get the plates?" Gemma was already moving toward the cabinets.

Bethany turned to Anna. "Would you like some?"

"Are you joking? I could eat the whole thing."

Mamm chuckled. "That's because you are eating for two."

Bethany and Anna shared a grin as Anna said, "That's what I keep telling my husband when he makes faces at my overflowing plate."

"Me too," Bethany said and giggled.

Gemma endured a stab of wistful envy. They had loving husbands to share their journeys into parenthood. She would travel that path alone unless she agreed to her father's plan. Was God leading her in that direction?

Marrying would allow her to keep her baby and remain near her parents and her friends. Agreeing to wed would lessen her father's displeasure. Would it be worth the trade-off? It was difficult to know what was best. The babe wasn't to blame but he or she would be a constant reminder of Gemma's fall from grace. For both Gemma and the man who wedded her.

Bethany and Anna were so happy about their pregnancies. Gemma wanted to feel that excitement, but she was afraid she never would.

Jesse stepped into Michael's house and heard the chatter of women pouring out of the kitchen. Jesse was happy to see Gemma in the midst of them. It appeared that she was fitting back into the community. Her friends had rallied around her. He was happy for her. There would be people who avoided her or spoke unkindly, but that would pass with time. Then he noticed she was standing a little apart from the group with her eyes downcast. There was something in her demeanor that seemed wrong.

She caught sight of him and smiled. His heart gave a happy leap. He had missed her companionship since returning to New Covenant. Finding time alone with her might not be easy but he was willing to try. Had she missed him? The hope that she had died a quick death.

Why should she? She was back among friends and family.

When they had been alone together in the wilderness, it was clear that she needed him. He knew what to do. How to take care of her. He knew how to find food and make a snug shelter. She didn't need any of that now.

He jumped when Michael patted him on the shoulder. "Hey, big guy. You're one for keeping secrets."

Jesse frowned. Did Michael know about Gemma's pregnancy? "I don't know what you're talking about."

"I see you making eyes at Gemma Lapp."

"I wasn't making eyes at her."

"Looked that way to me. You used to say she was annoying."

Jesse smiled. "She still can be."

"So, what is the story?"

"We are friends, nothing more."

"Friends?" Michael's eyebrows shot up.

Jesse scowled at him. "Is there something wrong with being Gemma's friend?"

Michael held up both hands. "*Nee*, not at all. I see my wife wants me." Jesse thought he heard Michael chuckle under his breath as he walked away.

"What are you mad about?" Gemma asked as she crossed the room.

"Michael was giving me a hard time."

"About what?"

"It's not important. What can I do to help?"

"You can help me hang the curtains up. You won't need a step stool."

"Lead on."

Gemma threaded the curtain rods through the pockets of the pale blue sheers and then gave them to Jesse. "How have you been?"

He hung them with ease. "Fine."

She chuckled. "I thought we weren't to use the word *fine.*"

"You can't. I can."

"How is that fair?"

"I'll think of a reason in a minute."

Shaking her head, she handed him the next set of curtains. "I've missed you, Jesse."

He paused with the rod in his hands. "You have?"

"Is that so surprising?"

"*Ja*, it is."

"I just feel like I can be myself with you."

He hung the curtain and they moved to the next window in the living room. Everyone else was in the kitchen. "Who are you being the rest of the time?"

"The disappointing daughter. The confused mother-bride-to-be. The waffling woman."

He crossed his arms over his chest and gave her a stern look. "Aren't you being hard on yourself? You have some difficult decisions to make."

"The bishop agrees that I should marry for the baby's sake."

"But you don't think so."

She gazed at him intently. "What do you wish your mother had done?"

"I wish she had found happiness in life instead of hiding from it."

Gemma laid a hand on his arm. "I wish I could have known you as a boy. I would have been your friend."

"That you are my friend now is enough." He turned back to the window, afraid to say more. He had grown to care for her more than he'd realized.

She handed him another rod. "Last one."

He hung it up. "Now what?"

She dusted her hands together. "Now we wait to see how things go on Sunday."

"Are you ready to face everyone?"

"Absolutely...not."

He tapped her nose with one finger. "You will be fine. If you are done with me, your father said he wants to talk to me about that property."

She smiled brightly. "He must be going to sell it to you. That would be—"

"Fine," he answered with a smile to match hers, and they both laughed.

Jesse left Michael's home with a bounce in his step. He had a feeling that Gemma was right and her father was going to sell him the land. He wouldn't overpay for it. He hoped Leroy would ask a fair price.

When he reached the Lapp place, he saw Leroy putting shoes on one of his buggy horses by the barn. His pair of dapple-gray draft horses looked on over the corral fence. Jesse walked up beside Leroy and waited until he had finished driving in the last nail.

He put the horse's foot down and straightened. "Thanks for coming by, Jesse."

"Can I give you a hand?"

"Nope, this is the last shoe. I wanted to speak to you about that property you are interested in."

"I'm willing to pay you a fair price."

"How does free and clear sound?"

Puzzled, Jesse shook his head. "I don't know what you mean."

"The property is my gift to you if you will marry Gemma."

Jesse's hands curled into tight fists but he managed to keep his voice calm. "That is a surprising offer but I'm going to refuse."

Leroy lifted his hat and raked his fingers through his hair. "Gemma has given you a disgust of her. I feared as much."

Jesse scowled at the man he called a friend. "It is not Gemma I'm disgusted with, Leroy Lapp. Your daughter is worth far more than eighty acres of farmland. If you can't see that, then I pray *Gott* opens your eyes to the treasure you are so willing to cast aside. Does the love and respect of your child mean nothing to you? Or is it that the respect of others means more?"

Leroy stood staring at Jesse with his mouth open. Jesse spun on his heel and walked away before he said things he would regret, hoping Gemma never learned of this conversation.

Sunday came much too quickly for Gemma's liking. News of her condition and confession had spread. She knew by the way her mother had returned tight-lipped from her quilting circle and by the way her parents spoke in hushed tones when they thought she might be listening. From what she was able to gather, there was a disagreement in the community about how her case had been handled.

She arrived early at Bethany and Michael's home because she needed to keep busy. It had snowed again during the night, and the world sparkled under a fresh blanket of white. She worked in the kitchen getting pies cut and bread sliced as the families arrived one by one. Many of the people she knew greeted her openly and she began to relax. It wasn't until the new families arrived that she was ignored when they brought their baskets of food in before the meeting started. She saw the unease on her mother's face and wished she knew how to smooth things over.

Out the kitchen window, she watched the men unloading the bench wagon and carrying the backless wooden benches into the living room for when the service would be held. Jesse was among them. He was easy to pick out from the men dressed alike in dark pants, coats and hats. He stood a head taller than everyone. Just the sight of him brought her comfort. She would have a chance to spend some time with him after the meal had been served. She kept that thought at the forefront of her mind.

When the benches were set up on both sides of a center aisle, the women dried their hands and tidied their aprons before they filed in to take their places on one side of the room. Many of the men were already seated.

Gemma had to take her place among the unmarried women while her mother and her friends sat in the front rows. She was relieved when Jenny squeezed in beside her.

Jenny grasped Gemma's hand. "I'm so happy you are home. I missed you."

Gemma squeezed the girl's fingers. "I missed you too," she whispered.

Her father, Bishop Shultz and Samuel Yoder came into the room and hung their hats on pegs by the door. The three men had been discussing the preaching that would be done that morning. None of them had any formal training in the ministry. They had been chosen by lot to bring God's word to the congregation. It was a lifelong appointment without pay or benefits of any kind. They spoke from the heart without notes or prepared sermons. It was a responsibility every baptized Amish man agreed to accept should he be chosen.

The preaching lasted for three and a half hours. Each man took his turn reading passages from the German Bible and explaining what those words meant to the congregation. Their theme was about forgiveness and the prodigal son. Gemma couldn't help but feel they were speaking about her. She laid a hand over her stomach. She also had to forgive in order to find peace. She let go of her bitterness against Robert.

After the service was over, Gemma headed to the kitchen again to help serve the meal. Her friends were already getting things set up. No one needed directions. Everyone simply pitched in and began working. Gemma saw they were running low on clean glasses. She opened the cabinet door above her to pull out another stack when two women bringing in the dirty dishes walked past her.

"It's astounding that the minister's daughter didn't have to make a public confession."

"It certainly doesn't seem appropriate to me."

Gemma closed the cabinet door. There was a sharp intake of breath, but she didn't see which woman made the sound. Her eyes were pinned to the floor as her face grew hot with shame.

"Would you have forgiven her?" Bethany asked in a tight voice.

Gemma glanced up. A woman in her midfifties stood holding a stack of dirty plates. Behind her, a younger woman Gemma thought must be her daughter stood with her arms crossed over her chest.

"Of course," the older woman said. "After a suitable period of shunning. That is how the bishop from our previous congregation would have handled it."

"A suitable period?" Gemma heard the anger in Bethany's voice and cringed.

"Five or six weeks."

"Then I'm thankful our bishop has a more forgiving nature." They all turned to see Jesse filling the doorway with a fierce scowl on his face. The women gaped as he moved to stand beside Gemma. He slipped an arm around her shoulder. She wanted to sink into him and hide her face, but she willed herself to remain still.

"I heard how you claim to have been lost in the wilderness together. What a cozy story," the young woman said with sweet sarcasm. "Perhaps the babe is yours."

Gemma gasped, ready to refute the statement, but Jesse spoke first. "The child is not mine by blood but should Gemma agree to marry me, the babe will become *my son* or *my daughter* and will be cherished in my home and in my heart for all my life. Of that you can be certain."

Gemma was too stunned to speak.

Bethany took a step toward the women with a frozen smile on her face. "I will certainly mention your criticism of Bishop Shultz's decision to him. What was your last bishop's feelings about people who disparaged him behind his back?"

The two women turned on their heels and left the kitchen without another word, taking the dirty dishes with them. Gemma shook her head sadly. "Bethany, you shouldn't defend me."

"Accept it and rejoice. Besides, I was defending Bishop Schultz, not you."

"Who are they?" Jesse asked.

Gemma looked through the doorway into the living room, where the women were collecting their children.

"Newcomers. Agnes Martin and her daughter, Penelope." Bethany waved one hand. "Pay them no mind. If their last congregation was so wonderful, why did they move here? And now I am being judgmental and unkind. I will go apologize as soon as I'm finished cleaning up."

"I think they are leaving," Gemma told her, unable to look at Jesse yet. Why had he implied she might marry him?

Bethany smiled. "What a shame. My apology will have to wait, won't it?"

Jesse turned to Gemma. "I'm going to take the bench wagon to your father's place. He said your mother has a headache and he is taking her home. I told him I'd see that you got home too. Would you care to ride along with me? We have a lot to discuss."

"We do. *Danki*, Jesse. I will be out in a few minutes."

He nodded and walked away.

Bethany sank back against the counter. "If you don't marry that man, you are a bigger fool than I can imagine. The way he spoke of your baby becoming his—it almost melted my heart. I could hear how much he wants to be a father. I never would have guessed that about Jesse. He would be a good father and a fine husband to you."

"He is a man with many layers, but I'm not going to marry him." She put on her coat and went out to meet him.

Chapter Eleven

Jesse stood beside the wagon, waiting for Gemma to come out. What was she thinking? Had she been appalled by his confrontation with the two women? He was a bit ashamed of letting his temper out, but he didn't like watching somebody be bullied without speaking up. Especially Gemma.

The door opened, and she came out. He silently helped her into the wagon seat and climbed up beside her. He picked up the reins and headed the team toward Gemma's home. After several long minutes of silence, he couldn't stand it anymore. "I reckon I should explain myself."

"You don't need to."

He glanced at her. "Why do you say that?"

"Because you spoke to defend me, and I thank you for that. I know you weren't serious about marrying me."

"Can I ask you something?"

"Of course."

"Do you still think about him?"

"Who?"

"The father of your child."

"Robert? Actually, I haven't thought about him much at all this week except to realize I must forgive him."

Jesse smiled to himself. "That's a good thing." He clicked his tongue to get the horses moving faster. "Have you given any thought to my proposal?"

"Why should I?"

"What would you say if I told you I was serious?"

She frowned. "Is this some kind of joke?"

"Nope."

Her eyes widened. "Are you out of your mind?"

"You proposed to me once, and I'm saying yes now."

She shook her head as if to clear it. "That's ridiculous. You can't be serious, Jesse. Stop teasing. It isn't funny anymore."

He turned the team into the lane that led to her house and drew them to a stop by the front gate. He got down and helped her off the wagon. He stood with his hands resting lightly on her shoulders. "I am serious, Gemma. I wish to marry you."

"Why?"

He smiled at her bluntness. "I like you. You need a husband and your babe will need a father. I know you don't love me. That doesn't matter. We get along quite well. I'm offering you a marriage in name only."

"What about more children?"

"One is enough for me. My farm isn't large. I don't have much to offer now, but I will take care of you. You'll never be hungry in my house."

"I don't know what to say?"

"I believe yes and no are the most often used replies."

"I need to think about this."

"Of course."

Gemma walked before him into the house. Her parents were in the living room. Gemma went and sat in a chair in the corner of the room with her head down and her hands clasped together in her lap. Her mother, Dinah, watched Jesse closely.

He rubbed his suddenly damp hands on his pants. What would her father think of his change of heart? It wasn't because of the land. Jesse would have to make sure Leroy understood that. He was doing it because Gemma needed him. "Leroy, I wish to marry your daughter. I am hoping you will see the benefits and encourage her to accept me."

Gemma clutched her fingers together tightly. "Oh, Jesse, don't do this."

Leroy stroked his beard. "You are a generous, hardworking man. I could not ask for a better son-in-law, but after what you said yesterday, you can see why I'm surprised to hear this. Have you changed your mind?"

"I have not. Our conversation yesterday has nothing to do with my decision today."

Gemma looked from one to the other. "What are the two of you talking about? What conversation?"

Jesse smiled at her. "It's not important. What is important is your answer."

Her father stared hard at Jesse. "Why do you wish to marry Gemma?"

"He is doing it because he feels sorry for me," Gemma said quickly. "I will be fine, Jesse. You don't need to take care of me anymore."

Her father frowned at her. "I must ask you again, Jesse. Why offer for my daughter's hand, knowing she carries another man's child?"

"I've decided I'm ready to settle down. I've never

found a woman who suits me. I believe Gemma and I will get along well once the scandal blows over."

"He doesn't love me, *Daed*," Gemma interjected. She fell silent beneath her father's glare.

"Love grows from respect," he said before turning back to Jesse.

Jesse's chance to wed Gemma did not hinge on what her father had to say. She had a choice. He didn't want her to feel pressured into marrying him. He wanted her to agree that this was best for her and the baby.

Her father turned to her mother. "*Mudder*, what is your feeling about this?"

"If she marries Jesse, I will see my grandchild as often as I want, but that is not a reason to wed. You must believe that God has chosen you for each other."

"That's why I can't marry you, Jesse. He didn't choose us for each other."

"I disagree. May I speak with Gemma in private?" Jesse looked from her mother to her father.

Her father nodded and beckoned to his wife. "Listen closely to him, Gemma. Jesse has a *goot* head on his shoulders. You have brought shame to this family. Your mother and I forgive you, but what you decide will ultimately affect us too. Do you understand that?"

She nodded.

Her parents left the room together. She held her hands wide. "I know you don't love me."

He pulled another chair over until he sat in front of her. He took her hands in his. "Love isn't necessary to have a good marriage. I care about you, Gemma. We are friends, remember? Why did God put us together in the wilderness if not to learn about each other and grow in our affections? You care about me, I know you do."

"And that's why I can see that you are making a mistake. There will still be talk. People will know you aren't the father."

"That's true, but the talk will die down in time and people will forget."

"Maybe they will, but can you forget he or she isn't your flesh and blood? Can you expect me to forget that?"

"In time, I hope we both look at the babe and see only the child of our hearts."

"I don't love you."

He flinched at the pain of her words. "I know, but we like each other, right? I won't expect what you can't give me. It will be a marriage in name only for the sake of your baby. Our baby."

She stood up suddenly. "I need some time. I can't make a decision today."

She rushed past Jesse and up the stairs, limping heavily. He heard her bedroom door slam.

Leroy and Dinah came back into the living room. "Well?" Leroy asked. He looked worn down and sad as did Dinah. Gemma's condition had inflicted a toll on her parents. Their disappointment had to be deep and soul shaking.

"She wants some time to think it over."

Her mother stared into Jesse's eyes. "I believe she will make the right decision. She is our only child and perhaps we have spoiled her because of that, but she has a good heart. If she rejects you at first, be prepared to be patient with her. Can you do that?"

He glanced up the stairs. "*Ja*, I can be patient. Tell her to come see me when she has an answer."

"My offer of the property still stands if she agrees," Leroy said.

His wife scowled at him. "I can't believe how foolish you are. Can't you see Jesse has her best interest at heart and not his own?"

Jesse smiled at her and nodded. "My answer is still the same. Keep your land. I will only wed Gemma if she wants to."

Gemma threw herself down on her bed and clutched the quilt tightly in each hand. She knew why Jesse had offered for her. He was still trying to protect her the way he had in the wilderness. It was noble, but she couldn't accept such a sacrifice from him. She wanted to keep the friendship they had found while they were snowbound in the cabin.

She turned over to stare at the ceiling. Would marriage allow them to remain friends, or would it change everything? It was easy to imagine spending her days keeping house for him, fixing his meals and helping him farm, but there was more to marriage than that. Didn't he deserve the chance to marry for love and be happy with a wife who loved him in return? If she wedded him, she was robbing him of that chance. She wouldn't hurt him in the long run because he was determined to help her now. She cared too much to allow that to happen.

The next morning, she made her way downstairs. It was late. To her surprise, her father was still sitting at the kitchen table. She poured herself a cup of coffee and sat down, expecting more of his silent treatment.

"How are you feeling?"

She looked up in surprise. "Not bad."

"Your mother had the worst morning sickness when she was pregnant with you. It went on for weeks."

A wry smile curved her lips. "Is that where I got it from?"

"Not from me. I'm never sick."

They both fell silent for a while. He cleared his throat and she expected him to speak but he didn't.

"How is Mother's headache?" Gemma asked to break the silence.

"Better once she didn't have to listen to the bishop's wife go on and on about her new grandbaby."

Gemma looked down. "I don't know what else I can say except I'm sorry."

"I too am sorry. I've been hard on you out of false pride. I hope you can forgive me."

"There's nothing to forgive." She managed a slight smile for him.

"Have you given thought to Jesse's proposal?"

"Only all night long. I'm going to see him now."

"What are you going to tell him?"

"I hope I'll have the right answer when I see him."

Jesse didn't think anything about Leroy's buggy turning into the shed building site. It wasn't until he heard someone cough that he stopped hammering and turned to see who it was. Gemma sat in the buggy with her hands clasped in front of her. She wore her gray cloak and her black traveling bonnet. "*Guder mariye*, Jesse."

"Good morning to you, Gemma. Have you come to any decision?" He held his breath, not knowing if he was pushing her too hard.

"I like you a lot, Jesse. I believe you will make a good father. But there is more to a marriage than that."

"I would try my best." He walked to the buggy.

She didn't get out. "Does it bother you that there would only be friendship between us, not love?"

It shouldn't have bothered him. Love wasn't something he claimed to want or need, so why did the lack of it trouble him? He shook off the foolish thought. "Love isn't necessary to start a marriage. Affection can grow over time. So can respect and compassion. These are things that make a strong marriage."

Was he convincing her? He pulled the buggy door open to help her down.

She braced her hands on his shoulders as he swung her off the seat and deposited her in front of him. He kept his hands on her waist. "I'm still waiting for an answer."

"I'm not trying to string you along. I have to make the right decision for me and for my child."

"I couldn't agree with you more. I'm a patient man." He leaned close to her ear. "Do I stand a chance?"

She tried not to smile but lost the battle. "A small one."

He could feel her wavering. "Give me that chance and I'll make a good life for you and your babe, I promise. I know I can make you happy, Gemma. We can build a good life here close to your family and the friends you love. Your mother will have her grandchild close by. Your little one will have Anna's and Bethany's children as playmates. We can even travel to Florida for a vacation once in a while. Please say you'll marry me."

Jesse had given her every reason to say yes, except the one she wanted to hear. That he loved her. She knew he didn't. She was foolish to think he might. Hadn't she learned her lesson yet?

If she said yes, it would be for the baby's sake and not because she was head over heels in love with Jesse. Love couldn't be trusted. Her baby would have a home, and she would have her family and friends near. She would have Jesse's companionship for the rest of her days.

"I'm giving you a chance to back out right now, Jesse Crump. You can live your life as a free man without any unwelcome burdens."

The corner of his mouth lifted in a slow grin that spread across his face as his eyes sparkled. "Sounds dull, don't you think? Who will I find to gather bark with me?"

She couldn't resist his smile. "You win, Jesse Crump. I will marry you."

"You will?"

"I will."

He wrapped his arms around her and pulled her close. Her cheek rested against his chest as he tucked her beneath his chin. "You won't regret this. I vow it."

She expected the hug but she hadn't expected it would feel so sweet or that she would want more.

The bishop came out carrying a sheet of plywood. "Jesse. Gemma, nice to see you."

Gemma glanced sheepishly at Jesse. "I've come to tell you I have accepted Jesse's proposal."

"That's *wunderbar*. Have you chosen a date?"

Gemma glanced at Jesse. He shrugged.

She turned back to the bishop. "I'll have to see what my parents want to do."

"Meet with me again when you have a day." He tipped his hat and walked on.

Jesse helped her back into the buggy. He held her hand a few moments longer than necessary. "I'll see you soon." He started to walk away.

"Jesse?"

He turned back to her. "What?"

"I promise to try to be the best possible wife." She meant it.

"And I promise to try to be the best possible husband."

Thirty minutes later, Gemma found her mother lying down with a cold compress on her forehead in her darkened bedroom.

"Oh, *Mamm*, do you have another headache? Can I get you something?"

Her mother held out her hand. "That's sweet, but I'm okay. What do you need?"

"I came to tell you that I've decided to accept Jesse's offer."

Mamm sat up. "You have?"

Gemma nodded and clasped her hands together.

"It won't be a big wedding since it will be rushed, but I want a nice one for you. Does Jesse have much family?" *Mamm* asked.

"Only his mother as far as I know."

"I can have everything ready in three weeks' time. Have you set a date?"

Gemma was pleased to see her mother so animated. "Not yet. We will want to visit with the bishop before we make any firm plans."

"Yes, of course. We'll need to start on your wedding dress right away. And we will need to pick out invitations and make a guest list. I hope that is enough time for your cousins in Pennsylvania to get here. We'll have to get those in the mail first. I need to make a list." She tossed back the quilt and got out of bed.

She embraced Gemma. "I have dreamed of your wedding for a long time. Bless you. I want you to be happy."

"I don't need a big wedding," Gemma said. She had caused so much grief for her parents. She had to hope this was the way to repair it. She would never cause her family such pain again.

Her mother patted Gemma's cheek. "The wedding won't be big, but it should be a happy day to remember all your life. Leave it to me."

Several days later Jesse drove briskly along the road that led past his house. Gemma sat beside him in the buggy. He was worried about what she would think of his home. It would be hers too. He hoped she would like the farm as much as he did. Since his proposal, she had been quiet and subdued, unlike the Gemma he knew, and he wasn't sure how to bring back his friend.

Bachelor, recluse, dog lover, Jesse was afraid his home showed the main aspects of his life clearly. He had intended to give the place a makeover before bringing a woman home, but there wasn't much time before the coming wedding. It was the custom for newlyweds to live with the bride's parents for several months or even a year after the wedding. He didn't want to wait that long.

He stopped by the gate, opened the buggy door and offered Gemma his hand. He prayed he wasn't about to make things worse between them. "This is my farm. Sixty acres. House, barn, chicken house, four outbuildings and a pretty view."

He was relieved to see a spark of enthusiasm come into her eyes. She placed her hand in his. "I'm glad you brought me here."

"I wanted you to see what you were getting into. It's not as fine as your father's house, but it's home."

"Will I be able to make changes? Oh, I didn't mean that as a criticism." She dropped her voice and her gaze.

He leaned close. "Gemma, I like a person who isn't afraid to tell me what they think."

She raised her eyes to meet his gaze. "Are you sure you do?"

"Of course. I like you, and you've given me a piece of your mind plenty of times."

She cracked a tiny smile. "Only when you needed it," she said sweetly.

"Needed it? Ha." He waved a hand toward the two-story farmhouse in need of a coat of paint, with mismatched shingles on the roof and overgrown trees sprouting along the foundation. His team of Belgian geldings stood in a corral by the barn, watching the activity with interest. He noticed the fence could use a coat of paint too. He had been letting the place go. "This is my humble home. Our home."

"It's nice," she said.

"That is not an honest opinion."

She gave him a cheeky grin. "Okay. It needs work, but it has wonderful potential."

He chuckled. "I would have stopped at *it needs work*. I haven't had much time or money to fix it up. I've been putting money aside for more land." He pushed away the thought that he could have gained what he wanted by accepting her father's offer. Gemma was here because she wanted to be, not because her father wanted her off his hands. She was here because Jesse wanted her to be a part of his life too.

Jesse opened the front door for his bride-to-be. He was tickled to see the sassy woman with witty comebacks starting to reemerge from the worried, subdued woman she had become in her father's house.

Gemma paused at the door of his home. She leaned forward and peeked in. "Is it safe?"

He shook his head as he placed a hand on her lower back and guided her through the door. "Depends on where you stand."

Her gaze went to the far wall, where the ceiling was marred by a large water stain that had made the plaster sag. A tiny frown creased her forehead. She slowly scanned the room, taking in the long worn-looking wooden table that had been handed down from his grandparents. It was stacked with groceries he hadn't taken the time to put away. She studied the fireplace and then the stove. Both needed a good cleaning. The corners of her mouth pulled downward. At the sight of Roscoe's food and water dishes by the table, her lips curled inward. She pressed them together hard.

"Are you pleased?"

She opened her mouth as if to speak, closed it and opened it again. "*Ja*. Of course."

Then she clasped her hands in front of her. He noticed she rubbed and twisted her intertwined fingers. He grinned. She wanted to say something else. There was a glint in her eyes. The woman he knew before she went away to Florida would never have held back her opinion in this manner. The words would have popped out before she had even thought through her comment.

And I would have grumbled at her for it. I was a fool. I reckon both of us have changed.

"Let me show you around. A woman should know her way around the house she is to keep. Don't you agree?"

She nodded, but before they could start the tour, Roscoe bolted in, knocking Gemma off balance. Instinctively, Jesse braced her.

"Oh," she gasped as she clung to him.

Roscoe sat facing them by the edge of the table, his bowl at his feet. He woofed once.

"No scraps yet, boy." Jesse moved away from Gemma to scratch the dog's head.

"He eats in here?" Her voice showed her disapproval.

"Of course." He hid a grin. She was going to learn that she could disagree with him without being chastised.

The Gemma he wanted to see, the one who aggravated him to the point of distraction, wouldn't allow a farm dog to eat in her kitchen. A smile grew in his heart. He hoped this tour would coax her out of her shell and get them back to the friendship they had enjoyed in the cabin.

"He sits at the table with me most nights. Just like a person. Don't worry. I don't think he'll mind having you join us."

Gemma approached the table and ran her hand along the back of the two chairs. "Join you?" She clasped her hands together again. "Does that mean we'll need to add another chair?" That was not what she wanted to ask or how she wanted to ask it. He could tell by the twitch in her jaw.

"I suppose so." He motioned toward Roscoe. "Go lie down." He held his breath.

Roscoe trotted to the bedroom. Gemma frowned as she examined the bare kitchen.

"What do you think? It needs a woman's touch, but you can give it a go if you want."

"Some curtains would be lovely."

"Curtains? I'm not sure that's necessary. Plain shades do well enough. Roscoe might pull them down." He folded his arms tight across his chest to keep from laughing at her expression.

"We'll have to get some china for that cabinet." She brightened as she gestured to the large empty china hutch nestled in a nook behind the dining table.

"China? I have these. Can't break them." He picked up a plastic dish, of which he owned only enough for him and Roscoe.

"But…" She started to say something, but hesitated.

"You wouldn't be able to reach all the shelves anyway, short stuff." He placed the dish on the top ledge. "Try."

Her eyes flashed in his direction. "Are you trying to pick a fight? Because if you are, you are about to get one."

He cocked one eyebrow. "No, dear."

"Don't *dear* me." She scooted past him into the living room and stopped short at the old worn-down couch under the window. Then she turned and looked in the other rooms.

When he'd moved to New Covenant, he hadn't thought of outfitting a home for a family. Any money he had went back into the farm. There was enough furniture for one man. That was all. He watched her face contort as she noticed the sparseness of the home. When she reached the first bedroom doorway, she let out a small shriek. He stepped up behind her and peered in to see Roscoe curled in the middle of the quilt on his bed.

"Good boy."

"Good boy?" Gemma asked in disbelief.

"He's lying down. He did as I told him. He'll get over and share the space with you when you're ready for bed."

"Is this where he usually sleeps? Because I'm not sleeping with a dog. Where is my room?" Her voice was rising. He smothered a grin.

"The next door down the hall. Where else would Roscoe sleep if not in your or my bed?"

"Outside! That's where animals sleep. And eat, for that matter. His job is to guard the farm. I don't want a dog slobbering where I'll be feeding the baby."

"That's not right. There's no bed for him out there."

"Actually, there's no bed for him in here. That is a bed for people, not dogs. I'm sure there is a perfectly good napping spot for him outdoors." That determined, bossy tone inched its way back into her voice.

He kept prodding. "It doesn't seem fair to make him sleep and eat outside."

She cocked her head and blinked. He turned away to keep from laughing. "Speaking of meals, I do expect breakfast at sunrise. Freshly baked bread, eggs and bacon will do. Roscoe prefers his eggs scrambled. I like mine over hard. How are you at housework?"

Jesse grabbed the broom that was standing in the corner. "I guess we will find out. We'll have your first lesson now." He pushed the broom toward her.

She crossed her arms and arched one eyebrow. "You intend to teach me how to use a broom? Are you serious?"

"We could start with the dusting, if you wish."

Her mouth dropped open.

"Or the cooking. There are several delicious ways to serve white pine bark and cattail roots."

The way her eyes narrowed told him she was finally onto him. A smile tugged at her lips and then blossomed into a grin. Her eyes sparkled. She jerked the broom from his grasp and beat at his boots until she backed him out the kitchen door onto the porch.

"Jesse Crump. I know how to cook a decent meal without boiling tree bark. I will sew curtains for the kitchen. Roscoe can eat his meals and take his naps on the porch, and if I can't reach the top shelf of the china cabinet, I will use a stepladder to retrieve my china myself."

He propped his hands on his hips and tipped his head. "Stepladder? What's that? I don't believe I've ever had the need for one of those before." He stepped up beside her and placed one palm against the porch ceiling.

"Show-off."

He gave a hoot of laughter.

"You're making fun of me." She turned her face away in mock anger.

"I'm not. I like a woman who knows how to laugh. You do that so well."

She raised the broom as if to swat him like an annoying giant housefly. He caught it and pulled her toward him. He leaned in until their faces were inches apart.

"I know it's not a cabin in the woods, but we can joke, laugh, tease each other, even argue within these walls and never worry about losing our friendship. Agreed?"

She laid a hand on his cheek. "Agreed."

"Welcome home, Gemma."

"I like the sound of that."

He gazed into her lively eyes and realized he was starting to fall for his bride-to-be. He was going to do everything within his power to see that she had a comfortable life and never regretted their marriage.

Was there a remote chance that she could someday care for him as more than a friend? If not, had he signed on for a lifetime of hiding his pain? It was wisest to remain her friend and never hope for more.

On Wednesday morning, Gemma and her mother were preparing to go into the city to start shopping for the wedding. Gemma had an OB-GYN doctor's appointment at ten o'clock that had been made by the emergency room nurse in Cleary. The day was snowy and gray, and it suited Gemma's mood. The doctor's visit was a reminder that her baby's life was always in danger.

Her mother's mare had already been harnessed to the buggy and she stood patiently waiting at the gate. The two women started out the door and met Jesse. He tipped his hat. "Leroy has asked me to drive you. I am ready when you are."

"That's very kind of you. I have a lot of errands today, and Gemma is to see the doctor."

He turned a look of concern on Gemma. "Are you ill? Is something wrong?"

She shook her head and replied meekly, "It is a simple pregnancy checkup. I'm fine."

"I would like to hear what the doctor has to say, if you don't mind."

"That is a *goot* idea," *Mamm* said as she climbed into

the back of the buggy. "You can get your marriage license today too."

"Don't we have to get blood drawn or something before we get married?" Jesse asked.

"Not in Maine," Gemma said. "I already asked Bethany about it."

It took almost an hour to reach the outskirts of Presque Isle. Fortunately, the traffic wasn't heavy. They visited the fabric store first and chose a periwinkle blue material for Gemma's wedding dress. After that, they found a printer that could do an order of a hundred invitations that same day. They would need to get them in the mail tomorrow in order to give family members in Pennsylvania and the neighboring Maine Amish communities enough notice to attend. Weddings were the most common way that Amish young people from different districts met each other and for far-flung relatives to reconnect.

They arrived at the obstetrician's office a few minutes before ten o'clock. Gemma filled out the paperwork required and waited nervously to see the doctor.

Dr. Thomas turned out to be a young woman with short dark curly hair who immediately put Gemma at ease. Following the examination, she had Gemma's mother and Jesse step into the room. "I'm pleased to meet all of you. I want to congratulate you on your new family-member-to-be. As the doctor in Cleary told you, Gemma, there is a problem with your pregnancy. In your case, you have what is called a partial placenta previa."

Gemma tried to absorb all the information the doctor gave her. She stressed the need for limited travel and bed rest as much as possible. It would mean a cesarean birth. Any labor could cause bleeding and jeopardize the life of both the mother and the baby.

"I understand you have a midwife in your community. She can manage you at home, but you will have to come here for the delivery. You are already twenty-six weeks along, and that is good. The goal is to get you as close to full term as possible and deliver you safely by C-section. I'm going to send some instructions home with you. It's important that you follow them. I'm also going to give you a steroid injection that will help mature your baby's lungs if it is born prematurely. Do you have any questions?"

After they left the office and reached their buggy, Jesse took Gemma's elbow to help her in. "That was a lot to take in. How are you?"

"I'm fine." It was a lie. She was terrified. She could lose her baby. The baby she hadn't wanted but had grown to love in spite of everything.

"I'm scared," he admitted.

Gemma nodded. "I am too."

Her mother took Gemma's hands between her own. "Our faith is in the Lord. In Isaiah 41:10, he tells us, 'Fear thou not; for I am with thee: be not dismayed; for I am thy God: I will strengthen thee; yea, I will help thee; yea, I will uphold thee with the right hand of my righteousness.'"

"I believe in the goodness of the Lord," Gemma said, struggling to find the faith beneath her words, but a deep sense of foreboding wouldn't leave her in peace.

Chapter Twelve

Gemma discovered that her family and friends had taken her doctor's instructions to heart. She wasn't allowed to lift a finger if anyone was around to watch her. Anytime she tried to do something for herself, she was scolded by her mother as if she were still an unruly toddler.

A week after her visit to the doctor, Gemma met the midwife, Esther Hopper. Esther was a jovial plump woman in her late fifties with short gray hair, who claimed her greatest joy in life was delivering babies.

Gemma was curled up on the sofa with a blanket over her lap, at her mother's insistence, when Esther breezed into the room. "Finally, I have a patient I don't have to track down."

Bethany and Anna followed the woman in bright pink scrubs beneath a red plaid coat into the room and took their places on each side of Gemma. Esther glanced at the group. "I believe I will just hold clinic here each time I need to see you ladies."

"What exactly is wrong with Gemma?" Anna asked. "She has tried explaining it to us, but we really don't understand."

"Gemma, may I discuss your case with your friends? I can't give them any information unless you allow me to. HIPAA and all that jazz. That would be the government regulations regarding patient privacy."

Gemma folded her arms across her chest. "I want them to know that I do not have to be chained to a bed or the sofa."

"Unfortunately, that is about the size of it. It is important that you don't do anything strenuous. I'm going to leave a cell phone with you, Gemma. I have your bishop's permission for you to use it in an emergency. I consider an emergency anytime you need to talk to me or anytime you have a question. My number is the first one. The only other number you should know is 911. At the first sign of labor, even if you are not sure it is labor, that is the number I want you to call. Understood?"

"Understood," all three of them said together and giggled.

Esther smiled. "You are blessed, Gemma, to have a support group at your fingertips. I'm sure you and your baby are going to be just fine."

After explaining Gemma's condition and using a nursing textbook illustration to help the women understand, she completed her paperwork and her exam of Gemma and pronounced her in excellent health. She brought out a small white boxlike machine from her bag. "This is a Doppler. It will allow the mother to hear the baby's heartbeat."

There was a knock at the door. Anna went to answer it. She came back into the room. "It's Jesse. May he come in?"

Gemma nodded. A few seconds later, he came in with his hat in hand. Esther introduced herself and said, "You are just in time." She positioned a wand on Gemma's tummy and immediately the *thud-thud-thud* of the baby's heartbeat filled the room. Gemma listened in awe.

"Is that her?" Jesse's voice cracked with emotion.

"Well, it might be a him, but yes, this is your baby's heartbeat. Amazing, isn't it? Every time I hear one I think how…amazing."

After Esther packed up her stuff and promised to return in two weeks, Bethany and Anna left with her. Jesse remained. He sat down beside Gemma. "How are you today? Don't say fine."

She kept her eyes downcast. The wedding was fast approaching, yet it didn't feel real. It would be a wedding without a courtship or a wedding trip because she would still be on bed rest in her mother's house until her babe was born. It was also going to be a wedding without love. Maybe it would be better to call off the ceremony until after the birth. She glanced at Jesse to tell him that and couldn't find the words. "I finished all the invitations."

"That's *goot*."

"I wanted to ask if you… Would you like me to send one to your mother? I don't have her address."

"Of course."

She handed him an envelope and he scrawled his mother's name and address across it. "I doubt she will come, but you never know." He handed it back.

"How have you been?" she asked.

"Busy. We have a lot of new orders. The bishop is thinking about hiring another man."

"It's wonderful that his business is doing well." She smoothed her hand over the blanket on her lap. He grasped her hand and held it gently.

* * *

"Gemma, is there something wrong?" Jesse asked. Her hand remained limp in his.

She didn't look at him. "*Mamm* has the wedding plans well in hand. The baby and I are doing okay."

"You seem distant."

"I'm right here." She pulled away from him.

"That's not what I meant."

She finally looked up. "You are worrying about nothing. I'm fine. I think I would like to take a nap now."

"Okay. I'll see you again tomorrow." He leaned over and kissed her cheek.

Her eyes filled with tears at the unexpected gesture. He took her hand again. "Tell me what's wrong. You can trust me. We are friends, remember?"

"What if I lose this baby? I listen to the doctor and the midwife and I'm afraid. What if we marry and then lose my child? Then you will be bound to me for no reason."

He adjusted the blanket over her shoulders. "We can't see the road ahead. We have to trust that we are walking the path meant for us. If the worst should happen— we will endure it. I will be bound to you because that is my choice."

"I'm just tired. Please go."

He didn't want to leave but had little choice. He left the Lapp farm and drove his buggy to Michael's place. Michael had a workshop attached to the house. Jesse entered through the side door. Inside the shop, the walls were covered with clocks in various stages of repair. A workbench sat in front of the large window. A half a dozen pocket watches sitting in padded boxes, a large magnifying glass and a jeweler's loupe were neatly arranged on it.

Across the room, Michael's dog, Sadie, lay curled on a rag rug in a patch of sunshine. Sadie got up and came to greet Jesse with her tail wagging. He scratched her behind her ears and patted her head. Satisfied with that much attention, she went back to her rug. No one else was around. Jesse was on the point of leaving when the door opened and Michael's brother-in-law, Ivan, walked in. He was intent on studying a beautifully etched gold pocket watch. He looked up and grinned. "Hey, Jesse, didn't see you there."

Jesse chuckled. "I don't hear that very often."

"I imagine not. What brings you here?"

"I wanted to speak to Michael."

Ivan put down the watch and turned his stool to face Jesse. "I heard you are getting married. Congratulations. I have to say, it came as a big shock to me."

"To me too. Sort of." Jesse sat down and leaned back against the workbench. He was always afraid of breaking something inside Michael's shop. He didn't see how his friend could enjoy working with things that were so small he needed a magnifying glass to put them together.

"Want to tell me about it?" Ivan asked.

"Actually, I was hoping for some advice from Michael."

"If you want advice about clocks, ask Michael. If you want advice about girls, I'm your man."

"How old are you?"

Ivan puffed up his chest, slipped his thumbs under his suspenders and stretched them out. "Almost sixteen, and the ladies love me."

"If I want advice on being a braggart, I'll know who to see."

Ivan chuckled. "I thought it sounded pretty good. I over did it, huh?"

"By quite a bit. Where's Michael?" Jesse asked.

"In the kitchen. I'll go get him."

After Ivan left, Jesse leaned forward and propped his elbows on his knees. He wasn't sure how much of the situation to share with Michael, but he needed help. When his friend came in, Jesse sat up straight. "Your brother-in-law is getting too big for his britches."

"You aren't telling me anything new. What's up?"

"I need some advice about Gemma. The closer the date of the wedding comes, the more remote Gemma seems."

Michael folded his arms over his chest. "You think she is getting cold feet? Marriage is forever. A lot of couples have second thoughts and doubts. You two must have them doubly so."

"Did you? Did Bethany?"

"I will admit to being nervous, but I never doubted that Bethany was the one for me. We were and still are very much in love. I don't know how it's possible to be much happier. Tell me something. Are you sure you don't love Gemma?"

Jesse rubbed his damp palms on his pant legs. His friend knew the reason he was getting married. "I care about her. She's cute and funny and her eyes light up when she sees me. She drives me crazy and makes me smile. I don't know if that is love, but I do know she needs someone to look after her and the baby. She is troubled, but she won't tell me about it. I thought you could ask Bethany to find out what Gemma is really thinking. If she is ready to call it off, I'll understand."

* * *

"Gemma, do you want to call off the wedding?"

Gemma was lying in bed in her room on the second floor of her mother's house. She glanced sharply at Bethany, who was sitting on a chair beside the bed. "Why would you ask such a thing?"

"Because Jesse asked Michael, who asked me to ask you if you want to call this thing off."

"Does Jesse want to?" Gemma's heart fell as she considered what that would mean. The marriage bans were to be read at the next church service.

Did it mean Jesse had changed his mind?

She looked at Bethany. "What if this is the wrong thing to do? Suppose he falls in love with someone after we are married. He'll resent me for denying him the chance at true love."

Bethany shook her head. "Not the Jesse I know. He doesn't hold a grudge. The same thing can face any couple. It is respect for God's law and respect for their partner that keeps them from acting on an attraction to someone else."

Gemma struggled to find something else wrong with marrying Jesse. "He's too big and tall. He makes me feel like a gnat beside him."

Bethany laughed out loud. "That is the lamest excuse I've ever heard for not marrying someone. I think you like Jesse Crump more than you're telling me and more than you'll admit to yourself."

Did she? The truthful answer was, yes, she did. She liked him a lot. Not in the same way as last year. That had been a girlish crush tied up with wishful thinking as much as anything. This was something deeper. Something real. And it changed things.

The more she grew to care about him, the more determined she became to avoid hurting him.

Bethany put her hands on her hips. "Are you asking me to ask Michael to ask Jesse if that's what he wants to do?"

"*Nee*, Jesse should be here after he gets off work today. I will ask him myself."

"That is the right answer. Is there anything else I can do for you?"

"*Nee*, I'm whining. I have vowed to do better, and already I am slipping."

"I would be out of my mind by now. I don't know how you can stay so calm."

"Because I must."

Bethany got up. "I'll be back tomorrow after church. Jenny and Ivan say hi."

"Bring them with you. I'd love to see them."

"They are excited about the wedding."

"I want all my friends in my wedding party. If there is going to be a wedding." Had Jesse really changed his mind? She chewed on her lower lip. A sharp pain ripped across her abdomen and she doubled over, clutching the covers to keep from crying out.

Bethany was at her side immediately. "What's wrong? Is it labor? Where is the phone?"

Gemma drew several quick breaths as the pain receded. "It's gone."

"Are you sure?"

"I think so. The phone is in the top drawer of my nightstand."

Bethany pulled it out and placed it in Gemma's hand. "Just in case."

Gemma's eyes filled with tears. "If I lose this baby, I don't know what I will do."

Bethany dropped to the bed and put her arms around Gemma. "You will do what women have done since the dawn of time. Keep on living. Have more children if God blesses you with them and know your babe is waiting for you in heaven."

"I didn't want it when I first found out. I wanted it to go away so I wouldn't be shamed."

"Which only proves that you are human. You want your babe now. You love your child, and he or she knows that."

"I hope so. I really hope so."

"I have to leave, but I'm going to get your mother to sit with you."

"She has so much to do already. I'm fine."

"Your *mamm* would forbid me to come again if I didn't tell her when her daughter needs her."

Bethany left, and a few minutes later Dinah marched into the room and up to Gemma's bedside. "It's the not knowing that's the worst, isn't it?"

Gemma nodded as tears slipped down her cheeks. Her mother gathered her in her arms and rocked her back and forth. "This is a hard time for you, I know. We have no way to see the future, so we fear what it holds. We make bargains with God. Save this child and I will give all my money to the needy. It's all right. Our Father understands our fears and our failings. He loves us just the same. We must humble ourselves before Him and pray that His will be done."

"What if I don't deserve this child?"

Her mother drew back. "What if you do?"

"I'm scared I won't be a good mother."

"We all are when that tiny naked thing is handed to us without a single set of instructions. And yet the world is full of grown people who walk and talk, so mothers do okay. *Liebchen*, I have more bad news."

"What now?"

"We don't have enough celery."

Gemma choked and then began laughing. "Oh, the horror of it. An Amish wedding without enough stewed celery to feed the guests. We'll be talked about behind our backs for years."

Jesse found Dinah and Gemma sitting beside each other on the bed, chuckling between sobs. They both had puffy red eyes. Fear hit him between the shoulder blades. "Is everything okay?"

"We don't have enough celery for the wedding dinner," Dinah said, getting up and walking out of the room.

"That is what you are crying about?"

Gemma wiped her face with her hands. "It's a disaster."

He sat down in the chair beside Gemma's bed. "I can arrange for a delivery of more celery."

She folded her hands on the quilt. "Do you want to call off the wedding?"

He tipped his head slightly, trying to read her face. "Do you?"

"I asked you first."

"Fair enough. I don't."

"Okay. Order more celery."

"That's it?"

"I can't think of anything else. Check with *Mamm*."

"Are we still okay?" he asked, not knowing what to expect.

"Are we still friends? We are, Jesse. We are."

Relief made him smile. "I'm glad, really glad. Someone asked me if we wanted a crib for the baby. Do you have one you want to use, or should I say yes?"

The light faded in her eyes. She traced the edge of the blocks on her quilt with one finger. "Let's wait on the baby things until—until after the wedding."

Chapter Thirteen

As was the custom among the Amish, Gemma and Jesse didn't attend the church service the day their intention to marry was announced. It was meant to give the engaged couple a day of rest before the rush of the final days leading up to the wedding, but Gemma had already had all the rest she could tolerate. She had convinced Esther to let her be up for a few hours while she cooked a meal for Jesse. Another Amish tradition. After that, she would go straight back to bed. Esther was going to stop in just to make sure she was following orders.

Gemma surveyed the food in the refrigerator. It was packed top to bottom with plastic containers, waiting to be served on Thursday. "What would you like to eat today?"

Jesse sat at the table, turning his fork around and around. "Doesn't matter."

He had retreated into his one-and two-word answers that made it impossible for her to tell what he was thinking. How had the wonderful bond they once shared vanished so completely?

"At least he didn't ask for pine bark," she muttered.

"What?" He looked her way.

"Nothing. Meatballs with rice sound okay?"

"Sure."

She measured out a pound of hamburger and formed it into balls, prepared the rice and some sliced vegetables, arranged the meatballs on top of the rice in a casserole dish and popped it into the oven to bake. After washing her hands, she set the kitchen timer and joined Jesse at the table.

"This is so nice." She sighed heavily and sat down.

"Spending the day with me, just the two of us?"

"That and cooking again. Standing at the sink. A hundred things I never thought I would miss until I couldn't do them."

The silence that followed proved she had missed a chance to connect with Jesse. She should not have lumped his company in with the kitchen chores.

"Have you heard from your mother?" she asked.

"Nothing."

"Did Dale get his truck fixed?"

"Yup."

She tapped her fingers on the tabletop. "More coffee?"

"Sure, but I can get it." He went to the stove and poured himself another cup.

He sat down with it but merely stared into the dark liquid. After a few minutes of silence, he looked at her. "Have you thought about names for the baby?"

She popped up and began searching in one of the cupboards. "I know I saw raisins."

She didn't want to pick a name to go on a headstone if the worst happened. She felt a twinge in her side. It subsided as quickly as it came on, but it was a pointed reminder of what could go wrong. She located the box she had been searching for. "Do you like raisins in your fruit salad?"

"Not really."

"Oh. Okay." She put the box back and returned to the table. Bracing her hands on her hips, she stretched her lower back.

"Are you hurting?"

In so many ways, Jesse. You have no idea.

She had spoken of her fear to him once. If she broadcast her concerns, they might come true. She didn't want Jesse to think she was whining about her condition. She would bear her fear in silence and humility. "I think I'll go and lie down. Call me when the timer goes off."

Gemma's next ten days were filled with watching everyone else make the final preparations for her big day. Hemming her wedding dress was all she was allowed to do. She'd chosen a deep blue material called Persian blue for her outfit and hoped that Jesse would approve. She was lying in bed or on the sofa as her friends helped her mother bake and clean the house. Jesse came by every day, but they seemed to have less and less to say to each other.

The day before the wedding, her married friends and members of the church arrived to prepare for the dinner. A meal would be served after the ceremony, but the celebration would continue long into the evening. A second meal would be needed for the guests who remained. When one of her mother's helpers didn't show up, Gemma was allowed back in the kitchen for a short time to wash dishes and ice the cake.

By the time the house settled in that evening, she

was dead tired and her feet were swollen. Although her sprain had healed, it still ached when she was up on her feet too much. Like now. She lit the lamp in her room and stared at the worn-out-looking woman staring back at her in the bedroom mirror. She stuck her tongue out at her reflection. "So much for a beautiful bride. I hope Jesse doesn't mind settling for a haggard-looking one."

Something rattled against her window. A few seconds later, the sound came again. What was going on? She went to the window and looked down. Jesse was searching for something at his feet. She raised the window and leaned out. "What are you doing?"

"Trying to see my fiancée. Come down."

As tired as she was, she still wanted to spend time with him. But why was he here? Had he come to tell her he had changed his mind? She wouldn't blame him if he had. She went downstairs and opened the back door. She held a finger to her lips as she slipped out beside him. "My *aenti* and cousins are sleeping on cots just inside. What do you want?"

He grasped both her hands in his. "An uninterrupted moment with my wife-to-be. Is that too much to ask?"

"I thought perhaps you had come to call it off."

"I promised I would take care of you, Gemma. I won't go back on that promise. Not now and not ever." He squeezed her fingers.

She was trusting him with her future and the future of her child. He was an honorable man and he would keep his word. "You deserve better than you are getting, Jesse Crump."

"I think the opposite is true. Want to go for a buggy ride? We won't really go anywhere. We'll simply snuggle together and pretend we are on a trip. Our wedding trip maybe. Where do you want to go?"

She rubbed her hands over her rounded belly. "Back to bed. I'm tired. All I want is a good night's sleep without someone kicking my ribs in one spot until they ache."

"It must be a girl, then."

She tipped her head. "Why do you say that?"

"I've often found women to be a pain in my side."

She grinned at him and he smiled back. He leaned in and kissed her before she knew what was happening. "Good night. Sleep well."

He walked away into the darkness. She wanted to call him back, wanted to recapture that flicker of attraction they had shared, but she knew she shouldn't. He was kind and considerate and funny. She didn't deserve it, but she wondered if he might have feelings for her just a little.

It proved to be a short night. Gemma was up at four thirty in the morning to wash, dry and put up her hair. She was dressed in her wedding dress and white apron with her newly starched *kapp* in her hand, staring out the window, wondering what Jesse was thinking, when Anna and Bethany came in to hurry her along. Both still newlyweds, the light of happiness in their eyes gave Gemma courage. She was doing the right thing. She would be a good wife to Jesse and never give him cause to regret this day.

Bethany took Gemma's hand. "It's time. Jedidiah has the buggy here for you. Let me pin your *kapp* on."

Gemma had asked Bethany and Michael to be members of her bridal party. Jedidiah Zook was acting as *hostler*, the driver for the group. The wedding would take place at Bethany's home while Gemma's mother readied their home for the wedding meal.

Gemma nodded. She was ready, but her fingers were cold as ice. Was a father for her child reason enough to wed Jesse?

She looked in the mirror, as she made sure her *kapp* was on straight. The woman looking back at her knew the answer. The real reason she was here was because she admired the man about to become her husband and wanted to provide the warm welcoming home that he had missed out on as a child. Maybe he didn't love her, but he cared enough to want to be her husband and to call her child his own.

Bethany squeezed Gemma's hand. "It will be fine."

"How can I be sure?"

"You care for each other, don't you?" Anna asked. "Love is sure to follow. I've seen the way Jesse looks at you."

Gemma looked out the window. "Jesse says love isn't necessary to have a good marriage."

Her two friends exchanged pointed glances. Gemma didn't want them to feel sorry for her. "He's a good man."

Gemma took a deep breath. The baby was only part of the reason for this day. With God's help, she would be a good wife and a good mother. She looked down at her expanding waist and wrapped her arms across her stomach.

"What's wrong, Gemma?" Anna took a step closer.

Gemma smiled at her. "I just realized that no matter what happens with my baby, she is here with me on my wedding day."

Anna grinned. "How do you know it's going to be a girl?"

Gemma closed her eyes. "Her father said so."

Jesse was waiting for her at the foot of the stairs.

He looked every bit as nervous as she felt, but he also looked wonderfully handsome in his new black suit, snowy white shirt and bow tie. He smiled and held out his hand. "Are you ready?"

She grasped his fingers tightly. "I am. Are you?"

"You are stuck with me. Who else will harvest pine bark for you?" They smiled at the shared memory. Some of their former closeness remained. She needed to hold on to his friendship and not want more.

She peered into his eyes. "We're going to be all right, aren't we?"

"I think so. I really think we are."

She wanted to believe him. Needed to believe in him. He truly cared about her and about her baby.

It was just after seven o'clock when they arrived at Bethany's home. The benches were being set up by Ivan and some of his friends. Additional seating had been rented for the day. All the downstairs rooms would be filled to overflowing with guests.

Bethany brought Gemma a chair and Jesse stood beside her. They greeted each guest as they arrived. The ceremony wouldn't take place until nine o'clock, but at eight thirty, the wedding party took their places on the benches at the front of the room, where the ceremony would be held. Gemma sat with Anna and Bethany on one side of the room, Jesse sat with Michael and Tobias on the other. Their *forgeher*—or ushers—Jenny and Ivan, made sure each guest, Amish and *Englisch*, had a place on one of the long wooden benches.

The singing began followed by sermons from her father and Samuel for almost three hours. Gemma tried to keep her mind on what was being said, but she could only think of spending the next sixty years with the man beside her. Of all the mistakes she had made in the past, this was the one thing she had to get right.

Finally, Bishop Schultz stood to address the congregation. "Brothers and sisters, we are gathered here in Christ's name for a solemn purpose. Jesse Crump and Gemma Lapp are about to make irrevocable vows. This is a most serious step and not to be taken lightly, for it is a lifelong commitment to love and cherish one another."

As the bishop continued at length, Gemma glanced at Jesse. He was sitting up straight, listening to every word. He didn't look the least bit nervous anymore. The bishop motioned for them to come forward.

Gemma knew the questions that would be asked of her and she answered them in a clear strong voice. To her relief, Jesse did the same. The bishop placed their hands together. "The God of Abraham, of Isaac and of Jacob be with you. May He bestow His blessings richly upon you through Jesus Christ, amen."

That was it. They were man and wife.

A final prayer ended the ceremony. The couple was whisked back to Gemma's home, where the women of the congregation began preparing the wedding meal in the kitchen. The men had arranged tables in a U-shape around the walls of the living room. In the corner of the room, facing the front door, the place of honor, the *eck*, meaning the corner table, was quickly set up for the wedding party.

He was married. Jesse waited for it to sink in. It hadn't yet. It didn't feel real. When the table was ready, Jesse took his place with his groomsmen seated to his right. Gemma was ushered in and took her seat at his left-hand side, symbolizing the place she would occupy in his life. A helpmate, always at his side through good times and bad. Gemma's cheeks were pale. Was the day too much for her? Under the table, he squeezed her hand. She gave him a shy smile in return.

Jesse spoke to the people who filed past. The single men among the guests were arranged along the table to his right and the single women were arranged along the tables to Gemma's left. Later, at the evening meal, the unmarried people would be paired up according to the bride and groom's choosing. Amish weddings were where matchmakings often got started, especially in a place like New Covenant where marriage-minded singles had to look far afield for mates. The non-Amish guests gathered together at tables and in groups as they wished. All the guests were invited to remain, eat and visit at their leisure by Gemma's parent.

Although most Amish wedding meals went on until long after dark, Gemma went around to bid their guests goodbye in the midafternoon. She had strict orders from her mother and the midwife to return to bed before the evening meal. She saw Jesse and her father deep in discussion. Jesse looked amazing in his new suit, and he had a smile on his face. A smile she was coming to adore, especially when it was directed at her. She decided not to bother them but to let *Mamm* know she was retiring. She looked over the crowd but didn't see her mother.

Dale crossed the room with a glass of punch in his hand and a wide grin on his face. "I can't believe the big man finally said 'I do.'"

Gemma smiled at him. "You have to take some of the credit for bringing us together, Dale."

He chuckled and raised his glass. "That's right. If I'd made it back to the truck that day, the two of you wouldn't have had a chance to get reacquainted like you did. Jesse's ended up with a pretty bride and a swell piece of property thanks to me."

"What property? Oh, did my father finally sell Jesse the land he wanted?" No wonder Jesse was grinning.

"Sold nothing. He gave it to Jesse free and clear. That's some wedding present."

A sense of unease crept over Gemma. Her heart began to pound. "My father gave it to him? Are you sure Jesse didn't buy it?"

"Jesse didn't have to spend a penny for it. You've got a real generous old man." Dale finished off his drink and gestured toward the serving table. "I'm gonna get a refill. Do you want something?"

To unhear what Dale had just told her.

Gemma's happiness drained away. She glanced to where her father and Jesse were still talking together. Her father's words echoed in her mind.

We won't have any success getting someone from here to marry her when word gets out. I'll have my brother in Lancaster find a fellow. There must be some man who will marry her once he learns he will inherit this farm one day. Had he made the same offer to Jesse, using the land Jesse wanted so badly?

Had Jesse accepted her father's offer? Was that why he had proposed? Not to give her child a name but to gain a valuable piece of land? Were his claims of affection as empty as Robert's had been?

She pressed both hands to her cheeks. It couldn't be true. Jesse wasn't like that. There had to be another explanation. She shivered as her hands grew cold. She had trusted him.

Jesse happened to glance her way. He spoke to her

father and started walking toward her. He stopped in front of her and tipped his head slightly to the side. "Are you okay?"

Ask him about it.

She shook her head. "I am going to lie down."

He took her hand. "Your fingers are like ice." He curled his large hand around hers.

Jesse held her hand as they walked up the stairs to her room. Tradition dictated that the couple would spend the night at the home of the bride's parents and help clean up from the festivities the next day. It wasn't going to be a traditional wedding night.

Jesse stopped outside her bedroom door. "Should I send someone up to stay with you?"

"*Nee*, go back down to our guests. Just because I can't be there doesn't mean you should miss it. I'm sorry your mother didn't come."

"Perhaps we can visit her after the baby is born."

Gemma nodded. "I would like that."

"You didn't get overly tired, did you?"

Was he truly concerned for her? "I feel perfectly fit, and I'm sorry I'm being sent to my room by the mean midwife. I know she has my best interest at heart."

Jesse laughed out loud. "I dare you to call her that to her face."

"I think not. It's good to see you smiling, Jesse. Are you happy?"

"I have a lot to smile about."

"You and my *daed* looked to be getting along well."

"I know you and he have had your differences, but Leroy is a generous man."

"In what way?" *Please tell me the truth.*

He cupped her chin in the palm of his hand. "He

has gifted me with his lovely daughter. She is mine to have and to hold for the rest of our lives. Here's to many more smiling days for both of us." He bent down and kissed her as thoroughly as she had wanted to be kissed by him for a long time. It didn't quiet the doubt flooding her mind.

"Did you get what you wanted, Jesse?"

He looked puzzled. "What?"

"Did you get what you wanted? My father offered you land to marry me, didn't he?"

His brows grew together in a fierce frown. "What are you asking?"

"Did you marry me to get the land you wanted so badly?" Her hands grew even more ice-cold. The silence stretched so long she thought she would scream.

"Is that the kind of man you think you married?"

She raised her chin. "Tell me I'm wrong."

"First tell me why you would think the worst of me? What have I done to destroy your trust?"

"I want an answer, Jesse."

Sadness filled his eyes. "So do I." He turned away.

She wanted to call him back but couldn't. What if she had been wrong to accuse him? Why couldn't he give her a simple answer?

"I'm going back to my place tonight. I think it best I stay there," he said. "Good night, Gemma."

She turned away and went into her room. She shut the door and leaned against it as tears welled up in her eyes. What had she done?

Chapter Fourteen

Jesse jerked upright out of a sound sleep. Roscoe stood beside the bed, howling a long drawn-out wail.

"What is wrong with you? Go lie down."

Roscoe slunk from the room. Jesse dropped back to the mattress and pulled his quilt up to his chin. Without his hound howling in his ear, he caught the sound of a siren in the distance. He sat up again. Was it coming closer? Roscoe raced to the front door and started barking. Jesse rolled out of bed and quickly pulled on his clothes. He hitched his suspenders over his shoulders and reached for his coat. "Quiet."

Roscoe stopped barking and Jesse heard the clatter of hooves galloping up his lane.

He pulled open his front door just as Ivan reined his horse to a halt. The boy hadn't taken time to put on a saddle. He slid from the horse's bare back and hurried to Jesse. "It's Gemma. Dinah says to come quick. I'll hitch up your buggy."

"Don't bother. Will your horse carry double?"

"I've never tried. You take him. I'll bring your buggy."

"Fine." Jesse sat down and pulled on his boots. He

gave a quick look around, found his wallet and hurried out the door. Ivan was still holding the horse's bridle. Jesse swung up onto the animal, who shifted uneasily under the unfamiliar weight. "Easy, boy."

Ivan handed him the reins and Jess headed the animal out the lane. He hadn't ridden bareback since he was a kid. If the horse dumped him, he would be sorry he hadn't taken a buggy instead. Reassured by the knowledge that Ivan would be coming behind him soon, he pushed the horse to a gallop on the snowy roadway.

Gemma must have gone into labor. How was she? Was the baby okay, or was it already too late? He prayed that God would spare both of them.

He shouldn't have been so angry with her. He could have easily said he turned down her father's offer, but would she have believed him? That she had questioned his honor and his motives hurt deeply, but none of that mattered now. She had to be okay.

He saw the flashing red lights of the ambulance reflected off the snow up ahead before he turned onto the highway. The siren stopped. They must have reached the Lapp farm. His horse tried to make the turn into Michael's lane and almost unseated Jesse. He was able to regain control and keep the animal on the highway, but he slowed his headlong gallop. The ambulance crew didn't need to pick up another patient.

Jesse drew the horse to a stop in front of the Lapp house. One of Gemma's cousins, he couldn't remember the young woman's name, took the horse's reins. "I've got him. Go on in."

"How is she?"

"I don't know." She led the skittish horse away.

Jesse strode into the house. Everyone was up and

milling in the living room. Leroy stood by the staircase, looking upward. Jesse laid a hand on his shoulder. "What happened?"

"We heard her cry out. Dinah ran upstairs and then shouted for me to call an ambulance. We forgot Gemma had a phone. I ran down to the phone shanty and made the call. It seemed to take them forever to get here."

"Can I go up?"

"The ambulance fellow said to keep the area clear. I think you should wait here. I'm so sorry for the way I treated her when she first came home. You were right. I didn't treasure my own child as I should have." He turned away, wiping tears from his eyes.

It was the longest fifteen minutes of Jesse's life. Finally, the men in uniforms appeared at the top of the stairs with a stretcher and quickly made their way down. Jesse caught sight of Gemma's pale face. Her freckles stood out in sharp contrast against her white skin. Her eyes were closed. "Gemma, it's Jesse. I'm here. You're going to be fine." He didn't know if she could hear him.

One of the men held an IV bag in his teeth as he maneuvered the stretcher off the stairs. Michael appeared beside Jesse. He took the bag and held it high.

"Thanks, buddy. Is the husband here?"

"I'm her husband. How is she?" Jesse asked, fearing the answer.

"We're gonna have to talk on the way. You can ride with us."

Leroy and Dinah held on to each other as the stretcher went past them. "Send us word," Leroy said as Jesse met his gaze.

"I will as soon as I can."

Bethany pushed a cell phone into his hand. "Esther's

number is in here. Contact her and she'll get a message to us."

After Gemma's stretcher was secured, Jesse got in beside her and the driver quickly closed the doors. The siren came on as the ambulance drove down the lane.

"What can you tell me about your wife's condition?" One of the men was listening to her heart while the other one was waiting for Jesse's answer.

"She has a partial placenta previa." Jesse did some quick math in his head. "The baby is twenty-nine weeks gestation."

He continued to answer questions when what he really wanted was answers of his own. "How is the baby?"

"We still have fetal heart tones, so that's good. Your wife is losing a lot of blood. She will likely go straight into surgery for a cesarean when we get to the hospital. They aren't equipped to care for premature babies for an extended time. If needed, a helicopter will be on the way from Bangor, and your baby will likely be transferred to the neonatal unit there."

Jesse nodded, trying to take in the information being given to him, but his eyes were glued to the machine over her head with bouncing lines moving across it. He knew it was Gemma's heartbeat, but he had no idea if it was normal.

He took hold of her limp hand. Her fingers were cold. He wanted to tuck them inside his shirt to warm them. It was a helpless feeling, knowing everything was out of his control.

The ambulance pulled into the emergency bay and the back doors were pulled open. Gemma was unloaded and wheeled into the hospital. He tried to follow but he was stopped by a security officer. "Your wife is being well taken care of. I need you to step over to the counter and give us some info."

Jesse gave them all the information he could. When he was finished, a volunteer took him to the surgical waiting room. He was the only one in it. Suddenly the pressure and worry of the day caught up with him. He sat abruptly on the couch as his legs gave out. They had to be okay. Both of them. He needed both of them.

Please, Lord, show mercy to my wife and to her child. They are in Your hands. Guide those who care for them that they may do Your will.

He sat and prayed silently for the two most important people in his life.

About twenty minutes later, he heard a commotion. He stepped to the door to check the hallway. Several people in hospital garb walked by. The piece of equipment they were pushing turned out to be an incubator. They went past him and through the doors leading to the surgery area.

It was a good sign that they needed an incubator, wasn't it? There wasn't anyone he could ask. Another twenty minutes went by and the group came out again. One of the women smiled at him. "Are you Jesse Crump?"

"I am."

"Would you like to meet your daughter?"

"Is she okay?" Joy nearly choked him.

"Come see for yourself."

He walked timidly toward them, not knowing what to expect. The woman moved aside so he could see into the incubator. He stared at Gemma's baby through the clear top. She was amazing. And beautiful. He had never seen such a tiny child. His finger was thicker than her scrawny legs. Her head was covered with thick brown hair that had a red tint to it.

"She has so much hair for an early baby."

"In my twenty years as a delivery nurse, I've never seen a preemie without a head of hair."

He smiled as he gazed at Gemma's daughter. Her face was heart shaped with a tiny bow mouth. There were wrinkles on her forehead that made him think of Gemma when she was angry. Taped to the side of her face was a clear tube with prongs that fitted in her nose.

The baby's eyes were closed. He couldn't tell their color, but her eyelashes were long and curved where they lay against her cheeks. Awed by the wonder of this new life, he knew without a doubt that she was God's greatest gift to him.

"You look like your mother," he told her.

She opened her eyes and blinked owlishly. Then she let out a hearty wail, letting the world know she had arrived. A wonderful warmth filled his chest as he fell head over heels in love with the most beautiful child he had ever laid eyes on.

He spoke to the doctor without taking his eyes off his child. "Is she going to be okay?"

"The steroids your wife received allowed her lungs to mature. She's getting a small amount of oxygen, but she is doing amazingly well for her size. She weighs three pounds and five ounces."

"A sack of sugar weighs more," he mused.

"We are taking her to Bangor to the NICU there. We don't have room for you on the helicopter, but we can arrange transportation to get you to the NICU today. She is ten weeks premature, but all her vital signs look good at the moment. A lot will depend on how well she does in the next forty-eight hours."

"We should get going," the nurse said. "Would you like to hold her hand before we go?"

He nodded. She opened one of the round windows in the side. Another nurse gave him some foam to rub on his hands. When it was dry, he reached in and touched his little girl. He laid his finger on her palm and she immediately grabbed hold of him. "You're strong. God be with you. I'll see you soon. Don't forget me."

The nurse closed the window. "Barring any serious complications, I like to tell the family to expect their baby to go home close to her due date."

"She might be in the hospital another ten weeks?"

"Give or take a few days, yes. Babies don't grow and mature any faster outside Mom than they do inside."

He would certainly need help from his community and others to cover her hospital bill, but he was not worried about the money. He would pay what he could. The bishop would collect alms to cover the rest. If it was more than the community could provide, a call would go out to all Amish communities to render assistance.

He looked at the doctor. "How is Gemma?"

"She lost a lot of blood, but they were able to stop the bleeding. She may be in the hospital for several days longer than normal."

The elevator doors opened, and he watched as they wheeled Gemma's daughter inside.

"Does she have a name?" the nurse asked.

He and Gemma had not discussed a name for the child. It seemed odd now to think how seldom Gemma had spoken about the baby. He glanced at the door. Did the baby look like her father? Only Gemma could answer that question. He hadn't given much thought to Robert, but he did now. Somewhere there was a man who didn't know that he had a daughter. One who hadn't been given the chance to see his beautiful child. If Gemma was right, the man willingly gave up any claim to his baby. Jesse would pray for him.

He looked at the nurse. "I will let her mother decide on a name."

"That's fine. I left some paperwork on Mom's chart. It has our contact information. Feel free to call and check on your daughter anytime of the day or night."

The elevator doors closed. He rubbed a hand over his face. The baby was okay. That was what everyone would want to know. Now he needed to see his wife.

He went back to the waiting room and got out the phone Bethany had given him. He dialed Esther's number. She answered on the second ring. He spent the next ten minutes updating her and having her relay messages to Gemma's family. When he hung up, a young man in green scrubs came into the waiting room. "You must be Jesse Crump." He held out his hand. "I am Dr. Brentwood. I have just finished surgery on your wife."

Jesse shook his hand. "How is Gemma? Can I see her?"

"She had a rough go of it, but I anticipate a full recovery. She needed several units of blood. Your wife will be in recovery for the next two hours. You'll be able to see her after that."

"Thank you, Dr. Brentwood. I appreciate everything you have done."

Knowing that he had two hours to wait, Jesse went in search of a cup of coffee and something to eat. When he reached the lobby, he saw a green van stop outside.

A half-dozen women wearing Amish clothing began getting out. He recognized Gemma's mother and her cousins who had attended the wedding.

Two of them carried large quilted bags over their arms. Dinah caught sight of him and hurried toward him. The other women followed her. They crowded around, asking about Gemma.

"She is in recovery. She will be there for another two hours. After that, she will be moved to a room. We will be able to see her then."

"Where can we wait?" one of her cousins asked.

He showed them to the waiting area. Dinah opened the bag she carried and withdrew several wrapped sandwiches. "I thought you might be hungry."

Someone else produced a thermos of hot coffee and disposable cups. He drank the coffee and tried to eat a sandwich, but he was too worried about Gemma. Her baby had been whisked away in a helicopter before she had even laid eyes on her. He knew that would be upsetting.

"Did you see the baby before they took her away?" Dinah asked.

"I did." He proceeded to tell them about Gemma's baby. He remembered her weight, but he didn't remember being told how long she was. They plied him for information until Dinah gently asked them to let him swallow a bite of his sandwich.

The time passed more quickly with company. He was surprised when a nurse came out to tell him he could see Gemma. He bolted out of his chair and followed her.

She lay on pristine white sheets. He thought her color was better than when she had left the house on the stretcher, but she was still pale. And beautiful. Tears filled his eyes as he pulled up a chair beside her bed. "Gemma. Open your eyes. Can you hear me, darling? It's Jesse."

Gemma heard Jesse's voice, but she couldn't make her eyes open. There was something important she needed to know. Something she had to ask him. She struggled again to open her eyes and he was there.

"Jesse?" Her voice came out scratchy and hoarse.

"Time to wake up, sleepyhead."

"Not yet." She drifted off for a few seconds and then opened her eyes wide. "The baby?"

"She's fine."

"A girl?"

"We have a *dochtah*."

"A daughter. You said it would be a girl. Where is she?" Gemma tried to raise her head. It was too heavy. She let it fall back. "Can I see her?"

"I'm afraid you can't see her yet." His voice held an odd quality that scared her.

"Why not? Why can't I see her? What's wrong?" She struggled to rise.

He gently restrained her. "Take it easy. She wasn't due for another two months, remember? She is premature. They can't take care of her at this hospital, so they have taken her to another one."

"Where?"

"Bangor."

"That's so far. She's all alone." A tear slipped from the corner of her eye.

"She isn't alone. She has some wonderful nurses and doctors taking care of her."

"That's not the same. Are you sure she is okay?"

She raised her hand and he took hold of it. He was so strong and so gentle. If only she could believe that his affection was real.

"I saw her before they took her away and she was hollering at the top of her lungs."

"That's *goot*, isn't it?"

"Very *goot*."

Gemma cringed with the rising pain. "She needs you, Jesse. You have to be with her."

"We will go see her together," he coaxed.

"*Nee*, you have to protect her. She needs you."

He bent close. "You need me here."

"I do, but she needs you more. Promise you'll go."

"I promise. Now, get some rest."

"Okay." Gemma closed her eyes and let her mind float away. *Why did you marry me, Jesse?*

Chapter Fifteen

By late that afternoon, Jesse was in Bangor at the medical center. Dale had been able to drive him, and Jesse was grateful to the bishop for arranging it. He went through the routine of filling out paperwork at the admissions office and then was asked to wait until a volunteer escort could show him to the nursery. All the while, his mind kept jumping back to Gemma. Was she doing okay? Was she in much pain?

He was torn between the need to be with his new wife and the desire to be with his new daughter. Gemma had insisted that he come to protect the baby. He didn't know what he could do that couldn't be done by the nurses and staff taking care of her but if his being here relieved Gemma's mind, he would make the long trip as often as she wanted him to.

An elderly man in a pink jacket arrived to show Jesse the way. As they walked together along a lengthy hall, the man cast a sidelong glance at him. "Are you Amish or Mennonite?"

"Amish."

"There aren't many of you folks this far north."

"There are more coming every year. The price of your farmland is reasonable and that makes Maine attractive to us."

"Are you a potato farmer?"

"I am. In the off-season, I build garden sheds and tiny houses at a business near my farm."

"I grew up on a potato farm. I'm old enough to remember my grandfather farming with horses. It's nice to see that coming back."

"Many of our *Englisch* neighbors in New Covenant feel the same way."

They stopped at an elevator and got on when the doors opened. The man selected the floor and pushed the button.

"I'm going to take you as far as the NICU doors," he said when the elevator stopped. He pointed the way, and Jesse stepped out. A receptionist sat behind a glassed-in desk. She opened a set of double doors and beckoned him inside. He followed her into the nursery, where she showed him how to scrub his hands up to his elbows and informed him he would do this every time he came in. He was willing to do whatever it took to safeguard his child.

Another nurse was summoned. She was a tall girl with a long black ponytail. She introduced herself as Jill and said she was Baby Crump's nurse. Her calm and friendly demeanor went a long way to soothe his worries.

At his daughter's bedside, he stopped in surprise when he saw the jumble of wires that were hooked to her. She was still wearing her oxygen tubing, but she was just as beautiful as he remembered. She lay on an open bed with a heating unit above her. An IV hung from a pole on a small machine that hummed and clicked softly. A white bandage on her arm held the IV in place. Behind her, a screen displayed several bouncing red lines and a lot of numbers that meant nothing to him. He stared at them, trying to make sense of what they were telling him.

"Mothers gaze at their baby's face. Fathers spend more time watching the monitors," Jill said with a chuckle.

"Then they must understand what the numbers mean because I don't," he admitted. "How is she doing?"

"Very well. She has some mild breathing problems, but the oxygen she is on is a small amount. Is her mother going to be nursing her or using formula?"

"I believe she will nurse her, but I don't know for sure. It will be several days before she can come here."

"It is almost her feeding time. Would you like to hold her?"

Excitement made him giddy. "Of course I would." His elation took a quick dive, tempered by uncertainty. "Are you sure it's okay?"

Smiling, Jill patted his arm. "I'll be right here. Have you heard of kangaroo care?"

He shook his head. "What does an Australian animal have to do with human babies?"

"That is what we call it when parents hold their baby skin to skin. We'll lay her on your bare chest and cover her with a blanket. Your body heat will keep her warm. The sound of your heartbeat will soothe her. We have found premature babies gain more weight and grow better with this type of contact. Want to try it?"

"Sure."

"We ask that you hold her for at least an hour. Do you have that much time today?"

"I have all the time she needs."

Jill grinned. "I like your attitude. I need to get her feeding ready."

The baby lay on her side with both hands tucked under her chin. He leaned in to speak softly to her. "*Goot* morn, *Liebchen*. Do you remember me? I'm your *daed*. Your father. I get to hold you today. Would you like that?"

Her eyes fluttered open at the sound of his voice, and she yawned.

Jill chuckled as she came back with the syringe filled with what he assumed was infant formula. "I don't think she's as eager as you are."

She indicated a recliner beside the bed. "Okay, Jesse, unbutton your shirt."

Feeling self-conscious, he sat still as a stone in the chair while the nurses transferred the babe. One of her wires came loose. Alarms sounded. He looked to Jill, who smiled reassuringly. "Just a loose lead. She's fine." She laid the baby on his chest and reconnected her to the monitor. The steady *beep, beep, beep* was comforting.

His large hands covered his daughter's entire body. She lay light as a feather against him. A rush of emotion filled his heart to overflowing, making it hard to breathe. Jill laid a warm blanket over the two of them, and the babe proceeded to make herself comfortable. She wiggled against his skin, her tiny fingers grasping handfuls of his chest hair. It was an amazing feeling, having her tiny warm body next to his heart. He wanted to hold on to this marvelous moment forever. He was holding Gemma's daughter. His daughter. It was everything he had imagined it would be and more.

Could she hear his heartbeat? Did she recall the

sound of her mother's beating heart? Sadness settled over him, dulling his happiness. He looked up at Jill standing close by. "It should be her mother holding her for the first time."

"Her mother held her safe and close for all these past months. It's okay for Dad to take his turn. Would you like me to take a picture for you?"

He considered her offer carefully. "If you make sure my face is not seen it will be acceptable. I'm sure her mother will want to know what she looks like."

As eager as he had been to see and hold his child, he was just as eager to get back to Gemma. Hopefully all of them would soon be together. He looked up when a man in a white coat stopped in front of him. He introduced himself as the baby's neonatologist and proceeded to update Jesse on the things that they were watching. It wasn't as good of a report as Jesse had been hoping to hear.

On the following morning, Gemma was sitting up in the chair for the first time when Jesse walked in. Relief and delight swirled through her body before she could tamp down her emotions. She wanted to fling herself into his arms, but she knew that wasn't going to happen. "How is she? I miss her so much and I've never even seen her face."

"I can help with that." He pulled a chair over to her and sat down. He wanted to kiss her; the need to hold her close burned in his chest but he didn't want to hurt her. He settled for a quick peck on her cheek when he was sure no one was watching. Public displays of affection between Amish adults, even married ones, were frowned upon. He longed to tell her how much she had come to mean to him, but the uncertainty between them kept him silent.

He took out his wallet and carefully removed the photograph Jill had taken of their baby. Only Jesse's fingers were visible in it. Gemma's hands shook as she took it and gazed at it with a look of endearing tenderness. Then slowly the joy in her eyes dimmed. "What's on her face? What's wrong with her arm? Is it broken?"

He had become accustomed to seeing the baby with all her tubing and equipment. He had to remember that Gemma had not seen any of it. "The little tube in her nose is giving her oxygen. That white bandage on her arm is to keep her from pulling her IV out. The blue tube in her mouth goes to her stomach. That's the way they feed her right now. When she gets a little bigger, they will use a bottle until you can nurse her. Isn't she beautiful? Her hair has hints of red in it. Her eyes are blue, but they told me all babies have blue eyes. I think she looks like you."

"You never met Robert. She isn't fine, is she? She's sick. They wouldn't be giving her oxygen if she was fine."

He had been trying hard to make it sound positive, but Gemma was right. "She's needing a little more oxygen today. Her blood levels show she may need a transfusion. They say it's not unexpected, and they still believe she's doing well. They just have to keep a close eye on her."

"You should be there. Why did you come back?"

"To see my wife. To bring her a picture of her daughter. I'm sure the bishop won't object to one photograph in a situation like ours. They are taking good care of her."

Gemma closed her eyes and nodded slightly. Was he telling the truth or trying to spare her? "I'm sorry. It was kind of you to think of me. I'm tired, that's all. Would you call the nurse to help me back to bed?"

"Sure thing." He rose and stepped out into the hall until he located a staff member. He waited outside the room while they moved her. Once she was back in bed, the nurse's aide opened the door. Gemma heard someone call his name. Michael, Bethany and Anna were coming toward her room. Ivan and Jenny followed behind them with a pair of bright pink balloons in hand. It's a Girl was written in gold lettering. Her parents came behind the children.

Gemma blinked away the moisture in her eyes. How could she tell her friends and family it was too soon to celebrate the birth of her baby? She couldn't. She would smile, thank them and keep her deep fear hidden from everyone, including Jesse. She was terrified her daughter was going to die.

Four days later, when Gemma was released from the hospital, she and Jesse made the long trip to Bangor with plans to stay for a week and perhaps longer in the accommodations the hospital provided for families with infants in the NICU. Jesse kept a close eye on Gemma. She was quiet and withdrawn. He worried that the trip was too much for her so soon after surgery.

She never complained, so he had little evidence to base his feelings on. Something just wasn't right.

When they were settled in the guest rooms, he went to the kitchenette and fixed them both a cup of hot tea. He offered it to Gemma. "It's not rose hip tea, but it's okay."

She accepted her cup gratefully. "It's hot and that's what counts. Our marriage isn't off to a very good start. You must regret marrying me."

"Of course I don't. I have a beautiful new daughter. Jill is going to ask me if we have picked a name for her yet. Shall we decide before we go over to visit her?"

"I'm not up to a visit just yet." She put her cup down.

Was she feeling worse than she was letting on? "That's fine. What about the name?"

"I won't know until I see her face. The picture was nice but seeing her in person will be best."

"That I understand. Can I do anything for you before I go over to visit her?"

She kept her gaze down. "I'm fine, Jesse. Stop worrying about me."

"If you say so."

"I didn't marry you to become a burden."

"You will never be a burden to me." He bent to kiss her cheek. "Get some rest."

She nodded meekly.

After he left their room, he stopped in the hospital lobby and placed a call to the phone shanty for Gemma's mother. He was worried that Gemma seemed detached from the baby. The NICU nurse had mentioned it happened occasionally when mothers didn't bond with their infants at birth. He left a message telling his in-laws that they had arrived safely and he would call again with an update tomorrow.

Jill was sitting beside his daughter's bed, writing on a chart when he came in. She looked up with a wide smile. "Your little one is off oxygen as of this morning."

"That's great." He couldn't stop his wide grin.

"Where is her mother? I've been looking forward to meeting her."

His smile faded. "The trip wore her out. She'll be in later."

Jill put down her pen and leaned on her writing desk. "Poor thing. What a rough delivery she has had. She'll feel better when she sees the baby."

"What else is new with my girl?"

"She's two ounces above her birth weight. To celebrate, I was going to make a card for her mother. I hate to ask, but do we have a name?"

He thought about it for a second. "Hope."

Gemma could change it if she wanted but that was how he saw this child. A gift of hope.

"Aw, I like that. It's not her feeding time, so you aren't going to be able to hold her."

"That's okay. I can admire her from afar."

Gemma woke in near-total darkness with her heart pounding in terror. Only a faint glow shone under the door of the bedroom. It took her a few seconds to figure out where she was. At the hospital in Bangor in one of the rooms reserved for parents of sick babies.

She checked the other bed and saw Jesse was sleeping sprawled across it. She eased out of bed and slipped her dressing gown over her long nightgown. She pulled her braid from beneath her gown and let it fall down her back. Her slippers were at the foot of the bed. She wiggled her feet into them and quietly left the suite. She had to get to the nursery. Her baby girl was dying.

The elevator seemed to take forever, but it finally opened on the correct floor. She spoke to the receptionist, who opened the door for her. Inside the unit, she had no idea where to go. She rushed over to the first nurse she saw. "Where's my baby? Is she gone already? Please tell me."

"Tell me your name and we'll see where your baby is."

"Gemma Lapp. I mean Crump."

"Ah, little Hope's mommy. Your baby is right over here." She led the way to where a babe with thick reddish-brown hair lay sleeping in an incubator. Gemma leaned close. Was this the same infant in the photograph? Had Jesse named her? Gemma looked at the nurse. "This is my baby?"

"Yes."

"Can I touch her?"

"First, I have to show you how to wash up. Then you can have a seat and I'll let you hold her."

"I woke up and thought something was wrong. I had to come see."

"A nightmare? They can feel so real sometimes. I'm Pepper. I'll be Hope's nurse until the day shift comes on. Where is Jesse?"

"I didn't wake him."

"He is such a good father. I wish there were more like him."

Gemma eased into a rocking chair. "I've never held her before."

Pepper opened the side of the incubator, deftly wrapped the babe in two blankets and laid her in Gemma's arms.

It was almost like holding nothing and the whole world at the same time. Gemma pulled the blankets aside to see her better. After gazing at her face, she started checking all her fingers and her tiny feet. "You're okay, aren't you? I had such a bad dream about you, but you're okay. My beautiful, beautiful baby girl. My Hope."

Gemma closed the blanket around her, so she wouldn't be cold. "I was afraid to meet you. Isn't that silly? You aren't a punishment. You're a pearl beyond compare. Look at your cute ears and your nose. I love every inch of you."

"She is a special gift from God to us."

Gemma looked up to see Jesse smiling at her. "She's amazing, Jesse. I didn't know."

He knelt beside her and cupped the baby's head. Gemma laid her hand over his. "Thank you."

"For what?" he asked, looking puzzled.

"For taking care of her while I couldn't."

"You are most welcome."

She gazed at her baby and then looked into Jesse's eyes. No matter why he had married her, she was in his debt. She wouldn't burden him with unwanted affection or question his motives. She would do all she could to give him a happy home, even if he never loved her. "I will be a good wife to you, Jesse."

He gazed at the floor for a long moment, then looked up. "Gemma, about the quarrel we had on our wedding night…"

She reached out and laid her fingers on his lips. "It doesn't matter. We are wedded, for better or for worse. Hope is who matters now."

He nodded and gave a half-hearted smile. It didn't erase the concern she saw in his eyes.

Chapter Sixteen

Jesse put in a call to update Gemma's parents and to ask for help. It produced immediate results. Dinah, Bethany and Anna arrived later that day to stay with and support Gemma. He was thrilled that she was bonding with Hope, but Gemma still wasn't herself. He put it down to the strain of the situation, but it didn't ease his mind completely. What was he missing?

She had become the most important person in his life. Was he in love with her? He wanted her to be happy. To smile and laugh and bicker with him the way she had when he gave her a tour of his home. Maybe he was being impatient. Maybe time was all she needed.

Remembering his vow to love and cherish his wife gave him solace. She needed her family and her baby now. Once life returned to normal, he and Gemma would have a lifetime to grow close once more. He longed to hear her say she loved him, but he was the one who had insisted love wasn't necessary in their marriage. He would wait until Hope was home and thriving before he asked Gemma for something she might not be able to give him. Her love.

On the following Monday, they all returned to New Covenant, leaving Hope in the skilled and kind hands of the NICU staff. Jesse needed to return to work. He faced rapidly mounting medical bills.

Gemma fought back tears as she left her baby. She barely spoke on the ride home, and he knew she was missing her baby. On Tuesday she seemed better, but he could tell was still depressed. They were both staying with her parents as was the custom for Amish newlyweds, but he had his own room. Gemma needed all the rest she could get. Her mother made sure she got it. He was glad for the added help in keeping Gemma's mind occupied while he was at work.

On Wednesday morning, Dinah caught him in the hall before Gemma was up. "I'm going to suggest a shopping trip to Gemma today. I want you to support the idea."

Did his wife enjoy shopping? He didn't know. The dwindling balance in his bank account gave him pause but if it helped Gemma, he wouldn't refuse. "A *goot* idea. Would you like me to take you?"

"I'll have Michael drive us. He mentioned he needed to go into town today and he has the patience needed to wait in the buggy while I'm in a store."

Jesse grinned. "Is this something I should cultivate?"

"Most definitely. We're going shopping for baby clothes and essentials. Gemma needs a gentle reminder that Hope will be home soon. She needs to concentrate on the future instead of bemoaning the fact that she doesn't have her child with her now."

"You've been a blessing to me, Dinah." Much more than his own mother, who hadn't come to the wedding or even acknowledged it.

"My *sohn*, you have been a blessing to me. More than you will know until you become a *grossdaadi*. When I looked upon the face of my grandchild, I knew it was God's way of giving me a glimpse into the joy that awaits me when I am called to my final home."

"I pray that is many years away." He folded his arms across his chest and stared at the floor as he framed his next question. "Does it bother you that I am not Hope's true father?"

When Dinah didn't answer, he looked up. She was smiling. She patted his cheek. "I forgot that. *Nee*, it bothers me not one bit. This is the last time we will think upon it, *ja*?"

"Ja," he agreed as his heart grew light. "Have fun shopping and bring a smile to Gemma's face if you can."

When his wife and Dinah left, he stopped by Bethany's and asked her to come with him to see Anna. When they were gathered around Anna's kitchen table, he sat forward in his chair and glanced between Anna and Bethany. "Have you noticed anything different about Gemma? Something that's not quite right?"

The two women exchanged speaking looks. Bethany nodded. "We have."

Anna laid her hands on the table. *"Subdued* is perhaps the word."

"Do either of you know what's going on?" he asked.

"Baby blues? She is going through a difficult time. You both are," Anna said quietly.

He nodded. "The midwife mentioned I should let her know if Gemma seems depressed. Maybe it is just the blues." That would get better with time.

"Have you told Gemma that you love her?" Bethany asked.

He shifted uncomfortably in his chair. "Not in so many words. I care for her and she knows that."

Bethany stabbed a finger in the air toward him. "You care for her. She *loves* you."

He sat up to stare at her. "Has she said this?"

Bethany relaxed her attitude. "Not in so many words, but I know my friend."

He glanced between the two women. "Why wouldn't she tell me how she felt?"

"Because yours wasn't a love match in the beginning, and you don't think love is necessary for a good marriage. Isn't that what you told her?"

"I admit I might not have known what I was talking about when I said it."

Anna nodded. "That's a smart answer. Remember, Gemma may be dealing with a lot of guilt too. I've read that mothers of premature babies often feel they are to blame for the early births. You saved Gemma's life in the storm. You married her to give her babe a name. You took Hope into your heart like she was your own. Gemma may not feel worthy of your affections."

He blew out a slow breath. "What do I do?"

The two women exchanged glances. Anna gave a slight shake of her head.

"What? Tell me," he insisted.

"Gemma married and became a mother all in one day," Bethany said. "She never had a chance to enjoy being alone with you. Her marriage was more of a contract than a courtship, and every woman wants to be courted, to be made to feel special by the man she adores. I'm not saying start a courtship now. You both have a lot on your plates, but when the time is right, you should set out to make her feel special."

"I have my work cut out for me, don't I?"

Bethany patted his hand. "I think you are up to the challenge."

Was courting his wife what he had to do to earn her love? He would try anything to regain their easy friendship and then let her know how much she had come to mean to him.

On her way back from their shopping trip, Gemma stopped off to see Bethany while Michael took her mother home. Bethany was scrubbing out her sink. Her bright smile lifted Gemma's spirits.

Gemma placed her packages on the table. "You have to see the cute clothes I found for Hope. It's hard to find preemie clothes. We had to go all over. I bought some material to make her a few outfits too. I know she'll outgrow them quickly."

"Did you enjoy yourself?" Bethany dried her hands on her apron.

Gemma thought about it for a second. "I did."

Bethany shook a finger at her. "I'm glad you're getting back to your old self. We were worried."

"I didn't realize I was worrying people. Who is *we*?"

"Your husband stopped in to ask Anna and me if we knew what was wrong with you."

Gemma spread out the first tiny pink dress. That Jesse was worried enough to seek the council of her friends surprised her. "I guess I've been worried about Hope. So many things could go wrong. She's so tiny."

"Is that all?"

"What else could it be?"

"That you are unhappily married?"

Gemma looked at her friend. "Don't think that. Jesse is a wonderful father, but..."

Bethany's eyes were full of sympathy. "But what?"

"He doesn't love me." Gemma shrugged. "That's the way things are and I have to accept that."

"My observation is that Jesse cares a lot about you. He wasn't faking that happy smile at his wedding."

"Maybe he had more things to smile about than getting married."

"What's that supposed to mean?"

"Never mind."

Gemma was too embarrassed to share what she suspected. Her father had practically sold her to Jesse. Was she worth eighty acres in Jesse's mind? At least something good had come out of their marriage for him. She managed a smile for her friend. "I'm going to make a few dresses for Hope out of this material. Do you like it?"

On her way home from her visit, Gemma stopped at the phone shanty and placed a call to the NICU. She was happy when Jill came on the line. "How is Hope today?"

"She's okay, except for a stuffy nose."

"Did she gain weight?"

"Let me look... No, her weight stayed the same."

"But she has been gaining every day." Concern inched its way into Gemma's mind. "Is it something serious?"

"Having a baby in an NICU is like riding a roller coaster. There are ups and downs. It's normal. Are you still planning on being here this weekend?"

"We are, and I'm going to stay until Hope is released." She wasn't going to be hours away if something did go wrong.

"That's good news. Hope will be happy to have her mommy here. Is Jesse staying too?"

"Ah, no. He has to work."

"Still, he'll feel better knowing you are with your daughter."

Gemma hoped that would be the case.

That evening she was packing her suitcase when Jesse came up to her room at her parents' home after work. She added some of the outfits she and her mother had purchased and the few she had sewn.

Jesse grinned. "She can't wear that many clothes in a weekend."

"I'm taking enough along for a month."

He looked puzzled. "For a month?"

She closed the top of her suitcase. "I'm going to stay there until she is ready to come home."

"I can understand why you want to do it."

"Bethany said you were worried because I have been depressed. I'm fine now. Oh, wait, I know how much you hate that word. I am feeling much less sad, and I'm eager to learn how to take care of my daughter. We can call each other every day."

She raised her chin, daring him to refuse to let her go. "I am going, and it doesn't matter what you say. You told me you admire people who speak the truth."

"I do. I will miss you."

It was nice to hear, but was it the truth? She picked up her nightgown and added it to the suitcase. "I will miss you too."

"Are you sure you want to do this?"

"What's the harm? If I get homesick, I'll come home."

"Then you should do what you need to do. I'll pack my things for this weekend and call for a ride."

* * *

Gemma's plan to stay with Hope for the next month or more surprised him. It would be good for both mother and babe; it made sense, but how would he and Gemma improve their relationship with so much physical distance between them? One phone call a day wasn't going to be enough. He wanted Gemma near him. He needed her. If only she believed that he had married her because he cared for her and not to gain land. How could he convince her?

On their arrival in the NICU in Bangor that evening, they were greeted with the distressing news that Hope's cold had worsened. Jill met them with a sober face. "We have had to move her into the isolation room. She has RSV. It's a viral infection that would be a cold for you or me but in premature babies, it can be very serious."

A chill ran through Jesse's body. Hope had come so far, but she was still so tiny. She didn't deserve a setback.

"Can we see her?" Gemma asked.

"Of course, but you will have to put on a gown, gloves and a mask." Jill led the way and Jesse followed, holding Gemma's hand. He knew by her grip that she was as worried as he was.

Hope was crying pitifully when they entered the special room designed to keep any contamination from spreading to the other babies. Gemma immediately went to soothe Hope and lift her out of her crib. The baby quieted, but she was still breathing hard. Her rib cage sank in as she struggled with each breath. Gemma gave Jesse a fear-filled look. It mirrored the dread in his heart.

Throughout the next two days, Jesse and Gemma held their daughter almost continuously. Being upright made the baby's breathing easier. She didn't fuss as much when she received her breathing treatments if someone was holding her. Jesse's heart broke each time she looked at him with her sad tired eyes. When the time came for him to leave, he sat holding Hope while Gemma was washing her hands.

After putting on her gloves, she stood aside. Jesse got out of the rocker and gently transferred Hope into Gemma's arms. She said, "Come here, my precious *bobbli*."

He dropped to one knee beside the chair and laid a hand on Hope's soft hair. "I can't leave, Gemma. She's not getting better. I'm worried about you too. You won't get enough rest if I'm not here to spell you."

"As much as you dislike the word *fine*, that's what I am today. Fine. My incision has healed. I'm getting stronger every day. I'm fine."

"That may be, but I'm not fine leaving you here alone. Marriage is a partnership. We will get through this together." He dropped a kiss on Hope's head.

"You love her, don't you, Jesse?" Gemma asked quietly.

"More than I ever thought possible. But you know how I feel, don't you?" He gazed into Gemma's eyes intently.

"I do. It's amazing—isn't it?—how much space someone so small can take up in your heart."

"And how much space is left over for the other people we love." He grew serious. Was now the time to tell her how he felt? "Gemma, I—"

One of Hope's alarms began ringing. Jesse looked at her monitor. He had learned the meaning of all the numbers and waving lines during Hope's first week in the unit. Most of the time, it was simply a false alarm that a wiggling baby could generate just by moving.

The monitor was over Gemma's head. She couldn't see the numbers. "What is it?"

"Her oxygen level is too low."

"Check to see if the lead is loose."

He did. It was secure. He could see the baby's lips turning blue as her numbers fell. Before he could call out, several nurses rushed to the bedside. One of them scooped Hope out of Gemma's arms and laid her in her crib. A few seconds later, a doctor hurried in. He listened to Hope with his stethoscope and scowled. "Call respiratory care. Have a ventilator brought in. We are going to intubate. Mom and Dad, I'm afraid you are going to have to step out."

"What's wrong?" Gemma demanded as Jesse helped her to her feet.

The doctor covered Hope's face with an oxygen mask. "We're going get an X-ray to be sure, but it sounds like her RSV has progressed to pneumonia. She's going to need help breathing."

A nurse touched Jesse's arm. "Please come with me. We'll take good care of her and let you come back in when we're done."

Jesse drew Gemma away with an arm across her shoulders. Outside the unit, the nurse indicated a waiting room. It was empty at the moment. Gemma turned her face into Jesse's chest and burst into sobs. He wrapped his arms tightly around her. "It's going to be okay. She's a strong girl."

Was he trying to reassure Gemma or himself? What was going on? How long before someone came to tell them something? He heard Gemma muttering prayers under her breath. He closed his eyes and prayed harder than he had ever prayed in his life.

* * *

After ten minutes of uncertainty, Jesse coaxed Gemma to sit down on the red sofa against the wall. There was a television playing in the corner, but Gemma ignored it. She dried her eyes and stared at the door. "I wish someone would tell us what's going on."

She heard the hum of a motor growing closer. The portable X-ray machine came down the hall, guided by a young woman. She pushed a button on the wall and went into the unit when the doors opened.

Jesse strode out into the hall to gaze into the unit until the doors swung shut again. He came back into the waiting room.

She looked at him hopefully. "Did you see anything?"

"Just a group of people around her bed." He sat beside Gemma. She wanted to be back in his embrace but didn't know how to ask.

She noticed his hands were clenched into tight fists. She laid her palm on one.

"I want to fight this battle for her too."

He leaned forward with his elbows on his knees and covered his face with his hands. A ragged sob broke free. Gemma threw her arms around him. If she needed comfort, he needed it too. "Don't cry, darling."

She drew his head to her shoulder. He wrapped his arms around her as his body shook with silent sobs.

"I can't—can't do anything for her. What good are hands as big as hams if they can't hold back the suffering she has to endure?"

They held on to each other through the longest hour Gemma had ever known until the unit doors finally opened again.

The doctor stood in the doorway with a faint smile on his lips. "She is on a breathing machine and resting much easier now that the vent can do some of the work. The X-ray does show pneumonia in her right lower lung. We've started medication to help clear it, but I think she's going to be fine."

"Can we come in?" Jesse asked, wiping his eyes.

"Give the nurses another ten minutes to get things cleaned up. I don't recommend you hold her today. Let her rest after this. If she is doing okay tomorrow, I think it will be fine."

"Danki," Gemma said.

The doctor nodded once and went back into the unit.

Gemma and Jesse stared at each other. Her relief was so profound she didn't know what to say.

He reached out and cupped her cheek. "I love you, Gemma. I think I've loved you since the day at the cabin when you knocked the cattail roots out of my hands and scolded me for getting frostbite."

She smiled softly. How could she have doubted this man? "I love you too."

They moved into each other's arms. Jesse kissed her forehead and held her tight. "I never want to let you go."

"That's fine with me, but I'm having a little trouble breathing." Her voice was muffled against his chest.

He chuckled as he loosened his hold. "Trust my Gemma to tell me what she thinks. I love that about you. I love everything about you." He drew a shaky breath. "I want to tell you about the land."

"You don't need to explain. I'm sorry I doubted your motives. I couldn't believe you wanted to marry me for myself alone. I didn't feel worthy of the sacrifice you were making. Jesse, I know in my heart that you are a man of integrity."

"Your father did offer me the land to marry you."

Her heart sank. "He did?"

"I refused and told him he didn't value the treasure he had in his daughter."

Her heart rebounded and thudded with joy. "I don't imagine he cared for that."

"I don't think he did, but he did give us the land as a wedding present. He said my farm wasn't big enough to raise a family on."

"I think it's a lovely farm. Although it is in need of some tender loving care."

He rested his forehead against hers. "You are worth far more to me than any amount of land in Maine."

She chuckled as all her doubts slipped away. "Of course I am. Farmland is dirt cheap up here. What would I be worth in Florida?"

"I believe the answer is in Proverbs 31:10. 'Who can find a virtuous woman? for her price is far above rubies.' Let's go in and see our daughter, shall we, my wife?"

"*Ja*, my husband."

Two and a half weeks later, Jesse opened the door to the suite where Gemma was staying. He'd gone back to New Covenant a week after Hope's recovery. He hadn't seen his wife or his daughter for a week. He dropped his duffel bag and held out his arms. Gemma rushed to hug him and gave him a quick peck on the cheek. "We have to get over to the nursery. The doctor wants a meeting with us."

"Now? I just got here. Can't I even say hello to you first?"

"Sorry." She raised her face for his kiss. It was still too brief before she pulled away, but it would have to do. "Come on. I want to find out what's going on."

"I thought you said she was getting well."

"She's been doing great. She weighs five pounds and seven ounces."

If his daughter was doing well, Jesse didn't understand what the rush was to see the doctor, but he hurried along beside his wife. In the unit, they were shown to a small office. The doctor came in a few seconds later. "Nice to see you again, Mr. Crump. I have some good news. Hope is ready to be discharged, and we need to make some going-home plans."

Discharged? They could take the baby home? Jesse glanced at Gemma. She was staring at the neonatologist like he was speaking Greek. Finally she said, "You mean Hope is well enough to go home? But she's so small."

"She is doing all the things we talked about. She is maintaining her temperature without heat. She is taking all her feedings and nursing well. And she is growing steadily. We can't do any better for her than you can."

Gemma clutched Jesse's arm. "It's too soon. We don't have anything ready for her at home."

The doctor grinned. "I suggest you get ready. She is going out the door on Monday morning."

On Monday afternoon, Dale Kaufman drove into the Lapp farm and stopped by the front gate. The farmyard was full of buggies and cars. "Looks like our new little gal has company already."

Jesse frowned. "The first thing they told us about taking her home was to avoid large crowds."

Gemma handed him the baby bundled up against the cold. "We can't stay in the car."

He took her hand and helped her out. The front door opened. Gemma's parents came out with Esther Hopper.

She stood back while Dinah and Leroy greeted the new arrival. Dinah took the baby from him and they all went into the house. It was empty.

Gemma looked around. "Where are the people who belong to the buggies outside?"

"In the barn," Leroy said, gazing fondly at the child.

Gemma and Jesse looked at each other. "What's going on?" he asked. "Why are people in the barn?"

"Because that's where it is warm enough to wait." Dinah smiled at Gemma. "Are you hungry? We have plenty of food."

Gemma cocked one eyebrow. "Do I have to go to the barn to get it?"

Dinah waved aside the question. "Of course not. I have some in the kitchen for you. I think we are ready to open gifts now. Esther, would you go tell the folks?"

"Gifts?" Jesse looked as puzzled as Gemma felt.

"This is your baby shower. Sit on the sofa with Hope so everyone can see her." She marshaled them to a place where the sofa had been turned to face the windows and opened the shades.

Esther went to the door. "She shouldn't be exposed to large crowds for a while, but everyone wants to see her."

Gemma's father pulled a cradle out from behind a chair. "Gemma, this cradle was made by your great-great-grandfather. I slept in it, as did you. May God grant you have many more children to rock to sleep in it."

"Now, my quilt," Dinah said. "This was made by myself and your cousins. By the way, there is a mud sale being planned in February by an Amish community in Ohio to raise funds for Hope's and Gemma's medical bills. We will have other fund-raisers soon. *Gott* provides."

One by one, the gifts from family and friends were displayed. There was a tap at the window. Gemma glanced up to see a dozen people lined up outside the windows, including the bishop, Mr. Meriwether, the grocer, Ivan and Jenny, their teachers and classmates from school, as well as Michael and Bethany. Everyone was bundled up against the cold. Bethany beckoned Gemma closer. Gemma handed the baby to Jesse. "Go show off your daughter."

He happily took Hope to the window and waited as guest after guest filed by to get a view of the newest resident of New Covenant. Gemma sat back and watched. She wouldn't say Jesse preened, but she had never seen him look so happy.

Two weeks after their arrival at her parents' home, Gemma and Hope were settling in well, except for one thing. Jesse had chosen to stay at his home until he had the place fixed up enough for his family to move there. While he came over every day, Gemma was wondering when she would be able to move into her new home.

She finished feeding Hope and was getting ready for bed on Saturday night when the sound of something hitting the window caught her attention. It sounded like a smattering of hail. She heard it again. What was going on?

She pulled up the shade. Jesse stood in the snow-covered garden below. A full moon hung low in the sky, making the scene almost as bright as day. She lifted the sash, letting in a rush of cold air. "Jesse Crump, what are you doing?"

"Dress warm and come out."

"Why?"

"Because I asked you to?"

"You will need a better explanation by the time I get down there."

"Come on. It's important."

She closed the window and quickly dressed. She pulled on long woolen leggings and put on her fur-lined boots. Hope was sound asleep in her bassinet beside her mother's bed.

Gemma tiptoed into her mother's room across the hall and gently shook her by the shoulder. "Mamm, wake up."

"What's wrong?" her mother whispered as she sat up.

"Nothing. Jesse wants me to come outside."

"At this time of night? What for?"

Gemma shrugged. "I have no idea. I left my door open. Will you listen for the baby?"

"Foolishness, if you ask me. Go, I'll keep an eye on her."

"Danki, Mamm." Gemma hurried down the hall to the front door, grabbed her coat and scarf from the peg and opened the door.

Jesse sat in a sleigh with one of his draft horses in harness.

Gemma came down the porch steps toward him. "What are you doing?"

"'Evening, Gemma."

She paused behind the gate. "Good evening to you. I don't understand."

"It's a right nice evening, isn't it?" His voice sounded strained.

"Nice enough for the dead of winter."

"I was wondering if you might like to take a sleigh ride?"

"Now?"

"That's how courting couples do it."

"Courting?" Her eyes widened.

"You never had a courtship. I thought you deserved one." Jesse held out his hand.

Gemma didn't hesitate. She pushed open the gate, took his hand and climbed in beside him. He spread a quilt over her lap. There were hot bricks on the floorboards to rest her feet on.

When she was settled beside him, he clicked his tongue and slapped the reins to set Goliath in motion.

At the highway, he turned south, away from the settlement. She couldn't contain her curiosity. "Where are we going?"

"Someplace we can talk without being interrupted."

"That could include ninety percent of the state of Maine." As if anyone was out and about at this time of night. He turned off on a road just beyond the Shultz place and then took the left fork behind their big white barn. The little-used road wound around the side of a hill and came out into a small meadow. A white-tailed buck stood browsing near the trees along the edge of the clearing. He bounded away in alarm.

Jesse drew his horse to a stop. "Will it bother you to walk a little ways?"

"I'll be fine."

"Not the *fine* word again."

"Okay. It won't bother me to walk."

"If you get tired or your ankle starts hurting, I'll carry you back to the sleigh."

She tucked that bit of information away to use later when she wanted to be held in his arms. At the moment, she was more curious about their destination.

Together, they walked side by side into the forest and down a faint path. The snow crunched under their boots. It wasn't long before she heard the sound of the water splashing over rocks. A few yards later, they came to an old stone bridge that spanned a rushing stream. They walked out into the middle of it, where Jesse stopped and leaned on the wall.

"How pretty it is here." Gemma stood beside him. The babbling of the water supplied the only sound. The air was motionless. The moon cast long shadows among the tall trees.

Jesse brushed the snow off the wall and sat on it. "I like to come here and think." He turned and pulled her to stand in front of him. He kept his arms around her and spoke softly in her ear. "Do you have any idea what kind of effect you have on me?"

"I hope that you view me as a dear friend." Her heart was beating so hard she feared he could hear it.

He smiled at her. "I don't think of you only as a friend."

He pulled off his gloves and cupped her face in his hands. "You and Hope have brought joy to me when I never expected to have it. I will never be able to thank God enough for bringing you into my life."

Before she could say anything, he bent his head and kissed her. His soft warm lips moved over hers, bringing a sensation of floating weightless in the night.

The sound of the rushing water faded away as

Gemma tentatively explored the texture of his lips against hers. Firm but gentle, warm and tender, his touch sent the blood rushing through her veins. Softly, slowly, his lips moved to her cheeks and then to the side of her neck. She didn't know it was possible for her heart to expand with such love and not burst.

When Jesse drew away, she kept her eyes closed, afraid she would see disappointment or regret on his face.

"Gemma, look at me," he said softly.

"I can't."

Old insecurities came rushing back to choke down her happiness. "You must be ashamed of my behavior."

"Why would you say that?"

"Because you aren't the first man to kiss me in the moonlight."

"Gemma, I will tell you this only once. It doesn't matter who kissed you first. I will be the man who kisses you next and last and every day in between for the rest of our lives. I love you, Gemma."

She circled his neck with her arms. "My dear Jesse. I love you more than life itself. I think I truly fell in love with you when you lifted me out of Dale's pickup and held me in your arms. You were so incredibly strong and gentle at the same time."

"Does that mean I may court you? Nod if you agree."

She smiled at his teasing, even though she saw the seriousness in his eyes. How was it possible to feel so happy?

"*Ja*, Jesse Crump, you may court me, but I warn you, I'm no great prize."

"I believe I get to be the judge of that." He nuzzled her cheek.

"How long will the courtship last?" She tipped her head so he could kiss her neck.

"Until the wedding."

"We're already married."

He drew back to grin at her. "Then there is no end in sight for us."

She rose onto her toes and kissed him with all the love she held in her heart for him.

He was the first to break away, drawing a deep unsteady breath that made her smile. He tucked her head beneath his chin. "I thought this was a romantic spot, but we should find somewhere warmer to continue our courting."

In the shadow of the trees, with the cold bright moonlight sparkling on the icy waters cascading below and his arms around her, Gemma had never been warmer in her life. "I'm fine."

"I'm happy for you, but my feet are freezing."

She chuckled. "You should have dressed warmer." He could always make her laugh. She loved that about him along with everything else.

He cupped her cheek with his hand. "I don't know why God chose this strange journey for you. From Maine to Florida and back just to end up in my arms."

"So that we'll never take each other for granted."

"That's what I think too." He bent and kissed her again.

She threaded her fingers through his hair and kept him close when he would have pulled away. "I plan to spend a lot of time kissing you, husband."

"*Goot*, for I plan to spend a little time kissing you back."

"Only a little?" She gave him a saucy grin.

He growled low in his throat. "God knew what he

was doing when He brought you back into my life. I reckon He knew I needed someone to drive me crazy." He lowered his head to kiss her again.

Gemma melted against him as her heart was swept away by the love that flowed between her soul and his. Being courted by Jesse Crump surpassed all her expectations. God had been good to her.

* * * * *

AMISH BABY LESSONS

Patrice Lewis

To God, for blessing me with my husband and daughters, the best family anyone could hope for.

Having then gifts differing according to the grace that is given to us, whether prophecy, let us prophesy according to the proportion of faith; Or ministry, let us wait on our ministering: or he that teacheth, on teaching; Or he that exhorteth, on exhortation: he that giveth, let him do it with simplicity; he that ruleth, with diligence; he that sheweth mercy, with cheerfulness.

—*Romans* 12:6–8

Chapter One

A crowd of people swirled around her on the hot train platform in Lafayette, Indiana, but Jane Troyer ignored them. The station was busy, with garbled announcements made over distant loudspeakers and the din of hundreds of passengers. Her head ached from the chaos. She sat alone on a bench next to her suitcase, trying not to give in to despair.

Running away from heartbreak was turning out to be harder than she'd thought. Moving to another town to live with her aunt and uncle had seemed like an easy solution. Until…

"*Geht es dir gut*? Are you all right?"

She lifted her head and saw a man in Amish suspenders and a straw hat, with a bag slung over one shoulder and a fractious baby in his arms. A streak of sweat ran down one temple and his blue eyes looked weary.

"*Nein*, I'm not," she replied. "Someone just stole my bag with all my money in it. I'm stranded here." She wondered why *Gott* had deserted her at this strange train station.

He bounced the baby. "Where are you going?"

"To visit my aunt and uncle in Grand Creek. It's about twenty miles away."

"I live in Grand Creek. Who are your aunt and uncle?"

"Peter and Catherine Troyer. They run a dry-goods store, a mercantile, in the center of town."

"They're practically my neighbors!" The man smiled. "I'd be happy to take you there." He swayed the baby in his arms.

"Will you?" She jumped up from the bench. "*Danke! Danke!*"

"You're welcome. But first I have some things to collect here at the station, some boxes." The baby gave a wail, and he grimaced. "They're large boxes too."

"Why are you picking up large boxes with a *boppli* in tow? That doesn't make sense." He seemed like he didn't know how to handle a baby. The baby seemed to know it too.

"Because there was no one to watch her. And I need the boxes. They're part of my business."

"Would it help if I held the *boppli*? That would free your hands."

Despite the infant's crankiness, the man seemed reluctant to relinquish his burden. "I wouldn't do that to you. She's irritable. She hasn't calmed down all day." As if to reinforce his words, the baby wailed, tears streaming down her face.

"That's okay. I don't mind." She reached for the child.

"Well, if you're sure…" He transferred the baby to her. "I hope you don't regret it. I'll be back in a few minutes."

Jane accepted the warm little bundle and cooed at the child. "Hush, hush…"

As the baby quieted, Jane looked up in time to see

the man's jaw drop. He snapped his mouth shut. "I've never seen her calm down that fast," he said in wonder.

"It's a gift *Gott* gave me." Jane shoved her eyeglasses higher on her nose. "Why don't I stay here while you get your boxes? That way I can make sure some other *Englischer* doesn't run away with my suitcase too."

"*Ja*. Here's her diaper bag." He removed the strap from his shoulder and dropped the bag on the bench. "I won't be long."

Jane sat down. She wondered why the man didn't have a beard. All Amish men grew their beards once they married, and certainly by the time babies came. And why was he trying to juggle an infant at the same time he was picking up large boxes from a train station? Why wasn't his wife caring for the child? She shook her head. None of it made sense.

The infant in her arms had large blue eyes, the wrinkled lids showing her to be very young, perhaps no more than a couple weeks old. At a time when most of her friends were married and starting families, Jane's arms had ached to hold her own baby, but that wasn't likely to happen anytime soon.

This visit to her aunt and uncle was to help her mend her broken heart. Her best friend had married the man Jane had spent so many years loving from afar. She didn't blame Isaac for never noticing her. Most men didn't. But it still hurt. Why had *Gott* made her so plain? She blinked back tears of self-pity.

Her mother always told her she made up for her lack of beauty with an abundance of character, but that was small comfort as her friends, one by one, settled into marital bliss, leaving her the sole unmarried woman from among her cohorts.

Her older sister Elizabeth, married now, was the beauty of the family. It was hard growing up in her shadow, even though her sister's character was just as lovely as her face. But Jane—who needed to wear glasses from a young age, then grew lanky and tall—felt awkward by comparison. Except when it came to babies. For whatever reason, her confidence soared with a baby in her arms.

The ironic thing was she was unlikely to ever have babies of her own. Marriage just didn't seem to be *Gott*'s plan for her.

The baby currently in her arms crinkled her face and started to wail again. Jane guessed she was hungry. "Where's your *mamm*?" she asked. Jane tried soothing the infant, but the *boppli* only wailed louder.

In desperation, Jane rummaged through the diaper bag and found two bottles.

Jane removed one, popped off the cap and determined it was the right temperature. She inserted the tip into the baby's mouth. The *boppli* immediately stopped crying and started suckling. A little piece of Jane's heart melted as she cuddled the infant.

"*Gut*, you found the bottles."

Jane looked up. The man hurried toward her, beads of sweat trickling down one side of his face. He was taller than her by several inches, which put him near six feet in height. He had the strapping look of a hardworking farmer. His dark blue shirt, damp from humidity, mirrored the dark blue of his eyes. But it still puzzled her why he had no beard. Married men grew beards.

"I loaded the boxes as fast as I could. Sorry to take so long..." he continued.

"Don't worry about it. I found everything I needed

in the diaper bag. But now you'll have to wait until she finishes eating."

"That's fine." He sat down on the bench. "*Ach*, what a day it's been so far." He heaved out an enormous breath.

"Bad day?" She shifted the infant. Her own troubles were forgotten for a moment as her curiosity got the better of her.

"You don't know the half of it. I'm grateful you minded the *boppli* while I collected my boxes." He fished a bandanna out of his pocket and mopped his face. "*Ach*, it's warm for this early in July."

"She's a *gut* baby," she offered. "No trouble at all."

"For you, maybe. For me, she's been nothing *but* trouble."

"My name is Jane Troyer, by the way."

"Levy Struder. The baby's name is Mercy."

"Oh, that's lovely." She smiled at the infant, whose eyes were half-closed as she concentrated on drinking her bottle.

"And apt. She needs all *Gott*'s mercy she can get."

Jane didn't ask for an explanation, but she put two and two together. Could Levy be widowed? He didn't act like a grieving man, but he *did* look like a harried one.

The baby pulled away from the bottle at last, so Jane took a clean cloth diaper from the bag and put it over her shoulder. She hitched up the infant over the cloth and patted her back. "I think she's ready to go."

"*Ja.* I'll take your suitcase. My buggy is this way."

Jane patted little Mercy's back until she heard a delicate *braaap*, then kept the baby there as she followed Levy toward a hitching post in the shade of a tree where a dozing horse stood hitched to a buggy.

He swung her suitcase into the back of the buggy, on top of a large number of big cardboard boxes. "I'll hold the baby while you get in."

She handed over the drowsy child. A large basket, padded with soft blankets as an impromptu cradle, occupied the seat. She moved it toward the back, climbed in and took the baby in her arms. Levy unhitched the horse, gave it a pat on the neck and climbed in beside her. He clucked, and the horse trotted out of the train station's parking lot.

"Ah, it's good to get away from there." Jane leaned back in the seat and cuddled the infant close to her chest. "It's been a long trip, and I don't like being among so many strangers." The horse pulled them through busy streets, laden with cars and stoplights and noise.

"You said you were robbed? What a bad start to your visit. How much money got stolen?"

"I had about fifty dollars in my bag." Her face hardened. "It was all I had."

"Did you report it to the station manager?"

"No. What could he do? The thief snatched my bag out of my hand and disappeared. By the time I would have found the station manager, my money would be far away."

"Did he steal anything else?"

"Just a handkerchief."

"There's a spare in the diaper bag if you need one." Humor crinkled his eyes. "I wonder if the thief was disappointed in getting only a handkerchief."

"Serves him right." Seeing the lighter side, Jane chuckled. "At least it was clean."

Levy guided the horse away from the station. "It will take about two hours to get to Grand Creek," he warned.

"I try not to make this trip any more often than I have to. I can't tell you how hard it was, driving here with Mercy in a basket."

"Why didn't you leave her with someone?" She paused, then decided to probe a bit. "Your wife?"

"I'm not married. This is my niece."

"Oh. I see."

She saw his mouth tighten, but he didn't explain why he was caring for his newborn niece, and she didn't ask where the baby's mother was.

"I had a *youngie* watching her," he explained, "but she's inexperienced with babies, and she was busy today anyway, just when I needed her most. I'm going to have to find someone more dependable."

"*Ach*, that's hard." She looked down at little Mercy in her arms. The warm bundle filled an empty hole in her heart, and she hugged the baby to herself. "Look, she's sleeping. She'll be quiet now the rest of the trip, I think."

Levy sighed. "I can't thank you enough. *Bopplin* are a lot harder than I thought."

"*Ja*." If this was his niece, why was he taking care of his sibling's child? There was some sort of mystery here.

He set the horse at a comfortable trot as the town fell behind them. He took a side road filled with rolling hills and broad farms. A slight breeze cooled the heat.

"So—what brings you here to visit your aunt and uncle?" inquired Levy. "Where are you from? Are you staying long with them?"

Jane took a moment before answering. She didn't want to start explaining why she'd taken such an extended trip or what she left behind. Now was not the time to explain her mixed-up love life.

"I'm from Jasper, Ohio," she answered. "It's about

a four-hour train ride from here. I told Onkel Peter I'd be happy to work in the store. He said he could use another clerk, and offered me a job." Anxious to avoid delving into her background, she changed the subject. "What is it you do?"

"Produce farming, with some accounting on the side. The boxes I picked up at the station hold crates and display materials for weekend sales at a farmer's market where I sell every Saturday through the end of October. Nearly all my yearly income is earned during the summer at the farmer's market, so it's a very busy time for me. As you can imagine, taking care of Mercy is going to be difficult."

Jane's brow furrowed. "Why are you taking care of her at all, if she's your niece?"

"Because my sister isn't here." His words were clipped.

All kinds of questions floated around in Jane's mind. If his sister wasn't here, what about the baby's father? Was the infant an orphan? It seemed Levy was being just as cagey about why he was caring for a young infant as she was in relating her reasons for leaving her hometown. "She's a beautiful baby" was all she said.

"Yes, she is. And she deserves more than being cared for by a bachelor uncle."

"Why haven't you asked someone to help you? The community must be full of women who would be happy to lend a hand."

"I... I've only had her a few days. The *youngie* I hired doesn't seem to be comfortable with an infant this young. I'm going to have to find someone more experienced." He gave her a sidelong look, then turned his attention back to the horse. The animal's hooves clattered in a comfortable rhythm.

Jane didn't ask the circumstances under which little Mercy was dropped in her uncle's lap. She would hear it soon enough. "*Ja*, it's unusual for a man to take care of a baby all on his own."

"It also gives me a new appreciation for young mothers." He steadied the horse as a car passed. "You're not married?"

"N-no." She kept her expression neutral. She had no intention of explaining herself. "I'd rather not discuss it."

His eyebrows rose. "Is there a story there?"

"If there is, it's none of your business."

"If you say so." He grinned, and Jane caught her breath. She didn't want to encourage any flirting. It made her uneasy. In her twenty-three years, she'd learned men didn't flirt with her. Men didn't court her. Men hardly paid attention to her at all—except to see her as a *useful* person, a woman willing to work hard. A woman willing to tackle difficult chores. It seemed to be her role in life.

She shoved her glasses back up her nose. "You're rude, Mr. Struder."

"And you're a mystery, Miss Troyer."

She hugged the baby closer, feeling as if the infant was a defense against unwelcome assumptions by Levy Struder. The unasked question hovered in the air—*Why don't you have any of your own?*—and she was grateful Levy didn't voice it. Instead, she turned the tables. "Mercy must have caused you quite a flurry of preparations, if she came to you unexpectedly."

"*Ja*, she did. I had nothing for a baby. It's hard to get

work done. I tried bringing her out into the fields with
me in her basket, but that only lasted a few minutes at a
time. I didn't realize how demanding young babies are.
Or how much women do to care for them."

"That's our secret weapon," joked Jane. "We make
it seem easy."

By the time they approached Grand Creek, Jane was
glad to see the familiar green fields, produce stands and
white farmhouses of an Amish community. Mercy woke
up and whimpered briefly, but she settled into Jane's
arms and seemed content to be held.

"I've never seen her so quiet." Levy waved at a distant acquaintance as they passed by on the road. "She's
been fussy since she came to me. Frankly, I was just
about at my wit's end."

"At this age, babies are pretty simple creatures," replied Jane. "Food, clean diapers, close body contact.
That's about it."

"I think it's a woman's touch too. She didn't seem
too happy to have me hold her."

"Maybe you need baby lessons." She smiled at the
thought of teaching this strange man how to care for an
infant. Caring for babies came to her so naturally that
even this unfamiliar baby lay content in her arms. It
was ironic that *Gott* would grant her the gift of soothing babies, but very little likelihood she would ever
have any of her own.

"Baby lessons. Maybe I do need them—" He interrupted himself, "Look! See that building over there?"
He pointed to a large squat brick commercial building
with a broad front porch at the town's crossroad. Colorful cloth swagging swooped between the porch col-
umns, lending the building an air of festivity. "That's

your aunt and uncle's store. But it's late, and they're closed. I'll take you straight to their house, if you like. It's not far."

"I'm just glad to see horses and buggies again." She gazed around at the wide, quiet streets arced over by generous shade trees. As they approached the far edge of town, lots gave way to small farms between five and fifteen acres.

"You said you came from Ohio? Does it have *Eng-lischers*? How many people live there in your town?"

"I'm guessing Jasper has five thousand people or so." She shoved her glasses up her nose. "Ohio is pretty crowded. This town seems smaller and more rural. I like seeing all these small farms. It seems things are spread out a bit more here in Indiana."

"Grand Creek has about two thousand people. I live on the outskirts, that way." He gestured. "Near your aunt and uncle."

"And you live by yourself?"

"*Ja.* I, uh… I do now."

Jane noticed his hesitation. Was he referencing his sister? She wondered at the secrecy.

Yet it was none of her business. She was here to heal, to work, to be useful—not to get involved in a stranger's problems. Starting over in a new town was better than stewing in heartbreak and unrequited love.

Soon a white two-story clapboard house came into view. It was set back from the road and shaded by huge maples, with generous front and back porches. "That's where you're going." Levy pointed. "There's your uncle in the yard, mowing the grass."

She peered through the late-afternoon sunshine and

saw her uncle's light blue shirt. His hair and long beard were grayer than she remembered.

"I haven't seen him in years!" Jane couldn't keep the excitement out of her voice. "The last time I saw Onkel Peter and Tante Catherine was three years ago, when my sister Elizabeth got married."

Levy turned the horse into the drive. "Everyone likes them, and their dry-goods mercantile does very well."

"Onkel Peter! Onkel Peter!" Jane waved.

Her uncle paused in his mowing and squinted. "Jane? Child, I thought you were coming by taxi."

"I was. Then an *Englischer* stole my money. This man, Levy, he found me and brought me along."

"*Ja*, I see that." Her uncle smiled. "*Vielen Dank*, Levy."

"Here, put the baby in the basket." Levy dragged the lined basket up front.

Jane laid the infant in the makeshift cradle. The child whimpered. "She might need her diaper changed," she warned Levy, who looked uncomfortable being in sole charge of the baby once more. Then she jumped out of the buggy and embraced her uncle.

"Your aunt will be very happy you're here," said Peter. "She's been talking nonstop about your visit."

But Jane was watching Levy. "Will you be okay?" she asked him.

"I'll be okay." He clucked to Maggie, the horse. "I hope!"

Jane heard Mercy's wailing as he drove away. She shook her head. "He's in trouble," she muttered.

Levy tried to ignore little Mercy's cries from her basket. The familiar tension and sense of helplessness enveloped him, as it had since the baby was metaphorically and literally dumped in his lap.

In contrast to his incompetence, this unknown woman, Jane Troyer, had an amazing ability when it came to soothing the infant.

What an odd package she was. Mousy brown hair, large glasses and amazing huge blue eyes. She was not beautiful, but there was something about her that piqued his interest. Her astounding aptitude with Mercy showed a maternal instinct he admired. Certainly she had more instinct than his sister Eliza had.

He compressed his lips. What was Eliza thinking, to send such a tiny infant to him? Did she think he was qualified to raise his niece, especially after the mess he'd made raising his own sister?

He hadn't asked to step into the role of surrogate father to his only sibling. But when his parents were killed in a buggy accident when he was eighteen, he'd thought himself capable of reining in a rebellious twelve-year-old sister.

He was wrong.

"*Gott*, forgive me," he whispered. Whether he required forgiveness for his thoughts about his sister, or his failure to raise her properly, it was lost in the anxiety of getting Mercy to stop crying.

He pulled Maggie, the horse, into the small barn and hopped out. Ignoring the squalling infant, he unharnessed the animal, led her into a stall, gave her a brief grooming, fed and watered her and opened the back stall door so she could access the adjacent pasture. Finally he collected the red-faced baby and diaper bag and headed into the house. By the time he sat in the rocking chair and got the baby to take a bottle, he was frazzled and exhausted.

Why had the young babysitter elected to bail on him today of all days?

He rocked the infant as she nursed, his thoughts racing through all the work he needed to get done, but couldn't. His income depended on selling his produce at the farmer's market, but he couldn't work if he had to care for Mercy. And if he couldn't depend on the teenage babysitter if she was going to flake on him when he needed her most. What could he do? He'd have to ask around to see who else might be available. Without finding Mercy a consistent caregiver, he couldn't work his farm, sell at the farmer's market, or do anything necessary to earn a living. A baby, he now realized, required almost constant care and attention.

His thoughts settled on Jane. She said she had a job at the Troyers' dry-goods store, but he wondered if she would be interested in taking care of Mercy instead.

It was worth asking her. No, it was worth *begging* her. He needed help. Now.

Chapter Two

U ncle Peter—a little more solid around the middle than last she saw him—picked up her suitcase and led the way into the house. "Sounds like you had quite an adventure."

"*Ja*. I'm glad to be here." She gazed after Levy's buggy as his horse trotted away. "But I'm worried about the baby."

"So are we. He just got her a few days ago. " Her uncle walked up the porch steps. "Come inside, your aunt is most anxious to see you."

Within moments Jane found herself enveloped in her aunt's embrace. "*Welkom*! *Welkom*!"

Jane hugged the woman hard and gave her a smacking kiss. "*Danke*! It's been so long."

Catherine's smoothed-back hair was still brown, but now laced with gray. Her blue eyes twinkled through the creases on her face. Motherly in the extreme, she insisted Jane sit and have tea and cookies.

Jane leaned back with a sigh. "*Ach*, it's good to be here. I'm grateful for the chance to get out of Jasper."

"It was that bad, then?"

"*Nein*, but it was getting…lonely. All my friends are married. Most already have babies. Hannah is expecting her first. *Mamm* thought I was becoming brittle. That's the term she used, brittle. She said my humor was getting sarcastic, and that would soon turn to bitterness. I had to ask myself, at what point do I give up and realize I have nothing in front of me? *Mamm* said I needed a change of scenery, so here I am."

Uncle Peter patted her hand before reaching for his mug of tea. "You're welcome to stay with us as long as you wish. With your cousins all out on their own, it will be nice to have a *youngie* in the house again. In the store too. We've been busy so far this summer."

"I'm looking forward to it. You'll have to teach me what to do, of course. My only job experience up to this point has been working with children, mostly babysitting."

"You always were *gut* with babies." Catherine chuckled. "I wonder if you shouldn't ask Levy whether he needs help. He's had a hard time coping, and the *youngie* he hired isn't very dependable."

"But what about the store? I don't want to leave you two in the lurch, since you're being kind enough to give me a place to live." Jane kept her voice casual. "Where's the baby's mother? Levy didn't go into any details."

Catherine exchanged a lightning glance with Peter. "I don't want to gossip, *liebling*, so that's a story you'll have to get directly from Levy."

"I'm a stranger, so I don't think he'll tell me. We only just met, after all."

"*Ja*, true." Peter stroked his beard. "But he's determined to raise the baby himself, which is causing all sorts of concern among the elders. The bishop tells him he should simply give the *boppli* to a family to raise."

"That makes sense," said Jane. "So what's the problem?"

"The problem is, he won't do it."

Jane raised her eyebrows. "He's going against the recommendation of the bishop?"

"*Ja.*" Peter looked troubled. "The bishop is looking at what's *gut* for the baby, but Levy insists his guardianship of the baby is only temporary and his sister will be back soon."

"I'm guessing Mercy was born out of wedlock?" It happened sometimes, Jane knew.

Catherine nodded and her eyes moistened. "We can only assume so. An *Englisch* woman knocked at Levy's door a couple days ago, handed him the baby and a note, then disappeared. The note only said the baby was Eliza's, but she was unable to care for her, so she wanted Levy to raise her since he was the one person she trusted above all others."

"Oh my." Jane whispered the words. "How sad." No wonder the man was at his wit's end.

"I know Levy blames himself for Eliza's behavior." Peter spoke into the poignant silence. "It's hard to watch him suffer, harder still to know what's happening with Eliza. I remember her as a sweet young woman. But after her parents died, she snapped. She became rebellious and fascinated with the *Englisch* world. Then one day she was gone. No one knows what happened to her, until suddenly a *boppli* shows up."

"It certainly puts things into perspective," ventured Jane. "What I left behind is nothing next to what Levy is facing."

"Jane." Catherine put down her mug of tea. "I know you're upset by what happened back home, when that man—what was his name, Isaac?—married your best friend. But you're here now. You can have a useful life with us."

Useful. Jane was coming to hate that term. It seemed being *useful* was all she was good for. "Of course, Tante." Useful, not pretty. Useful, not interesting. Useful, not marriageable. "But I do find it humiliating that Isaac never had eyes for me, only my best friend. Sometimes I get a little mad at *Gott* for making me so plain."

"*Liebling*, I don't think you're plain." Catherine looked troubled. "Besides, you know *Gott* sees what's on the inside, and someday you'll meet a man who sees that too. Have you prayed?"

"Of course. But if *Gott* has answered my prayers, I haven't noticed yet." The moment the words were out of her mouth, she felt ashamed. Her mother had warned her that her sharp tongue was changing from witty to harsh. "I'm sorry, Tante Catherine."

"*Gott* is bigger than us. I'm sure He understands being angry."

A clock chimed over the kitchen sink, and Catherine and Peter both glanced at it.

"The chores!" her uncle exclaimed. "I have to get to the milking."

"Can I help?"

"*Ja, danke.* Sometimes I get a little tired of doing the milking all by myself."

Jane rose from her seat.

"I'll take your suitcase upstairs." Catherine also stood up. "Go on, get the chores done and I'll have a nice meal ready when you're finished."

Jane followed her uncle and took a clean bucket from the kitchen counter, then strode behind him toward the small barn behind the house. "How many cows do you have?"

"Just three now. We're slowing down. How many does your father keep?"

"Ten, so milking three won't take long with both of us."

The doe-eyed Jerseys chewed their cud in the shade of a fine maple tree behind the barn. Clipping halters to lead ropes, Jane and her uncle led two of the animals inside and tied them to a rail. With an ease born of experience, she sat on a low crate and wiped down the animal's udder, then zinged the warm milk into the bucket.

"So Isaac got married, eh?" Uncle Peter asked as he began milking.

"*Ja.*" Jane sighed. "And I'll admit, I'm angry about it. To be fair, I don't think he ever knew I loved him. But it hurt when Hannah—my best friend—fell in love with him. It was too hard for me to be around them anymore. I had to leave."

"It sounds like you're angry with your friend Hannah. But no one understands the chemistry of the heart except *Gott*. Things will work out, *schätzchen*. Meanwhile, your aunt and I couldn't be happier to have you staying with us as long as you like."

With her forehead pressed against the cow's flank, she felt the pressure of tears at her uncle's kindness. "*Danke*, Onkel Peter. I'll help out every way I can."

"And I hope you'll have some fun too. There are many activities for the *youngies* around here. In fact, there's a barbecue this Friday evening, so you can start getting acquainted with people your age. Who knows, maybe…" He trailed off.

"Maybe *not*," she replied, following her uncle's unspoken wish that she might meet someone special. "Right now I don't want to meet anyone. I'd rather work in your store. That's all."

"Your time will come, child." Her uncle's words were gentle and teasing.

Jane felt better. "*Ja*, I know. Sometimes I just get impatient." She squeezed out the last few drops of milk. "Do you want me to get the other cow?"

"*Nein*, I'll finish up. You're probably tired after your journey anyway. Tell your aunt I'll be there in a few minutes."

Jane released the cow and seized the bucket filled with warm, foamy milk. The early July twilight enveloped her as she walked back to the house. She paused a moment to admire the tidy, widely spaced farmhouses set back from the gravel road with small holdings tucked in back. Crickets chirped from hidden ditches, and robins hopped along lawns and fence posts. She saw the familiar huge gardens and small fields of corn and oats.

In the large airy kitchen, Aunt Catherine took a bubbling casserole dish out of the oven. The rich smell of cheese filled the air.

"Macaroni and cheese!" exclaimed Jane. "You remembered!"

Catherine laughed. "Of course I remembered your favorite dish."

Jane knew the cheddar cheese was homemade from the output of the cows she'd helped milk. The top of the dish was crusty with a mixture of breadcrumbs and Parmesan cheese.

Jane set the bucket of fresh milk on the counter. "Show me around the kitchen so I know where everything is."

The spacious kitchen was painted in cheerful shades of sage and cream, with a large, solid table and six upright chairs dominating the center. Streams of evening light poured through the window over the sink. Her aunt opened cupboards and drawers until Jane was familiar with the layout. Uncle Peter came in and set two more buckets of milk on the counter. Catherine strained the milk through a clean cloth, then poured the milk into large jars and put them down in the cool cellar. Jane set the table.

After a silent blessing, Catherine dished up the food. Jane forked some pasta into her mouth. "Oh, Tante Catherine, no one makes this better than you."

Then she paused. From outside, she thought she heard the thin distant wail of a crying baby.

Peter cocked his head. "Is that…?"

Jane heard the wail grow louder, then a knock came at the kitchen door. Peter jumped up and answered it.

Levy stood on the small porch, looking harried. The baby wailed in his arms. "*Gut'n owed*, Peter," said Levy politely. "Is your niece in?"

"*Ja. Komm* in." Peter stood aside as Jane rose to her feet.

Levy stepped into the kitchen. "*Gut'n owed*, Jane."

"*Gut'n owed*." She wiped her mouth and put the napkin on the table. "Is there something you need?"

"I need a nanny." His words were blunt and held a note of desperation.

She gaped. The poor man certainly looked stressed

beyond belief, and Jane wondered if the infant had stopped crying since she last saw him.

"You need a nanny?" she parroted. "Now?"

"*Ja*, now. This instant. I can't seem to make her stop crying."

More from instinct than anything else, Jane reached for the child and cuddled her. "Shh, *liebling*, shhh…" She swayed the baby in her arms.

Within half a minute, the baby calmed down and fell into a peaceful silence.

She looked up and saw the same stunned expression on Levy's face he'd worn when she'd quieted the baby at the train station that afternoon.

He snapped his jaw closed. "How do you do it?" he asked in wonder. "I haven't been able to soothe her at all."

"I've always been able to calm babies," she replied simply. "I used to babysit all the time, and often mothers hired me to help when they had a newborn."

"Levy, we're just sitting down to eat dinner." Catherine pointed to an empty chair. "Have you eaten? You're welcome to join us."

"*Ja*, *danke*, I will. I've been too busy with the *boppli* to think about food."

Catherine fetched another plate and some cutlery, then dished up a portion of the casserole for Levy.

With the quiet baby in her arms, Jane sat back down. "You said you need a nanny, and I can understand why, but I came here to work in Onkel Peter's store."

"I know. But Peter—" he turned to the older man "—I'm in desperate need of help. You know how busy I am this time of year. I can't tend the garden or harvest crops or even sell at the farmer's market while caring for an infant."

"*Ja*, I see that. But the decision is Jane's."

Levy turned to her. "What do you say?"

Jane looked at the warm, trusting baby in her arms. The infant's eyelids drooped, and she seemed moments away from nodding off to sleep. "I think, if you can spare me from the store, I'd like to take care of her. She's a darling *boppli*. And maybe I can give Levy some baby lessons." She glanced at him.

"*Danke*." Levy looked relieved beyond words. "Later this evening, maybe you can come to the house and I'll show you around. *Danke*," he babbled again. "*Vielen Dank*."

Catherine chuckled. "Eat," she told him, "before the food gets cold."

When the meal was over, Jane rose to help with the dishes, but Catherine waved her off. "Why don't you go with Levy now and see what he needs you to do?"

"Actually, I've got the barn chores to do first." Levy stood up and placed his napkin on the table. He looked at Jane. "Can you give me half an hour or so?"

"*Ja*, sure. Do you want me to bring the baby with me? She's sleeping right now."

"*Nein*, if she's sleeping, I'll just lay her in her crib. Here, I'll take her."

Having seen his previous reaction to the infant, Jane considered it a minor miracle the infant didn't wake up when she transferred her to her uncle's arms. "First baby lesson," she told him. "Support her a bit more under the head, like this." She positioned his arm more securely around the baby.

"*Ja*, that feels better." He looked at the child, and for the first time Jane saw tenderness on his face toward his niece. He raised his head. "Half an hour then?"

"I'll be there."

"Catherine, *danke* for supper." He smiled. "I didn't realize how hungry I was."

Catherine flapped a hand. "Go on, now. It was nothing."

Cradling the infant, Levy touched the brim of his hat and departed.

"Whew." Jane sat down. "Looks like I have a job."

"The *boppli* needs you more than we do," affirmed Peter. "I think you made the right decision."

"Will this leave you in a lurch, since I was supposed to work in the store?"

"*Nein*, we'll be fine," said Catherine. "And your uncle is right. The *boppli* needs you. So does Levy." She chuckled.

"I offered to give him baby lessons," Jane commented. "Looks like that's what I'll be doing."

"He needs them, for sure and certain. *Nein*, *liebling*, don't worry about dishes. Why don't you go unpack until it's time to go to Levy's? Your suitcase is upstairs, second bedroom on the left."

Jane climbed the stairs and found the bedroom, glowing and quiet as the late-evening sun streamed in the window. It was plainly furnished with a colorful quilt on the bed, a chest of drawers, a rocking chair and some hooks on the wall for clothing.

With one suitcase, it took her no time to unpack. Before heading back downstairs, Jane stepped into the bathroom to splash her face and tidy some stray wisps that had escaped her *kapp*. She gave herself one hard look in the mirror and turned away. She didn't like mirrors. It only reminded her of what she lacked.

In the kitchen, Aunt Catherine was just finishing the dishes. "I guess I'll be going. Where is Levy's house?"

Catherine wiped her hands on a dish towel, then pointed. "It's the little farm at the end of this road, maybe half a mile away. White house, big front porch, look for the row of sunflowers growing next to the ditch in front." Her aunt winked. "And *gut* luck."

"*Danke.*" Jane chuckled and set off.

She set off toward Levy's house, looking around with interest at her new community. The small town had large homes and neat gardens. Fireflies began flickering over the lawns and fields. Some children played in the spacious front yard of a nearby house; their shrieks and laughter drifted over the road. There seemed to be far fewer *Englischers* living here in Grand Creek than in her hometown in Ohio.

Just ahead, two young women about her age and wearing *kapps* walked toward her. They paused as Jane passed by. "*Gut'n owed!*" one of them said. "Are you visiting here?"

Jane stopped. "*Ja.* I'm Jane Troyer. I just arrived to stay with my aunt and uncle, Peter and Catherine Troyer."

"*Welkom.* I'm Sarah. This is Rhoda…"

Jane chatted with the women for a few minutes. Sarah invited Jane to the same barbecue her uncle had mentioned earlier.

She thanked her for the invitation, then headed on toward Levy's house. She felt the warmth of acceptance and had a feeling it would be no trouble fitting into her new home. Despite the loneliness she sometimes felt as one by one her friends got married and started families, there was a certain excitement about being in a new place and meeting new people.

And she would no longer have to see Isaac, giddy

about his new bride. She wouldn't have to witness Hannah's excitement at her first pregnancy. She would no longer have to pretend to be indifferent.

Yes, a whole new community full of new people was just what she needed.

The glow of the kerosene lamp lit the living room as Mercy cried in Levy's arms. He paced back and forth, trying to calm the infant. She'd woken up the moment he'd stepped into the house. Why? What was he doing wrong?

When he heard a knock at the door, he sighed with relief.

Jane stood on his porch, her glasses reflecting the lamplight from within. "Isn't this where I left you?" she joked.

He thrust a hand through his hair and gently bounced the baby. He spoke without greeting. "I've fed her, diapered her. I don't know why she won't stop crying."

"Sounds like she's overly tired. Here, let me take her."

Glad for the break, Levy handed over the infant and stepped away from the door, inviting her inside.

"Shhh, shhhh," Jane whispered. She cradled the baby, swaying a bit as she walked. Levy gestured toward a rocking chair, and she sank down and rocked, cuddling the infant against her chest and murmuring soothing nonsense.

Within moments, Mercy's crying stopped and her little face relaxed.

Levy dropped into a chair opposite. He felt exhausted. "How can you do that?"

"As I said, it's my gift. Enough said." Her voice was clipped.

Levy noticed her curtness, but was too tired to analyze it. "Then I think I've discovered my anti-gift. With me, she won't calm down at all. I can't thank you enough for agreeing to care for her."

Jane set the rocking chair in motion again. "Is there no other woman who can take this baby? It's not going to be easy for a single man to care for her, especially since, as you've said, you have to run your business."

"I'm discovering that. You arrived just as I was going to look for someone else to care for Mercy. That makes you an answer to prayer."

"I've been told I'm good at being *useful*." He thought he saw her eyes tear up, but wasn't sure since she ducked her head to look at the baby. "She's starting to fall asleep, see?"

Levy leaned back in his chair. "It seems like I've been walking her for hours. That's an exaggeration, but not by much. What hours can you work? I'm warning you, I may overwork you."

"My schedule is open. I can work whenever you need me. Within reason," she added.

"What time tomorrow do you want to start?"

"I can be here by eight in the morning. Would that be all right?"

"I hate to ask, but could you make it closer to seven? The days have been very hot lately and I'm trying to get work done outside before the sun is high."

"*Ja*, I can do that."

He nodded, filled with gratitude at this strange woman who had saved him. "Now here's an important question. Can you work Saturdays?"

"I suppose so. But why Saturdays?"

"Because if you remember, I have a booth at the

farmer's market. I spend most of my week gearing up for it. Many *Englischers* come to buy produce, so I'll be busy, from dawn until dusk. That's probably when I'll need you the most."

"I'll have to ask my aunt and uncle. Forgive me, Levy, but would it be easier..." She trailed off and didn't finish.

"Let me guess. You were going to ask why I don't give Mercy to another family to raise."

"Well...*ja.*"

"*Ja* sure, it would be easier. That's what the bishop wants me to do. But I won't. Not yet. Not until I know whether or not my sister..." He didn't finish his words, unwilling to reveal the deep emotion behind his determination to keep the baby. "If my sister ever comes home, I want her to see I've risen to the challenge of caring for her child."

He was relieved when Jane didn't pursue the matter further. His reasons were his own, and whatever difficult path he had set himself, he was trying to follow it.

"Well, I'll help however I can." Jane shifted the sleeping baby from the crook of her arm to over her shoulder. The infant gave a small sigh and didn't wake. "I think I'll enjoy caring for her."

"I'm grateful." He saw beyond the plain features and thick glasses of this young woman, and noticed instead her sweet expression as she held the baby.

"Well." She rose from the rocking chair. "Where does the *boppli* sleep? I'll put her down."

"In here." Levy picked up the oil lamp and led the way to a bedroom off the kitchen. "This is my room, and it's easiest to have her with me for now."

Late-evening shadows had darkened the room, but

he put the lamp on the dresser near the crib so she had light. Jane leaned over and placed the slumbering infant on the mat. She covered her with a light blanket, then tiptoed out of the room.

Levy heaved a sigh as he replaced the lamp on the table. "Ah, *danke*. She's been fussy all day, and I still have barn chores to do."

"Hopefully she'll sleep through the night, so doing chores shouldn't be a problem. I expect she's still getting used to the changes around her. Babies are creatures of habit, so the more she can stay on a regular schedule, the calmer she'll be." Jane walked toward the front door, then turned back to him. "I'll be back tomorrow morning at seven. You can show me where everything is—her formula, diapers and such."

"*Ja*, that's fine. And Jane, *danke*. I had no idea I was so bad with babies."

"Do you still want lessons? Baby lessons?"

"*Ja*. I don't have a choice."

"Then we'll start tomorrow. Don't worry, Levy. If you're determined to raise the baby, you'll learn fast. *Gude nacht*." She smiled and walked out the door.

Levy watched the tall, slender figure walk down the darkening street. Jane wasn't pretty in the conventional sense, but she had a remarkably calming quality about her. Not just with Mercy, but somehow he felt more composed in her presence.

He shook his head. There was more to Jane than met the eye, that was for sure. He was just very grateful she'd agreed to care for Mercy.

Jane retraced her path down the quiet road toward her aunt and uncle's house. No streetlights or car headlights broke the darkness, but fireflies twinkled over the fields and warm lamplight shone from windows.

So she had a job now, a job where she could be *useful*. Levy needed help, no question. In addition to caring for little Mercy, she was glad Levy wanted some parenting lessons. All in all, it had been an eventful day, and she realized how tired she was.

But being *useful* kept darker thoughts at bay. She tried not to think of the cozy home she'd left behind, with her mother and father, her younger sisters, her brothers. Her married older sister was expecting a baby. And Jane would miss all that.

When her *mamm* half-jokingly offered to arrange a marriage for her, Jane knew it was time to leave. She wasn't sure an arranged marriage was the right thing for her, at least not right now.

Here in this new community, she wouldn't linger over the past. She would look only at the present—her new job, becoming acquainted with people her age, spending some time with her aunt and uncle. Yes, she had a lot on her plate, and she was grateful for it.

Maybe caring for little Mercy full-time would fill the ache that came from knowing she was unlikely ever to have a baby of her own.

Chapter Three

Early the next morning, Jane walked toward Levy's home. Mist burned off from across the fields, and the sun shone through it in streaming bars of light. The air was cool and fresh. She walked up to the house and knocked on the front door.

"Come in!" he called.

Morning sunshine poured through the windows as she walked in, lighting a room that was comfortable but not clean. Dusting and sweeping, apparently, had gone by the wayside with little Mercy's arrival.

"In here!" called Levy.

Jane dropped the bag she'd carried onto the floor and followed his voice into the bedroom off the kitchen. Levy was changing the baby's diaper.

"At least she's not crying," observed Jane, leaning against the doorframe.

"*Ja*, something of a marvel. All right, *geliebte*, almost finished…"

"You're actually not bad at that." Jane watched as he tucked the cloth diaper neatly into a diaper cover around the baby's bottom and fastened the straps.

"Amazing what I've learned since Mercy arrived," he admitted. He slipped a flannel dress over the baby's head and pushed her little arms into the correct holes.

"Where did you get the diapers and baby clothes?"

"People in the church donated them. I had to buy the bottles and formula, though." He lifted the baby up.

"Here, I'll take her," Jane said.

Levy placed the baby into Jane's arms, and her heart melted a bit at the sweet-smelling little bundle. "Goodness, she's such a precious baby."

"*Ja.* When she's not crying, that is." He ran a hand through his hair. "She's just a whole lot more work than I ever anticipated."

"Well, it doesn't sound like you had any warning."

"That's an understatement. Let me show you around, so you know where to find things."

Jane trailed behind as he showed her where the baby's diapers, formula, bottles, clothing and other things were located. She was pleased to see the bouncy seat on the table, which would allow the infant to be present during meals or other kitchen activities.

"I know it's awkward to be in someone else's home," he concluded, "especially since you're just settling in with your aunt and uncle."

"*Ja*, I was going to ask about that. Do you mind if I go back and forth between here and there?"

"*Nein*, of course not. I trust you to do whatever you need to do with Mercy." He glanced at a clock over the kitchen sink. "But I need to get to work. Will you be okay on your own?"

Jane chuckled. "Probably better than *you* are on your own."

His eyes crinkled with amusement. "Help yourself

to anything in the kitchen, and feel free to explore the house and property." He picked up his hat, plopped it on his head and strode out the door.

Jane watched as he seized several garden tools and walked toward fields planted deep with corn and other vegetables. Beyond the barn she saw fenced pastures where three cows and their calves grazed. A rooster crowed from a coop near the barn, and she saw a tangle of fencing that could only be a pigpen. In all ways, Levy's property was a typical Amish small farm.

She looked down at Mercy, who gazed back with unfocused eyes. Jane dropped a kiss on the baby's nose. "It's just you and me, little one. What shall we do first?"

She began by taking Levy up on his offer and exploring the house. It was smaller than most Amish homes, just two dusty, unused bedrooms upstairs, a cellar below, and the rest of the living quarters on the first floor, including the master bedroom he shared with the infant. A treadle sewing machine occupied one corner of the living room. A small room off the living room turned out to be an office. From the ledgers and notepads, she concluded it's where he did his accounting work.

Mercy looked ready to fall asleep, so Jane sat in a rocking chair until the baby drifted off. She noticed the film of dust on the furniture, the unswept floors, the clutter of unwashed dishes in the kitchen sink. Levy needed more than a nanny for this motherless infant— he needed a housekeeper. She wondered why he wasn't married. Unlike her, he was an attractive person. Surely some woman would notice that?

When Mercy had fallen asleep, Jane laid the baby in her crib, then tackled the house. She explored the basement and found shelves of canned food and jars of dried beans, as well as hundreds of empty canning jars. Selecting some split peas and a jar of canned ham, she went upstairs and started making some split-pea soup for lunch. She washed the piles of dishes. She dusted and swept the entire downstairs.

Mercy awoke with a wail, so Jane changed her diaper and sat down in the rocking chair to feed her a bottle. It was then that Levy returned.

"Soup!" He sniffed the air. "I didn't expect you to cook, Jane, but it sure smells good."

"What would you normally eat midday?"

"Just a sandwich or two." He ladled the steaming soup into a bowl. "And you did the dishes!"

"This house needs a woman's touch." Jane lifted the bouncy seat on the table and laid Mercy in it. "There, *liebling*, now you can watch as we eat."

"Was she good this morning?"

"Like gold. She's such a sweet baby."

Levy closed his eyes for a silent prayer, then swallowed a spoonful. "It was *Gott*'s will you got stranded at that train station. Already I don't know what I'd do without you."

For just a moment, Jane's heart gave a thump. Whatever happened, she wouldn't let herself become attracted to Levy. She wouldn't. "I'm grateful for the job." Her remark was deliberate, to remind Levy she worked for him and nothing else.

"Mercy seems happy too." He toyed with the baby's feet, encased in thin flannel socks. "Maybe she knows she's no longer subject to a fumbling bachelor's care. How late can you work?" he added.

"What time do you normally finish working outside?"

"Dinnertime, though I often do an hour or two of accounting afterward."

"Maybe I should put it this way—what time do you feel up to taking over Mercy's care?"

He rubbed his chin, a look of frustration darkening his blue eyes. "To be honest, I don't feel up to it at all, but I know that's not a realistic attitude. I can't keep you here around the clock."

"I wasn't joking about offering baby lessons, if you really want them."

"I don't have a choice at this point, especially since I plan to keep her."

"But for the time being, how about I stay until after dinner? I don't mind cooking."

"*Danke*. Since you didn't sign up for cooking meals, I can pay you a bit extra."

"Can you afford it?" She clapped a hand over her mouth. "That was rude. I'm sorry. Your finances are none of my business."

He laughed. "Don't worry, I'll manage."

"Then *ja*, *danke*. And in addition to cooking, I can do housekeeping—laundry and dishes and tidying up."

"I think we'll get along together well. I'm grateful, Jane."

"Forget the gratitude and just show me where you keep your washing machine. I'll do a load of laundry this afternoon."

The swing-handled nonelectric washing machine was stored in a shed off the back porch. After Levy went back to work, Jane fed Mercy, changed her diaper then strapped the baby back in her bouncy seat on the porch. Jane sang as she washed a load of diapers, more for Mercy's sake than her own. Then she washed some of Levy's clothes and hung them to dry on the clothesline.

"Come on, *liebling*, let's go look at your uncle's garden and see what we can find to make dinner." She lifted the baby over her shoulder, picked up a large basket and walked out to the gated space filled with vegetables.

However messy Levy's house had been, his garden was a thing of beauty, tidy and weeded. Jane spied the prolific zucchini and decided to make zucchini casserole for dinner. She filled her basket with four of the green squashes, then dug up a couple of onions and some garlic. Back in the house, she had the casserole assembled within a few minutes and popped it into the oven to bake.

Mercy started to fuss, so Jane eased the baby onto her shoulder and sat down in the rocking chair, humming lullabies and rocking the child. The afternoon was warm and Jane was tired. Her humming grew slower and softer.

Next thing she knew, she blinked her eyes open to see Levy standing nearby.

"Oh." She felt her face grow warm. "I must have fallen asleep."

"Don't worry about it."

"The casserole…!" The infant gave a small start at Jane's small cry of alarm but didn't wake up.

"It's out of the oven and on the warming rack."

She settled back into the chair and shook her head. "I can't imagine why I did that, falling asleep on the job, I'm so sorry…"

"Jane, I can see how much work you've done this afternoon. Don't apologize." He grinned. "It was actually rather a sweet sight, coming in to find you both asleep."

Her face flushed warmer. "*Ja*, well, I'll just go put Mercy in her crib."

She stood up and kept the infant cradled on her shoulder, but the moment she stepped foot in the kitchen, she stopped in her tracks. "What on earth…"

"I'm not a total klutz in the kitchen." Levy chuckled.

The table was neatly set for two, and the casserole was covered and on the stove's warming rack.

"You didn't have to do this…" she began.

"Why not? Stop feeling guilty, Jane. It didn't take me long."

She nodded and disappeared into the bedroom to lay Mercy in her crib. She took a few deep breaths before leaving the room. Falling asleep her first day on the job—how embarrassing.

When she reemerged, Levy dished up the food and filled the plates. Jane bowed her head for grace, then reached for her fork. "Your garden is beautiful. After seeing the state of your house, I didn't expect it to be so nice."

"*Ja*, I'm more of an outdoorsman than an indoor one. I can weed all day, but I don't see anything that needs doing inside."

"Which is why everything was so thick with dust." Jane swallowed a bite. "But it will be easier to keep up now that I cleaned everything."

"Oh, did you clean everything?"

She chuckled. "Typical man who doesn't see dust bunnies until they're big enough to bite. Don't worry, I took care of them."

"And you did laundry too. And made lunch and dinner. And took care of Mercy."

"And you worked in the fields all day. We both have our jobs, then."

"Still, you seem like a very organized person."

Jane's smile faded. "I've been told I'm a very *useful* person."

"Is that such a bad thing?"

"*Nein… Nein*, I guess not." *Unless it came from the man she loved.* She shoved the thought of Isaac behind her. "So I guess I'll accept being useful."

"Being useful has its advantages."

"And it's what I'm good at. I try not to be bitter about it." She hadn't meant to be so open with Levy.

He raised his eyebrows. "Bitter? Why would you be bitter about something like that?"

"It's nothing."

"Does this reference have to do with your mysterious past that we talked about yesterday on the way home from the train station?"

"Maybe." She rose, trying not to feel flustered. "Are you finished? I'll wash up before I head home."

"You're changing the subject, but that's okay. I'll take advantage of the baby sleeping and start my accounting work."

As Jane washed and rinsed bowls and cutlery, she found herself grateful for Levy's restraint. He clearly wanted to know about her past, but didn't probe. Levy was the last person she wanted to learn about her background.

With just two people to feed, dishes took only a few minutes. Jane peeked in at the baby and found her still sleeping. She frowned and wondered if such solid napping this late in the afternoon meant Levy might be in for a long night with a wide-awake infant. She'd have to work harder to get little Mercy on a better sleep schedule.

"I'll head home now," she announced to Levy. Late-evening sunshine poured into his office window.

He looked up from a scattering of papers, pen in hand. "*Vielen Dank* for everything you did today, Jane."

"I'll be here around seven o'clock tomorrow morning. But since tomorrow is Friday, I should let you know I was invited to attend a barbeque tomorrow evening. It would be a good chance for me to get to know some of the young people around here."

He frowned. "Fridays are busy for me, since that's the day I prepare for the farmer's market."

"Well, I'll be here all day. I'll just be leaving a bit early, is all."

He looked doubtful. "All right, then. Good night."

Why would Levy seem unhappy that she had a social event planned? Jane wondered at his odd reaction. She walked back to her aunt and uncle's house and found them relaxing with hot cocoa and the *Budget* newspapers on the front porch.

"How did your first full day of work go?" asked Catherine.

"Fine." Jane plopped down in a spare rocking chair and sighed. "And I got a raise, so to speak. Levy's house was a mess, so he offered me extra pay to add cooking and housekeeping duties in addition to watching the baby."

Catherine chuckled. "He's had his hands full, no doubt."

"Why isn't anyone else helping him?"

"I think it just hadn't gotten to that point yet," her aunt replied. "He was obviously going to need help the moment Eliza sent the baby to him, but I think he had a crazy idea he could do it all himself. Now he's finding he can't, and that's just when you arrived."

"I think Levy doesn't believe me when I say she's easy to care for, though my arms got a little tired with carrying her so much."

"Would you like a baby sling?" Catherine asked. "I still have one tucked away."

"*Ja*, I'd forgotten about those! That would be wonderful."

Catherine disappeared for a few minutes, then came back out to the porch carrying a soft cotton garment. "You remember how to wear this, right?"

"I think so." Jane slipped the sling over her shoulder and mimed cradling an infant in it. "I'm surprised you still have this."

"It's been a while since I used it, but with three grandchildren so far, I still use it occasionally. Remember, until she's old enough to sit up, you carry the baby either like this, or like this." Catherine demonstrated infant positions.

Jane nodded and copied her actions. "This will help a lot, since it means I can carry Mercy while working around the house. Levy did tell me I was free to bring her here, or go anywhere I want with her too."

"Then that sling will be useful everywhere."

Jane winced at the term *useful* but didn't say anything. Instead, she looked over the peaceful lawn illuminated by late-evening sun and sighed. Overall she was glad to be here in Grand Creek. But was this the best place for her? Only time would tell.

* * *

When she arrived at Levy's the next morning, she found him outside near the barn constructing something. Mercy was strapped into her bouncy seat nearby.

"*Guder mariye.*" Without asking, Jane removed the infant from the seat and lifted her into her arms.

"*Guder mariye.*" Levy stopped working and fished out a red bandanna to wipe a trickle of sweat from beneath his straw hat. "*Ach*, it's going to be a hot day. Already the sun is warm."

"What are you building?"

"Remember those boxes I picked up at the train station? It's a new booth for the farmer's market." He pocketed the bandanna. "Just confirming, you said you can work on Saturdays, *ja*?"

His eyes had dark circles around them, and Jane wondered how many times he'd gotten up with the baby. But she frowned. Just how much time was this job going to entail? Would she ever have a day off?

"I can work Saturday," she assured him. "And perhaps in exchange I can take a day off during the week." She paused as he looked unhappy. "Levy, I can't work here every day, all day. I have a life too."

"*Ja*, I know." The strain increased on his face. "Though I work every day, and I don't know what I'll do without you."

"You may have to hire someone else for the days I take off."

"Maybe." He didn't look happy as he glanced upward at his construction project. "This is almost finished. I'll spend the rest of the day picking and crating up the produce I'll sell tomorrow."

"What will you sell?"

"Corn, onions, garlic, some late strawberries, raspberries—lots of raspberries, they're peaking now—tomatoes, lettuce, spinach..." he continued, ticking down the list of foods.

"Definitely sounds like you have a full day ahead of you." Jane glanced at the baby. "Will it be convenient for me to leave by six o'clock tonight so I can make it to the barbecue?"

He shoved a crate. "Why are you going to that?"

She arched her eyebrows at the question. "That's kind of rude. Why shouldn't I go? I think it's important to meet others in the community."

He frowned. "Seems a very frivolous thing to do."

"Fortunately, it's not your place to dictate what I can and cannot do." Jane's voice was tart.

He scrubbed a hand over his face, but remained silent.

Jane knew he was tired. "I can work tomorrow, don't worry."

Levy just nodded and went back to his work.

She didn't see him until lunchtime. She caught glimpses of him outside, picking corn or gathering tomatoes or plucking raspberries.

"Do you need help?" she asked, as he wolfed down the grilled cheese sandwiches she'd made for lunch. "It's an awful lot of work for one man to do alone."

"You're helping enough, trust me." He wiped his mouth and gulped the milk from his glass. He glanced at the clock. "Back to work."

It was her first glimpse into the heavy schedule Levy set himself. All day long, he picked fruits and vegetables and hauled them back to the cool barn. The delicate raspberries he brought into the house, and Jane put them down in the basement. Levy didn't complain about the workload, but Jane could tell he was stressed.

She did a load of laundry, gave the house a quick dusting and sweeping, made a hearty dinner, washed the dishes and made sure Mercy was bathed and diapered.

"Don't forget," she reminded him toward evening. "I'll be leaving in a few minutes."

"Oh that's right." He made a face of dismay. "That means I'm back to taking care of the baby."

"I know you're busy, but ultimately she's your responsibility, not mine." Jane tried not to let her temper rise. "I can't work all the time."

"Well, *I* work all the time."

She lifted her chin. The martyr act wouldn't work on her. "That's your choice. Now, what time do you need me here tomorrow?"

"Early, if you can. The farmer's market opens by nine o'clock, so I plan to leave here by seven at the latest. You'll have to pack a diaper bag for her…"

"Diaper bag?" Jane raised her eyebrows. "You mean I'll be working the market with you? I thought I'd just stay home with the baby. Wouldn't that be easier?"

"Surprisingly, no. A second pair of hands is best, if for no other reason than the occasional break." He offered a thin smile.

Quickly, she adjusted her thinking. Working at a farmer's market actually sounded like fun. "I'll be here by six thirty then. That way I can handle the baby while you pack the wagon."

His nod was curt. "*Danke.*"

"Good night, Levy." She handed him Mercy.

Her annoyance faded as she walked back toward her aunt and uncle's. His apparent objections to her attending the barbecue seemed deeper than mere inconvenience regarding childcare or a busy schedule. Was there a problem with the *youngies* in town? Instinct told her it was something more. She wondered if she'd ever learn what it was.

As Levy watched Jane walk away, he couldn't shake the eerie feeling he was watching his sister walk away to attend a *youngie* event. Eliza had always been keen to get away from him, from her home, from her responsibilities. For a fraction of an instant, he saw his sister's retreating figure instead of Jane's.

Then he shook his head and snapped out of it. It was unfair to project his worries over Eliza's fate on the woman who had kindly taken on the chore of caring for her baby. Jane was nothing like his sister. She was steady, levelheaded and incredibly efficient.

For once, Mercy lay quiet in his arms. He looked down at her tiny face, trying to see his sister in her features, wondering where Eliza was and if she missed her baby.

Then he looked up, but Jane had already disappeared down the road. He was glad she was coming to the farmer's market with him tomorrow—for deeper reasons than merely caring for the baby.

He didn't want to examine those deeper reasons. Not yet.

Chapter Four

That evening, as Jane got ready for the barbecue, she tried not to be annoyed at Levy. He was stressed, no question. Most Amish men worked hard, but it seemed to her Levy worked *too* hard. It was tough enough to operate a small farm solo. Throw in the complication of an abandoned baby, and it was a recipe for strain and pressure.

Her thoughts went to the barbecue and all the people she would meet.

"Are you nervous?" Catherine asked.

"*Ja*, maybe." Jane washed her face and tidied her hair at the kitchen sink as her aunt lingered nearby. "Back home, I knew everyone. Here I don't. It's just something I have to face, getting used to a new crowd."

"They're a nice group." Catherine handed Jane her *kapp*. "I'm sure you'll have fun."

"Except I'll feel guilty all evening, leaving Levy in charge of Mercy. He wasn't happy about it." Jane pinned on her *kapp* and slipped a clean apron over her dress.

"He's going to have to get used to caring for her,

that's all there is to it." Her aunt gave her directions to the host farm. "Have fun at the barbecue, *lieb*."

"*Danke*." Jane kissed her aunt's cheek and set off down the road.

The farm hosting the barbecue was a mile away. Catherine had told her the Yoder family, with four teenagers still at home, enjoyed hosting *youngie* events. Already dozens of people were gathered in the front yard under the shade trees. Jane thought she was looking forward to the event, but now that it was at hand, she wondered if she would fit in. It was one thing to grow up in a community and know everyone since birth. But she knew no one here. She shoved her glasses higher on her nose, took a deep breath and walked on.

Sarah, the young woman she'd met earlier, spied her right away. "You came!"

"*Ja*, thank you for letting me know about it." Jane glanced at the young people milling about, chattering, laughing, roasting hot dogs over a pit fire.

"I'll introduce you around, if you like," offered Sarah.

"I'll never remember everyone's names," warned Jane. "But please introduce me."

What should have been a fun evening with new friends was anything but. Jane felt shy and awkward despite the support of Sarah and Rhoda, who took her under their wing.

"I feel like I'm sixteen instead of twenty-three," she groused to Sarah as she sprawled on the lawn with her new friends, learning each of their stories. "Will I ever grow out of being awkward, do you suppose?"

"I'm sure it's just because you're in a new place," soothed Rhoda. "You'll fit in just fine when you have a chance to know more people. That's why I think you should keep coming to singings and other *youngie* events. How else will you get to know anyone?"

"*Ja*, true…" Jane trailed off, thinking about Levy's awkwardness while being in sole charge of the baby.

"Besides, we're glad you've come." Sarah spoke with such simple sincerity that Jane's eyes felt hot. She loved the Amish sense of community.

"And it seems it was *Gott*'s will to find a job the moment I arrived too," she replied. "Levy Struder—do you know him?—he's taking care of his sister's child. He hired me as the baby's nanny."

"Oh, Levy, he's a *gut* man," said Sarah.

"He seems a little old to be single. Why isn't he married?" Jane asked, trying to keep her question casual.

"It all goes back to his sister," Sarah answered, nibbling a cookie. "He practically raised her after their parents died, and when she left for her *Rumspringa* and didn't come back, he took it very hard. I think he's afraid he'll mess up with everyone—a wife, his own children—so he never sought out the responsibility of a family. Which is pretty ironic, since he loves kids."

"Yet he thinks he can raise little Mercy on his own," observed Jane. "He refuses to give her to another family to raise."

"He's really eaten up by guilt over his sister," said Sarah. "He can't bear the thought of giving up his sister's baby."

"Did she…ah, was she not married?" asked Jane.

"I don't know." Rhoda looked troubled. "No one knows for sure, but why else would she give up her baby if she had a husband?"

"Well, I'll do the best I can for the *boppli*, but I

hope Levy remembers I'm just the nanny, not the baby's mother."

"What do you mean?"

"He's very busy running his business. Two businesses, actually. Plus the baby isn't sleeping through the night. I could literally have the care of her for twenty-four hours a day, seven days a week, and I don't think it would be enough time for him. Each evening when I go home, I feel guilty for leaving Mercy to Levy. I think he's scared to be in sole charge of her."

"Did you have a hard time getting away to come to the barbecue tonight?" asked Rhoda.

"*Ja.* I mean, he didn't argue with me, but he got an odd look on his face." Jane mimicked Levy's expression so accurately the other girls laughed.

"I hope you can keep coming to the *youngie* events." Sarah looked around at the chattering groups of young people lit up by the flickering flames of the pit fire. "We have activities just about every week during the summer. A lot of people knew someone was coming to stay with your aunt and uncle, and we were anxious to get to know you."

She felt a quiver of unease. It seemed her adolescent awkwardness had never left her. She'd never really cultivated the social graces, and now she had to plunge outside her comfort zone. Had she made a mistake to leave home where she knew everyone, to immerse herself with strangers?

Yet Rhoda was right. If she didn't keep coming to these events, how else would she get to know anyone?

"It's late." Rhoda climbed to her feet and dusted off her dress. "It's been so hot lately, so we work outside in the garden in the early morning. I'd best get home."

Others were departing as well, carrying empty food containers and walking through the darkness toward their homes. Jane walked alone—it was something she was used to—and headed for her aunt and uncle's house.

In a moment of insight, she realized why she'd cultivated being *useful*. It covered for her plain looks, her awkward social skills. Everyone needed a *useful* woman.

She had been useful back home in Jasper. She would be useful here in Grand Creek, too.

She had cause to regret her decision to be useful by the next morning.

She arrived at Levy's to find the baby wailing in her bouncy seat on the porch. Levy was loading boxes and baskets of produce into the wagon, which was already hitched to the horse.

"She's all yours," he snapped, his face tense. "I've got a lot to do before we leave."

Jane didn't say a word. Levy's anxiety had communicated itself to little Mercy, and the baby cried louder.

She picked up the infant and cradled her in her arms. "I'm here, hush now, hush…"

It took some time for the infant to calm down, and even then she was edgy and cranky. Jane stayed out of Levy's way while he dashed around. Instead, she concentrated on packing what she needed for the baby: a diaper bag with bottles of formula, several changes of clothing and diapers, a light blanket, the sling, the padded basket used as a cradle and the bouncy seat. For herself and Levy, she packed a large lunch since she suspected he'd forgotten about food for himself.

Levy poked his head through the kitchen door. "Can you be ready in five minutes?"

"I'll be ready." Slipping the baby into the sling, Jane picked up the diaper bag and a food hamper and walked outside.

The wagon was loaded to capacity with the shelving, displays, chairs, tools, a scale and all the other accoutrements of a farmer's market booth. Boxes and crates and baskets of produce bulged at the corners. He'd even stuffed two bales of straw into the side. Jane managed to wedge the food hamper and diaper bag in a tight corner.

"Here, I'll hold the baby while you climb up." Levy appeared from the barn, mopped his brow with a bandanna and took the baby while Jane scrambled onto the wagon seat. She leaned down and took Mercy and settled the baby back into the sling while Levy stepped up, took the reins and started the horse down the road.

"Sorry I was so busy. I overslept," he apologized.

"Let me guess—Mercy was up during the night?"

"*Ja.* I meant to get up much earlier, I fell back asleep after feeding her, and the next thing I knew the sun was already up when I opened my eyes. I dashed around getting all the chores done, but I'm afraid I didn't have much time to devote to the baby, except for feeding and diapering her."

"Well, don't worry about her for now. I'll take care of her." She thought about her conversation with Sarah and Rhoda last night at the barbecue, about Levy's determination to keep the baby. Personally she thought the bishop was right and Levy should give Mercy to another family to raise. It was clearly too much for him to run his business and care for such a tiny infant.

But he'd already told her he didn't want to give Mercy up without knowing if his sister would return. Plus he was a stubborn man. She looked down at the baby in the sling. The child's eyes were heavy. After the anxious atmosphere of the morning, she seemed ready to sleep. Jane chose not to voice her doubts about Levy's decision to keep Mercy. "I'm grateful for the work, and I enjoy caring for the *boppli*, however long the arrangement lasts."

"Right now I'm too busy to think long-term. All I know is…" His voice trailed off.

Jane glanced at him, then looked out at the scenery going by. She promised herself not to bring up his sister anymore. The subject was clearly too personal, too raw for him. He wouldn't give up Mercy because doing so would be giving up on Mercy's mother, his sister. That much was obvious.

"I'll do my best to ease your burden," she said instead. "I like caring for babies."

"*Danke.*"

She lapsed into silence as Mercy fell asleep. Feeling the precious weight against her chest, her feelings toward the baby—already warm—altered. There were worse jobs than to act as a surrogate mother to this baby.

The farmer's market was held in a shady park that took up nearly one entire city block in an otherwise quiet residential neighborhood. A section was fenced off for Amish horses and buggies, and the parking lot was for vendors only.

"Do customers have to park on the streets?" inquired Jane, looking around.

"*Ja.* The whole farmer's market takes on an air of a festival every weekend. They even arrange for some children's entertainment, clown shows and such." Levy guided the horse through the parking area. "It's a whole lot more popular than the size of the town suggests. I'm fortunate it's so close by."

A clatter of other wagons crowded the streets, and Amish families started setting up their own stalls and booths. Levy called out to a number of them.

"*Hei*, what a lot of vendors!" Jane exclaimed. The place was packed.

"Ja. You won't believe the crowds that will come later," Levy answered.

He pulled up by an empty space and climbed down from the wagon, then raised his arms for Mercy. Jane handed him the sleeping infant, then climbed down from the wagon and took the baby again. "What do you want me to do?"

"I have to figure out how to set up this new booth. While I work on that, can you unload boxes of produce? Or would that be too much while you're holding the baby?" He seemed to be over his earlier dark mood.

He grinned at her, which made Jane catch her breath. Levy's rare smiles transformed him from a rather grim man to an unnervingly handsome one. His dark blue eyes glinted in the dappled sunshine. To hide her reaction, she concentrated on slipping Mercy into the padded basket Levy used as a makeshift cradle without waking her. "*Nein*, unloading boxes shouldn't be a problem. I'll just make sure she's safe in the shade by that tree."

With Mercy sleeping in the basket, she deposited the diaper bag and food hamper nearby, then began unloading crates of produce while Levy figured out how to assemble his new booth.

The park was busy with vendors setting up. The scope of the market amazed her. Dozens of booths were being assembled. Not all were run by Amish families. She saw many *Englisch* farmers as well, setting out crates of tomatoes, corn, peppers and other vegetables and fruits. A few early shoppers wandered around, but most sellers weren't quite ready to open for business yet. She received friendly nods and greetings from neighboring sellers.

"Here, can you hold this?" asked Levy. He indicated a pole. "I need to fasten these two pieces together. *Ja*, just like that."

Jane helped balance various components while the booth took shape under Levy's hands.

Finally he stepped back. "What do you think?"

"It looks *gut*!" she replied. "I don't know what your previous booth looked like, but this seems spacious and welcoming."

"*Danke*." He began setting out baskets of tomatoes, propped up at an inviting angle on a display rack. "I think it will work out well."

Jane began hauling boxes of produce over, but then Mercy woke up, so instead she grabbed one of the two folding chairs Levy had brought and set it next to the nearby tree. She found a bottle of formula in the diaper bag and settled in to feed the *boppli*.

"What's that?" Levy pointed to the hamper next to the diaper bag.

"Lunch. And breakfast, for that matter."

"*Gut*! I completely forgot." He smiled at a family who wandered by and stopped to examine the produce for sale.

"Does this farmer's market have an official opening

time?" Jane settled the baby more comfortably in the crook of her arm.

Levy waited until the potential customers moved on, then he dove into the food hamper, pulled out some biscuits and began eating. "I was so busy this morning I didn't have time for breakfast. As for when it opens— it's somewhat informal, though vendors are asked to finish unloading and move their cars and wagons by 9:00 a.m. We have to stay until five o'clock, though, by the rules."

"Rules? Is it that structured?"

"*Ja.* We sign an agreement. I can understand why they have these rules, otherwise a vendor might depart early and leave a big gaping hole where his booth was. Good morning!" he added to a young mother with two children in tow.

Once Mercy was fed, Jane slipped the infant into the sling and helped Levy stock the booth, spreading out the fresh fruits and vegetables in beautiful eye-catching displays.

"Having you here is sure useful," he murmured as the crowds grew thick. "It's nice to have another pair of hands to help out."

She flushed with pleasure, even at the term *useful.* "I'm still learning," she warned him. "I've never worked with customers before."

"Then you're a natural. Keep it up."

His praise was all she needed to redouble her efforts. Watching Levy sell his farm produce was a revelation to Jane. His booth was thronged almost from the beginning, and he easily outsold nearly every other vendor in the park. It was easy to see why. Unlike most Amish men, he was not reserved, but animated. He joked, he chatted, he bantered. She estimated half his customers were regulars, but several times she noticed people stopped at the booth because they wondered why it was so crowded.

And she knew it would have been extraordinarily difficult for him to function this way without someone watching Mercy.

Jane stayed busy too. When Mercy was quiet—either tucked in her sling or resting in the cradle basket—she helped weigh and bag produce, make change and restock the crates and baskets with fresh food. But she lacked Levy's easy way with strangers, especially *Englischers*.

During a rare quiet moment, she collapsed on the chair. "How do you do it?" She gulped water from a jar. "You behave like you've had classes in salesmanship."

"In a way I have." He bit into a sandwich. "When I first started selling here, my booth was right next to an older man—an *Englischer*—who was retiring and moving to Florida. His name was Robert and he was wonderful with customers. He wasn't pushy, he was friendly. I watched him and learned. It's a little difficult for me—I'm not a salesman by nature—but this is how I make my living, and if I'm going to sell produce, I have to sell it in the very best way possible. It puts me way outside my comfort zone, for sure and certain. I'm grateful to *Gott* for putting my booth next to Robert's. If I'd been anywhere else, I never would have watched him in action and seen how well he did."

"Did he know you were watching him?"

"Of course. In fact, he spent the whole summer

coaching me. He gave me pointers and tips for improving my sales. I'd never done anything like this before, so it was a steep learning curve. But I find it tiring. By the end of the day, I'm wiped out and need a whole week to recover."

"I can understand that." The crowds were hard for Jane to get used to as well. "I'm surprised this little town has so many people coming to its farmer's market."

"They advertise farther away, in many communities around here. I've had people tell me they drive an hour to get here so they can stock up on their week's groceries. The success of this little market far surpasses the boundaries of the town, for sure and certain. The people who run the market know what they're doing."

Their brief respite ended when more people stopped by to browse the produce, and Levy's booth stayed busy until late in the afternoon.

"What did you do with Mercy last week?" she asked at one point, after the baby woke up from a nap and cried until Jane fed her again.

"The teenage *youngie* I hired watched her," he admitted. "I didn't have a choice. You can see how busy I am on market days. They're $3.99 a pound," he told a customer, smiling as he sold the last of his raspberries. "But having you here changes the whole dynamic, even with the *boppli*. I'm not nearly as stressed."

Jane quivered. His gratitude seemed to hold a note of something more, something deeper than just recognition that she was a useful sales associate. Or was she imagining it?

The pressure of customer demands didn't ease until just before the market was due to close. But Levy seemed in no hurry to break down and pack up any remaining inventory. "Always be the last to close," he explained to Jane. "That's another trick of the trade Robert taught me. You'd be surprised how many times people want to make one last purchase before they leave for the day."

This proved true when not one, but *three* late customers cleaned out the rest of Levy's tomatoes, corn and onions. Other booths were in a state of disassembly, but Levy's little store was still open for business.

With the clock edging toward 5:30, a weary Jane laid Mercy in her cradle basket and helped Levy collect what small amount of produce remained unsold.

"I'll go hitch up Maggie and get the wagon," he said.

Left alone, she stacked what she could and repacked their food hamper. After a few minutes, Levy guided his horse and wagon nearby, and they began disassembling the booth components and loading them into the wagon.

Finally they started for home. "That was intense." Jane sighed.

"*Ja.* I think it's more intense because they only hold the farmer's market on Saturdays. So many of their vendors are Amish and we won't work on the Sabbath, and people know that, so everyone crowds in to make their purchases on that one day."

"Do you like selling there?" Jane waved to another departing vendor.

"It's not a question of like, it's a question of practicality. It's convenient." Levy stopped at an intersection, then guided the horse through. "During the summer and early fall, I earn almost my entire year's income from the farmer's market or Community Supported Agriculture subscriptions. That means I have buyers who take excess produce every week."

"And during the rest of the year, you supplement your income with accounting?"

"*Ja*. It gets very busy before tax day, so I do a lot of bookkeeping over the winter. It's been a precarious income, but this is the first year I've done better financially."

"Seeing how hard you work makes me feel guilty for accepting money to nanny the baby." She hugged the quiet baby resting in her arms.

"You work hard too. I think it's *Gott*'s timing. My business started doing well just when I needed to hire a nanny. We roll with the punches in this life, dealing with whatever *Gott* hands us."

"*Ja*, I suppose." She lapsed into silence, idly watching the town pass by. Finally she thought to ask, "I assume you won't need me tomorrow on the Sabbath?"

"Well, I wouldn't *say* that." Levy's mouth curved into a thin smile. "But it's the Sabbath. I can't ask you to work on your day of rest."

"But no rest for the weary *onkel*, eh?"

"Right. I'll cope somehow."

Jane had her private doubts that he would be able to, but she let it go.

He dropped her off directly at her aunt and uncle's house. "*Vielen Dank*, Jane. You were incredibly helpful and useful today." He touched his hat brim, spoke to the horse and drove away.

Jane stared after him. *Useful* again. She blinked back tears and realized she didn't want Levy to appreciate her *useful* qualities, but perhaps something more.

All day long she had worked side by side with Levy.

Perhaps it had been her imagination, but she got the impression he was appreciating her for more than her usefulness. Now, it seems, she was wrong.

A small part of her wanted him to appreciate her for more than that.

Chapter Five

Sabbath mornings were different from the rest of the week. Jane looked forward to the church services. It was more than a chance to take a break from the relentless work, to focus on *Gott*, to pray.

It was also a chance for the community to come together, for her to see the friends she'd made and perhaps meet new ones. The thought made Jane clasp and unclasp her hands in her lap. Making new friends was difficult for her.

Wearing clean clothes and a freshly starched *kapp*, she rode with Uncle Peter and Aunt Catherine toward the home of the Millers, who were hosting the week's worship service. Many buggies joined them on the road as they headed out, with occupants waving greetings.

"*Ach*, there's young Lydia Yoder with Jacob. Looks like she's about to have her baby any day now," commented Catherine.

Jane peered around the edge of the buggy and saw a pretty young matron, heavily pregnant. "Is it her first?"

"*Ja*. She's very happy."

"And there's Phillip Herschberger." Uncle Peter

waved an arm. "He broke his leg last month. I think he'll be getting the cast off shortly."

"And that's the Stoltzfus family. They own the hardware store near our store."

"I see Moses Bontrager." Uncle Peter nodded toward an incoming buggy. "He's been down with the flu. I'm so glad to see him up and about."

So the comments about friends and neighbors in the community continued all the way to the Sabbath service. The older Miller boys directed buggies and horses, and men unhitched their animals and led them into a spacious shady corral for the day. Uncle Peter swung out of the buggy, handed down Jane and Catherine and unhitched his own horse.

Back in her hometown of Jasper, Jane had loved Church Sundays. People came together for a single purpose—worship—but it was so much more. It was a reinforcement of their identity, a chance to visit and strengthen bonds of friends and family and an opportunity to learn who might need help.

And now she had to join a whole new community. Jane resisted the urge to cling like a child to her aunt's skirt and hide from strangers, as she used to do with her mother. She was a grown woman, and grown women weren't supposed to be tongue-tied or self-conscious.

Everywhere she looked, people clustered in groups, chatting in subdued tones. Many women carried covered bowls and platters of food into the Millers' kitchen, even though the service was being held in the large barn, where benches had been set up the day before. Children ran around, their shirts or dresses as colorful as flowers.

There were so many new people to meet, many of

whom were her age. Jane's heart should have swelled with the thought of new acquaintances who would not consider her a useful person, but instead a fun, even enjoyable person—but she was fooling herself. With sudden insight, she realized one of the reasons she made herself useful was that she knew she'd never be popular. She didn't have the slightest idea how. So…she found other ways to be valuable to the community instead.

Despite the bustle, there was an air of solemnity. It was Sunday, the day to formally worship *Gott*. Socializing would come later, after the service.

Jane spotted Sarah and Rhoda, but there wasn't time to speak with them before the community filed into the Millers' barn and found places on the benches. She spotted Levy carrying Mercy, the only one on the men's side holding a baby. He gave her a nod and settled down on a bench.

Jane found it very coincidental that the deacons settled on the biblical theme of service and how to use one's gifts to the service of *Gott*.

Jane's gifts—of soothing babies, of being "useful"— sometimes seemed like curses. Over the years, she'd struggled with a defiant spirit that rebelled against being plain, against the expectation from others that she enjoyed the hard work, that she never minded the times romantic dreams took a back seat to utility.

But there were times she longed to stop being viewed as merely useful and start being viewed as a woman with hopes and dreams of a family of her own. None of that was possible if she shrank from meeting new people.

Her friend Rhoda said it best at the barbecue a few days earlier. *"That's why I think you should keep com-*

ing to singings and other youngie events," she had advised. *"How else will you get to know anyone?"*

So she sat and listened to the sermon and grappled with the awkward longing to get to know more people, which fought against the biblical call to service.

The worship service ended and people rose from their benches, stretching and talking.

Rhoda beckoned her over into the yard before the meal started. "Come here, Jane! I want you to meet some people."

Jane hesitated, fighting a desire to avoid the laughing, chattering groups. But she mastered her reluctance and prepared herself to endure her inevitable lack of social graces.

Rhoda introduced her to more young people their age, pulling her toward the more gregarious of the bunch. She received numerous invitations.

"We're having a barbecue—can you come?"

"I'm going to the singing next week, will you be there?"

"Everyone's going to the hot dog roast at the Herschbergers', can you make it?"

Jane smiled through clenched teeth. Of *course* she would attend all these events. How else would she get to know anyone? And if a young man among the group should ever see beyond her glasses and plain features, perhaps she might have a hope for a family someday. The only way that would happen was if she forced herself to become a social butterfly.

At last she excused herself from the group and caught up with her aunt. She began bringing food out of the kitchen to the long tables set up under the shade of some trees.

"It's too nice a day to be inside. I'm glad we're eating outdoors." Jane placed a platter of fried chicken next to a bowl of potatoes.

"*Ja*, it's been so warm lately." Catherine wiped a bead of sweat from her forehead with a corner of her apron. "It looks like you've made some friends."

"I'm trying. I've received a lot of invitations."

"That's *gut*. You're a bit on the shy side, child, so going to social gatherings will help."

"I hope so. Everyone seems very nice." Jane bit her lip. "I just feel so awkward. It was bad enough back in Jasper, so why did I think it would be easier here, with a bunch of strangers?"

"It's putting you outside your comfort zone, for sure and certain," chuckled Catherine.

Jane remembered Levy using that very phrase when it came to learning salesmanship at the farmer's market. "*Ja*. That's exactly it. When will that end?"

"I don't know, but perhaps you'll meet a special young man at one of these gatherings."

"Don't get your hopes up." Jane spoke with a tartness she hadn't intended. "I'm sorry," she added.

Her aunt smiled. "I think things will get easier for you the more you go."

"I'm sure you're right."

"Come now." Aunt Catherine gestured. "Let's eat. People are starting to sit."

Everyone except Levy. Jane saw him at the edge of the large yard, standing under a tree, gently bouncing the baby. He looked ill at ease. Jane thought about taking over the care of little Mercy, and her conscience stung as she justified not following through. It was her day off, after all. And Levy had gotten enough baby lessons from her that he should be able to wrestle with his tiny bundle of responsibility.

Shouldn't he?

Juggling the baby in his arms, Levy watched the young people gathering around Jane. It concerned him to see her mingling with so many *youngies*. From where he was, he couldn't tell if she was enjoying it or not. He realized he didn't want Jane to be popular among her peers. Popularity wasn't necessarily a good thing.

His sister, Eliza, had been a popular young woman, and look what had happened to her.

He fought the instinctive reaction down. Jane wasn't like Eliza. She was a baptized member of the church, while Eliza was not. Still, it worried him.

Mercy stiffened in his arms, and her tiny face screwed up. She began to wail. Levy unslung the diaper bag from his shoulder and seated himself on the grass, rummaging for a bottle of formula. The minute the tip was in her mouth, she stopped crying.

Despite himself, he softened. Caring for a baby was a lot more work than he'd ever anticipated, but it had its redeeming moments. This was one of them. He even fancied he could see a resemblance to Eliza in the infant's features.

Did his sister think about what she was missing? Did she regret not seeing Mercy's first smile, her first step, her first word…

It was hard to think about that. He said a silent prayer for his sister's health and safety.

"There, little one," he crooned.

"You're getting good at that," said a voice.

Levy looked up to see Peter Troyer, Jane's uncle. "I don't have much choice." He lifted the baby into his arms.

"Seems like you're getting more comfortable holding her," Peter chuckled. "Though it was definitely an odd sight, having a baby on the men's side during worship."

"I felt pretty funny about it," admitted Levy. "But it's not as if I could ask Jane to take the baby for me. She's entitled to a day off like anyone else."

"I'll admit, Catherine said she was itching to give you a hand. But sometimes a man has to just cope, no matter whether it's babies or crops, ain't so?"

"*Ja.*" Levy bounced the baby. He liked Peter Troyer. He was a solid man who never shirked his responsibilities, and managed to keep a twinkle in his eye and a grin on his face. "I'll admit, this little one has her good and bad moments. When she's not crying, she's cooing. It melts the heart."

"It's *Gott*'s way of keeping us from doing our children harm," chuckled Peter. "Come, we're deciding on the Church Sunday hosting schedule. We need your voice."

Levy drove his buggy home with Mercy asleep in the basket he used as a traveling cradle. He'd gotten through the entire church service with minimal fussing on the part of the baby. He was rather pleased by this accomplishment. Maybe Jane's baby lessons were sinking in.

The *boppli* remained asleep as he parked the buggy in the barn and unhitched the horse. Not until he entered the house did she open her blue eyes. She wasn't quite ready to smile yet—she was too young—but that would come soon enough.

"*Ach, liebling*, I need to think what to do with you," he murmured to her as he lifted her from her basket to the bouncy seat on the kitchen table. He sat down in front of her and toyed with her tiny foot. "What's a bachelor uncle going to do with a baby girl?"

He always thought his adult life would follow the usual course of events—courtship, marriage then babies. But here he was, unmarried and with a baby to care for.

The usual twist of agony at the thought of his sister's fate hit his gut. After their parents had died in that horrible buggy accident, he honestly thought he could handle raising Eliza. At eighteen, he believed he was grown up enough to handle the responsibility.

But Eliza's headstrong behavior taught him differently. Never easy to handle, the grief of losing her parents at the age of twelve meant she no longer had the steady guiding hands of their mother and father to rein in her rebellious nature.

That's why seeing Jane surrounded by *youngies* at the Sabbath service disturbed him. All he could see was his sister…until she was gone.

And now… He tickled Mercy's little foot. And now Eliza had a baby she couldn't raise, and he had her baby who he refused to give up. It was all very confusing and frightening.

What was a bachelor uncle to do, indeed?

Jane showed up at Levy's farm bright and early one morning a few days later. She felt refreshed by the sunny weather. But Levy, she soon found out, had gotten out of bed on the wrong side.

"Just overwhelmed, I guess," he replied when she

asked what the matter was. "I have so many things to do. Here." He thrust Mercy into her arms. "I'm already late milking the cows." With that, he stalked out of the house.

Jane stared after him. Perhaps it was her imagination, but it seemed his moodiness sprang from a different reason than his workload.

She gently bounced the baby. "Your uncle is cranky this morning." She touched the infant's nose. "But I'm not going to let him get to me. C'mon, I suspect it's time to wash some diapers."

Jane washed and hung the baby's laundry, then gathered other dirty clothes, swept the house, fed Mercy, put her down for a nap and made lunch. Whatever the cause of Levy's attitude, she would respond by making him a good meal.

She did not, however, eat lunch with Levy. She settled in the living room rocking chair to feed Mercy a bottle of formula.

He didn't say a word, either before or after the meal. Instead, he finished eating, put his plates in the sink and went back to work. As Jane washed the dishes, she looked out the kitchen window and noticed the raspberry bushes loaded down with fruit. She knew how difficult it was to keep up with berries when they peaked.

Picking up Mercy and tucking her in the sling, she descended into the cellar. "Let's go look for canning jars," she told the baby.

The high windows in the home's foundation gave dim light, and Jane was gratified to find hundreds of empty canning jars, which doubtless had belonged to Levy's mother. She picked up a box holding a dozen jars and brought them back upstairs. Then she took a bucket, went out to pick raspberries and came back in to set about making raspberry jam.

In the midst of the hot and sticky process, Levy suddenly entered the kitchen. "I owe you an apology, Jane," he stated without preamble.

Stirring the boiling jam, Jane looked up and wiped a trickle of sweat off her forehead with the back of her hand. "Oh?"

"*Ja*. I worry about my sister, and sometimes I project my worries about her on to you. It makes me bad-tempered, and I'm sorry for that."

Now that she was a bit more familiar with his background, Jane understood his fears. "But I'm not your sister. And I'm not doing anything against the *Ordnung*."

"Neither did she, until she left. But she was always going to *youngie* events. I thought she was on the path toward baptism, but I was wrong."

Jane softened. He was clearly tormented over the fate of his sister, not Jane's social life.

"I have three sisters," she said. "If any of them disappeared into the *Englisch* world, I would be frantic with worry too. Do you want to talk about it, or is it too painful?"

"Too painful." He pinched the bridge of his nose, then dropped his hand. "How many *brüder und schwestern* do you have?"

"Five. Three sisters, two brothers. My older sister is married and expecting her first baby. I'm the second oldest. My younger sisters and my brothers, they're all teenagers." She smiled. "It's a lot for my parents to handle at once."

"Do you miss them?"

"*Ja*, sure, of course. But they're all *gut kinner*. They don't give my parents any trouble."

"Unlike my sister." He removed his hat, stared at the straw brim for a few moments then plopped it back on his head. "I need to get back to work." He stalked out the side door.

Watching him stride away toward the fields, Jane wondered why he felt the sudden need to apologize. But she was right—if anything happened to her sisters, especially her younger sisters, she would be panicky. It seemed he bore a lot of guilt over Eliza's fate. It must have been difficult to try to be a parent at such a young age. She supposed she could understand his odd quirks of behavior. Besides, his moods were none of her business. She was here to watch the baby and make herself useful. Nothing more.

By the time the jam was ready to jar, it was time to start dinner. She strapped the baby to her bouncy seat on the kitchen table, ladled hot jam into sterilized canning jars and set them in a pot of water to boil and seal. Then she made a simple dinner of grilled cheese sandwiches and tomato soup.

Levy came in carrying two buckets of fresh milk, which he strained into oversize jars and set down in the basement to allow the cream to rise.

"I can make butter tomorrow if you have enough cream," Jane offered when he came back up.

"*Danke*. I think there's enough." He sniffed. "Dinner smells good. I'm starving."

While he ate, Jane lifted the jars of jam from the water bath and set them on a towel to cool.

"What inspired you to make jam?" Levy spoke with his mouth full.

"The amount of raspberries left unharvested. It seems sinful to let them go to waste."

"This time of year there are more raspberries than I can sell, and they have to be picked fresh for the farmer's market." He rubbed his chin. "Maybe I can sell your jam too."

"I can keep picking berries through the week, then, and make more jam. Be sure to build in the cost of the jars and lids, since they're yours. I found them in the basement."

"I'll split the money with you, then. My supplies, your labor."

"Deal."

She felt a tentative truce was in effect, so she sat down and reached for a grilled cheese sandwich. Between them, the baby rested in her seat, making small motions with her hands.

"May I ask you a question?" Levy asked as he spooned up some soup.

"*Ja.*"

"Why are you here? What I mean is, why did you decide to come to stay with your aunt and uncle?"

It was the last question Jane expected, and she nearly choked on her sandwich. "Why do you want to know?"

"Just curious. Is it a big secret or something?"

"*Nein… Nein*, not really."

He raised his eyebrows. "Yet it seems you left something behind in Ohio. Did I hire a woman of questionable background to watch Mercy?"

"Of course not." She looked away, then heaved a

sigh. "The truth is, the man I loved married my best friend. End of story."

"Whoa. Sounds more like the beginning of a story to me."

"I would rather not talk about it. It's painful and it's something I chose to leave behind me. It comes from having a best friend who was pretty. Very pretty. And that's all I'll say about the matter." She stood up. "In fact, it's time for me to go. Leave the dishes. I'll do them tomorrow. Mercy's been fed and diapered. See you tomorrow."

She practically ran from the room and down the porch steps. Walking toward her aunt and uncle's house, she was angry at how she'd handled his question.

Her heart was pounding like it was going to pop out of her chest. What did it matter if Levy knew about the reason why she came to Grand Creek? It was not, after all, a deep dark secret.

Yet she realized Levy was the last person in the world with whom she wanted to discuss her love life—or lack thereof. How awkward was it, after all, to discuss it with her employer? She had no intention of baring her soul to him.

Thoughts of Isaac receded as she began thinking more and more about Levy. Despite his stubborn refusal to give Mercy to another family to raise, he had many excellent qualities. He was hardworking, devout, loyal, clever, dedicated and—when he chose to be—kind. His rare smiles lit up his face and made her heart beat faster.

What did that matter to her? He didn't see her as anyone attractive or interesting. And she refused to engage her heart where it wasn't wanted. She did not intend to turn Levy into another Isaac, longing for a man who didn't see her as a woman but merely as a tool.

"What is the matter with me, *Gott*?" she whispered. She seemed to settle her interest on men who didn't— or couldn't—return the interest. Was she unlovable? Or was she destined only to love those who couldn't love her back?

Chapter Six

With some amusement, Levy watched Jane flee from the house. So she'd left her heart behind in Ohio, had she? Smiling, he shook his head at her embarrassment. And found himself curious about her.

He was determined to pry those secrets out of her one way or another.

He went about caring for Mercy—a bit more comfortable now, thanks to Jane's baby lessons—and barely paid attention to why he was so interested in Jane's past.

Because he *was* interested. Not just in her life before she got to town, but in her. She was a unique package, unlike any woman he'd met before. On the surface she seemed quiet and demure, even plain. But underneath? He sensed a strong streak of stubbornness and, more importantly, strength. Strength of character, strength of integrity. He admired that in a woman.

He grinned at Mercy as she tried out a tentative smile at him. She was certainly an adorable *boppli*. "Come, little one," he said as he gathered her up in his arms. "Let's think of a way to pry your nanny's story out of her, shall we?"

* * *

When she arrived at her aunt and uncle's, Jane found Catherine just making some tea. "*Gut'n owed*, how went your day?"

"Fine. Fine." Jane gulped.

Catherine looked at her. "What happened?"

"Oh nothing." Jane dropped down into a chair. "Except I dodged some questions from Levy about why I left Jasper and came here. It was…awkward."

Her aunt prepared a second mug of tea and placed it on the table for Jane. "Why was he asking?"

"It just came up."

Her aunt frowned. "Was he flirting?"

"No!" Her denial came too quick. "Of course not."

"Because if he was, you could do worse," continued her aunt. "Levy's a *gut* man."

"Tante Catherine, please. Don't play matchmaker."

"*Ja*, sure." Her aunt looked unconvinced. "But you're young and pretty, so it's normal for me to wonder who'd make a *gut* husband for you."

"Pretty? I'm nothing of the sort." Jane shoved her glasses back up her nose. "Don't you know lying is a sin?"

"I'm not lying, *liebling*. You just have no confidence in yourself."

"Maybe not." Jane toyed with the tea strainer in her mug. "Years of experience, I guess."

Catherine sipped her tea. "There's been no one special for you? No rides home from singings?"

"*Nein*." Jane laughed with the very tinge of bitterness that had concerned her mother. "And the ironic thing is, my gift from *Gott* is I'm wonderful with babies. I can soothe any baby. I figured that out when I started babysitting for neighbors. Then I began getting hired as a mother's helper for women who'd just had babies. I don't like to think it's *hochmut* that I'm so *gut* with *bopplin*, but it's my gift. That's why Levy asked me to care for little Mercy. But am I likely to have *bopplin* of my own? *Nein*…" Her voice rose.

"Jane, stop it." Catherine spoke sternly. "You're being melodramatic now. You don't know what *Gott* has in store for you, but it's not likely to be a life of minding other peoples' babies. You're only twenty-three. There's plenty of time yet."

"Easy for you to say…"

"Jane, do you remember your baptism?"

Startled at the abrupt change of subject, she stared at her aunt. "Of course."

"Do you remember what you promised during the ceremony?"

"*Ja*, sure, I remember."

"What *did* you promise?"

"To walk with Christ and His church, to remain faithful through life until death, to confess Jesus is the Son of *Gott*, to abide by the *Ordnung* and be obedient and submissive to it…" It wasn't hard to rattle off the vows she'd taken, even though her baptism had been four years ago.

"*Gut*. You do remember. Then why are you failing to keep those vows?"

Jane's jaw dropped open. "What do you mean?"

"I mean, you're fighting *Gott* every step of the way. You fought Him when Isaac married your best friend. You fought Him over coming here to stay with us. You're fighting Him now, by questioning your appearance and your talents."

Chastened, Jane remained silent while she tried to process her aunt's words. They stung. "So you're saying it's *Gott*'s will that I'm a spinster and likely to remain so?"

"I don't presume to know *Gott*'s will. But—this is the thing you're forgetting—*neither do you*."

Tears welled up again, and one large one slid down her cheek and onto the table.

Catherine's face softened. "You're impatient, child. You want it all now and aren't willing to wait for *Gott* to work according to His will, not yours."

Jane heaved a huge and shuddering sigh. "You're right, Tante Catherine. I *have* been railing against *Gott*. It's just been so hard watching my sister and all my friends get married. Isaac and Hannah were the last straw."

The older woman patted Jane's hand. "Don't think we aren't thrilled to have you stay with us, no matter what difficulties you left behind in Jasper. But that's all behind you now. You have a whole new life to look forward to here. You need to have more confidence in yourself, child."

"I guess." Jane wiped her eyes. "I can't help but wonder if the people I've met so far are just being friendly because I'm new in town."

"Nonsense. You're not making friends out of pity, you're making friends because people like you. New friends are *gut* to have. I'm glad to see you so outgoing."

"It's a struggle," Jane admitted. "But Rhoda—she's one of those new friends—told me I wouldn't get to know everyone unless I went to *youngie* events. She's right. I know I have to get out more, even if Levy doesn't think so."

Her aunt raised her eyebrows. "Levy doesn't think it's good for you to have friends?"

"Well *nein*, he didn't quite say that. But he admitted he was projecting his sister's behavior on me. He apologized later and said he kept thinking about how his sister was so sociable right before she disappeared."

Catherine looked thoughtful. "*Ach*, poor man. And poor Eliza. He's right, she was very sociable. I think he believes that's when she started going down the wrong path. Most of the problem is he doesn't know where she is or what she's doing. The fact that she sent a baby for him to raise breaks his heart because he worries that the worst possible fate has befallen her."

"I had a lot more sympathy for him after I envisioned how I would feel if any of my sisters left the community." Jane sighed. "My problems seem a lot less important by comparison. I'll try to have a better attitude, Tante. I don't know what *Gott* has in store for me, but I'll try to be more patient."

Levy found himself looking forward to seeing Jane the next morning. He was determined to learn something about this mysterious past she'd alluded to.

But that would have to wait. He had work to do, and he felt the familiar stress arise as Mercy seemed inconsolable that morning, wailing without end.

Jane entered the house without knocking. "I could hear her crying from the road," she observed. "Apparently those baby lessons I've been giving you haven't sunk in yet."

He handed over the baby, and as if on cue, Mercy quieted down right away. He shook his head. "I don't know how you do it."

"Then you need more lessons." She gave him a

cheerful smile. "Is there anything special you'd like for lunch?"

"Uh, no…" He thrust a hand through his hair. "You seem chipper this morning. Are you feeling okay?"

"Never better." She gave him a sunny smile and turned toward the kitchen. "If I'm making butter this morning, maybe I'll use some of it for biscuits with lunch. Biscuits and gravy. And maybe a potato casserole too."

"*Ja*, that sounds *gut*." He gave her a puzzled look and left the kitchen.

All morning as he hoed and weeded and picked and cultivated, he wondered about her change in attitude. Yesterday afternoon she seemed anxious. Today she was cheerful. What a mercurial woman she was.

"The man I loved married my best friend," she'd said yesterday.

Evidently that had been painful enough to send her fleeing from the security of her hometown, her parents and siblings, her church.

He found himself wondering just how attached she still was to this man she'd loved.

Before he knew it, it was lunchtime. When he returned to the house, he entered the kitchen and saw newly churned butter in a bowl on the counter, and fresh biscuits and gravy on the table. Jane was just pulling a potato casserole from the oven. Mercy sat quietly in her seat on the counter, watching Jane with large blue eyes.

"I don't know how you do it," he repeated as he washed his hands at the sink. "You get all this work done and Mercy stays quiet. With me, she never settles down."

"I'm sure part of it is because you're still nervous

with her." Jane brought the bouncy seat and baby to the table, and placed Mercy in the middle as a centerpiece.

After the silent blessing, Levy reached for the biscuits. "So…why are you so cheery today?"

"I had a nice discussion with my *tante* yesterday after work," Jane admitted. She dished some potato casserole onto her plate.

"Does this have anything to do with the topic you avoided with me yesterday evening?" He split open the biscuits and ladled gravy over them.

He watched the changing expressions on Jane's face as some of her cheer seemed to evaporate. "I don't want to talk about it."

But Levy was determined to get her to open up—not just to satisfy his own curiosity, but because a small part of him wondered if his failure to listen to his sister's concerns when she was younger might have played a factor in her disappearance.

Jane was not like Eliza, of course. But perhaps she would like a sounding board just the same.

"So how long were you in love with that young man from your hometown?" he asked abruptly.

She glared at him. "Excuse me?"

"You heard me. How long were you in love with him?"

"Levy, that's none of your business."

"Maybe not, but don't you think it would be good to unburden yourself? You seem weighed down with something."

"I'm *not* burdened."

"Then why are you so defensive?" He took a bite of a biscuit.

"Because… Because…" He saw tears in her eyes.

He suddenly felt bad that her mood had taken a

downturn, but he persisted. "Look, Jane, after seeing what happened to my sister, I think it's important to share burdens. It helps lighten the load. Won't you tell me?"

She stared at her plate, and Levy wondered if she would refuse to answer. Mercy gave a coo into the silence.

Finally she spoke in a low voice, still staring at her plate. "We went to school together, me, Isaac and Hannah. I had a crush on Isaac since I was, I don't know, maybe thirteen or fourteen. But he only had eyes for Hannah."

"Did he know how you felt?" Levy kept his voice gentle.

"Hannah is beautiful, and I'm… I'm not. I can't blame him for wanting to marry her."

Ah, so that was the crux of the matter. Jane thought she wasn't beautiful.

"And you think this Isaac only married your friend because she was prettier?" he persisted.

"It certainly was a factor in his decision. Why wouldn't it be?" Jane raised her head.

"If that was his only reason for marrying your friend, then he's a fool," proclaimed Levy. "Seems rather shallow."

"Maybe so, but what does it matter?" She shoved her glasses farther up on her nose. "It seems to be the way men think." She gave him a grim smile. "But you'd know that better than I would."

"*Nein*, I wouldn't. That's not the way I think." He saw skepticism on her face and continued, "You know very well *Gott* only sees the inside of a person, not the outside."

"*Ja*, sure. I'm grateful beyond words too, or I'd be in trouble. But it also meant Isaac only had eyes for Hannah, not me. And I didn't realize how much that hurt."

"And so you came here."

"My *mamm* said I needed a change of scenery because I was growing bitter and cynical."

"And what do you think of Grand Creek so far?"

"From what I've seen, I like it. Everyone seems very friendly. Speaking of which," she added, in a clear attempt to change the subject, "I've been invited to a hot dog roast this evening."

Instantly stress flooded through him as the implication sank in. "Oh. That means I'm in sole charge of Mercy."

"I'm sure you'll do fine."

"It's not just her physical care, though you've seen how bad I am at that. But I was going to work later into the evening and try to get a jump on things."

"In other words, you want me to work late." There was a touch of annoyance in her voice.

"*Nein... Nein*, I didn't say that..."

"Look, would it help to take Mercy with me?"

"Take a baby to a *youngie* event?" He raised his eyebrows.

She took another bite of casserole, then tickled Mercy's feet. "At this age, she shouldn't be much trouble."

"Are you sure? Because I'll freely admit, it would be a big help if you did."

"*Ja*, why not? If nothing else, it will be an experiment to see how she does. And since I've been invited to a singing on Friday, if tonight works well, I'll bring Mercy again. That way you'll be completely free to do whatever you need to get ready for the farmer's market."

"You're turning into quite the social butterfly." He didn't want to admit why Jane's popularity bothered him.

"It isn't easy, believe me." She looked at her plate. "I'm shy by nature, but I want to get to know people. It gets me…" She raised her head, and he saw a twinkle of humor in her eyes. "It gets me outside my comfort zone."

He remembered telling her that's what he had to do while selling his produce at the farmer's market.

"*Ja*," he agreed. "If you can take Mercy, you could combine business with pleasure. You can attend your *youngie* events, and I can get some work done."

"Are you finished? I'll wash up." She rose.

"*Ja. Danke*, lunch was delicious." He snatched up his hat and stepped out the door.

Back in the fields, he grabbed a hoe and applied it to the weeds. He realized he was discomfited by Jane's plans. But he was in no position to question her social life.

He tried not to think of his sister's popularity and where it had ultimately led. But Jane wasn't Eliza. He didn't have responsibility for her, not as he'd had with Eliza.

The fact that he had messed up when raising his sister was something he tried not to dwell on.

But it wasn't always easy.

Before she left for the hot dog roast, Jane packed a diaper bag with everything she could possibly need for the infant. She made dinner for Levy. She folded diapers and stacked them near the baby's crib. With Mercy tucked in the sling, she swept the house and porch.

When she was ready to leave for the event, she carried the baby and the diaper bag out to the barn where Levy was milking the cows. "I'm leaving now. I'll be back no later than 8:30. Your dinner is in the oven, warming. Don't worry about the dishes. I'll do them in the morning."

He barely looked up from his task. "Fine. Have fun."

She shrugged and set out for the function. Whatever Levy's issue with her attending *youngie* events, he couldn't fault her for neglecting her job.

The hot dog roast was held at the farm of Sarah's parents. Sarah was the first to spot her when she arrived. "You came! Oh, let me see the baby. Isn't she darling!"

Mercy was passed from person to person and cooed over. "She's so cute."

"What a joy!"

"She's such a quiet baby!"

Mercy didn't cry during any of these exchanges. When she finally found her way back into Jane's arms, Jane settled the baby in the sling and joined Sarah and Rhoda around a pit fire, where everyone held hot dogs on forked sticks over the fire.

"Is Levy glad you took the baby with you tonight?" asked Sarah.

"I guess. He's not pleased I'm here at all."

Her new friend looked surprised. "Why not?"

"I don't know. He acts like a bear with a sore paw whenever I mention coming to any singings. He seems to think I'm acting like his sister did before she disappeared."

"Levy's so *serious*," observed Rhoda. "And you're just the opposite. How do you two get along?"

"By not seeing each other much during the day. He's

outside working, I'm taking care of Mercy in the house. End of story."

Sarah raised an eyebrow. "Any sparks between the two of you?"

"Lots. But not the kind you mean. There are times he drives me crazy, other times he's amazing to watch in action, like when he's at the farmer's market. Then it's like he's a different man."

"In a good way or a bad way?"

"Just a different way. He becomes far more animated, jokes and banters a lot with the customers and sells like crazy."

"He's interesting, all right." Sarah bit into a cookie. "I don't know him very well, but I've never heard anything bad about him. No one blames him for what happened with his sister. We all know he did the best he could with her."

"Maybe that's why he gets bothered when you attend *youngie* events," remarked Rhoda. "He's used to acting like a father."

"Well, he's not *my* father," Jane said as she laid Mercy on a soft blanket on the ground.

"*Nein*, but he's used to being a father to his sister. That's probably why he does it." Rhoda looked down at Mercy. "I wonder if Eliza will ever come back for her baby?"

"Did you know her?"

"Eliza? Of course. Everyone knew her. She was quite the social butterfly."

"That's the term Levy used with me," said Jane. "What was she like? Besides being a social butterfly, as you called her?"

"She was always laughing, always smiling, but she

didn't much like working hard. Except sewing. She was very *gut* at sewing. Levy works all the time, so he used to get frustrated at her laziness. She kept up the garden pretty well, but I remember seeing the inside of their house once, and it was dusty and she had dirty clothes in her room. She didn't like cooking either." Sarah rubbed her chin. "I mean, neither do I, but that doesn't mean I won't do it. She was very stubborn about not doing things she didn't like. But with just the two of them, her and Levy, there's a lot to do even on a small farm. Maybe that's what drove her away, thinking she would have it easier if she lived among the *Englisch*."

"I wonder if she'll ever return to Grand Creek," Jane murmured.

"I think part of him thinks she won't," said Sarah. "That's why he's so determined to keep the baby. Maybe he feels he shouldn't fail the second time around."

"Yet I'm doing all the work with her." Jane tickled Mercy under the chin.

"I admire that you're nannying her," commented Sarah.

"What do you mean?"

"I mean, I think it would be hard to be a nanny, especially to a *boppli* this adorable. What if you fall in love with her? You're not her *mamm*. It's just a job. When the time comes, you'll move on, and what will happen to Mercy then?"

Shaken, Jane looked at the happy infant cooing on the blanket. "You're right. And it would be very easy to fall in love with her. But what choice do I have? What choice does Levy have? He can't take care of her by himself, not if he wants to be able to work."

"*Ja*, it's a problem all right." Sarah dangled a leaf over

the baby's face, though Mercy couldn't quite focus on it. "It would be hard, in some ways, if Eliza ever *did* come back. It wouldn't be so hard now since Mercy is too young to know any different, but what would happen if Eliza came back when Mercy was older?"

Sarah spoke nothing but the truth—and where did that leave her, Jane? She hadn't planned on staying with her aunt and uncle forever. She missed her own family.

But leaving Mercy would mean depriving the baby of the only mother figure she'd known. With unease, Jane wondered if it wouldn't be better to leave sooner rather than later, before Mercy would know the difference. If Levy was determined to raise his niece, then he'd better take to heart those baby lessons.

"I think we're going to have rain tomorrow." Rhoda pointed overhead at the darkening sky. "Maybe even tonight. That's *gut*, we need it."

"I should probably get going." Jane rose to her feet. "I told Levy I'd bring Mercy back home by 8:30 so he could put her to bed."

"Are you coming to the singing on Friday? It's at my house," urged Rhoda.

"I hope so. I'll probably have to do the same thing and bring Mercy with me, but I'd like to attend."

"Everyone is so glad you're here," Rhoda stated. "We want you to come to every gathering!"

She smiled her thanks. "I'll come as often as I can. Come on, little one, let's go see your uncle." She lifted Mercy off the blanket and slipped her into the sling. "*Gude nacht.*"

She walked the half mile or so back to Levy's home. The clouds overhead thickened and a wind gusted up. Jane picked up her pace.

She hesitated at Levy's front door. Lamplight shone from within. She knocked before walking in. "Levy? I've brought Mercy home."

Levy emerged from the small room he used as an office. "*Ja, danke.*"

"Do you want me to change her diaper before I go?"

"*Nein*, I'll take care of it." His face was a neutral mask. He didn't ask her about the gathering, didn't ask how Mercy had behaved. He simply held out his arms to take the baby.

"I'll be here tomorrow then." Feeling peeved, she hung the baby sling on a hook by the door and left.

Would it kill Levy to show any warmth or appreciation? Would it pain him to inquire how her new friends were or how many people had attended the hot dog roast? As she stomped down the road, she admitted his lack of interest bothered her.

Levy didn't see Jane disappear into the night. He saw his sister Eliza walk away. For one moment, the two women merged in his mind, and he shook his head to dispel the illusion.

He knew he was projecting his fears and concerns about Eliza's behavior on to Jane, and that wasn't fair.

He looked at the sweet baby in his arms. She looked ready for sleep, her eyes just about drooping. He searched her features again for any traces of his sister, and believed he saw a similarity. Or was he imagining things?

He sighed and went about preparing Mercy for bed. How much did the baby resemble her father?

He shied away from speculating on the circumstances of Mercy's birth. He loved his sister with a fierce devotion, a bond made stronger after he stepped into the role of guardian when his parents died. His failure to rein in Eliza's wild adolescence weighed on him like a stone. He still blamed himself for her departure.

If Mercy was born out of wedlock as he suspected, then Eliza might never return to the community.

Yet he desperately hoped that one day Eliza would return to claim her baby, even if it meant facing down the inevitable gossip. That, more than anything else, accounted for his stubborn refusal to give Mercy to another family to raise. However irrational, Mercy was a link to his lost sister. If he gave up Mercy, he gave up all hope of seeing Eliza again.

He kissed the *boppli*'s forehead and laid the sleepy infant in her crib. He would never give up Mercy, because he would never give up hope that Eliza might return.

Chapter Seven

In the morning Jane opened her eyes and saw it was raining, no surprise after the change in weather she saw the night before.

"It is a gift from *Gott*, as we need the rain," Uncle Peter commented at breakfast, sipping coffee and looking at the gray weather outside.

"It's going to keep Levy indoors, though," muttered Jane.

Her uncle raised his eyebrows in a silent question.

She explained, "I've come up with a daily routine with the baby, and he's likely to get in the way."

"Well, it's his house. And his niece."

"*Ja*, I know." Jane scrubbed a hand over her face. "I'm sorry, Onkel Peter. It's just that…well, Levy and I don't always get along."

"He has a lot on his mind."

"I know, so I try to be understanding about it." Jane glanced at the clock. "But I'd better get going. I try to be there by seven."

Donning a cloak and taking an umbrella, Jane headed out toward Levy's house. The fields around her, even under a gray sky, greened up as the rain washed away dust and soaked the thirsty soil. Jane breathed deeply in the moist fresh air and vowed to keep her temper in check today.

Surprisingly, Levy was feeding the baby when she arrived, sitting with Mercy in the rocking chair as she drank a bottle of formula. "*Guder mariye,*" she said. "Do you want me to take over?"

"*Ja,* please. I haven't milked the cows yet."

Mercy fussed when the bottle slipped out of her mouth, but Jane traded places, settled into the chair and continued feeding her. "You milk three cows, right?"

"Right. It takes me about half an hour."

"Have you had breakfast?"

"*Ja.*" He crammed his hat over his curly hair. "Back in a while." He left for the barn.

When he returned with buckets of fresh milk, Jane was in the kitchen putting together lunch, with Mercy secure in the sling against her chest.

Levy stood in front of the sink, staring out the kitchen window at the pouring rain. "I won't get much done today," he muttered.

"Is it such a bad thing to take a day off?" Jane asked.

"I already have a day off," he replied. "On the Sabbath. The rest of the time, I'm on a tight schedule to get everything done in time for Saturday's market. You know that."

"Unfortunately, it doesn't look like you have a choice." She gestured toward the window.

"I know."

"Don't you have anything that needs doing in the barn?" she hinted.

He quirked an eyebrow at her. "Trying to get rid of me?"

"Well, *you* may not be able to work, but I'm still on the clock. And you're in the way." She tempered her words with a half smile, but truthfully her schedule was easier without Levy's constant hovering—even if it was, as her uncle pointed out, his house.

He moved away from the sink. "What is it you do all day?"

"What I always do," she retorted. "But normally you're outside."

"*Ja, ja,* you're right. I'm sorry, that was a *schtupid* thing to say." He shrugged. "I'll be in the barn."

What is it you do all day? In the now-silent kitchen, Jane snatched up dirty dishes and dumped them in the sink.

Whatever he found to do in the barn only kept him occupied for an hour, then he was back in the house. Jane pushed aside a strand of hair that had escaped her *kapp* as she chopped bell peppers and onions for a casserole. "Are you up for a trip to town?" she asked.

"*Ja,* I suppose. What do you need?"

"Formula for Mercy. We're running low."

"And it would get me out of the house, right?"

"Why yes, it would." She smiled and kept chopping.

"I have a few other things I could pick up as well. *Ja,* I'll go into town."

He grabbed his wallet and headed back for the barn. Jane sighed with relief.

Why was he so restless today? Whatever the cause, she was glad when she heard the clip-clop of hooves pull away from the house.

Levy hitched up his favorite mare, Maggie, to the buggy and swung into the seat.

He felt so restless today. He also couldn't believe he'd insulted Jane in such a way. *What is it you do all day?* How dumb could he be? He knew exactly what she did all day.

He trotted the horse toward the center of town.

His errands were trivial, but he lingered in the hardware store. He avoided the Troyers' dry-goods store.

It was with some relief that he saw friends hailing him from under a café awning where they lingered over coffee.

"Do you have time to join us?" asked Thomas.

"*Ja.*" Levy dropped into a chair. "This rain is keeping you from working outside too?"

"For sure and certain." Thomas winked. "And *alle daag rumhersitze macht em faul.* Sitting all day makes one lazy. I could be doing things in the barn, but I blame Paul here for dragging me into town on the pretext of going to the bank. Next thing I know, I'm drinking coffee."

Levy chuckled. He'd known Thomas Lapp and Paul Yoder since they were boys. They always managed to cheer him up, no matter what.

"How goes fatherhood?" asked Paul.

A waitress took his order and departed. Levy removed his hat and hooked it on the back of his chair. "Better, now that Jane's doing most of the hard work."

"Babies can be tough." Thomas tugged his beard. "My Annie, she juggles both our young ones very well, but it is definitely easier with two people at hand."

"Our third is due in about a month." Paul sipped his beverage. "Louisa is wonderful with the kids. My eldest boy, he's now old enough to follow me around the farm. He's a joy, as is my little girl. But tiny babies... they're best left to the *frauen*."

Thomas chimed in. "Have you considered giving Mercy to another family?"

Levy shook his head. "*Nein*. She stays with me. She's all I have of Eliza."

"Then it's good you have Jane to take care of her. Everyone says she's wonderful with babies." Paul grinned. "Better than you!"

The words were meant to be teasing, Levy knew, but they still stung. He drew his brows together. "So I'm a little awkward with Mercy. I haven't had any practice before this."

"Will Jane stay? Does she seem content to be Mercy's nanny?"

"*Danke*," Levy said to the waitress, who placed a coffee cup before him. "*Ja*, she says so. At this point I don't know what else I can do but keep her on."

"Why, is there a problem?" Thomas's brows arched upward. "Everyone talks well of her. Is she hard to get along with?"

"*Nein*, not exactly," Levy hedged. "I'm paying her a little extra to handle housekeeping chores as well, and she's been very good about it. It's just that..." He stopped and stared out at the downpour just outside the café awning.

"Just that what?" prompted Paul.

"I don't know," he went on. "I can't put my finger on what's wrong. She's always wanting to go to singings and get-togethers. Last night she went to a hot dog roast and took Mercy with her. I can't say she's neglecting her job because she's not. It's just that..."

"...that you're thinking of Eliza," finished Thomas.

Levy felt his face flush. "It's true," he admitted.

"Is that a good enough reason to work against the best interests of the baby?"

Levy scowled. "I'm *not* working against her best interests. Jane's doing a fine job with her."

"But what are Jane's plans?" persisted Thomas. "You hired her right off the train, and she started working because she knew you were desperate. But she's under no obligation to stay. She can do whatever she wants."

Paul chimed in. "Remember, she's young and single, and there's no reason she shouldn't enjoy herself by socializing with other *youngies*." His expression altered. "Why do you object to her going to *youngie* events so much?"

"I don't."

Thomas chuckled. "Don't you know lying is a sin, Levy? Why does it bother you when she has some fun, especially since they're all chaperoned events?"

Levy remained silent, since he had no real answer for Thomas's question. He took another sip of his coffee.

Eager to change the subject, Thomas asked, "How goes the farmer's market sales?"

Levy was grateful for the conversation shift, and a few minutes later, they all parted ways.

He left his horse hitched out of the weather in the open-sided shed provided by the café and ducked into a small grocery store to buy formula for Mercy. He considered it bad luck when he bumped into Bishop Kemp.

"Ah, Levy!" exclaimed the venerable man. "I was going to call on you, but now I see you here."

"Bishop." Levy shook hands. "Quite the weather outside, ain't so?"

"*Ja*. I wanted to ask how it is with your sister's baby?"

"Uh, fine. Jane Troyer is doing an excellent job caring for her."

"*Gut, gut.* But Levy, you know that can only be a temporary solution." Bishop Kemp stroked his beard. "The *boppli* needs stability. Have you thought about getting married?"

"Married?" Levy's voice went high-pitched.

"*Ja,* of course. Married. That way the baby can have both a mother *and* a father."

"That's not a *gut* reason to get married." He scowled.

"Then you need to seriously think about giving Mercy to a family who can raise her." The bishop's voice was gentle and persuasive.

"That's not acceptable either." Levy scowled harder.

"Levy, are you listening to yourself? You're not being logical. You can't take care of her on your own—not if you have to work on the farm all day—so as I see it, you have three choices. You can get married, you can put her up for adoption or you can hire a succession of nannies."

Levy was silent, glowering.

The bishop continued. "Let me ask you this—why are you determined to keep Mercy? What's wrong with putting her up for adoption with another family?"

"She's all I have of Eliza."

"*Ja,* that's what you have said. So let me ask you a very, very hard question. Will you do a better job raising Mercy than you did raising Eliza?"

He stared, wide-eyed. "I don't know," he groaned.

Bishop Kemp laid a hand on Levy's shoulder. "I'm sorry to bring up such difficult things, my *sohn,* but you have to be practical. If you let her be adopted, nothing says you have to stay entirely out of her life. You can be as involved as you want. But the best thing you can give that *boppli* is stability…and you don't have that right now."

Levy's mouth pinched. "I know you're right, but it causes me physical pain to think about giving her away."

"Well, nothing must be decided right now. If Jane Troyer is doing as *gut* a job as you say, then you have time to think things through. But Levy, don't wait too long to decide. The longer you wait, the harder it will be on Mercy."

"*Ja*, I know." Levy squared his shoulders. "I'll give it some thought, Bishop Kemp. And meanwhile, I'll continue to pray for Eliza."

Levy purchased the formula, then returned to his buggy. He unhitched Maggie and drove home through the rain.

"You're not being logical." Bishop Kemp's voice echoed in his ears as Levy reached home. He guided the horse into the barn and unhitched her, then spent more time than necessary grooming and feeding the mare. He oiled the harness and hung it on its hook. He even wiped down the buggy. Anything to avoid going into the house.

But when he could find no other excuse to putter around the barn, he placed his straw hat firmly on his head and walked into the house.

Jane was in the kitchen, which smelled of fresh-baked cookies. A huge platter of them rested on the table. She sat reading a book, a mug of steaming tea at her elbow.

"So *this* is what you do all day," he teased.

She raised her head. "*Ja*. That's after I made lunch, swept and dusted, did a load of laundry and hung it in the basement, and made cookies. Have one, they're oatmeal-raisin."

"*Danke*." He picked one up and leaned against the counter while he ate it. "Is Mercy napping?"

"*Ja*." She paused. "Levy, what's bothering you?"

"What makes you think something's bothering me?"

"You're jumpy as a cat today, and so critical. Have I done something wrong?"

The woman was too insightful. Not for anything would Levy confess his true concerns. "*Nein*." He knew his voice sounded curt. "You've done nothing wrong. I, uh…have some things to do in the barn."

He fled the house.

Jane was far more upset by Levy's dark mood than she expected. Tears welled in her eyes, and she wiped them away.

Through the kitchen window she saw Levy pause in the doorway of the barn, just out of the relentless rain. Whatever "things" he had to do in the barn didn't seem urgent, as he simply stood there looking into the dark interior.

A grumble of thunder came from a distance, and still he stood motionless in the doorway. Jane admitted to herself why Levy's brusqueness hurt so much. She had begun to pin romantic hopes on the man where none existed.

"Jane, you *schtupid* fool," she whispered. "Wasn't Isaac enough? Do you need to get kicked in the shins by Levy too?"

It became very clear to Jane that she wanted Levy to see her as a woman, an interesting woman, an attractive woman…not a "useful" woman. But now, it seemed, even her usefulness was limited. *What is it you do all day?*

Through the window she saw him turn and head back to the house. She composed herself just before he opened the kitchen door and strode back in.

He filled the kettle and set it on the stove to heat, pulled out a mug and a tea bag, then sat down across the table from her. "Can we talk?"

"*Ja.*" She suppressed the shuddering breath that preceded a crying jag. "I want to know what I've done wrong."

"You haven't done anything wrong, Jane. I'm just worried about Mercy's future." He rubbed his chin. "I bumped into the bishop in town. He asked me why I didn't give Mercy to a family who could raise her. It's a lot harder than I thought to be her guardian, and now I'm questioning my decision. The bishop still wants me to reconsider."

"But you're stubbornly refusing to do what's right for Mercy."

"Yes, I am." His face grew stern. "I love my sister. I love her more than anything. A little frightened part of me is worried that if I give Mercy away, I'm giving away all hope of seeing Eliza again. I keep wondering where I went wrong with her, what I could have done differently."

"Levy." Jane stood up as the kettle started to sing. She poured water over his tea bag. "Will you tell me what happened with you and Eliza? How you came to take care of her? Explain to me why you're so determined to keep a newborn baby."

"How much have you heard from others?"

"Not much. Just some gossip. Everyone thinks highly

of you, and even if they disagree with why you're keeping Mercy, they understand it."

Levy looked surprised. "That's *gut*, I suppose."

Jane sipped her tea. "All I know is you'd taken care of your sister since your parents died. She left, never came back and you only heard from her when she sent the baby into your care."

"That's the gist of it." Levy dipped his tea bag in and out of the cup, staring at the darkening water. "My parents died when a car hit their buggy. That was ten years ago. Eliza was twelve years old at the time, and I was eighteen. My parents only had two children. When they died, it was just Eliza and me."

"How did Eliza take your parents' deaths?"

"Very hard, as you can imagine. We both did, but she was at a more impressionable age. I stepped into a fatherly role for Eliza." He closed his eyes. "I guess I wasn't very good at it."

Filled with compassion, Jane touched his hand briefly. He opened his eyes and looked at the spot she'd touched.

"Up until about the age of fifteen, she was fine. I'd already been baptized, and I thought she was on the same path. A nice young man named Josiah was interested in her. But then she hit a rebellious phase, running around with other *youngies*, neglecting her chores, acting disrespectfully. I just didn't know what to do, how to cope." His voice trembled.

"My friend Sarah said she left on her *Rumspringa*."

"*Ja*, that's right. She was taking classes to be baptized, but one day while in town she met an *Englischer*, and next thing I knew she was gone. I can only presume Mercy is the result of that relationship. It…it kills me to think of Eliza, alone and pregnant…and all because I didn't know how to handle a teenage girl."

Jane tried to be sympathetic. "With *Gott*, all things are possible. Eliza may come around…"

Levy laughed bitterly. "And be accepted by the community? I don't think so."

"Don't be so sure. If she was never baptized, she can still return and be forgiven for her sins. I think you might be too hard on her."

"Wouldn't you be?" He fixed her with an angry glare. "If you were in my shoes, could you speak so easily of forgiveness?"

"Maybe not." Jane sighed and took a sip of her tea. "I would be devastated if either of my two younger sisters followed the same course Eliza did. But you can't see into the future, Levy, nor can you change the past. If I were in a position to counsel you, I would tell you to forgive yourself for what happened in the past, and pray for what might happen in the future."

He pinched the bridge of his nose. "Why should *Gott* listen to me?" he muttered.

She was surprised to hear him say such a thing. "*Gott* always listens!"

"Then where is my sister?"

"*Gott* knows, and He's got His hand on her. Don't lose your faith, Levy—it's the most important thing you have."

"I'm trying not to." He stared at his mug. "But it's hard. I worry she's alone in some big city."

"The one thing to remember is Eliza is not a child any longer. She's a grown woman, and she's making her own way in life. It may not be a way you approve of, but it's her life."

"But not her child?"

"Maybe not."

Levy sighed. After a long pause, he asked, "Jane, that's another thing I wanted to ask—how long do you think you'll be able to work as Mercy's nanny? I need to think about Mercy's future, and that means finding out how long you anticipate staying."

"I don't know." She toyed with her spoon. "Originally I wasn't going to stay more than a few months. I like this community, I like the people I've met, I like my work, I love my *tante* and *onkel*…but I was born and raised in Ohio and want to keep the option of going home. But already I can see this will be a problem—not just because of my future, but because of Mercy's."

"So can you give me a deadline for when I should look for a replacement? Are you thinking two months? Three months? Four months?"

"It's too hard to predict. But one thing is certain. Without a mother in the picture, someone permanent, it's going to be hard having a series of nannies go in and out of her life."

"I know…"

Just then the infant started crying from the bedroom. Jane rose to her feet. "As I told you before, however long I'm here, I'll continue to care for Mercy as if she were my own." She bit her lip. "In fact, it will be hard to give her up when the time comes."

Chapter Eight

Jane changed the baby's diaper, then settled into the rocking chair to give her a bottle. She watched the baby as she drank. Her tiny hands looked like stars.

She'd told Levy the truth. It would be very hard to give Mercy up when the time came. She realized she was falling in love with this precious and sweet *boppli*.

"I think when your belly is full, I'm going to give you a bath," she crooned. The infant's large blue eyes gazed upward as she sucked on the bottle.

When the formula was gone, Jane placed a clean diaper over her shoulder and placed the baby over it, patting the tiny back until she emitted a satisfactory *braaap*.

When she returned to the kitchen, Levy was gone. Jane warmed some water and padded a washbasin with a towel. She filled the washbasin with hot and cold water until she was satisfied with the temperature.

"C'mon, little one, let's get you washed." Jane gathered clean clothes, a washcloth, a cup for rinsing and other accessories.

Mercy enjoyed the bath. She smiled and cooed as Jane soaped her little body, then rinsed her off, protecting her eyes with the washcloth. As she worked, Jane felt the warmth of love steal over her for this tiny *boppli*. No matter what her future held, it would be hard to stop caring for Mercy.

She dressed the baby, then placed her in her bouncy seat on the kitchen table. She started to cook dinner when she heard a knock at the door.

Picking up the baby, she went to answer. Her friend Rhoda stood on the porch, panting, a dripping umbrella at her side. "We're having another singing in the Millers' barn since it's too wet to work outside," she gasped, grinning. "I ran all the way over here to ask if you can come. It starts in an hour, and if you can come, bring something to eat since we'll all have dinner there."

"*Ja*, I think so. I'll have to make dinner for Levy, but that sounds like fun."

"*Gut*! See you there."

When Jane closed the door and returned to the kitchen, Levy was there, rain dripping off his hat brim. He looked at her unsmiling. Then he turned to wash his hands at the sink.

"I'll make double the amount of dinner and bring half with me to the singing tonight," said Jane.

"That's fine." He wiped his hands on the dish towel.

"I can bring Mercy with me, if you like."

"Great."

A wave of pity came over her. "Levy, I know you're upset by what the bishop said. But try not to worry about Mercy's future. *Gott* will provide."

"*Ja*." He looked down at the dish towel in his hands. "I know. I've been praying for clarity, for guidance. I just don't see the right path yet."

"You will, I'm sure. And for the moment, Mercy's in *gut* hands." Jane patted the *boppli* on the back.

Levy looked at her, and she saw gratitude in his eyes. "Whatever happens in the future, I thank *Gott* I saw you that day at the train station."

Jane held his eyes a heartbeat longer than required before she dropped her own gaze. "*Ja.* Well, I guess I'll start dinner."

Levy disappeared into his office. The rain pattered on the roof, and Jane opened the kitchen window a bit to let the moist warm air into the house. She tried not to think of that vulnerable raw emotion she saw in his eyes. She tried not to dwell on how her own heart responded.

She set the table for Levy, packed the extra food into an insulated carrier and tucked it inside Mercy's diaper bag. Then she slipped the *boppli* into the sling, and put on her cloak to protect both of them from the rain. She stopped at the doorway to Levy's office, where a lamp lit the inside against the gloomy afternoon, illuminating an account ledger.

"I'll be leaving now. I've left dinner for you on the table."

"*Danke.* Have fun." He gave her an abstracted smile, then continued scratching in the ledger with a pen.

She picked up her umbrella and the diaper bag, and set out for the Millers' farm.

It pained her to see Levy hurting. And she wondered what else she could do to help this man, whom she was growing to care for.

She saw many young men and women walking toward the Millers', with umbrellas bobbing from different directions. The large barn doors were wide open in welcome. Jane stepped inside, shook the rain off her umbrella and stacked it near the doorway with dozens of others.

The Millers had set up boards across sawhorses along the outside walls of the main part of the barn. Jane joined the groups of chattering, laughing young people placing food along the boards. For such a spontaneously arranged function, a lot of people had come. The rain pounded on the roof overhead, but inside the barn the energy was high.

"What's wrong?"

Jane turned and saw Rhoda. "What do you mean, what's wrong?"

"You were standing there like you're angry."

"Oh, nothing. Just some moodiness from Levy, that's all." Jane gave Mercy a little bob in the sling, but the baby was cozy and alert.

"Is he still giving you grief about attending *youngie* events?"

"Not so much. But he's…" Jane trailed off. Gossiping was a sin, and she'd nearly gossiped about Levy's private struggle. "Well, he just has a lot on his mind," she went on.

Some others clustered around Jane, cooing at the baby, so she took Mercy from the sling and allowed her to be passed from arm to arm. Free of the infant, Jane found herself surrounded by several young men, who engaged her in conversation.

These were the same young men, she realized, who seemed to hang around every event she'd attended so far. Caught up in the notion she was plain, it dawned on her that she was, for the first time in her life, attracting male attention.

This was reinforced later when Sarah sidled up and whispered, "I think Charles is interested in you."

"What? Really?" Jane refrained from glancing over at the young man. "I thought it might be David, since he's been at my side the whole evening."

"Him too. And maybe even Daniel. But not Josiah. I thought he was too heartbroken still, but now he may be courting."

Josiah? Jane's ears pricked up. That was the young man Levy's sister had left behind when she disappeared into the *Englisch* world.

"Which one is Josiah?" she asked Sarah.

The young woman pointed to a nice-looking man with straight brown hair. He sat with another young woman, talking. "He was stuck on Eliza for a long time," Sarah stated. "But now maybe things will be different. I hope so. He's a *gut* man. Come on, the singing is just getting started."

The mishmash of chairs and benches filled up as the young people seated themselves, most with hymn books in hand. Jane took Mercy back and found herself with Sarah and Rhoda, while the young men seated themselves opposite, with Jane's admirers sitting as near to her as was possible in the barn.

The group sang vigorously for half an hour before breaking for something to drink, and Jane found herself once more the center of attention. She remembered telling Levy of the need to step outside her comfort zone, and she realized it was getting easier to do as she chatted with her new friends.

Jane noticed Josiah glance at her, then look away. She suspected it was because he knew she held Eliza's baby. He remained with the young woman she'd noticed earlier.

The group sang some more, then broke for the meal. Jane went into a quiet corner so she could change Mercy's diaper and feed her.

Sarah kept her company while the baby drank her bottle. "I saw Charles whispering to his brother and glancing your way," she confessed. "I wouldn't be surprised if he was thinking about courting you."

The thought was not exciting, though she liked Charles well enough.

Sarah's teasing grin faded. With feminine precision, she asked, "Is it Levy?"

"What? No!"

Her friend's eyebrows arched. "Well, then, is Levy interested in you?"

"As a nanny, yes. As a woman, of course not."

"What makes you so sure?"

"We're like oil and water. He doesn't like it when I attend *youngie* events, and I don't like his moodiness."

"Okay, if you say so." Sarah grinned.

"Stop it," ordered Jane. "Don't create something that isn't there."

"I don't think I have to." Sarah's eyes twinkled. "You say boys never paid much attention to you before, but why bother with boys if a decent man like Levy finds you interesting?"

To her annoyance, Jane felt her face flush. "He doesn't. He just finds me *useful*."

"And how do you feel about Levy?" Sarah asked her.

Jane looked down at Mercy. "It used to be I wanted to strangle him half the time. Now, that's not the case.

I know he's wrestling with what to do with the *boppli*, and that means he's sometimes hard to be around."

"I can imagine. Is she done drinking her bottle? I saw some walnut brownies on the table."

Jane returned the empty bottle to the diaper bag and hoisted Mercy over her shoulder, burping her as she went. She joined Sarah in line for food.

And when Charles offered to carry her plate, citing her full hands with the baby, she thanked him and wondered what it would be like to be courted. By anyone.

The rain continued to fall as she set out to return to Levy's after the singing. It wasn't terribly late and the skies were gloomy, but not pitch-dark. Jane had no trouble seeing the road as she walked back. Mercy slept in the sling, snug against Jane's body.

As she approached Levy's house, she saw he had set a lamp in the window for her. That thoughtful gesture touched her.

She let herself inside, making sure to create a lot of noise so Levy knew she was back. Soon he emerged from the kitchen, coffee cup in hand, as she closed the door behind her.

"How was the singing?" he asked.

"It was fun. Lots of people." She paused for effect, then added, "Lots of cute boys too."

His mouth thinned. "How nice."

"And Sarah pointed out Josiah to me. It looks like he might be courting someone."

Levy nodded. "I'm sure that's for the best. He took Eliza's departure hard."

"He seemed to avoid me. I think it's because I had Eliza's baby with me." She patted the baby's bottom through the sling. "But everyone else loves her. She gets passed around and fussed over."

Jane made her way to the kitchen, where she placed the diaper bag on a chair. "I'm going to diaper and feed Mercy, then put her down. I think she's quite tired."

By the time the *boppli* was fast asleep in her crib, it was pitch-dark outside with the rain still falling. "I can drive you home in the buggy," offered Levy.

"*Nein, danke.* I know the way and can probably walk it quicker than it would take you to hitch up the horse." Jane swung her cloak around her shoulders and fastened the clasp. "I'll see you in the morning. Hopefully the rain will have stopped."

She picked up her wet umbrella from the porch and started walking toward her aunt and uncle's house. She was later than usual and hoped they hadn't worried.

"It was an impromptu singing," she explained after arriving home. "I'm sorry I didn't let you know, but it was so much fun!"

Uncle Peter chuckled. "This rain put off a lot of work today, so I'm glad the Millers donated the use of their barn for a singing."

Jane removed her damp cloak and hung it to dry on a peg near the front door. "I was happy to have something to do, since Levy was hanging around the house all day and driving me nuts."

Peter raised his eyebrows. "Does he often drive you nuts?"

"*Ja.* We seem to rub each other the wrong way."

Her uncle looked concerned. "Is it too difficult to work for him? You can come work in the store anytime, you know."

"*Nein*, I couldn't do that to Mercy. It would mean

leaving her in the clutches of an incompetent uncle."
She made a face, then chuckled. "Don't worry, Onkel
Peter. Levy is outside in the fields most of the time any-
way, and Mercy is a joy."

"Well, if you're sure…"

"I'm sure." Jane yawned. "*Gude nacht*, I'm off to
bed." She kissed her aunt and uncle on their cheeks
and went upstairs.

Jane woke to a day that dawned sunny and humid,
with the earth giving off moisture after the relentless
rain of the past few days.

As soon as Jane arrived at the farm, Levy was frantic. "I have tons to do," he said. "I missed a whole day
of work yesterday, so I have to get moving if I'm going
to have enough to sell at this week's market."

"Anything I can do to help?"

He paused and looked at her. "Would you be able
to pick raspberries and work on jam? We can sell it on
Saturday."

"Sure. It's not hard to do with a baby in the sling, or
on a blanket in the shade."

"Then yes, that would be great. *Danke*."

He seemed to have gotten over his moodiness from
yesterday, Jane thought. She fed and diapered the baby,
tidied the house, then bundled Mercy in the sling,
grabbed a blanket and a couple of buckets and headed
outside to the raspberry patch.

The day was warm, and she was glad some of the
patch was shaded by a generous maple tree. She stripped
Mercy down to just her diaper and laid her on a blanket under the tree and picked nearly two gallons of berries before the baby got squirmy and Jane was sweaty.

"Wow, that's a lot of berries." Levy came around the corner of the house and peered at the buckets.

"It will certainly add to your inventory of things to sell on Saturday, once I get these turned into jam. Is it lunchtime already?"

"If my growling stomach is any indication," he joked, and just then, Jane's own stomach made noises. They both laughed.

He glanced at the baby. "It's not too hot out here for her?"

"No worse for her than for you or me." Jane leaned down and lifted Mercy, whose face was beaded with sweat. She wiped the infant with a corner of her apron. "But *ja*, she seems warm. I'm ready to go inside."

She slipped Mercy into the sling and picked up one of the buckets of berries. Levy grabbed the other and she followed him into the kitchen.

"It's just going to be sandwiches for lunch today." She put the baby in her bouncy chair on the table and bustled around the kitchen, preparing food.

Levy washed his hands and made himself a sandwich from the ingredients Jane laid out. He sat at the table and looked at Mercy. "She seems awfully quiet today."

"She's probably just warm." Jane sat down and took a bite of her own sandwich. "She was quiet while I was picking raspberries, which was *gut*."

Levy gulped some cool water and finished his sandwich. He grabbed a few oatmeal-raisin cookies from the supply Jane had made yesterday. "I'm heading back to work."

Jane looked at the buckets of raspberries and sighed. Making jam was hot work, and it was already a hot day.

At least Mercy stayed quiet while she worked. It took

all afternoon, but Jane preserved sixteen pints of jam from the berries she'd picked that morning.

She shoved a damp strand of hair off her forehead as she surveyed her handiwork, satisfied. The jars were lined up on the countertop, cooling on a towel. They looked like jars of rubies. That should bring in a nice bit of extra income for Levy—and herself.

She washed up and glanced at Mercy, who had fallen asleep in her bouncy chair. Jane frowned. The child looked flushed. She laid a hand gently atop the baby's forehead and nearly gasped at the heat she felt. Mercy had a fever! A high fever! While she was busy working on the jam, the infant entrusted to her care was burning up with fever.

Moving fast, Jane took some of the boiling water from the stove and poured it into the same washbasin she'd used to bathe the baby yesterday, then diluted it with cool water until the bath was just a bit cooler than tepid. She laid a padded towel into the water.

Then she unstrapped the baby and lifted her up. Mercy whimpered but didn't wake. Jane stripped her bare, then laid the baby into the water, pouring liquid over the heated limbs and belly. Mercy woke up, her eyes glazed with fever, but didn't cry.

"Please, *Gott*, let her get better," Jane whispered. "Please, *Gott*, let her get better..."

Guilt plagued her. If she'd only paid attention to the baby, not the jam, not her tangled feelings about Levy, not her own fatigue. The baby. Her sole focus should have been the baby.

Jane spent twenty minutes trying to cool down the child. At last she lifted her out of the water and wrapped her in a dry towel, then scoured the house for medicine, anything to lower her fever. She found nothing.

By the time Levy came back in from his work, sweaty and dirty, she was nearly frantic with worry. "Mercy's sick," she told him. "She has a high fever. Do you have any baby ibuprofen in the house?"

"*Nein*, I don't." Concern written on his face, he peered at the infant's flushed skin. "Should I hitch up and go buy some?"

"I think so, *ja*." Jane placed the baby over her shoulder and patted her back. "Whatever you do, make sure you don't get aspirin—babies can't have it. It should be ibuprofen. And if you're going out, can you stop at my aunt and uncle's and let them know I might not be home tonight? I want to stay with her."

"*Ja*." Levy snatched up the sweat-soaked straw hat he had just discarded and put it on his head. "I'll be back as quick as I can."

While he was gone, Jane bathed Mercy once again in cool water, praying the fever would lessen.

Levy came back much sooner than anticipated, panting. "We're taking her to the hospital," he said without preamble. "Catherine said fevers in babies this young are an emergency. Peter is asking an *Englisch* neighbor to drive us over there."

Panic clutched Jane at the thought of Mercy being in danger. "I'll pack a diaper bag."

She ran around the house, gathering bottles and formula and clean diapers and other necessary items. And all the while she berated herself for her lack of vigilance. If only she hadn't picked raspberries. If only she hadn't made jam. If only...

"Jane, calm down." Levy, still filthy from his outdoor work, watched her frantic movements.

She stopped in her tracks and covered her face with her hands. "Please, *Gott*, let her be okay," she whispered. She looked at Levy and felt the pressure of tears. "I feel like it's my fault she's sick."

"*Nein*, it's not. Babies get sick sometimes." He cocked his head toward the screen door. "I think I hear the car. Let the doctor tell us why she's sick before you start blaming yourself. *Komm*."

Chapter Nine

Levy carried the packed diaper bag and Jane carried Mercy, who wore nothing but a diaper and a thin blanket. Jane barely saw the car's driver, but she thanked him in a shaky voice for agreeing to drive them to the hospital.

"I've got kids. I understand," he said.

The driver raced through the streets until he reached Grand Creek's small hospital, and pulled right up to the emergency room entrance. Jane scrambled out right behind Levy.

"This baby has a high fever," Jane told the receptionist.

"Are you the mother?"

"No, I'm the nanny…"

"I'm the baby's uncle and her legal guardian." Levy spoke over her shoulder.

"The fever spiked up this afternoon," Jane told her. "I've been giving her cool baths but it's not making a difference."

A nurse came through the double doors. "How old is the baby?"

"She's about four weeks old."

The professional nodded. "It's good you brought her in. At that age, fevers can be serious. We'll check her for infection." Then the nurse whisked Mercy deeper into the hospital while Levy started filling out the inevitable paperwork.

Jane huddled on a waiting room chair, feeling helpless and vulnerable…and guilty. The baby's unusual lethargy should have tipped her off.

"Still blaming yourself?" Levy dropped into the seat next to her.

"*Ja*. I should have noticed she was sick sooner than I did."

"Funny, I've been thanking *Gott* you noticed as quickly as you did."

A doctor came out the double doors. "Mr. Struder?"

Levy jumped up. "*Ja*, that's me."

She smiled reassuringly. "I want to let you know what we're doing with little Mercy."

Jane stood up too. "Will she be okay?"

"Very likely. It's a good thing you brought her in right away. A baby's body is less able to regulate temperature than an adult's, so it can be more difficult for them to cool down during a fever. Their bodies are naturally warmer than an adult's body because they are more metabolically active, which generates heat. Was she in the sun much today?"

"I had her outside," confessed Jane, feeling miserable. "She was lying on a blanket on the grass, but it was fully in the shade all the time. A huge maple tree…"

"Then it's not sunstroke. Don't worry, having her in

the shade outside didn't cause this to happen, so don't beat yourself up."

"We were at a singing a few nights ago," she recalled. "She was being passed around to a bunch of people who wanted to hold her. Could she have picked something up?"

"It's hard to say at this point," said the doctor. "By itself, a fever does not necessarily mean a serious illness. If the baby's behavior is normal, they're likely to be okay. But with infants this young, it's best to err on the side of caution."

"What will you test her for?" asked Levy.

"The biggest concern is meningitis," replied the doctor. "It's a bacterial infection of the membrane that covers the spinal cord and the brain. Untreated, it can be very serious. But if treated, recovery is almost always complete. I'm grateful you got her here as quick as you did. When babies get sick, they get sick fast."

"How long will she have to be here?" asked Jane.

"Until we get the tests run." The doctor looked at Levy. "You said you're the baby's legal guardian, yes? Where is the mother?"

"I don't know." Levy looked distressed. "I haven't spoken to my sister in years."

"So you don't know your sister's current medical condition?"

"No."

The woman continued, "I hope I'm not scaring you. The good news is the vast majority of infants with fevers have mild infections like colds or stomach viruses that resolve in a few days without any problems. And the other good news is that even more serious infections are treatable. The earlier we start treating them, the better the chances the baby will be fine."

"So now we just have to wait?" asked Jane.

"I'm afraid so." The doctor looked sympathetic. "That's the hardest part, I know. There's a coffee shop just down the street if you're hungry, but otherwise you can make yourself comfortable in the waiting room."

After the doctor left, Levy looked at Jane. "Are you hungry?"

"I honestly haven't stopped to think about it."

"Well, I am." He plucked his shirt. "I'm also sorry I'm so dirty and sweaty, but appearances were the last thing on my mind. Still, I have some money in my pocket, so let's go get something to eat."

Jane walked with Levy to the air-conditioned restaurant and slid into a booth with a sigh. "I'm still beating myself up."

"That makes two of us." Levy removed his straw hat and placed it beside him on the booth seat. "I keep wondering..." He trailed off.

"Wondering what?"

"Wondering if I'm cut out to be a father."

"No one is cut out to be a father—or a mother—when it first happens."

"Then how do people do it?"

"They learn on the job, how else? The only difference between you and other people is you didn't have nine months to mentally prepare yourself like most dads do."

"True." He stared at the cutlery on the table. "This made me realize how much Mercy has come to mean to me. I've grown to love her so much. I suppose that's another thing new dads do."

"Of course." Jane closed her eyes for a moment. "I'm the same. She's such a lovable baby. Despite the oddness of how she arrived, it's like she was meant to be here."

When she opened her eyes, she saw Levy watching her. "That's something I hadn't thought of," he admitted.

"What's that?"

"That you—as the nanny—might fall in love with Mercy."

"I've taken care of a lot of babies over the years, but never as a full-time job. It's an occupational hazard I didn't anticipate."

"Then how will you—" He was interrupted by the waitress, who came to take their order. After she departed, Levy continued, "How will you handle it when it comes time for you to leave this job?"

"I don't know." Pain stabbed her in the heart at the thought of leaving Mercy…and Levy. "I haven't thought that far ahead. Falling in love with Mercy wasn't what I'd planned."

Levy sighed. "Life certainly has a way of becoming complicated. I'm a simple man. I prefer a simple life. I didn't anticipate something like this."

"It's been a stressful day," she acknowledged. "And depending on how long the tests may take, I think I'll spend the night here. You've got work to do on the farm, including milking the cows. I'm the logical person to stay with her."

He nodded. "I won't argue. I'm grateful, Jane. I don't know how I'd do this without you."

When the food was delivered, Jane bowed her head and prayed for Mercy's health. Then she unfolded her napkin and glanced around the restaurant. "I wonder how many people here have friends or relatives in the hospital."

"I don't like hospitals." Levy bit into his hamburger. "They remind me of when my parents were killed."

She couldn't imagine the pain Levy must have been through in his life. No wonder he was so adamant about keeping Mercy despite all the difficulties involved.

She looked at him, sitting across the table from her. He was not pleasing to the eye at the moment. His face was streaked with grime from the day's work, his shirt was filthy, his hair plastered to his head from the shape of the straw hat.

Yet he had strength and maturity in his face, a sense of purpose and determination. The burdens and responsibilities he took on in his life, he took very seriously.

She compared him to Isaac, and realized with a sense of shock that, next to Levy, Isaac was still a boy, at least in her memory. Levy was a man. And despite the dirty clothes and face, he was a handsome man.

She sighed as she took a bite of her own food. The last thing she needed was to start thinking about her boss in that way. She had enough on her plate right now—and so did Levy.

When they returned to the hospital, Mercy was still undergoing tests and the receptionist instructed them to be seated. An hour passed, then two. Finally a doctor emerged from the swinging double doors. "Mr. Struder?"

Levy bounced to his feet. "*Ja?*"

Jane rose too.

"I'm Dr. Forster." He shook hands with Levy, then Jane. "I want to let you know the baby is stabilized. We have her on an antibiotic IV drip and we've managed to control her fever. The good news is we've ruled out meningitis, which was the most serious threat."

"Thank *Gott*," whispered Levy, pinching the bridge of his nose.

"Do you know what caused the fever?" asked Jane.

"Are you the mother?"

"No, I'm the nanny."

"The baby's mother is my sister," explained Levy. "She is…well, I don't know where she is. A few weeks ago she sent the baby to me to raise. I hired Jane to care for her."

The doctor nodded. "That helps us decide a couple of things. I'll be honest, Mr. Struder. The baby may have a condition she picked up from her mother during the birth itself. Since we don't know your sister's prenatal health, we have to make sure the baby didn't pick up a pathogen of some sort. This can mean mild symptoms for the mother, but much more serious implications for a baby."

Levy paled. "How serious?"

"Try not to worry." The doctor held up a hand. "Much of what we're doing is ruling out what she *doesn't* have. But because newborns with high fevers can be at risk, we tend to be pretty aggressive in our evaluation and treatment. So far we've ruled out meningitis and pneumonia, but some of the tests require lab cultures, and those take time. This is why I recommend we keep her here in the hospital until we get the test results back, which won't be until tomorrow, or the next day at the latest."

"I've already told Levy I'll stay with the baby," Jane told him. "He has farm animals to take care of."

"That's fine. We can provide a bed for you in the

baby's room. Since the baby is familiar with you, she'll be calmer under your care anyway."

Levy looked at Jane. "I'll have to figure out some way to get home…"

"How did you get here?" inquired Dr. Forster. "Did you use a horse and buggy?"

"No, an *Englisch* friend drove us in."

"I can call a car to bring you home," offered the doctor.

"Thank you, I would appreciate that."

After the physician left to make arrangements, Levy dropped into a chair. "I'm trying not to think how much this will cost," he muttered.

Though medical costs were often shared by the community, Jane understood the reluctance to add to anyone's financial burden. "It's better to have a healthy baby," she told him. "It sounds like it could have been very, very serious if we hadn't brought her in."

"*Ja*, you're right. And *Gott* will provide us the way to pay for everything. But it also means I'll need to work harder at the farmer's market." He quirked a grim smile at her. "Those pints of raspberry jam will be very welcome in the booth."

"Well, I won't take any money for the ones that sell." Jane dropped down into the chair next to him. "It will all go toward the hospital costs."

He didn't argue.

A nurse emerged. "Mr. Struder, a car will be here in a few minutes to bring you home."

"Can I see Mercy?"

"Of course. But don't be alarmed by her appearance."

Jane's stomach clenched as she and Levy followed the nurse into the bowels of the hospital.

Stepping into Mercy's room, they saw her lying in a crib. Wires connected her to monitors. She was sleeping.

"She's tired out from the tests," said the nurse. "Sleeping is the best thing she can do right now. It'll help her heal."

"I hate seeing her here," Jane confessed.

"But she's improving. Unless she takes a turn for the worse, and we don't expect that to happen, we'll keep her on antibiotics for another twenty-four hours or so. By then we'll have some of the lab results back. If things look positive, we can release her while we wait for the rest of the cultures to come back." The nurse smiled. "I expect you'll be able to bring her home twenty-four hours from now, though she'll need some follow-up visits."

Levy nodded and Jane saw him swallow. "It scares me to think what might have happened if we hadn't brought her in."

"Older babies can spike a fever of unknown origin, and while it's a little scary for the parents, it generally passes without a problem," said the nurse. "But in newborns, fevers can be life-threatening. We may not find out what caused it, but the critical thing is to either treat—or rule out—the very serious illnesses."

Levy reached out and gently cupped Mercy's head with his hand, and Jane saw his lips move in prayer. Then he stepped back. "I'd best get home. I have a lot of work to do." He looked at Jane. "I'll come back with the buggy tomorrow afternoon."

"*Ja.*" She watched as he turned and made his way out of the hospital room. "He's so worried," she murmured.

The nurse heard. "He's the uncle, right?"

"*Ja.* And part of his worry stems from not knowing where his sister is, the baby's mother."

The nurse's expression was sympathetic. "He seems like a good man."

"*Ja*, he is."

The nurse grew brisk. "I'm assuming you don't have a change of clothes, but we can give you a hospital gown to sleep in for the night, if you like. We also have a small library if you'd like something to read while you're here."

"Thank you."

The nurse showed Jane where the bookshelves were located, then departed for her duties. Jane chose a few books as well as a Bible, then returned to Mercy's room.

It seemed very strange to sit in a chair beside the baby's crib, confined to a cheerful but serious hospital room full of unknown equipment.

With some relief, she heard Mercy stir and whimper, then the whimper turned into a thin fretful cry. A different nurse came hurrying in.

Jane felt helpless. "Is she okay?"

"Seems so." The nurse read various monitors over the crib. "Yes, I think she's just hungry. And wet."

"Can I change her? And feed her?"

"Of course. Holding her is about the best thing you can do right now, though you'll have to be careful of her IV tube and the wire connections."

The nurse provided a tiny disposable diaper, which Jane—used to cloth diapers—managed to fit onto the baby. The nurse showed her how to avoid tangling with the tubes and wires while she picked Mercy up and cradled her.

She sank down into the room's comfortable glider

rocking chair while the nurse prepared a bottle of formula. Mercy was fretful until Jane slipped the tip into the baby's mouth. Immediately she started sucking.

"Ah, that's a good sign. She has an appetite," said the nurse. "Hold her as long as you like. She'll enjoy the body contact. I'll check up on you in a few minutes."

Jane leaned back, watching the infant's face as she nursed. Mercy's eyes stayed closed, and she seemed tired, but there was no question she was hungry. She nearly finished the bottle.

Jane flipped a hospital towel over her shoulder and lifted Mercy onto her shoulder, careful not to touch the IV tube and monitor wires, and patted her back until she burped. Then Jane slid Mercy down onto her chest and rocked as the baby relaxed into sleep.

Slow tears trickled down Jane's face as she realized how much Mercy had come to mean to her. She blessed her Aunt Catherine for encouraging them to take the baby to the hospital right away. What would have happened if she had kept her home, only to have her take a turn for the worse?

Now thanks be to *Gott*, this precious, vulnerable bundle was still alive and resting against her chest. Jane didn't want to let her go.

Exhausted, she dozed until the nurse came in. "Everything all right?"

Jane blinked. "*Ja*. She fell right asleep after her bottle. Should she go back to her crib or can I keep holding her?"

"Oh, hold her, by all means. Babies do best when they're held and loved." The nurse moved about the room, taking notes, straightening some items. "Can I bring you some dinner?"

"No, thank you, I already ate."

"Some tea, perhaps?"

"Oh, thank you. That would be wonderful."

So the nurse brought Jane a paper cup of steaming water and a little basket filled with tea bags and sugar packets, which she placed on a small sturdy table near the rocking chair. She helped prepare the tea, since Jane was unable to use both hands to make the tea herself. Then she brought the small pile of books Jane had borrowed and set them on the table as well.

"You look like you've done this before," Jane said, smiling.

"Yes, we often have parents staying with their sick babies. They usually don't want to do anything but hold them."

Jane rested her hand on Mercy's back. "I can understand why."

"But she's not your baby? You're the nanny?"

"*Ja*, but it's not hard to fall in love with something this precious."

The nurse smiled. "This baby is in good hands."

Left alone, Jane sipped her tea and managed to thumb open one of the books. Mercy breathed easily, and the horrible fever heat had left her body.

The words of the book blurred as Jane's thoughts wandered. It was true what she'd just admitted to the nurse: she had fallen in love with Mercy. She supposed it would be hard not to love the vulnerable motherless infant with such a sweet disposition.

Back in Jasper, as her friends started to get married and have families, Jane felt left behind. Her *Gott*-given gift to soothe babies had been appreciated by her friends whenever they'd needed an extra pair of hands, but Jane had never fallen in love with the babies she'd cared for. She'd never experienced motherly love and, after Isaac married Hannah, she wondered if she ever would.

Until now.

A slow tear leaked out of the corner of her eye. This baby wasn't hers. It wasn't even Levy's. It was Eliza's. If the mysteriously absent sister ever decided to return to Grand Creek, wouldn't she want her baby back?

Levy was another difficulty. Despite his prickly personality and touchiness over how he'd raised his sister, he was a good man…a fact not lost on Jane. She'd seen him at his worst, and his worst wasn't bad. She was trying hard not to fall in love with him. Levy saw her as a *useful* person, just as Isaac did. Not as a potential wife. Falling in love with him would be as painful as losing Isaac.

It seemed her new life here in Grand Creek was turning out to be just as complicated as her life in Jasper.

Chapter Ten

Jane ended up holding Mercy in her arms most of the night, dozing in the rocking chair and keeping the baby snuggled against her chest. A nurse came in every couple of hours to check on Mercy and examine the IV. She seemed pleased at the baby's progress. Jane changed the infant's diaper once and fed her twice during the night.

"A healthy appetite is a good sign," the night nurse assured her when she came in during her rounds and saw Jane feeding Mercy. "She looks like she's progressing well."

As the sun rose over the cars in the parking lot outside the hospital window, Jane laid the sleeping baby in her crib and stretched her cramped muscles. Heavy-eyed, she stumbled into the bathroom, removed her *kapp*, splashed water on her face, tidied her hair and made herself neat. Looking in the mirror, she winced at the dark circles under her eyes.

By the time the doctor came in on his morning rounds, Mercy was awake and quiet.

"Let's see how she's doing. She looks better," said Dr. Forster. He went to the baby in the crib and did a brief exam while Jane watched. The physician took Mercy's temperature, listened to her lungs, examined her eyes and mouth, and smiled.

"She's a fighter, this kid," he told the hovering Jane. "I think we can take her IV tube out, but I'd like to keep her on the monitors. We'll get some of the lab results back today, which will give us some indication what may have caused the fever. But if she continues improving and shows no more signs of fever throughout the day, I see no problem with discharging her this afternoon."

"That's a relief. I've been so worried." She closed her eyes and whispered a prayer of thanksgiving.

"You look like you were up all night with her." The doctor eyed her.

"*Ja*, I just dozed in the rocking chair but held her all night."

He smiled. "I wouldn't be surprised if that contributed to Mercy's improvement. Many people underestimate the importance of holding a baby as a factor in their healthy development. I see a lot of mothers who put their babies in cribs or strollers or playpens, but seldom hold them. Physical contact is especially important for babies who are bottle-fed."

"I use this a lot too." Jane rummaged in the diaper bag and plucked out the sling. "I can carry her around while doing chores."

"Excellent." Dr. Forster glanced at his watch. "You're probably in for a boring day until Mercy is discharged this afternoon."

"I have books to read." Jane gestured toward the pile. "Do you have many Amish patients?"

"Of course. Since I'm a pediatrician, I treat many

farm kids for injuries or illnesses." He smiled and then left Mercy's room to continue his rounds.

As predicted, it was indeed a boring day for Jane. Hours later, Dr. Forster came back, holding a file, just as the nurse poked her head in the door. "Dr. Forster? Mr. Struder is here, the baby's uncle. Did you want to talk to him?"

"Yes, can you bring him in?"

The nurse disappeared and reappeared a few minutes later with Levy. He was much cleaner than yesterday and wore a fresh shirt, though he also had circles under his eyes. Jane's heart jumped when he walked in.

Dr. Forster shook his hand. "Did you have a bad night's sleep?" he quipped.

"*Ja*, I kept imagining the worst." He peered at Mercy. "Is…is she better?"

"Much better, and I'll be discharging her shortly. However, I'd like some way to get hold of you in a hurry if the remaining lab results come back with anything alarming." He held up a hand. "I don't anticipate that happening, but I'll need some way to reach you. Do you have a neighbor with a phone?"

"*Ja*. They don't live next door, but they're not far away."

"Do you know their phone number?"

"No, but I can get it."

"Then here's my business card. That way if something comes up, you can reach me."

"*Ja*, sure." Levy slipped the card into a pocket.

"Now let's discuss follow-up care…"

He spent several minutes relating what additional symptoms to watch for, and urged Levy to bring the baby in for a follow-up appointment at the hospital's attached clinic the next week.

"I have a question," said Jane. "Levy sells produce at the farmer's market on Saturdays. It's helpful to have another person work the booth with him, so I bring Mercy and help when needed, though most of the time he's the one interacting with customers. Would it be all right to bring Mercy to the farmer's market by Saturday, or is it better for us to stay home?"

"Assuming she acts healthy and shows no signs of additional problems, I see no reason why you can't resume your normal activities," said the doctor. "However, I wouldn't let anyone else hold her."

Levy looked relieved. "Thank you. That will be a big help."

"Can she go outside?" persisted Jane. "The reason I ask is the nurse mentioned the fever probably didn't come from sunstroke, but I want to make sure I'm not making anything worse. Is it okay to bring her outside? I put her on a blanket in the shade. Otherwise I'll keep her in the house."

"No, by all means feel free to bring her outside. But yes, keep her fully in the shade, especially since it's been so hot lately."

"*Danke.*"

The doctor smiled and shook both their hands. "Check out at the registration desk before you go, and we'll see you in a week."

Levy picked up the diaper bag. Jane slipped Mercy into the sling and walked out of the room that had seen such drama in the last twenty-four hours.

Leaning back in the buggy seat, Jane sighed as Levy

clucked to the horse and guided her out of the hospital parking lot. "I'm glad that's over. I don't like hospitals."

"Neither do I. *Ach*, what a rotten night I had, not knowing what was going on. I can't imagine it was any better for you."

"Actually, it probably was. I didn't get much sleep, of course, but at least I knew what was going on." Jane peered at Mercy, snug against her chest in the sling. "Remind me to thank the *Englisch* neighbor who drove us in yesterday. I was so distracted I didn't even catch his name."

"Well, we have to talk to him anyway to ask him to leave his phone number with the hospital, so that would be a good time."

"I'll bring him baked goods or jam in thanks."

"Just so you know, I let your aunt and uncle know you were at the hospital last night."

"*Danke*! I forgot all about them. I'm glad you let them know." She fell silent a moment and watched the town transition from city streets to rural roads. "So how far behind did you fall on the farm work?"

"It's going to be a challenge to have enough for Saturday's farmer's market," he admitted. "Between the rain and the hospital, a lot of this week was shot. I'm trying not to worry about money."

"What can I do to help?" she said. "I can't leave Mercy alone in the house, of course, and I don't want to expose her to full sunshine after what happened, but is there anything I can do to be—" she paused over her word choice "—useful?"

"The raspberry jam will be a huge help. If you can continue picking raspberries and turning them into jam, that would be wonderful. Whatever jam doesn't sell can be held until the following week, since it won't go bad. But with the amount of raspberries coming in at the moment, it's the only way to use them up. I'll pick some for selling fresh on Friday."

"*Ja*, I'll keep making raspberry jam then. But I'll make sure to pick them earlier in the day before it gets terribly hot."

Levy sighed, then asked Jane, "What about this evening? You've been on duty nonstop for thirty-six hours with the baby at the hospital. Should I take you straight home?"

Every instinct cried out for rest, but Jane knew Levy was already overstressed, and she wouldn't feel right going home while he watched Mercy. "I have an idea," she offered. "Let's go by your place first and let me pick up that portable crib and some other things for the baby, then take us both to my aunt and uncle's. She can spend the night with me. That way my aunt can fuss over her while I get cleaned up, and I'll be able to keep an eye on her all night."

"*Ja*, that would be great." Levy spoke with obvious relief. "*Danke*."

Half an hour later, having picked up what she needed for the baby, Levy pulled the horse to a stop in front of the Troyers' home. Her aunt popped out of the house. "You're here!"

"*Guder nammidaag*, Tante Catherine." Jane gave Mercy to Levy while she climbed out of the buggy, then took the child while he hopped down and unloaded the baby supplies. "I'm going to keep Mercy here for the night, if that's all right with you."

"*Ja*! Of course! Here, I'll take the *boppli*." She took

the child into her experienced arms and started cooing at the tiny alert face.

"I'll be over tomorrow around seven in the morning," Jane told Levy. "That way I can start picking raspberries before it gets too hot."

"*Ja, danke. Vielen Dank* for everything." He gave her a long look, filled with something Jane didn't understand, then clucked to the horse and started down the road.

She stared after him for a moment, then turned to her aunt.

Catherine looked at Jane hard. "Seems like you've been awake all night. Am I right?"

"Close to it, *ja*." She punctuated this by a huge yawn. "I didn't even sleep in a bed, but held Mercy all night in a rocking chair."

Her aunt nodded with the wisdom of experience. "I've done that, though never in a hospital room. Come inside. I know your uncle wants to hear everything that happened."

Over dinner, with Mercy secure in her bouncy seat on the table, Jane related the last twenty-four hours. "With Mercy's hospitalization and his primary source of income at the moment coming from the farmer's market, he's stressed about money."

"It's up to Levy to figure out his finances," Peter said firmly.

"Your uncle is right." Catherine took a bite and spoke with her mouth full. "If Levy's going to keep this little *boppli*, he's going to have to figure out how to juggle all his commitments."

Her aunt paused for a moment, then continued. "I wonder if he's waiting for Eliza to come back?" she mused. "I mean, clearly he's nurturing some sort of hope for his sister's redemption."

"That young woman who didn't see the need to be baptized," growled Uncle Peter with uncharacteristic hostility. "She could have married Josiah Lapp, who's a fine *youngie*, but instead she left Grand Creek for the *Englisch* world and now Josiah is interested in the Miller girl."

Jane's ears pricked up. "Did this Josiah Lapp lead her on or anything?"

"*Nein*, just the opposite. Eliza was something of a flirt, but Josiah was stuck on her something fierce. When she left, it took him a while to get over it."

Perhaps Jane's sympathies should lie more with Josiah than with Eliza, since she too had been jilted by the person she loved. Well, she could hardly call it *jilted* if Isaac had never realized she was in love with him. Still, she felt a stirring interest in Eliza's fate.

"Well, whatever happened, she had a beautiful baby." Jane touched Mercy, and the infant immediately clasped her finger with a tiny hand. "She's such a joy to take care of. When she's not spiking a fever, that is."

Catherine chuckled. "You always had a gift for babies. Maybe someday…"

For once Jane didn't feel the familiar stab of pain. "Maybe someday I'll get married and have some of my own?"

"I'm sorry, child, I shouldn't have said that."

"Don't worry. You reminded me what I'd forgotten for a bit, that I should turn my future over to *Gott*. I'm willing to wait and see what He has in store for me," Jane said, then added, "And that's the first time I've felt optimistic about it too."

"*Gott* works in mysterious ways," Peter told her. "And who knows, maybe He'll restore Eliza back to the community, in which case she can raise her own baby."

Jane thought about the mysterious Eliza as she prepared for bed. She settled Mercy into her portable crib and slid between the sheets, watching the baby, grateful she seemed fully recuperated from her illness.

How would she feel if Eliza suddenly returned and claimed the baby as her own? She had every right to raise her own child, but Jane knew it would be a difficult thing to stop caring for this infant who had come to mean so much to her.

Along with Levy.

Jane rolled over and stared at the dark ceiling. Crickets chirped outside her open window, and she heard the hoot of an owl from a distance. She blasted herself for falling in love with another man like Isaac, who only saw her as "useful."

What was the matter with her that she could be "useful" but not lovable?

Chapter Eleven

Uncle Peter drove her and Mercy to Levy's farm the next morning, since Jane couldn't walk there while carrying the baby equipment and the baby.

"*Danke*," she told her uncle as he unloaded the portable crib, diaper bag and bouncy seat on Levy's front porch. "I'll be home this afternoon."

Levy wasn't in the house. Jane walked through the quiet home, noting dirty dishes in the sink and a small pile of laundry on the floor. She smiled despite herself at his clear lack of domestic skills.

Before doing anything else, though, she carried buckets, a blanket and the baby outside to harvest raspberries before the day got too hot. She settled Mercy in the shade and began picking.

By the time Levy returned from the fields, the sun was high and her buckets were full. Mercy's diaper needed changing, and the baby began making noises indicating she was about to go into a full-fledged crying jag until her belly was filled.

"Here, I'll take the berries," offered Levy. "You take care of Mercy."

"*Ja, danke*, she's hungry and wet." Jane picked up the baby and returned to the house. She changed her diaper and settled into a rocking chair with a bottle of formula.

"No problems?" Levy settled onto a chair near the rocker as the baby nursed.

"*Nein*, she slept all night. Whatever caused the fever, it doesn't seem to be causing any additional problems."

He sighed with a relief Jane fully understood. "I'm grateful to *Gott* it wasn't worse. I don't know what I'd have said to Eliza if something happened to Mercy."

"And you have no possible way to get in touch with your sister? No address?"

"No." He stood up and returned to the kitchen. "I'm going to make myself a sandwich and get back outside. I have a lot to do to get ready for the farmer's market."

"I'll make jam this afternoon."

"*Ja, danke.*"

Within a few minutes, he was gone and the house fell silent.

When Mercy fell asleep after her bottle, Jane laid the baby in her crib and commenced a quick housecleaning, ending with hanging laundry on the line. Then she started to make the raspberry jam.

Levy was grateful Jane arrived a bit earlier than normal on Saturday morning. "I've got your jars of raspberry jam already packed," he told her. "If you can take care of the baby, I'll finish loading the wagon."

"*Ja*, let me have her." He handed Mercy into her capable arms, and Jane slipped the infant into the sling.

"I've got a few more crates to pack, then we can be on our way," he added.

"What can I do?"

"I don't have Mercy's diaper bag or the lunch hamper packed. Can you work on those?"

"*Ja*, sure." She disappeared into the kitchen. He paused for a moment to admire her figure in the tidy green dress, then continued loading crates of lettuce and early carrots, flats of raspberries, fresh corn and tomatoes. In plenty of time, he was able to get the wagon on the road.

"Mercy seems fully recuperated." Levy guided the horse through an intersection. "But the back of the booth is well-shaded, and you might want to keep Mercy there rather than expose her to the crowds."

"*Ja*," agreed Jane. "I don't want her to pick up any germs."

"She's fortunate you're here to care for her." Levy kept his eyes on the horse's ears. The compliment fell clumsily from his lips. He covered the awkward moment by adding, "Still, I think I'm going to ask you to conduct a small experiment whenever Mercy is napping. How would you like to act as a scout?"

"A scout?" She glanced at him. "What do you mean?"

"I mean someone who can walk around the market. I'm always so busy at the booth that I seldom get to see what other people are selling."

"Are you thinking in terms of adding to your booth's inventory?"

"*Ja*, something like that." Finances had been on his mind a lot. "I have the hospital bills to pay off, so I want to learn what other things besides produce sell. Your jam is selling so well that I'm thinking it's time to go beyond just fruits and vegetables."

Jane chuckled. "So you want me to be an undercover spy."

He smiled. "Exactly."

"I'd be happy to. I'll wait until the crowds are thickest, and I'll see what people are buying the most of."

"*Danke.*"

The next few hours were busy. Following the unspoken pattern from the last few weekends, he set up the booth while Jane unloaded crates of produce. Once the booth was assembled, she joined him in stocking the display units.

"Here, you might like this." He held up a hand-lettered sign. "I made it last night."

"'Fresh Homemade Raspberry Jam,'" Jane read out loud. "'Meet the Expert Jam-Maker in Person.'" Her eyes crinkled in amusement. "Do you think it will help?"

"Can't hurt." He grinned and hung the sign over the jars of ruby-red jam.

Then, as customers started trickling and then flooding the market, he switched on his consummate salesman personality.

"It's like you become a whole different man," Jane said to him during a lull.

"What do you mean?"

"When customers come into the booth, it's like you flip a switch. You're teasing and talkative, but without being obnoxious or pushy."

So she'd noticed. Levy couldn't help but be pleased. "Do you wish I could stay that way all the time?"

"No. It's effective while selling something, but it's not who you are. I… I like the other man better. The real you." She looked away, her cheeks turning pink.

A group of customers entered the booth and distracted him. He began to talk with them, while thinking about Jane's shy blush. He found he liked the idea of making her blush.

* * *

Jane stayed in the back of the booth, keeping Mercy in her sling unless she had to feed or diaper her, and watched as fruits and vegetables disappeared with magical speed. Levy had to constantly restock his inventory.

She hadn't meant to reveal that she liked the real Levy. The words just came out. She was glad when some customers had distracted him. Least said, soonest mended, as her mother always observed.

At a time when Mercy was sleeping in her basket and the crowds were at their heaviest, Levy gave her a nod and she slipped out of the booth. She avoided the Amish booths because she knew they sold similar items, but she was curious about the *Englisch* booths.

It was an eye-opener. Creative entrepreneurs sold everything from baked goods to soaps to knitted items to crafts, even gourmet dog biscuits.

Several items caught her eye as something Levy could do. She saw gift baskets packed with edible goodies, both fresh and baked, which sold briskly.

And eggs. Why wasn't Levy selling eggs? She saw cartons of farm-fresh eggs in nearly every bag a customer carried.

And potted plants. Jane saw a booth selling potted herbs that was busy with customers.

And baked goods. Cookies, breads, rolls, muffins, cupcakes and other items sold well.

And cut flowers. Women bought them in bulk.

And packages of dried herbs. Jane knew Levy grew some herbs, but he didn't sell any. Why not?

And dried glass gem corn. Jane knew this variety grew well in Indiana. People seemed to like it for decorative purposes. Levy didn't have any growing, but perhaps next year…

Her mind buzzed with the potential of how Levy could expand his sales. If he had hospital bills to pay off, he could put a lot more items up for sale and earn more money.

She returned to the booth in time to help him handle another surge of customers. "Yes, those are $2.99 a pound," she told a lady, slipping behind the table. She paused to check on Mercy, who slept soundly in her carrier basket, and turned back to the customer.

To her surprise, his signage drawing attention to the "Expert Jam-Maker" had garnered much more attention than she'd anticipated. Many people, mostly *Englisch* women, asked her how she made it. Jane was floored. Who didn't know how to make raspberry jam?

But she explained the steps to dozens of women as well as a few men over the course of the day. And the jars of jam disappeared until there were only two left.

And those final jars were snapped up by a grandmotherly woman late in the afternoon. She exclaimed over the jam and told Levy how much she used to enjoy making preserves with her mother and grandmother.

"Come back in a couple of weeks when the blueberries are ripe," Levy told her. "Jane makes blueberry jam that simply melts in your mouth."

"I will!" The woman tucked the jam into a canvas bag. "I don't do a lot of canning anymore, so I'll look forward to it."

After the happy customer departed, Jane eyed Levy. "You've never tasted my blueberry jam."

"*Nein*, but can you tell me it won't be anything but delicious?"

She laughed. "Well, I have to admit your sign worked. You sold seventy-five jars of jam!"

For the rest of the afternoon, sales were brisk and Levy seemed pleased as one item after another sold out. As was his usual custom, Levy was the last booth to break down at the end of the day, and he netted two extra sales as a result.

"Whew." With the wagon packed and the horse hitched up, Levy slumped as he directed the animal toward home. "This is why I look forward to the Sabbath. I'm always so tired by the end of farmer's market day."

"And I'm about to make you even more tired."

"What do you mean? Are you talking about your scouting expedition this afternoon?"

"*Ja.* There are many things you shouldn't even think about selling. A lot of vendors do, as you put it, 'the buy-and-sell.' Obviously there are no oranges grown in Indiana," she joked.

He chuckled. "*Ja*, I hope the vendors aren't trying to pass those off as what they grew themselves."

"And several booths sold things like crafts and homemade soaps. I assume you're not interested in competing."

"No. I don't have the time or the interest."

"But there were a lot of things you might consider. Eggs, for example. Why aren't you selling eggs?"

He looked bewildered. "Everyone sells eggs."

"And everyone sells out. Bring what eggs you have. Trust me, they'll sell."

He rubbed his chin. "I'll have to get cartons. They sell empty cartons at the feed store in town. What else did you see?"

"A few things you might think about for next year,

but too late for this year. For example, you've seen glass gem corn, right?"

"*Ja.*"

"One booth had ears for sale, and the vendor was selling lots of them. The *Englisch* like to use them for decoration."

"Hmm." He looked thoughtful. "It would be easy to plant that next summer, though I'll have to check the pollination timing. I can't have it crossing with my sweet corn. What else?"

"Flowers."

"Flowers?"

"*Ja*, cut flowers. Zinnias, daisies, black-eyed Susans, sunflowers, sweet peas, that kind of thing. All the *Englisch* women were buying them by the armfuls. Of course, that's more for next year too, but it's something to think about."

"*Gut, gut.* I can plan for next year. But what about this year?"

"Herbs. People are crazy for herbs. I notice you have some in the garden, so you might pot some cuttings and sell those. Rosemary, sage, thyme, parsley, mint, basil. It's a little late in the season, but I'll bet they'll sell. And dried herbs as well. I saw a lot of demand for dried herbs."

He nodded. "That wouldn't be hard to do."

"And baked goods. I saw people selling bread, cookies, cupcakes, rolls, muffins, cinnamon rolls, all kinds of things."

He shook his head. "That's not something I can do. I'm no good at baking."

"But I am."

He glanced at her. "You're doing enough, Jane. Not

only are you taking care of Mercy, but you're doing the housework and making jam."

"*Ja*, sure, but you've got some hospital bills to pay off. Right now I think we both need to do as much as possible to sell things and pay off those bills. You don't want to make Mercy's hospital stay a burden to the rest of the community unless it's absolutely necessary."

He looked troubled. "I know. You're right. But it's a lot of extra work."

"Of course it is. But what we need to do is sit down and plan out each day's work. I can establish a baking schedule and make things to sell. Same with the jam. You can add dried or potted herbs to your schedule as well as picking fruit for me to make into jam."

"That sounds *gut*. I wonder too—would your aunt and uncle like to send some of their dry-goods inventory over and we can sell some of those for a small commission?"

"You know what might work better? How about if we start looking at some of the things women in the church make already—dolls or small quilts or other sewn goods? You could buy them wholesale and sell them at your booth."

"*Ja*." He gave a dry chuckle. "I just bought this new booth. But I have a feeling I'm going to have to get a bigger one."

"What about your old booth? Is it still usable?"

"*Ja*, but it's too small."

"But can you add it to your new booth?"

"Hmmm." His brow furrowed. "Not to the side—the spaces on either side of me are rented. But maybe I can go deep. I could connect both booths into a deeper space. Fresh produce and baked goods could be up front, and dry goods and other things like that could go farther in." He looked out into the distance, and Jane could almost see the gears in his brain churning. "I'd have to make new signage inviting customers to walk all the way to the back, but it would open up a lot more display space…"

"We'll make this work, Levy."

He sighed. "I've never had a partner before. Always, I've been on my own."

She was startled. "I'm not your partner, Levy. I'm just Mercy's nanny."

He went silent. She worked so well with him, sometimes she suspected he forgot.

And, if she were truly honest with herself, so did she.

Jane set herself daily tasks toward providing more products to sell at the market. Levy busied himself with combining his old and new booths into one larger booth.

"Come see what you think!" he called into the house on a Wednesday afternoon.

Jane picked up the baby and walked out to where he had set the booths up near the barn. "*Ach*, it looks *gut*!" she exclaimed.

He had reconfigured the two structures to allow display racks down the length of both sides, with a small area in back where non-sale items such as chairs, the diaper bag and other personal things could be stored behind a screen. The booth was now ten feet wide and twenty feet deep.

"See, these curtains will hide the unsold produce." He lifted a length of cheerful red gingham skirts tacked across the bottoms of the displays. "I can stack crates of fruits and vegetables under here, and they'll stay cool and shaded and out of sight. But everything will be easy to restock. The sales table and scale will be here. Your jams can be displayed there. These shelves above will be for potted herbs. Next year if I have more to sell, such as cut flowers or decorative corn, I can add bins to this area." He pointed. "And I'll put up signs here and here with arrows pointing inward, so people know they can walk all the way to the back."

"It looks *wunnerschee*," enthused Jane. "It will make a huge difference in your sales, Levy, I'm sure of it."

"I can't wait to try it out this Saturday." Levy looked up at the slatted roof topped with burlap, which offered shade but allowed breezes to flow through. "I think it will work."

"By the way, don't forget Mercy has a follow-up appointment with the doctor this afternoon."

He groaned. "I forgot." He took off his hat and scratched his head in frustration. "And I have a lot to do." He thought for a moment, then said, "Are you comfortable driving yourself to the doctor? Maggie the horse, she's well trained and easy to handle."

"*Ja*, sure, I've driven a buggy a fair bit. I'll take her in myself."

Jane gave herself plenty of time to get to the hospital for Mercy's checkup. Levy was right: the horse was easy to guide. In the hospital parking lot, she hitched Maggie under the shade of a large tree at a rail set up for the town's Amish population. She slipped Mercy into the sling, took the diaper bag and went into the hospital.

Dr. Forster was delighted to see the baby. "You'll be happy to know all the tests came back negative," he told her as he laid the infant on a padded table and examined her. "We may never know what spiked that fever, but I can't tell you how glad I am to see her looking so healthy. No more issues?"

"No. None." Jane related the week's events.

The doctor picked up the infant and cuddled her for a moment, then handed her to Jane. "This baby is lucky to have you caring for her, Miss Troyer. Keep on doing the excellent job you're doing."

"Thank you, Doctor." Jane slipped the baby into the sling. Then she shook the doctor's hand and made her way out of the hospital.

In the midst of processing the fruit for jam the next day, Jane heard a knock at the door. She wiped away sweat from her forehead with her sleeve and felt a moment's annoyance. She didn't look her best and she was in the middle of a messy project. The propane cookstove was laden with large pots of water heating toward a boil, and one huge pot in which she was stirring crushed berries. She sighed, washed her hands and went to answer the door.

"*Guder nammidaag*!" sang her friends Sarah and Rhoda when Jane opened the door. "We've brought company!"

"Come in, come in!" Jane spoke with cheer, but her heart sank when she saw the other visitor was Charles, the young man who had paid her such attention at the singing. "I'm in the middle of canning jam, so let's visit in the kitchen."

Jane was able to conjure up a plate of cookies. The baby woke up, and soon enough she was being passed around by the young women. Little Mercy smiled with all the attention.

Charles didn't say much, but his eyes followed Jane's

every move as she stirred the mashed raspberries on the propane stove and added the sugar and lemon juice. Jane was conscious of his interest, his scrutiny, his flattering attention. Yet after all she'd been through with Mercy in the hospital and then ramping up making items to sell at the farmer's market, he seemed to pale in comparison to Levy's constant industry and hardheaded common sense.

"We haven't seen you for the last few days," Rhoda said.

"It's been so busy here. It's the height of the berry season and work has been nonstop."

"Where's Levy now?" asked Sarah.

"Berry picking," Jane replied. "He's getting the last of the raspberries, but their season is mostly over. Now the blueberries are starting to peak, and he has a lot of blueberry bushes. He's also selling a lot of the fruit fresh. You know Mercy had to spend a night in the hospital, *ja*? It put Levy behind schedule, so we've both been working twice as hard to make things to sell at the farmer's market."

"Do you go too?" inquired Charles. "To the farmer's market, that is?"

"*Ja*." Jane smiled at the young man. He was nice-looking but seemed boyish in comparison to Levy. "I don't really do any of the selling, but it's helpful to have another pair of hands. And do you know what Levy did?" She gestured toward the kettle of boiling fruit. "He made a sign saying 'Meet the Expert Jam-Maker in Person!' that he hangs when he puts the jam out for sale. I've learned a lot of *Englisch* don't make their own jam, and I get so many people asking questions."

Sarah and Rhoda chuckled at the story. But Charles, she noted, had to force his smile. She nodded to herself. *Gut*. He understood the subtle innuendo and unspoken nuance of the tale, and picked up the message that she, Jane, was tied up with Levy's business plans and therefore not available as a romantic interest. She felt a little bad, but she didn't want him harboring any thoughts she wasn't interested in sharing.

Besides, there were lots of other girls in the *youngie* group. Prettier girls. Jane knew she only stood out because she was new in the community, but she had no illusion about her looks and knew Charles could get any number of other young women to return his affection.

The pot on the stove boiled, and Jane stirred in the rest of the sugar and kept stirring for about a minute before she removed the pot from the heat and skimmed off the foam. She set out the pint jars she'd sterilized earlier and began filling them with a wide-mouth funnel while the group chattered behind her.

"Ah, that's the hardest part of the jam done." She wiped sweat from her forehead and lifted the lid off the pots of water to check the temperature. She capped the jam and lifted the jars into the pots.

"How many pints of jam do you hope to make?" inquired Sarah.

"As many as we have raspberries for," Jane replied. She replaced the lids on the pots and dropped onto a kitchen chair with a sigh. "I'll repeat this process tomorrow with whatever berries have ripened. *Ach*, I'm tired. It's such a busy season for Levy, and now I understand why."

"I suppose we should leave you to your work then." Rhoda finished eating the last of her cookie.

"I'm glad you visited." Jane spoke the truth. She liked Sarah and Rhoda, and it was good to clear the air with Charles. "I don't know how many *youngie* events I'll be able to attend for the rest of the summer since it's so busy here, but I'm sure that will change after the harvest season is over."

"*Ja*, we'll let you know what's planned. We'll see you on Church Sunday."

Jane saw her friends out the door, then returned to the kitchen. Little Mercy began making hunger noises, so Jane prepared a bottle, checked the status of the jam and took the baby into the other room so she could settle into the rocking chair while she fed her.

She rocked and smiled. She realized the visit from the three people cheered her up. They hadn't forgotten her. And Charles—well, he was a nice young man. He would have no trouble finding someone to court.

It just wasn't going to be her.

"This new booth arrangement is working better than I'd hoped," Levy murmured to Jane on Saturday, as he watched the crowd. "Sales are better than ever."

Jane scanned the customers. "Everyone seems to like it."

Levy watched the play of dappled sunshine on Jane's face and realized how much he enjoyed working with her. Her industriousness—especially while caring for an infant—staggered him. And her help during these busy summer months was yielding astounding results. He realized she had a head for business that exceeded his own. She was smart, savvy and intuitive.

He listened as customers expressed appreciation for the new booth layout. "You can thank her," he often said, waving a hand toward Jane. "She's the genius behind the design."

The first time he said that, he saw the glow of appreciation on her face. For a moment he was poleaxed and realized how very pretty she was. It was something he had no time to dwell on, because of how quickly customers bought things. Every pot of herbs sold. So did every jar of jam and every last baked good Jane had made. He sold out of corn, beans, peas, raspberries, blueberries, tomatoes and almost all the other produce.

At the end of the day, after the wagon was packed, Levy clucked to the horse to start for home. "I don't think I've ever had such *gut* sales."

"We need to ride this wave." Jane gently bounced Mercy in her lap. "If you keep this up, the hospital bills will be paid in no time."

"Rebecca Yoder said she had some fabric items she'd be interested in selling. A few dolls, a couple of baby quilts, that kind of thing."

"And my friend Sarah has some small rag rugs she said we could display."

"The raspberries are about done, but the blueberries are starting to peak. Are you up for making blueberry jam?"

"Of course."

He smiled. "I don't know how I would manage without you, Jane. *Vielen Dank* for all your help."

"This is fun. A lot of work, *ja*, but it's a direct connection—providing what people want."

She lapsed into silence, holding the baby close while she watched the passing town. Levy snuck looks at her, wondering why on earth she ever thought herself plain. There was a sparkle to her, an animation he admired. Yet she also had a soothing presence, a calming influence.

He remembered her uncertainty about how long she

planned to stay in Grand Creek. He realized how much he was depending on her—not just as Mercy's nanny, but for her assistance at the farmer's market, for her business instincts, for her industriousness. And maybe, just maybe, for herself.

"Jane," he said, "I know you said you didn't know how long you would stay in town. Is it possible for you to stay until after the farmer's market season is over?"

She turned toward him, her blue eyes bright behind her glasses. "When does the market end for the season?"

"The last weekend in October."

"That's three months off."

"*Ja*. Were you planning on leaving sooner?" His heart sped up as he waited for her answer.

"I don't know." She spoke thoughtfully. "I miss my family, of course, but I can see why you'd need me to stay until the season is over. Let me think on it."

"*Ja, danke*." He knew he couldn't push, but he also knew he wanted her to stay.

For a long time.

Chapter Twelve

"She's really starting to hold her head up now. Look at that." Jane pointed.

It was late September. Mercy lay on a blanket on her stomach under the shade of the maple tree. As Levy walked up, sweaty and dirty from a day in the fields, she raised her head and smiled at him.

He sat down on the grass to rest for a moment. "What a little beauty."

"Nearly three months old already." Jane dangled a small toy before the infant. "It seems like July was just yesterday, when I started taking care of her. She's growing so fast."

He looked out at the verdant garden and fields as the sun dropped lower in the sky. "I wonder if Eliza ever wonders about Mercy and how she is."

"Every single day, I would imagine."

He stayed silent a few moments, gazing to the west. "The pumpkins are starting to turn orange," he commented at last. "I think a few might be ripe enough to bring to the farmer's market this Saturday."

"You seem tired." Jane also thought he looked distracted and moody, but it would have been rude to mention it.

He sighed. "I am. Since I combined the booths a couple months ago, sometimes it's hard to keep up with the increased sales. Still, I'm grateful to *Gott* for everything. This summer has been the most profitable it's ever been. I've been able to pay every bill to the hospital myself so far, without having to ask the community to help."

Jane knew that was a huge motivating factor behind his hard work. He had no wish for his sister's baby to be a financial burden on his church family.

"Well, only four more weeks to get through." Jane's voice wavered for a brief moment. In four weeks—in theory—Levy would no longer need her help in nannying Mercy. Their work schedule throughout the summer had meshed so seamlessly that it was hard to imagine not seeing him on a daily basis. The very thought made her heart lurch in her chest.

She thought she'd learned her lesson back home in Ohio. Why did it seem she was destined to fall in love with men who didn't see her as a woman? Levy, she knew, appreciated her help in everything from Mercy's care to the items she made to sell. He was, by every indicator, an excellent boss.

It wasn't his fault she had fallen in love with him.

But she kept her emotions in check. She'd grown up a lot over the summer and refused to become the lovelorn figure she was when she first arrived. Besides, Levy had given no indication he returned her affections, and she wasn't about to make a fool of herself. Again.

She forced her mind back to the present. "I'm going

to start making peach chutney this week," she said. "The peaches are beautiful. All your fruit trees are doing well."

He gave a small groan as he rose to his feet. "*Ach*, my sore muscles. There are some crates of peaches in the basement, ripening," he added. "Go ahead and use those."

She watched as he went back to work. That was another thing she'd come to admire over the last two months. His work ethic. He never seemed to stop. She didn't think she'd ever met a man as hardworking as Levy.

By the time Saturday rolled around, Jane had pulled together fifty pints of peach chutney, two dozen pints of applesauce, two dozen pints of tomato salsa and three dozen quarts of apple pie filling.

In addition to the full bounty of a September harvest, Levy had expanded into offering packets of seeds for customers to purchase. He made brown-paper envelopes, and on each envelope he wrote out the types of seeds and basic planting directions. Jane used a tiny green ribbon to close the flaps.

The booth, when it was set up at the Saturday market, was packed to capacity with goods for sale.

"There." Levy finished tying some corn stalks for decoration at the booth corners before the market opened. He took off his hat and wiped a hand across his brow. "Let's pray sales are *gut* today."

By the time they were ready to break down in the late afternoon, nearly everything had sold. The packets of seeds were especially popular, another component that surprised him. "Unbelievable," he muttered to Jane. "Seeds are available everywhere. Why would people buy so many here?"

She picked up the one remaining unsold packet. "These look *gut*. And people know the seeds come from your farm. I've come to realize how many people like knowing the sources for things."

"I've never had a summer like this." He started breaking down the booth components so they could be loaded into the wagon. "*Ach*, I'm glad tomorrow is the Sabbath."

"*Ja*, it will be good to rest."

Jane helped him load the boxes and crates, and the wagon started for home.

Jane thought Levy still seemed distracted, almost nervous. "I'll throw together a quick dinner before I go home tonight," she offered.

"*Danke*," he answered, then fell silent.

She didn't know what to make of his behavior. He didn't seem angry. She'd had no cross words with him in weeks. They seemed to work well together. What could possibly be wrong?

When he pulled up to the house, Jane took Mercy inside and started dinner while Levy groomed and fed Maggie and put the booth away for the week. By the time he came inside, she had the table set.

Levy sluiced his face at the sink as Jane pulled food from the oven. He sat down at the table and fidgeted. He shuffled. He fretted.

"Levy, are you *oll recht*?" she asked after they'd said grace. "You seem as nervous as a cat." She poured herself some milk.

"*Ja*, sure." He took a bite, then laid his fork down. "Jane, I have a question for you."

"*Ja*? What is it?"

"Would you consider marrying me?"

Jane couldn't believe what she was hearing. "What? Did I hear you right?"

"Yes."

"Levy, where did this come from?"

"I think it's a logical question. You're so good with Mercy. You're amazing in everything you do…"

Jane's temper rose. If she had ever entertained any hopes about her and Levy, they were dashed on the rocks at the bottom of her heart. There was no mention of love, of warmth or affection or anything else upon which a stable long-term marriage could be built.

Her answer was short. "No."

He winced. "I'm sorry I asked so bluntly, please won't you reconsider…"

"Levy, do you expect me to marry someone who only sees me as a baby nurse?" She got to her feet so fast the chair went flying and crashed to the floor. Mercy whimpered.

He looked surprised. "Just a baby nurse? Jane, hasn't it been obvious that my feelings for you have grown over the summer?"

She stared as her heart continued to pound in thick, painful thuds. "No. It *hasn't* been obvious."

"I thought we were getting along so well…"

"Sure, as an employer and employee. Not as a husband and wife."

He, too, rose to his feet. "Then I've been remiss. I've… I've never courted before. This is new territory for me."

For Levy to admit such a weakness drained Jane's anger. But the tiny portion of her heart that longed for romance shrank from him. Her mind flip-flopped this way and that, trying to come to terms with this new development.

"Besides," he added, "I can't take care of the baby on my own."

Her heart sank. *Useful* again. Never romantic.

And yet…and yet…was that really such a bad thing? She loved him, and even if he didn't return her feelings, they got along well and had the baby to unite them. Could such a marriage work?

"That's what the bishop is urging you to do, ain't so?" she asked. "Marry?"

"*Ja*. If you marry me, we can raise Mercy together." He raised an eyebrow. "That's the most logical, rational solution to the problem."

She lifted her chin. "If you want a logical, rational answer, then here's mine. I can't help but feel this proposal springs from guilt. I think your guilt over what happened to your sister is coloring your views on what's important to the baby. You insist on keeping Mercy rather than letting her be raised by a family…"

"But I *am* her family!"

"*Nein*, you're her uncle who has a living to make and can't take care of an infant on your own. You're doing the best you can, but it's impossible to care for the needs of a baby while you work a farm."

"But wouldn't marrying me solve that problem?"

"Marriage is permanent. It's a lifelong commitment. There would be no going back. That's a lot to ask of me."

"Jane." Levy placed a hand on her arm, and his voice was gentle. "Are you saying you have no feelings for me?"

She stared at his hand and her throat thickened. "I…

I don't know," she stammered. "All I know is men don't look at me twice because I'm plain. To suddenly believe you want to marry me for anything else besides a built-in nanny is hard for me to comprehend." Tears welled up in her eyes.

He tipped her chin up so her eyes met his. "You keep thinking you're plain, and I don't understand why. You've never been plain to me."

Coming from any other man, Jane wouldn't have believed that statement. But with Levy...well, it was possible he spoke truly. She knew she had fostered respect from him through the summer. Could it have grown into something more?

She stepped back and broke contact, though her skin tingled where he had touched her. "Levy, this is so sudden. I can't give you an answer yet."

"Then think about it. Tomorrow is the Sabbath. Let *Gott* guide your thinking, and we can talk on Monday."

"*Ja. Gut.*" She backed up another step, suddenly desperate to get away. "Then I'll leave Mercy to you. *Gude nacht*, Levy." She turned and fled.

Her footsteps pounded in her ears as she walked home. She felt a need to talk things over with her aunt. She needed the calm, levelheaded advice of the older woman to get over this hurdle.

Walking into her aunt and uncle's house, she found them sitting in the living room with newspapers. "Tante Catherine, can I talk to you?" Her voice sounded strained even to her own ears.

Her relatives raised their heads. Uncle Peter looked at her face and rose from his chair. "I just remembered

I have some work that needs doing in the barn." He left the room. Jane made a mental note to thank him later.

"You're white as a sheet," observed Catherine. "Sit down, child, and tell me what happened."

Jane sat down and promptly burst into tears.

Catherine handed her a handkerchief and stayed quiet while Jane continued to cry.

"Tell me what happened, *liebling*," she said after the storm had passed and Jane wiped her cheeks dry.

"Levy asked me to marry him," Jane blurted out.

Catherine's eyebrows shot up into her hairline. "What!"

"That was pretty much my reaction. Essentially he wants a built-in nanny-housekeeper for Mercy, and this was the most logical, rational solution he could think of."

"Did this happen just out of the blue?"

"*Ja*." Jane toyed with the handkerchief. "And…and I don't know what to do. I don't understand why he thought I would agree to a one-sided marriage…"

Catherine snapped her head up. "One-sided?"

Jane fell silent.

"One-sided?" persisted her aunt. "What do you mean, one-sided?"

Jane heaved a shuddering sigh. "Just what I said. I've fallen in love with Levy—and the baby as well—but I don't know that I want to accept a marriage proposal when he doesn't return the sentiment."

"Oh *Schätzchen*. No wonder you're so upset. Here he could be offering you the moon and the stars, if only the sentiment was behind them."

"*Ja*. Exactly. Oh, Tante, what should I do?" The tears

started again. "To Levy, I'm just another 'useful' person, just like I was with Isaac. Why don't men see me as a woman? Why am I always nothing more than a tool?"

"Are you sure he has no feelings for you? Levy's aware of the commitment behind a marriage. Surely he wouldn't propose if he didn't feel some affection for you?"

"He says he does, but I don't know that I believe him."

Catherine raised her eyebrows. "Why wouldn't you believe him?"

"Look at me. I'm as plain as a box of nails. Levy is a handsome man. He could ask any woman in this town to marry him, and stand an excellent chance she'd say yes. Why should he love someone like me?"

Catherine's voice grew stern. "Jane, stop it. You've always doubted your worth, all because you've been comparing yourself to your friend after she married Isaac. You've got your own type of beauty, and you're nowhere near as plain as you seem to think. And Levy has worked closely with you for months now. Don't you think he's smart enough to see what's inside you?"

"I…"

"But you don't believe him."

"Maybe that's the problem. I don't believe him. I don't believe anyone like Levy would want to marry me."

"You're being a fool, Jane." Catherine's voice was firm.

The verbal slap was exactly what Jane needed. She raised her head and looked at her aunt. "Do you honestly think it's worth accepting Levy?"

"I honestly think it's worth considering. Believe it or

not, *geliebte*, that may not be a bad way to start a marriage. You're good with the baby, that's why he needs you. I'm not saying you should accept his proposal, but nor should you necessarily dismiss it as hopeless. Happy marriages have been built on far less in our community."

"But unhappy marriages have been built that way too."

"*Ja*, sure. But would you truly be unhappy with Levy? He's a *gut* man."

"I agree. And I don't know." Jane stared at the floorboards at her feet, pleating the damp handkerchief, her mind churning. "I guess you're right," she said at last. "If I have any consolation, I imagine Levy is going through similar mental turmoil. And he has no one to talk it over with except a three-month-old *boppli*."

"I have no doubt that things will work out for the best, child." Catherine leaned forward and planted a kiss on Jane's forehead. "Let the matter rest with *Gott*. He'll provide the answer."

Lying in bed that night with her hands stacked beneath her head, Jane tried to pray for guidance. But in the wee hours of the night, tossing and turning and unable to sleep, Jane started questioning her personal insecurities and fears…and her reasoning took another turn.

What if she *did* accept Levy? What if she did enter into marriage, allegedly for the sake of Mercy? Was Aunt Catherine right when she said happy marriages were built on less?

Would it be so bad, being yoked to Levy? There was much to admire about him. People spoke highly of him in the community. He worked hard, was loyal and never shirked what he saw as his responsibilities.

And if he thought she was a worthwhile partner, maybe they could build a life together.

She fell asleep and dreamed Mercy was her baby... hers and Levy's.

Chapter Thirteen

Heavy-eyed, Jane stumbled over to Levy's on Monday morning. She dragged her steps, reluctant to have to think about his proposal.

Approaching Levy's house, she took a deep breath and stepped into the kitchen.

Mercy was strapped in her seat, quiet and content. Half-finished seed packets were scattered all over the table in the process of being assembled for the farmer's market. But Levy sat, his hands buried in his hair, staring at a piece of paper on the table before him. Jane's greeting died on her lips as he didn't appear to notice her at all.

The tension in the room crackled through the silence. Finally she spoke. "Levy?"

He jerked his head up, his eyes wide and startled. "What?"

His face held an extraordinary mixture of bleakness and hope, and instinct told her it came from the paper on the table.

"What's the matter?"

He looked dazed. "What?"

"What's the matter?" she repeated. "Are you *oll recht*?"

Levy remained silent a moment, then touched the paper. "I just received a letter from my sister."

"Your sister!" It was the last thing Jane expected.

"*Ja.*"

What did Eliza want after all this time? Would Levy's long-lost sister return to reclaim Mercy? She put her thoughts aside and walked into the kitchen. At least one problem was solved. Levy's marriage proposal appeared to be shelved for the moment. "So she's okay?"

"It seems so." Levy scrubbed a hand over his face. "She wants to come home."

"Home? Meaning here in Grand Creek?"

"*Ja.*"

Jane kept her voice neutral. "Then that solves one of your problems, ain't so? You won't have to pay a nanny anymore."

Levy focused on her. His eyes had dark circles under them. It appeared he'd slept no better than she had over the last couple of nights. "I owe you an apology, Jane. I stepped way over the line on Saturday, as a Christian and as a friend and as a man. It won't happen again."

Jane felt her heart break. It seems she wasn't even good enough for Levy's lame marriage proposal. Caring for babies, yes. Marriage, no.

At her silence, Levy lifted the sheet of paper. "But you're not out of a job, not yet. It will take her a while to get back. She said she anticipates being here a week from Tuesday."

"Where is she now?" Jane spoke with care, trying not to let her voice betray her emotions.

"She doesn't say, but the stamp on the envelope says Seattle."

"Seattle! So far away!"

Mercy began to whimper, and Jane guessed the baby needed her diaper changed. Glad for an excuse to leave the room, she lifted the infant out of the bouncy seat and took her into the bedroom to change her.

Eliza. Coming home. Doubtless to claim her baby. Jane took her time cleaning Mercy and putting a fresh garment on her. She slipped the baby over her shoulder and felt tears prickle her eyes at the thought of no longer having the sole care of this precious child.

"I need to get to work out in the fields," Levy called out from the kitchen. "I've already had breakfast."

"*Ja, gut.*" Jane took a deep breath and reentered the kitchen. "Do you want me to can more chutney or pie filling today?"

"If you would. I'm harvesting as fast as I can in the garden and orchard, so we'll have lots to sell on Saturday."

The work must go on. Despite the ricocheting of emotions, the work must go on.

Jane was grateful to *Gott* she hadn't said anything to Levy about her possible acceptance of his marriage proposal. It was best if those thoughts were kept to herself, to her heart alone. She drew in a deep breath, slipped Mercy into the baby sling and went to bring up more canning jars from the basement.

When Levy came in for lunch, she initiated the subject to avoid the subject of marriage. "You must be very happy your sister is coming home."

"*Ja.* And no. It's complicated."

Jane paused. "But you've done nothing but beat yourself up over her since I met you. How can you not be happy she's returning?"

"Because I don't know what she's returning from. There have been horrible situations where a *youngie* left the community, got involved in drugs or crime, then tried to return and fit in. It was often a disaster."

"But you don't think Eliza got mixed up in any of that, do you?"

He fixed his gaze on her. Then looked pointedly at the baby.

Jane bit her lip. He had a point. "Did she say anything about her circumstances in her letter?"

"*Nein*, just that she's ready to come home and be baptized." He picked at his food in silence for a few moments. Then he said, "It's going to take Eliza some time to resettle, for sure and certain."

"And she'll live here? With you?"

"*Ja*, of course. This is her home, every bit as much as mine."

Which would leave no room for the nanny. At some level, Jane realized why Eliza's return disturbed her. She was jealous.

Oh, not of the life Eliza had lived out in the *Englisch* world. Instead, Jane was jealous about the baby. Jane would never in a million years let Levy or anyone else know how much she dreaded the thought of Eliza's return. It wasn't that Eliza would put her out of a job. She could start working at her aunt and uncle's mercantile store. But she'd grown to love Mercy, now sleeping and secure in her crib. The *boppli* was blessedly unaware of the kaleidoscope of emotions swirling around her caregivers.

Levy returned to work. Jane concentrated on making more peach chutney for sale at the farmer's market.

By the time evening rolled around, Jane's wounded

feelings were humbled as she saw how preoccupied Levy was, between news of his sister and the weekly strain of preparing for the farmer's market. Her life might be emotionally complicated, but it was nothing next to Levy's—not just concern about Mercy, but about finances and his sister's forthcoming return. He had a lot on his plate, and she didn't have to add her injured feelings on top of everything else.

By the time he sat down to dinner, he seemed more centered as well. "I think I got a lot done today," he said after the silent blessing, reaching for a bowl of green beans.

"Will Eliza be able to work the farm with you?" asked Jane. "It seems you're in desperate need of an additional pair of hands."

"*Ja*, no doubt. But I don't know what will happen when she gets here, even whether she'll want to take over Mercy's care."

Jane startled. "Surely she will. It's her daughter." She looked at little Mercy, snug in her bouncy seat in the center of the table. The infant batted at the colorful toys on the bar above her. Soon the baby would be sitting on her own, then graduating to a high chair as she learned to eat solid food. "And it won't take long to love this *boppli*."

Levy laid down his fork. "I hadn't stopped to think about that, or even how difficult this will be on you."

Jane looked down at her plate as tears stung her eyes. "It's hard not to fall for something this sweet," she admitted.

There was a short and pained silence. "I don't know what Eliza will do with Mercy," Levy warned. "She has every right to take over the care of her own child."

"Of course. But…" She looked at him with swimming eyes. "But if she does, I'll probably go to work in my uncle's store. Or go home to Ohio, back to my family. It would be too hard to see Mercy on a daily basis but not take care of her anymore."

He was silent a few minutes, eyes on his food. "Things will change after Eliza gets home, for sure and certain," he admitted. "She hasn't been here while I built up the business—the produce sales, the farmer's market, even the bookkeeping I do. I don't know what she's been doing while out in the *Englisch* world."

Jane could see why Levy had his doubts about Eliza's return.

Not wanting to offend, she just said, "It's in *Gott*'s hands. For all you know, Eliza wants to walk the straight and narrow path from now on. She could be a huge asset to the business side of things. You just don't know until she returns."

He looked troubled. "I realize that. And I aim to give her every chance—not just to settle back into the church and the community, but to help on the farm and help with the market." His mouth thinned. "But one thing I do know. It will be like having a stranger in the house again. I don't know how much she's changed, if her values are different, what her work ethic is like. I don't know her anymore, and she doesn't know me or how much I've changed. I haven't seen her in three years. That's a long time."

Her heart ached for him. She could see the love for his sister warring with the reality of his work demands. "If I may ask, Levy, why the sudden doubts? Since I've known you, you've done nothing but express regret about the mistakes you think you made in raising her. Eliza coming home is a *gut* thing, *ja*?"

"I think it's because it's now real. Now I have to deal with her."

"Don't be surprised if she's stronger and more mature than you imagine," advised Jane. "If she's been out in the *Englisch* world, it means she's changed. Hopefully any harsh experiences she had have made her grow up into a young woman of strength. In other words, don't condemn her before you see her. You might be pleasantly surprised."

Jane struggled with herself for a few minutes, then added, "But whatever happens, Levy, please don't carry a burden of guilt around anymore. Eliza is her own person. You did the best you could after your parents died, and my hope is Eliza knows that and is grateful. Besides, how many *youngies* go crazy and leave for the *Englisch* world and do *schtupid* things with their lives, and who come from loving, intact homes? No one but *Gott* can change how a young person feels or behaves. Maybe *Gott* finally worked on Eliza."

"I hope so." He sighed. "I sincerely hope so."

On the walk back to her aunt and uncle's that evening, Jane reflected on her own dread of Eliza's imminent return. It was more than the possibility of losing Mercy. It was also the possibility of losing Levy. Awkward marriage proposal or not, she knew she was in love with him. But Eliza's return meant Levy's attention would be understandably divided by the needs of his sister.

In other words, she was jealous.

Maybe it was time to return to Ohio, to her parents and siblings, to her home. The emotions that had sent her fleeing here seemed eclipsed by the emotions she struggled with now.

Jane was ashamed of herself. Jealousy was an ugly emotion. She knew that from experience after watching Isaac fall in love with Hannah. The way she'd coped from that debacle was to leave Ohio and come here to Grand Creek.

Now it seemed she would be coping with her current jealousy the same way, by leaving. How could she stay and face the man who no longer even had the pretext of caring for the baby as the basis of his marriage proposal?

Once again, it seemed everything she cherished, longed for, hoped for, wished for was being snatched away. She had a moment of blazing anger at *Gott* for doing this to her…again.

She was a baptized member of the community, and her faith in *Gott* wasn't diminished. But she was angry at His hand in all this. Why couldn't Eliza have just stayed away?

The moment the thought went through her mind, she was ashamed of herself. She should be praying for Eliza's redemption, not her estrangement. Yes, jealousy was an ugly emotion.

These thoughts were not resolved by the time Jane returned to Levy's the next day. He was in the kitchen heating a bottle for Mercy. "She took a tiny bit of solid food this morning," he told her. "Eliza will be so glad she's healthy and developing normally."

"*Ja*, we must thank *Gott* Eliza will be happy." Jane heard the jealousy in her voice and turned away in shame.

Silence fell in the kitchen, and finally Levy asked, "Jane? What's the matter?"

"Nothing." To her frustration, she felt tears welling up in her eyes and refused to turn around to let Levy see them. Instead, she busied herself gathering the ingredients for making the bread she hoped to sell on Saturday.

"Are you worried about Eliza coming home?"

"*Nein*, why should I be?"

"You're not a very good liar, Jane."

She jumped, then froze when she felt his hands on her upper arms as he came up behind her. He continued gently, "I know this is hard on you, with the likelihood Eliza will take over Mercy's care. But I don't think I realized *how* hard it would be for you."

Her shoulders heaved as a sob rose in her throat. With an inarticulate sound, Levy spun her around and pulled her against his chest. Jane's pent-up emotions finally released and she burst into tears.

He stroked her back and just let her cry. A part of Jane was relieved he thought she was weeping solely over the loss of Mercy. But much of Jane's despair was the imminent loss of Levy as well—the daily interactions, the seamless work, the shared meals, the mutual concern for the baby. How long could she stay in Grand Creek if those things were no longer hers to enjoy?

The pressure of his arms and the gentle stroking on her back were too much. Not trusting her reaction to his touch, she pulled away, fished a handkerchief from her pocket and removed her glasses to mop her face. "Sorry," she murmured.

"Don't be." He stepped back. "Eliza's return will throw a wrench into a lot of things. I've been thinking it over too, and finding myself hoping she doesn't disrupt my routine to the point where I can't make a living."

"What do you mean?" She blew her nose.

"I mean, she'll need a lot of support as she transitions back into the community. I'm the logical person to give her that support. But you've also seen the tight deadlines I deal with as I prepare for each week's farmer's market. If that deadline is interrupted and I'm not ready, I don't earn money. The rest of the year I'm more flexible, but these farmer's markets bring in the bulk of my income for the year. Eliza has no idea how tight my schedule is."

In an odd way, it helped to know she wasn't alone in realizing how much Eliza's return would complicate things. "And you said she'll be here next Tuesday?"

"*Ja.*"

"Then I will plan to not come to work that day. You and Eliza will have much to discuss."

"I'm pretty much resigned to the fact I won't get much work done that day." He glanced at the clock. "Which means I'd best get back to the fields right now."

Jane needed a huge batch of dough for bread to sell at the farmer's market. While the dough rose, she fed and changed Mercy, then slipped the baby into the sling while she did a quick once-through on housecleaning. By the time Levy came in for the evening, ten loaves of bread were cooling on racks, and she had made meat loaf with green beans for supper.

She hoped Eliza would be able to take over these tasks. Levy needed the help.

After Jane left for the day, Levy spread a small blanket on the floor and put Mercy down on her stomach so she could practice lifting her head. The *boppli* smiled readily now, and he was less clumsy with her since Jane's baby lessons were so effective.

"What will your *mamm* think of you, do you suppose?" he asked the infant. "Will she think your bumbling uncle did an okay job?"

He himself was still mulling through the ramifications of his sister's return. He recognized part of his ambivalence was wondering where Jane would fit into his life after Eliza came home.

If Eliza slipped back into the role of mother—and he fully expected she would—where did that leave Jane? Levy realized how much he had come to look forward to seeing the woman on a daily basis. Whatever Eliza chose to do after she came home, Jane's schedule would naturally change. And Levy wasn't sure how he felt about that.

He sighed as he dangled a toy in front of Mercy. The infant raised her head and focused on it, but didn't quite have the strength or coordination to reach for it yet. That would come. She was in all ways a healthy baby, hitting all the developmental milestones she was supposed to hit—or so Jane told him. And he trusted her to know. Her gift with babies was uncanny.

She had a gift for more than babies. Since her involvement with the produce stand at the farmer's market, his income had gone up tremendously. He had just paid off the last of the hospital bills, something that would have taken him a year to do. But thanks to Jane's hard work, business sense and presence in the booth, his sales had quadrupled. And she did it all while raising a baby not her own.

He remembered looking at Jane months ago when she first came on as Mercy's nanny and thinking there was more to her than met the eye. Now that he knew her so much better, that opinion hadn't changed.

He knew beneath those thick glasses beat the heart of a warm, wonderful woman.

Chapter Fourteen

On the day before Eliza's arrival, Jane made sure Levy's house was spotless. She dusted and swept Eliza's bedroom, and made up the bed with fresh sheets and a cheerful quilt. She topped off the room's kerosene lamp and made sure the globe sparkled. She swept the house, did laundry and cleaned the kitchen.

And when Levy came in from his day's work, she hugged Mercy to her chest, kissed the child and handed her to Levy.

"Jane, wait!" he called as she marched out the front door. But she didn't answer. Instead, the tears poured from her eyes as she walked back to her aunt and uncle's house.

Feeling bleak, Levy watched Jane walk away with an air of finality that disturbed him. Mercy cooed in his arms, quiet and content, but he knew that wouldn't last as the child would soon miss the security of Jane's embrace and her confident care.

He paced around the kitchen, already missing Jane's vivacious presence. He didn't like the way she'd left.

He knew she was bothered by Eliza's upcoming return, but why couldn't she just give him a few days to get reacquainted with his sister and then get things back to normal?

He looked at the baby in his arms. What was "normal"? This whole summer had been anything but normal. He knew Jane loved Mercy very much. But would Eliza love Mercy too? Or had that bond been severed?

He sighed and put the baby in her bouncy chair, then poured himself a cup of coffee, sat down and played with the baby's toes.

"Your *mamm* is coming home," he told her. Then he wondered if that was true, or if Mercy's mother had just walked out the door. Who was Mercy's real mother?

Restless, he unstrapped Mercy and lifted her to his shoulder, then went upstairs to his sister's bedroom to get it ready. He was certain it needed dusting, and of course the bed needed to be made…

He stopped in the doorway, dumbfounded. The bedroom was pristine, with clean sheets and a bright quilt, a vase of flowers, a polished kerosene lamp on the dresser and not a particle of dust visible anywhere.

This was Jane's doing, of course. She might be filled with sorrow, but that didn't prevent her from making sure Eliza would be welcome in her own home.

He swallowed hard. Jane was a treasure. And it hit him how much he wanted to keep that treasure.

The question was, how?

Eliza arrived the following morning by taxi. She wore a blue Amish-style dress, but no apron—and no *kapp*. Her dark blond hair was pinned back in a bun, and her blue eyes were wary. She looked world-weary and cautious, as if unsure of her welcome. Above all, she looked older. During the time she'd been gone, she'd grown from a teenager into an adult.

"Eliza!" Levy rushed out the door and scooped his sister into an embrace.

Eliza hugged him tight and began to cry. "*Brüder!* I didn't know if you'd want me back."

"How could I not?" He drew back and watched the tears course down her cheeks. "This will always be your home."

"But I've been gone so long, and so many things have happened."

"Well, you're home now." He fished a clean bandanna from his pocket and handed it to her. "Come inside, we have a lot to talk about."

"Levy…" Eliza stood rooted on the side of the road. She twisted the handkerchief in her hands. "Mercy… is she okay? Is she here?"

"*Ja*, she's here. She had a good nanny while you were gone."

Eliza nodded, then followed him through the side door into the kitchen. Mercy was strapped to her bouncy seat on the table. She had reached the age where she could bat at the rod of colorful shapes above her.

"My baby," whispered Eliza. Her hands trembled as she lifted the infant out of the seat and cradled her on her shoulder. The young woman started crying again. "She's grown so much, and I've missed it all."

Levy poured two cups of coffee and led the way into the living room, where Eliza settled into the rocking chair and cuddled the baby. Levy set one mug on the small table near her elbow.

"We have lots to discuss." He sat down in an easy

chair. "First and foremost, what are your plans? You said you want to be baptized. Is it true?"

"*Ja*." Eliza spoke without hesitation. "I want to visit the bishop tomorrow. I need to confess my sins and start the classes."

Levy closed his eyes. So *Gott* hadn't deserted him—or Eliza—after all. He opened them to see his sister cradling her child with adoration in her eyes.

"I'll have to learn to take care of you, *liebling*," she crooned to the infant. "It's been a long time since I changed your diaper, or rocked you to sleep…"

"It might be hard at first to settle back into the community," he warned. "Having an out-of-wedlock baby is…"

"Out of wedlock?" Eliza raised her head, shock on her face. "She's not out of wedlock. I was married."

It was an understatement to say Levy was surprised. "Married! Then how…"

Eliza sighed. "Let me start at the beginning. It's a long story."

She spoke nonstop for almost an hour. There was a whirlwind romance with an *Englisch* man, a hasty marriage, early pregnancy, then abrupt widowhood.

Eliza wept as she finished her story.

"When Mercy was born, I knew I couldn't care for her. Bill—that was my husband—came from a broken family, and at any rate they lived all the way across the country. I was too humiliated to return to Grand Creek. You're the only person I trusted to raise her right," she concluded, "so I sent her to you."

"It surprised me, for sure and certain," Levy admitted. "Suddenly I had a newborn arrive on my doorstep. I didn't have any idea how to take care of her, but fortunately I hired a neighbor's niece who agreed to be the baby's nanny. I realized I couldn't work and take care of Mercy at the same time."

"What kind of work are you doing? I'm completely out of touch."

While Levy filled her in on his business development for the past few years, he watched his sister's face. The tenderness with which she held her baby was a good sign.

It was only when he began explaining about Mercy's care that he understood the growing sense of unease within himself. Eliza's natural desire to care for her own child meant Jane would no longer be needed.

"…and the nanny's name is Jane," he concluded. "She's been very helpful with the farmer's market—she makes jam, bread, cookies, that kind of thing, which have sold very well."

"She sounds like a *wunderbar* nanny," observed Eliza. "And…and maybe I can find a job and help contribute to the finances."

"But then who will take care of the baby?"

Eliza flushed. "That was the problem I faced in Seattle. I couldn't work and take care of her at the same time either."

"Eliza…" Levy hesitated. "I'm glad you're home. I've prayed to *Gott* for your redemption, and He's answered my prayers. I look forward to seeing you baptized."

He saw tears fill her eyes. "There are times I can't remember why I thought it was so important to leave. It's hard out there in the *Englisch* world. There are so many things that separate someone from their faith. My husband…" She hesitated. "He wasn't religious, and it was one of the things I most regretted the moment we were married. Despite my rebellion, I never questioned my faith. But he didn't believe in *Gott*, and his attitude started to wear me down. That's why I named this baby Mercy. I want faith always to be a part of her life."

"It's good you're back, then."

"Levy, I have to ask… Is Josiah Lapp married?"

Levy put down his mug. It was easy to see where Eliza was going with this train of thought. "*Nein*. Not yet, at least. He's been courting a young woman, though, so I wouldn't get your hopes up."

"I won't. Still, I… I want to see Josiah, to apologize. I know he thought about me as part of his future, and I ruined that. I won't interfere with whomever he's courting, of course, but he's been on my conscience."

"You'll see him on Church Sundays."

"*Ja*, but it's not like we'll have much of a chance to talk privately. Or rather, I'll understand if he avoids me."

"Then maybe you should just ask him if you can meet later on. But Eliza, you need to make good choices from now on."

"*Ja*, I plan to." She bit her lip. "Sometimes I think how different my life would have been had Josiah and I gotten married, if I'd stayed behind and accepted a quiet, calm life instead of one filled with drama and angst. Why I ever thought drama and angst were preferable to peace, I don't know."

"You really *have* grown up, little *schweschder*." He smiled.

"I didn't have much of a choice." She kept her eyes on the baby. "But now I have to find work. Maybe we should keep the nanny so I can look for a job?"

"Maybe we should. She's been a blessing. I don't know what I would have done without her."

Eliza peered at him closely. "That sounds like more than just professional gratitude."

"It might be." He didn't deny it. "She's amazing with the baby, she's amazing in the home and the garden and the farmer's market. She's an amazingly hard worker. She's also kind and generous and funny."

"So my big *brüder* has fallen in love at last." Eliza smiled through her tears.

In love? Levy froze. With blinding clarity, he realized his sister was right.

Jane, with her glasses that always fell down her nose. Jane, caring for Mercy with a competency that came naturally. Jane, teaching him what he needed to know to tend to the infant. Jane, making bread and cookies and jams to sell. Jane, shoring him up whenever he was down.

He felt dazed he hadn't recognized this before. His eyes unfocused as he realized how much he had come to love the tall, gawky woman who had saved him when Mercy arrived. "*Ja*," he said slowly. "I think I have." His heart started pounding. "I don't think I realized just how much I loved her until now." A grin spread across his face.

"Does she return the sentiment?"

His smile was wiped away as he recounted his clumsy marriage proposal from ten days before. "I don't know."

"Then you need to find out. After *Mamm* and *Daed* died, you put your life on hold to finish raising me. I paid you back by rebelling and running away. As a result, I missed out on a great many things, including raising my child." She hugged Mercy closer. "I also missed out on marrying Josiah. Don't make the same mistakes I did. It's okay to admit you love this woman. If that's the case, you need to let her know."

"I need to think on this." He still felt dazed at the realization of his feelings for Jane. "I need to figure out what to do…"

"What is there to figure out? If you love her, then court her. Just don't wait too long."

"So now my baby *schweschder* is advising me?" Levy beamed.

"Your baby *schweschder* has been a fool her whole life." Eliza smiled through tears. "If I can keep even one person from making a bad decision, then it will make me happy. If you love this woman, don't let her get away."

Jane rattled around her aunt and uncle's store, restocking shelves and trying not to obsess about what was happening in the Struder home. Would Eliza want to care for her own baby? Jane assumed she would. If that was the case, she certainly was out of a job.

She realized there was something she could do: pack.

She would ask Uncle Peter to take her to the train station tomorrow. She had told Levy she would stay until the farmer's market season ended at the end of October, but things had changed now that Eliza was home. If she left, she wouldn't have to bear the pain of watching Mercy back with her mother. Nor would she have to see Levy, who could now concentrate on rebuilding his family. Yes, it was better if she left.

"So you're serious about going home, then?" asked

Aunt Catherine that evening as Jane helped wash the supper dishes.

"*Ja*, I think it best."

"Is it Eliza?"

Jane nodded. "I assume she wants to raise her own baby, in which case I'd only be in the way."

"You could work with us in the store."

"And see Mercy on Church Sundays but know she's not mine?" Pain shot through her at the thought. "And you know how I feel about Levy. I… I can't bear to be around either of them if…" Her voice trailed off and she blinked back tears.

"I'm sorry it didn't work out, *liebling*."

At her aunt's gentle tone, a single tear rolled down Jane's cheek. She wiped it away and dried another plate. "It seems *Gott* hasn't decided what to do with me yet. Maybe I'll find the answer back home in Ohio."

"I know you don't want to hear this, Jane, but I think you should talk things over with Levy before you go."

"Why? What can he possibly say? 'Stay because you're *useful*'? No. I won't have it."

"So you intend to just leave without explanation?"

"It sounds rude, but I think it's best. I can always send him a letter later on, but for now, I don't want to see him. Or Eliza."

"I think you might be turning Eliza into a bigger problem than she really is."

"She's Mercy's mother. That's not a problem, that's a fact. I'm not needed anymore." She spoke in a tight, controlled voice.

"You're always needed, Jane." Catherine's voice was gentle.

Jane felt ashamed. She leaned over and kissed her

aunt on the cheek. "You and Onkel Peter have been so good to me. I honestly didn't expect to fall in love with anyone while here in Grand Creek, but that's what happened. But Levy never looked at me as a woman. Even his offer of marriage was based purely on his need for a permanent nanny. Everything has changed with Eliza's return, and I can't stay here when I'd be seeing Levy daily and knowing I'm not even *useful* to him anymore."

Catherine sighed. "Well if you're sure, I'll let Peter know. I'm sure he can take you to the train station tomorrow."

"*Danke*, Tante Catherine." Jane put away the last dish. "I'll go finish packing."

Wednesday dawned bright and sunny, with a hint of a breeze and a promise of a beautiful autumn day. Levy bent over the tomato plants in the field, trying not to wonder where Jane was. He worked methodically, filling baskets with ripe tomatoes. He would transfer the tomatoes to crates and stack them in the cool dark basement until the Saturday market.

Jane's absence preyed on his mind. With Eliza home, it was obvious Jane was staying away. He told his sister she was probably working at her aunt and uncle's store.

Eliza had walked over to talk with the bishop. She also told him she wanted to visit the Troyers' store to meet and thank Jane.

He looked up as Eliza came walking through the garden rows, carrying Mercy over one shoulder. "How did your meeting with the bishop go?"

"It went well. Better than I hoped, in fact. I told him everything that happened since I left Grand Creek." She patted the baby's back. "In some ways I think he was relieved to know about the circumstances around Mercy's birth. Most importantly, he's going to put up the possibility of my baptism to a church vote. If the decision is unanimous, I'll start classes toward baptism."

"*Ach*, that's *gut*. The bishop is a fair man. I'm glad he's working with you on this."

"Also, I stopped by the Troyers' store and had a talk with Catherine Troyer. She's willing to have me work in the store if I can figure out who can take care of Mercy."

"Won't Jane do it? I have a feeling she'd be more than happy to continue caring for her."

"Jane's gone. Catherine said Peter is taking her to the train station—"

"What!" Levy jerked upright and the basket tipped over. Crimson tomatoes rolled away. "What did you say? Jane's gone?"

"*Ja*. I wanted to thank her for taking care of Mercy, but Catherine said Peter had left about an hour before. I guess she's returning to Ohio."

Levy stood frozen, frantic thoughts racing through his mind. He felt stunned by the loss.

"Levy, what's the matter?"

"She can't go. She can't." His lips felt cold, his hands numb. The thought of not having Jane nearby made him realize just how much she meant to him. Why had he never said anything to her? Why had he left her in doubt as to his feelings? Without question she felt he'd just moved beyond needing her now that Eliza was home. "She *can't* go," he repeated in shock.

"But she's on her way home. Levy…" Eliza reached out and touched his arm. "Are you that much in love with her?"

"*Ja*." He refused to admit how close to tears he felt.

"Why did she leave so quickly? Why didn't she let me know she planned to leave?"

"Sounds like you two need to talk."

"How can we talk if she's already at the train station?" snapped Levy, glaring at his sister.

But the young woman smiled with the wisdom of hard knocks. "But she's *not* at the train station. Not yet. If Peter's been gone only an hour by this point, then they still have some distance to go…"

"…and I might be able to catch up with them." Suddenly sure, Levy yanked off his gloves, dropped them to the ground and sprinted toward the barn.

Chapter Fifteen

Levy wanted Jane. He needed her. These last few months of daily contact cemented how strongly his feelings toward her had grown.

His favorite mare was a former harness racer, able to achieve high speeds at a trotting pace. Levy had never considered the animal's pedigree very impressive before, but today he blessed her heritage.

As he urged his horse to pull the buggy faster, he regretted his clumsy marriage proposal of a couple weeks earlier. What was he thinking, destroying her hopes for a stable loving partnership by pitching nothing more than a convenient business arrangement? Convenient to him, perhaps, but insulting to her.

How she felt about him, he wasn't quite sure. He'd pushed her patience more than she deserved, taken advantage of her skills and talents in creating items to sell at the farmer's market, without considering the workload he'd placed on her. In all ways, he'd taken her for granted. And now he might be paying the ultimate price—losing her—if he didn't catch up with her in time.

An Amish buggy loomed ahead. Levy pulled up alongside, but it proved to belong to Eli Herschberger, his graying beard forking in the breeze. "In a hurry!" he called to the older man, flourishing a hand and urging his horse to higher speeds.

If he failed to catch up with Peter's buggy, if Jane departed on the train before he had a chance to explain, what would he do? He realized he wanted nothing more than Jane at his side for the rest of his life. But first he had some apologizing to do.

As they sat in the buggy together, Jane's uncle told her, "You are loved, child, never forget that."

"*Ja, danke.* I know." She touched his arm. "But sometimes the love of relatives or even the love of children simply isn't enough."

Uncle Peter sighed. "Well, our home is always open if you ever change your mind and want to come back…"

A car raced past them, just one of many on this busy road as they got nearer to the train station.

"I forget how noisy it is here." Jane shook her head. "I'll be glad to get back to Ohio and see *Mamm* and *Daed.*"

"Your aunt and I were discussing who we might hire in the store," remarked Peter. "We thought perhaps Eliza might be interested."

"Levy's sister?"

"*Ja,* sure. Why wouldn't she work for us? She needs a job."

"But who will take care of the baby?"

Peter rubbed his chin. "I don't know if that's been solved, so perhaps it won't work out after all. But Catherine's minding the store by herself right now, and as

I'm sure you're aware from working the farmer's market with Levy, it's tough working solo."

Jane frowned. "And she's alone because you're taking the time to drive me to the station…"

He patted her hand. "I'm glad to do it, niece."

But Jane wasn't placated. Her sigh was both bitter and frustrated. "It seems I have a habit of sowing problems and discontent wherever I go."

"You do nothing of the sort. For the time you were here, you solved a great problem. It just wasn't *our* problem, true, but you helped Levy when he badly needed it."

"And now he doesn't need me anymore—" She broke off, startled to hear fast-approaching hoofbeats behind them.

Uncle Peter directed his horse to a wide spot off the road to make room for the passing buggy, but instead the vehicle slowed down and came alongside them. Jane peered around the corner and her jaw dropped. "Levy!"

He called "Whoa!" To the panting horse and pulled the animal to a stop as Uncle Peter did the same.

"Jane, I need to talk to you."

Her face shuttered. "Why? What is there to say?"

"You won't know until you hear, right?"

"I'm on my way home to Ohio."

"*Ja,* I know. But you're not going."

Her mouth thinned. "You have no right to tell me what I can and cannot do."

"You're right, I don't. Then let me ask. *Please* don't go." He climbed out of the buggy and approached her.

"What are you doing?"

"Asking your uncle if he'll be kind enough to let me drive you home."

"Levy, I have my plans."

"*Ja*, you probably do. But you haven't heard *my* plans."

Something in the tone of his voice made her pause.

"I certainly wouldn't mind getting back to the store," Uncle Peter said to Jane. "Your aunt is working by herself."

Jane sighed and climbed out of the buggy, taking Levy's outstretched hand as she stepped down.

"Thank you, Peter," Levy said. "I'll bring her back."

Uncle Peter turned his horse around, crossed the street and headed back toward Grand Creek.

"What's this all about?" asked Jane. She tried to deny the searing hope that trembled at the edge of her soul. Why had Levy run after her? Why had he stopped her plans to return home?

"I need to let Maggie rest a bit." Levy gestured toward a nearby park with generous shade trees and a hitching post for Amish buggies. "Will you let me rest her?"

"Of course." Avoiding him, she turned and patted the animal's sweating neck.

Leading the horse, Levy walked toward the cool oasis. Jane, silent but with her emotions in chaos, walked on the other side of the mare.

Levy hitched the animal to the hitching post and sat down on a bench. Jane perched at the other end.

"I…" His voice came out as a croak, and he cleared his throat. "I have to apologize," he began.

"For what?"

"For many things, but first and foremost for that clumsy marriage proposal I made a couple weeks ago. I've been beating myself up over it ever since."

Jane's emotions cooled. Is that what this was all about? "You already apologized, remember? You're forgiven."

"*Nein*, I'm not. I don't deserve to be. I've had a hard time in the past, forgiving myself. I spent so many years taking on the blame for what Eliza did. But where you're concerned, I don't want to look ahead to years of regret. I can't mess this up again. I can't let you go, Jane."

Her heart began hammering. Levy was still being awkward and clumsy in some ways. But he was trying very hard to say something very important. Above all, Jane did not want to misunderstand his intent. "What do you mean?"

"Jane…" He groped for her hands, held them firmly in his. "I want to ask you again to be my wife. Not as a business arrangement, not as a permanent nanny to Mercy, but because I love you."

Her jaw dropped open in shock. She spent a few moments simply gaping at him. "Levy, where did this come from? I thought you didn't like me."

"Didn't like you!" He stared. "Nothing could be further from the truth! Jane, I've worked with you for months now, and everything you do is wonderful. Everything. Your wit, your intelligence, your dedication to Mercy, your business sense, your hard work—everything. I haven't found anything about you I couldn't admire. It was only when Eliza told me you were going home that I realized how much I loved you."

Conflicting emotions warred within her. This change of feeling on his part was so sudden, so unexpected, that she didn't know what to say. For one of the few times in her life, she was speechless.

At her silence, she saw panic cloud Levy's face. "Please, Jane, say yes."

"I… I…" she stuttered.

His grip tightened on her hands, then he released them and half turned away. "So I misread the situation." He dropped his head in his hands in despair. "I embarrassed you again with my clumsiness. I'm so sorry."

"Levy, this is all so unexpected," Jane choked out. "I was going home because I was convinced I meant nothing to you…"

He raised his head. "You mean the world to me, Jane. You mean the moon and the stars to me."

She couldn't help but smile a bit at his melodramatic turns of phrase. Then she turned serious. "Levy, what about your sister? What about Mercy?"

"I don't know yet. She seems anxious to become a mother to her own child, but she'll need help. She talked to your aunt about working in the store…"

"But if she works in the store, what about the baby? Who's going to take care of her?"

"That's part of the problem. She wants to contribute, but doesn't quite know how. Jane, there's something else you should know. Mercy wasn't born out of wedlock. Eliza was married to an *Englischer*, but he died in a car accident while she was pregnant."

Jane gasped. "*Ach*, how sad!"

He closed his eyes and pinched the bridge of his nose. "It's very complicated. She has a long road ahead of her, but at least she wants to stay and be baptized."

"Then *Gott* did answer your prayers."

"*Ja*, as far as Eliza is concerned." He looked at her. "I'm still waiting to see if He answers my prayers as far as you're concerned. I'm waiting to see if Mercy's beautiful nanny will become my wife."

Maybe it was the hand of *Gott* reaching out, but she suddenly felt more confident of her path.

But she warned him, "I can be stubborn and hot tempered…"

"Welcome to the club."

She laughed at that. "Levy… I… I have a confession to make. I thought about accepting your marriage proposal a couple weeks ago until the letter from your sister changed things."

He couldn't have looked more surprised than if she'd clobbered him over the head. "But you turned me down!"

"*Ja*, with some hotheaded words, as I recall. But later I talked things over with Tante Catherine. I thought about it all through the night and decided a one-sided marriage could eventually be made to work."

"One-sided? You mean…?"

"*Ja*. I fell in love with you a long time ago, Levy. But I felt you didn't see me as a marriageable woman, just a *useful* one." Her old bitterness still tinged the word. "I couldn't seem to escape the curse of being *useful* but not *lovable*."

A tremulous smile lit his face. "So…has *Gott* answered my prayers?"

"*Ja*. I will marry you, Levy."

Epilogue

"It's lovely." Aunt Catherine laid out Jane's blue dress. "Eliza did a beautiful job sewing it."

"I feel a little guilty, not sewing my own wedding dress." Jane fingered the dark blue fabric which, she knew, brought out the color of her eyes. "But Eliza is such a fine seamstress, and she really wanted to make the dress. I think it's one of her ways to thank me for taking care of Mercy for her."

"Eliza has certainly settled down. I'm glad she's one of your wedding *newehockers*."

"And my younger sisters are the other two attendants."

"Your parents seem to like Levy very much. I'm so glad." Catherine dropped a kiss on Jane's forehead. "You and Levy will be very happy, I'm sure."

Jane hugged herself, her face aglow. "It's a dream come true. I should have known *Gott* had a plan for me. And Levy. And Eliza. And Mercy."

Catherine chuckled. "I must say, you make one of the happiest brides I've ever seen. And by this time tomorrow, you and Levy will be bound forever." Catherine's eyes crinkled. "You're both *gut* for each other, that I can plainly see."

"She's *gut* for me," said Levy, coming into the room.

"No doubts about your future wife?" teased Catherine.

"Are you kidding? *Gott* gave me the most beautiful bride in the world."

Jane felt her heart well up with love for this man who thought her beautiful.

Aunt Catherine looked from one to the other, then murmured, "I think I hear Peter calling me," and escaped from the room.

"Tomorrow." Levy smiled at her.

"Tomorrow," breathed Jane.

Just after noon on the following day, Bishop Kemp stood before the gathered community and concluded his sermon on the merits of marriage.

"Levy and Jane, please come forward," intoned the bishop.

Attired in her new blue dress, Jane stood up and faced the leader of their community. Beside her, Levy also stood.

"You have heard the ordinance of wedlock within the provisions of our faith," Bishop Kemp said. "Are you now willing to enter wedlock together as *Gott* in the beginning ordained and commanded?"

Levy spoke first. "*Ja.*"

Jane spoke next. "*Ja.*"

The bishop directed his next words to Levy. "Do you stand in the confidence that this, our sister, is ordained of *Gott* to be your wedded wife?"

"*Ja.*"

The bishop turned to her. "Do you stand in the confidence that this, our brother, is ordained of *Gott* to be your wedded husband?"

Ordained of Gott. Never were there truer words. This man to whom she was joining herself was, indeed, ordained by *Gott.* Jane fought back tears. "*Ja.*"

The bishop continued with the vows. Then he took her right hand and clasped it with Levy's. His grip was strong, sure, confident. Jane smiled up at the man now joined with her for the rest of her life.

"...be with you and help you together and fulfill His blessing abundantly upon you through Jesus Christ. *Amein,*" concluded the bishop. He wiped a tear away and smiled at the couple.

She looked at Levy, the strong, handsome man who had chosen her—a plain Jane—as his wife. Above all, she wanted to lean in and kiss him, but that wasn't done at a wedding ceremony. Instead, she turned her attention to the bishop for the closing formalities.

Levy's hand was warm around hers. She was now something she never thought she would be—Levy's wife—and she closed her eyes a moment. "*Danke, Gott,*" she whispered.

"*Ja,*" Levy whispered back. His hand tightened over hers. "*Danke.*"

* * * * *

LOVE INSPIRED

Stories to uplift and inspire

Fall in love with Love Inspired—
inspirational and uplifting stories of faith
and hope. Find strength and comfort in
the bonds of friendship and community.
Revel in the warmth of possibility and the
promise of new beginnings.

Sign up for the Love Inspired newsletter
at **LoveInspired.com** to be the first
to find out about upcoming titles,
special promotions and exclusive content.

CONNECT WITH US AT:

 Facebook.com/LoveInspiredBooks

 Twitter.com/LoveInspiredBks

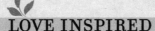
"What do I need to know?" Hannah faced him then, her big blue eyes full of expectation. Randy liked that about her. She didn't hide anything.

Well, everyone hid something. He'd certainly been hiding something for years—from this town, from his friends, even from his brother.

So what? It was nobody's business.

"Let's start with the basics." He gave her a quick tour. Her presence was making his pulse race. He didn't like it or the reason why it was happening.

Hannah's cell phone rang. "Do you mind if I take this?"

"Go ahead." He backed up to give her privacy, busying himself with a box of nets, but he could hear every word she said.

"You're kidding," she said breathlessly. "That's great news. Yes…Right now? I'd love to…You're serious? I can't believe it…"

Finally, she ended the conversation and turned to him with shining eyes. "That was Molly. She has a dog for me."

"Another puppy?" He placed the box on the counter.

"No, a retired service dog." She looked ready to float through the air. "I've been on the adoption list forever. The ones that have become available all went to either their original puppy raiser or someone higher on the list."

LIEXP0422

"Won't the dog be old?" Why would she want someone's ancient dog that might not live long?

"Some of them are. This one is eight. Too old to be placed for service, but he's still got a lot of good years left."

Something told him that even if the dog had only a couple of good months left, Hannah would be equally enthusiastic.

"I'm going to go pick him up." She lightly clapped her hands in happiness, and he kind of wished he could go with her.

"Let me get you the store key, then."

"Oh, wait." She winced. "I didn't think this through. Is there any way I can bring him with me to the store? He passed all of his obedience classes years ago. I'm sure he wouldn't cause any trouble. I just can't imagine bringing him home and then leaving him by himself all day before he has a chance to get to know me. He's used to being with someone all the time."

"Of course. Bring him." He'd always liked dogs. His customers wouldn't mind. In fact, they'd probably linger in the store even more because of him. Maybe he'd get a dog of his own after he moved into the new house. It was a thought.

"Thanks." She came over and gave him a quick hug. "I'll open the store tomorrow at nine. You're closed on Sundays, right?"

"Right." He stood frozen from the shock of her touch as she hurried to the back. The sound of the screen door slamming jolted him out of his stupor.

Hannah almost made him forget he wasn't like any other guy.

And he wasn't.

He had a secret. And that secret would stay with him until the day he died.

When that day came, he'd be single.

He had to be more careful around Hannah Carr. There was something about her that made his logic disappear like the morning dew. He couldn't afford to forget he couldn't have her.

Don't miss Guarding His Secret
by Jill Kemerer, available June 2022
wherever Love Inspired books and ebooks are sold.

LoveInspired.com